NEXT

MICHAEL CRICHTON

NEXT

HarperCollins*Publishers*

HarperCollins*Publishers*
77–85 Fulham Palace Road, London W6 8JB

www.harpercollins.co.uk

Published by HarperCollins*Publishers* 2006

Michael Crichton asserts the moral right to
be identified as the author of this work

A catalogue record for this book
is available from the British Library

ISBN-13 978 0 00 724099 9
ISBN-10 0 00 724099 6

Printed and bound in Great Britain by
Clays Ltd, St Ives plc

This book is proudly printed on paper which contains wood
from well managed forests, certified in accordance with
the rules of the Forest Stewardship Council.
For more information about FSC,
please visit www.fsc-uk.org

Mixed Sources
Product group from well-managed
forests and other controlled sources
www.fsc.org Cert no. SW-COC-1806
© 1996 Forest Stewardship Council
FSC

This novel is fiction,
except for the parts that aren't.

The more the universe seems comprehensible,
the more it also seems pointless.

—STEVEN WEINBERG

The word "cause" is an altar to an unknown god.

—WILLIAM JAMES

What is not possible is not to choose.

—JEAN-PAUL SARTRE

NEXT

Prologue

Vasco Borden, forty-nine, tugged at the lapels of his suit and straightened his tie as he walked down the plush carpeted hallway. He wasn't used to wearing a suit, though he had had this one, in navy, specially tailored to minimize the muscular bulk of his body. Borden was big, six-four, two-forty, an ex–football player who worked as a private investigator and fugitive-recovery specialist. And right now, Vasco was following his man, a thirty-year-old balding postdoc, a fugitive from MicroProteonomics of Cambridge, Mass., as he headed right for the main room of the conference.

The BioChange 2006 Conference, enthusiastically entitled "Make It Happen Now!" was being held at the Venetian hotel in Las Vegas. The two thousand attendees represented all sorts of biotech workers, including investors, HR officers who hired scientists, technology transfer officers, CEOs, and intellectual property attorneys. In one way or another, nearly every biotech company in America was represented here.

It was the perfect place for the fugitive to meet his contact. The fugitive looked like a dink; he had an innocent face and a little soul patch on his chin; he slouched when he walked and gave the impression of timidity and ineptitude. But the fact was, he'd made off with twelve transgenic embryos in a cryogenic dewar and transported them across country to this conference, where he intended to turn them over to whomever he was working for.

It wouldn't be the first time a postdoc got tired of working on salary. Or the last.

The fugitive went over to the check-in table to get his conference card to drape around his neck. Vasco hung by the entrance, slipping his own card over his head. He'd come prepared for this. He pretended to look at the event roster.

The big speeches were all in the main ballroom. Seminars were scheduled for such topics as "Fine-Tune Your Recruiting Process," and "Winning Strategies to Keep Research Talent," "Executive and Equity Compensation," "Corporate Governance and the SEC," "Patent Office Trends," and "Investor Angels: Boon or Curse?" and, finally, "Trade Secrets Piracy: Protect Yourself Now!"

Much of Vasco's work involved high-tech firms. He had been to these conferences before. Either they were about science or business. This one was business.

The fugitive, whose name was Eddie Tolman, walked past him into the ballroom. Vasco followed. Tolman went down a few rows and dropped into a seat with no one nearby. Vasco slipped into the row behind and sat a little to one side. The Tolman kid checked his cell phone for text messages, then seemed to relax, and looked up to listen to the speech.

Vasco wondered why.

The man at the podium was one of the most famous venture capitalists in California, a legend in high-tech investment, Jack B. Watson. Watson's face was blown up large on the screen behind him, his trademark suntan and striking good looks magnified to fill the room. Watson was a young-looking fifty-two, and assiduously cultivated his reputation as a capitalist with a conscience. That appellation had carried him through a succession of ruthless business deals: all the media ever showed were his appearances at charter schools, or handing out scholarships for underprivileged kids.

But in this room, Vasco knew, Watson's reputation for tough deal making would be foremost in everyone's mind. He wondered if Watson was ruthless enough to acquire a dozen transgenic embryos by illicit means. He probably was.

However, at the moment, Watson was cheerleading: "Biotechnology is booming. We are poised to see the greatest growth of any industry since computers thirty years ago. The largest biotech company, Amgen, in Los Angeles, employs seven thousand people. Federal grants to universities exceed four billion a year on campuses from New York to San Francisco, Boston to Miami. Venture capitalists invest in biotech companies at a rate of five billion a year. The lure of magnificent cures made possible by stem cells, cytokines, and proteonomics are drawing the brightest talent to the field. And with a global population growing older by the minute, our future is brighter than ever. And that's not all!

"We've reached the point where we can stick it to Big Pharma—and we will. Those massive, bloated companies need us and they know it. They need genes, they need technology. They're the past. We're the future. We're where the money is!"

That drew huge applause. Vasco shifted his bulk in his seat. The audience was applauding, even though they knew that this son of a bitch would cut their company to pieces in a second if it suited his bottom line.

"Of course, we face obstacles to our progress. Some people— however well intentioned they *think* they are—choose to stand in the way of human betterment. They don't want the paralyzed to walk, the cancer patient to thrive, the sick child to live and play. These people have their reasons for objecting. Religious, ethical, or even 'practical.' But whatever their reasons, they are on the side of death. And they will not triumph!"

More thunderous applause. Vasco glanced at the fugitive, Tolman. The kid was checking his phone again. Evidently waiting for a message. And waiting impatiently.

Did that mean the contact was late?

That was sure to make Tolman nervous. Because somewhere, Vasco knew, this kid had stashed a stainless steel thermos of liquid nitrogen that held the embryos. It wasn't in the kid's room. Vasco had already searched it. And five days had passed since Tolman left Cambridge.

The coolant wouldn't last forever. And if the embryos thawed, they would be worthless. So unless Tolman had a way to top up his LN2, by now he must be anxious to retrieve his container, and hand it over to his buyer.

It had to happen soon.

Within an hour, Vasco was sure of it.

"Of course, people will try to obstruct progress," Watson said, from the podium. "Even our best companies find themselves embroiled in pointless, unproductive litigation. One of my startups, BioGen, in Los Angeles, is in court right now because some guy named Burnet thinks he doesn't need to honor the contracts he himself signed. Because now he's changed his mind. Burnet is trying to block medical progress unless we pay him. An extortionist whose daughter is the lawyer handling the case for him. Keeping it in the family." Watson smiled.

"But we will win the Burnet case. Because progress cannot be stopped!"

At that, Watson threw both hands up in the air, waving to the audience as applause filled the room. He almost acts like a candidate, Vasco thought. Is that what Watson was aiming for? The guy certainly had enough money to get elected. Being rich was essential in American politics these days. Pretty soon—

He looked over, and saw that the Tolman kid was gone.

The seat was empty.

Shit!

"Progress is our mission, our sacred calling," Watson cried. "Progress to vanquish disease! Progress to halt aging, banish dementia, extend life! A life free of disease, decay, pain, and fear! The great dream of humanity—made real at last!"

Vasco Borden wasn't listening. He was heading down the row toward the side aisle, scanning the exit doors. A couple of people leaving, nobody looking like Tolman. The guy couldn't have gotten away, there was—

He looked back just in time to see Tolman moving slowly up the center aisle. The kid was looking at his cell phone again.

"Sixty billion this year. Two hundred billion next year. Five hundred billion in five years! That is the future of our industry, and that is the prospect we bring to all mankind!"

The crowd suddenly rose to its feet, giving Watson a standing ovation, and for a moment Vasco could no longer see Tolman at all.

But only for a moment—now Tolman was making for the center exit. Vasco turned away, slipping through the side door and out into the lobby, just as Tolman came blinking into the bright lobby light.

Tolman glanced at his watch and headed down the far corridor, past big glass windows that looked out on the red brick campanile of San Marco, re-created by the Venetian hotel and lit brilliantly at night. He was going toward the swimming pool area, or perhaps the courtyard. This time of night those spaces would be crowded.

Vasco stayed close.

This was it, he thought.

In the ballroom, Jack Watson paced back and forth, smiling and waving to the cheering crowd. "Thank you, that's very kind, thank you . . ." ducking his head a little each time he said it. Just the right amount of modesty.

Rick Diehl snorted in disgust as he watched. Diehl was backstage, taking it all in on a little black-and-white monitor. Diehl was the thirty-four-year-old CEO of BioGen Research, a struggling startup in Los Angeles, and this performance by his most important outside investor filled him with unease. Because Diehl knew that despite the cheerleading, and the press releases with smiling black kids, at the end of the day, Jack Watson was a true bastard. As someone put it, "The best I can say about Watson is, he's not a sadist. He's just a first-class son of a bitch."

Diehl had accepted funding from Watson with the greatest reluctance. He wished he didn't need it. Diehl's wife was wealthy, and he had started BioGen with her money. His first venture as CEO had been to bid on a cell line being licensed by UCLA. It was the so-called Burnet cell line, developed from a man named Frank Burnet, whose body produced powerful cancer-fighting chemicals called cytokines.

Diehl hadn't really expected to land the license, but he did, and suddenly he faced the prospect of gearing up for FDA approval for clinical trials. The cost of clinical trials started at a million dollars, and went rapidly to ten million a pop, not counting downstream costs and after-marketing expenses. He could no longer rely solely on his wife's money. He needed outside financing.

That was when he discovered just how risky venture capitalists considered cytokines to be. Many cytokines, such as interleukins, had taken years to come to market. And many others were known to be dangerous, even deadly, to patients. And then Frank Burnet had brought a lawsuit, casting doubt on BioGen's ownership of the cell line. Diehl had trouble getting investors to even meet with him. In the end, he had to accept smiling, suntanned Jack Watson.

But Watson, Diehl knew, wanted nothing less than to take over BioGen and throw Rick Diehl out on his ass.

"Jack! Fantastic speech! Fantastic!" Rick extended his hand, as Watson came backstage at last.

"Yeah. Glad you liked it." Watson didn't shake his hand. Instead, he unclipped his wireless transmitter and dropped it in Diehl's palm. "Take care of this, Rick."

"Sure, Jack."

"Your wife here?"

"No, Karen couldn't make it." Diehl shrugged. "Thing with the kids."

"I'm sorry she missed this speech," Watson said.

"I'll see she gets the DVD," Diehl said.

"But we got the bad news out there," Watson said. "That's the point. Everybody now knows there's a lawsuit, they know Burnet is a bad guy, and they know we're on top of it. That's the important thing. The company's now perfectly positioned."

Diehl said, "Is *that* why you agreed to give the speech?"

Watson stared at him. "You think I *want* to come to Vegas? Christ." He unclipped the microphone, handed it to Diehl. "Take care of this, too."

"Sure, Jack."

And Jack Watson turned and walked away from him without another word. Rick Diehl shivered. Thank God for Karen's money, he thought. Because without it, he'd be doomed.

Passing through the arches of the Doge's Palace, Vasco Borden moved into the courtyard, following his fugitive, Eddie Tolman, through the nighttime crowd. He heard his earpiece crackle. That would be his assistant, Dolly, in another part of the hotel. He touched his ear. "Go," he said.

"Baldy boy Tolman has reserved some entertainment."

"Is that right?"

"That's right, he—"

"Hold on," Vasco said. "Just hold that thought."

Up ahead, he was seeing something he could not believe. From the right side of the courtyard, he saw Jack B. Watson, accompanied by a beautiful, slinky, dark-haired woman, merging with the crowd. Watson was famous for always being accompanied by gorgeous women. They all worked for him, they were all smart, and they were all stunning.

The woman didn't surprise Vasco. What surprised him was that Jack Watson was heading directly toward Eddie Tolman, the fugitive. That made no sense at all. Even if Tolman were doing a deal with Watson, the famous investor would never meet him face-to-face. And certainly never in public. But there they were, on a collision course in the crowded Venetian courtyard, right before his eyes.

What the hell? He couldn't believe it was going to happen.

But then the slinky woman stumbled a bit, and stopped. She was wearing a short, skintight dress and heels. She leaned on Watson's shoulder, bent her knee, showing plenty of leg, and inspected her shoe.

She adjusted her heel strap, stood up again, and smiled at Watson. And Vasco glanced away from them and saw that Tolman was gone.

But now Watson and the woman crossed Vasco's own path, passing so close to him that he could smell her perfume, and he heard Watson murmur something to her, and she squeezed his arm and put her head on his shoulder as they walked. The romantic couple.

Was all that an accident? Had it happened on purpose? Had they made him? He pressed his earpiece.

"Dolly. I lost him."

"No prob. I got him." He glanced up. She was on the second floor, watching everything below. "Was that Jack Watson that just walked by?"

"Yeah. I thought maybe . . ."

"No, no," Dolly said. "I can't imagine Watson's involved in this. Not his style. I mean, Baldy boy is heading for his room because he has an appointment. That's what I was telling you. He got some entertainment."

"Namely?"

"Russian girl. Apparently he only likes Russians. Tall ones."

"Anybody we know?"

"No, but I have a little information. And I got cameras in his suite."

"How'd you do that?" He was smiling.

"Let's just say Venetian security isn't what it used to be. Cheaper, too."

Irina Katayeva, twenty-two, knocked on the door. In her left hand she held a bottle of wine, encased in a velvet gift bag with drawstrings at the top. A guy of about thirty answered the door, smiled. He wasn't attractive.

"Are you Eddie?"

"That's right. Come on in."

"I brought this for you, from the hotel safe." She handed him the wine.

Watching all this on his little handheld video monitor, Vasco said, "She gave it to him in the hallway. Where it would be seen on the security monitor. Why didn't she wait until she was in the room?"

"Maybe she was told to do it that way," Dolly said.

"She must be six feet. What do we know about her?"

"Good English. Four years in this country. Studying at the university."

"Works at the hotel?"

"No."

"So, non-pro?" Vasco said.

"This is Nevada," Dolly said.

On the monitor, the Russian girl went into the room and the door closed. Vasco turned the tuning dial on his video monitor, picked up one of the inside cameras. The kid had a big suite, close to two thousand square feet, done in the Venetian style. The girl nodded and smiled.

"Nice. Nice room."

"Yeah. So, you want a drink?"

She shook her head. "I don't really have time." She reached behind her back and unzipped the dress, left it hanging from her shoulders. She turned around, pretending to be puzzled, allowing him to see her bare back all the way down to her buttocks. "Which way is the bedroom?"

"This way, baby."

As they went into the bedroom, Vasco again turned the dials. He saw the bedroom just as she was saying, "I don't know anything about your business, and I don't want to know. Business is *so* boring." She let the dress fall. She stepped out of it and lay down on the bed, naked now except for high heels. She kicked them off. "I don't think you need a drink," she said. "And I know I don't."

Tolman threw himself on her, landing with a kind of thud. She grunted and tried to smile. "Easy, boy." He was panting, gasping. He reached for her hair, to caress her. "Leave the hair alone," she said. She twisted away. "Just lie down," she said, "and let me make you happy."

"Aw, hell," Vasco said, staring at the tiny screen. "Do you believe that? He ain't even a minuteman. When a woman looks like that, you'd think—"

"Never mind," Dolly said, over the headset. "She's getting dressed now."

"So she is," he said. "And rather hurriedly, too."

"She's supposed to give him half an hour. And if he paid her, I didn't see it."

"Me neither. But he's getting dressed, too."

"Something's up," Dolly said. "She's walking out the door."

Vasco thumbed the tuner, trying to change to a different camera. All he got was static. "I can't see shit."

"She's leaving. He's still there. No, wait . . . he's leaving, too."

"Yeah?"

"Yeah. And he's taking the wine bottle with him."

"Okay," Vasco said. "And where's he going with it?"

Frozen embryos in liquid nitrogen were transported in a special stainless steel thermos lined with borosilicate glass called a dewar. Dewars were mostly big affairs, shaped like milk jugs, but you could get them as small as a liter. A dewar didn't have the shape of a wine bottle, because they had a wide-mouth cap, but it would be about the same size. And would fit in a wine sack for sure.

"He must be carrying it," Vasco said. "It must be in the sack."

"I figure," Dolly said. "You see 'em yet?"

"Yeah, I do."

Vasco picked up the couple on the ground floor, near the gondola stand. They walked arm in arm, the guy carrying the wine bottle in the crook of his arm, keeping it upright. It was an awkward way to carry it, and they made an odd-looking pair—the beautiful girl and the diffident, slouchy guy. They walked along the canal, hardly glancing at the shops as they passed them.

"On their way to a meeting," Vasco said.

"I see 'em," Dolly said. Vasco looked down the crowded street and saw Dolly at the far end. Dolly was twenty-eight, and completely ordinary-looking. Dolly could be anybody: an accountant, girlfriend, secretary, assistant. She could always pass. Tonight she was dressed Vegas-style, teased blond hair and a sparkly dress with cleavage. She was a little overweight, which made the impression perfect. Vasco had been with her for four years now, and they worked well as a team. In private life, they got along only okay. She hated that he smoked cigars in bed.

"Heading for the hall," Dolly said. "No, they're doubling back."

The main hall was a huge oval passageway, high gilded ceiling, soft lights, marble pillars. It dwarfed the crowds that moved through it. Vasco hung back. "Change their mind? Or they made us?"

"I think they're being careful."

"Well, this is the big moment." Because even more than catching the fugitive, they had to know whom he was turning the embryos over to. Obviously someone at the conference.

"Won't be long now," Dolly said.

Rick Diehl was walking back and forth along the shops by the gondola canal, holding his cell phone in his hand. He ignored the stores, which were filled with expensive stuff of the sort he never wanted. Diehl had grown up as the third son of a Baltimore physician. All the other boys went to medical school and became obstetricians, like their father. Diehl refused, and went into medical research. Family pressure eventually drove him to move West. He did genetic research at UCSF for a while, but he was more intrigued by the entrepreneurial culture among the universities in San Francisco. It seemed like every professor worth his salt had either started his own company or was sitting on the boards of several biotech firms. At lunch, the conversation was all about tech transfer, cross-licensing, milestone payments, buyouts and payouts, foreground and background IPRs.

By then Karen, Rick's wife, had come into a substantial inheritance, and he realized he had enough capital to get started. The Bay Area was crowded with firms; there was intense competition for space and hiring. He decided to go to the area north of Los Angeles, where Amgen had set up their huge facility. Diehl built a terrific modern plant, put bright research teams in place, and was on his way. His father and brothers came to visit. They were duly impressed.

But . . . why wasn't she calling him back? He looked at his watch.

It was nine o'clock. The kids should be in bed by now. And Karen should be home. The maid said she had gone out an hour before, she didn't know where. But Karen never left without her cell phone. She must have it with her. Why wasn't she calling him back?

He didn't understand it, and it just made him nervous as hell. Here he was, alone in this damn city, with more beautiful women per square foot than he had ever seen in his life. True, they were plastic, lots of surgery, but they were also sexy as hell.

Up ahead, he saw a schlumpy guy walking with a tall chick who was striding along on spike heels, and she was just a knockout: black hair, smooth skin, and a hot, lean body. The schlumpy guy must have paid for her, but even so, he clearly didn't appreciate her. He was clutching his wine bottle like it was a baby, and appeared so nervous he was almost sweating.

But that girl . . . Jesus, she was hot. Hot, hot . . .

Why the hell, he thought, wasn't Karen calling him back?

"Hey," **Vasco said.** "Looky look. It's that BioGen guy. Walking around like he has nothing to do."

"I see him," Dolly said. She was about a block ahead of him.

"Nope, never mind."

Tolman and the Russian girl walked right past the BioGen guy, who did nothing but flip open his phone and dial. What was his name? Diehl. Vasco had heard something about him. Started a company on his wife's dough, and now maybe she was in control of their marriage. Something like that. Rich broad, old Eastern family, lots of money. Those broads could wear the pants.

"Restaurant," Dolly said. "They're going in that Terrazo place."

Il Terrazzo Antico was a two-story restaurant with glassed-in balconies. The décor was whorehouse modern, gilded everything. Pillars, ceiling, walls: every surface covered with decoration. Made Vasco jumpy just to look at it.

The couple walked in, right past the reservation desk, heading for a side table. And at the table, Vasco saw a heavyset guy who looked like a thug, dark-skinned and heavy-browed, and the thug was looking at the Russian girl and practically licking his lips.

Tolman marched right up to the table and spoke to the dark-skinned man. The guy looked puzzled. He didn't invite them to sit. Vasco thought, *Something's wrong.* The Russian girl had stepped back a pace.

At that moment a flash went off. Dolly had snapped a picture. The Tolman kid looked, took it all in, and bolted.

"Shit, Dolly!"

Vasco started running after Tolman, who was heading deeper into the restaurant. A waiter held up his hands. "Sir, excuse me—"

Vasco knocked him flat, kept right on going. Tolman was ahead, moving slower than he might, because he was trying not to shake his precious wine bottle. But he didn't know where he was going anymore. He didn't know the restaurant; he was just running. *Whang* through swinging doors, into the kitchen, Vasco right after him. Everybody was yelling at them, and some of the cooks were waving knives, but Tolman pushed on, apparently convinced there was some sort of rear entrance to the kitchen.

There wasn't. He was trapped. He looked around wildly. Vasco slowed. He flashed one of his badges, in an official-looking wallet. "Citizen's arrest," he said. Tolman cowered back by two walk-in freezers and a narrow door with a slim vertical window. Tolman went through the narrow door and it closed behind him.

A light blinked by the door.

It was a service elevator.

Shit. "Where does this go?"

"Second floor."

"Anywhere else?"

"No, just second floor."

Vasco pressed his earpiece. "Dolly?"

"I'm on it," she said. He heard her panting, as she ran up stairs.

Vasco positioned himself in front of the elevator door and waited. He pressed the button to bring the elevator down.

"I'm at the elevator now," Dolly said. "I saw him; he went back down."

"That's a tiny elevator," Vasco said.

"I know."

"If he's really got liquid nitrogen with him, he shouldn't be in there." A couple of years back, Vasco had chased a fugitive into a laboratory-supply warehouse. The guy had nearly suffocated after he locked himself in a closet.

The elevator came down. As soon as it stopped, Vasco yanked the handle to open it, but Tolman must have pushed an emergency switch, because the door wouldn't open. Vasco could see the wine sack on the floor. The velvet had been pushed down to reveal the stainless steel rim of the dewar.

And the top was off. White steam around the opening.

Through the glass, Tolman stared at him, wild-eyed. "Come out, son," Vasco said. "Don't be foolish."

Tolman shook his head.

"It's dangerous," Vasco said. "You know it's dangerous."

But the kid pushed a button, and the elevator started back up.

Vasco had a bad feeling.

The kid knew, all right. He knew exactly what he was doing.

"He's up here," Dolly said, standing on the second floor. "But the door won't open. No, he's going down again."

"Go back to the table," Vasco said to her. "Let him go."

She realized at once what he was talking about. She hurried back down the plush red velvet staircase to the ground floor. She was not surprised to see that the table where the thuggish man had sat was now empty. No thug. No beautiful Russian girl. Just a hundred-dollar bill tucked under a glass. He'd paid in cash, of course.

And vanished.

Vasco was now surrounded by three hotel security guys, all talking at once. Standing half a head above them he yelled for quiet. "One thing," he said. "How do we get the elevator open?"

"He must have hit the override."

"How do we get it *open*?"

"We have to kill the power to it."

"Will that open it?"

"No, but then we can wedge it open, once it's stopped."

"How long will that take?"

"Maybe ten, fifteen minutes. Doesn't matter, this guy isn't going anyplace."

"Yes, he is," Vasco said.

The security guy laughed. "Where the hell can he go?"

The elevator came down again. Tolman was on his knees, holding the glass door shut.

"Get up," Vasco said. "Get up, get up. Come on, son, it's not worth it, stand up!"

Suddenly, Tolman's eyes rolled up into his head and he fell onto his back. The elevator started to rise.

"What the hell?" one of the security men said. "Who is he, anyway?"

Ah shit, Vasco thought.

The kid had pushed some override that had jammed the elevator circuits. It took them forty minutes to get the doors open and haul him out. He was long since dead, of course. The instant he fell, he was immersed in 100 percent nitrogen atmosphere, from the liquid nitrogen that was streaming from the dewar. Because nitrogen was heavier than air, it progressively filled the elevator from the bottom up. Once the kid flopped on his back, he was already unconscious, and he would have died within a minute.

The security guys wanted to know what was in the dewar, which was no longer smoking. Vasco got some gloves and pulled out the long metal stick. There was nothing there, just a series of empty clips where the embryos should have been. The embryos had been removed.

"You mean to say he killed himself?" one of the security men said.

"That's right," Vasco said. "He worked in an embryology lab. He knew about the danger of liquid nitrogen in a confined space." Nitrogen caused more laboratory fatalities than any other chemical. Half the people who died were trying to rescue co-workers who had collapsed in confined spaces.

"It was his way out of a bad situation," Vasco said.

Later, driving home with him, Dolly said, "So what happened to the embryos?"

Vasco shook his head. "No idea. The kid never got them."

"You think the girl took them? Before she went to his room?"

"Somebody took them." Vasco sighed. "The hotel doesn't know her?"

"They reviewed security cameras. They don't know her."

"And her student status?"

"University had her as a student last year. She didn't enroll this year."

"So she's vanished."

"Yeah," Dolly said. "Her, the dark-skinned guy, the embryos. Everything vanished."

"I'd like to know how all this goes together," Vasco said.

"Maybe it doesn't," Dolly said.

"Wouldn't be the first time," Vasco said. Up ahead, he saw the neon of a roadhouse in the desert. He pulled over. He needed a drink.

Division 48 of Los Angeles Superior Court was a wood-
paneled room dominated by the great seal of the state of
California. The room was small and had a tawdry feeling.
The reddish carpet was frayed and streaked with dirt. The wood veneer
on the witness stand was chipped, and one of the fluorescent lights was
out, leaving the jury box darker than the rest of the room. The jurors
themselves were dressed casually, in jeans and short-sleeve shirts. The
judge's chair squeaked whenever the Honorable Davis Pike turned away
to glance at his laptop, which he did often throughout the day. Alex
Burnet suspected he was checking his e-mail or his stocks.

All in all, this courtroom seemed an odd place to litigate complex
issues of biotechnology, but that was what they had been doing for
the past two weeks in *Frank M. Burnet v. Regents of the University of
California*.

Alex was thirty-two, a successful litigator, a junior partner in her
law firm. She sat at the plaintiff's table with the other members of her
father's legal team, and watched as her father took the witness stand.
Although she smiled reassuringly, she was, in fact, worried about how
he would fare.

Frank Burnet was a barrel-chested man who looked younger than
his fifty-one years. He appeared healthy and confident as he was sworn
in. Alex knew that her father's vigorous appearance could undermine
his case. And, of course, the pretrial publicity had been savagely negative. Rick Diehl's PR team had worked hard to portray her dad as an

ungrateful, greedy, unscrupulous man. A man who interfered with medical research. A man who wouldn't keep his word, who just wanted money.

None of that was true—in reality, it was the opposite of the truth. But not a single reporter had called her father to ask his side of the story. Not one. Behind Rick Diehl stood Jack Watson, the famous philanthropist. The media assumed that Watson was the good guy, and therefore her father was the bad guy. Once that version of the morality play appeared in the *New York Times* (written by the local entertainment reporter), everybody else fell into line. There was a huge "me, too" piece in the *L.A. Times*, trying to outdo the New York version in vilifying her father. And the local news shows kept up a daily drumbeat about the man who wanted to halt medical progress, the man who dared criticize UCLA, that renowned center of learning, the great hometown university. A half-dozen cameras followed her and her father whenever they walked up the courthouse steps.

Their own efforts to get the story out had been singularly unsuccessful. Her father's hired media advisor was competent enough, but no match for Jack Watson's well-oiled, well-financed machine.

Of course, members of the jury would have seen some of the coverage. And the impact of the coverage was to put added pressure on her father not merely to tell his story, but also to redeem himself, to contradict the damage already done to him by the press, before he ever got to the witness stand.

Her father's attorney stood and began his questions. "Mr. Burnet, let me take you back to the month of June, some eight years ago. What were you doing at that time?"

"I was working construction," her father said, in a firm voice. "Supervising all the welding on the Calgary natural gas pipeline."

"And when did you first suspect you were ill?"

"I started waking up in the night. Soaking wet, drenched."

"You had a fever?"

"I thought so."

"You consulted a doctor?"

"Not for a while," he said. "I thought I had the flu or something. But the sweats never stopped. After a month, I started to feel very weak. Then I went to the doctor."

"And what did the doctor tell you?"

"He said I had a growth in my abdomen. And he referred me to the most eminent specialist on the West Coast. A professor at UCLA Medical Center, in Los Angeles."

"Who was that specialist?"

"Dr. Michael Gross. Over there." Her father pointed to the defendant, sitting at the next table. Alex did not look over. She kept her gaze on her father.

"And were you subsequently examined by Dr. Gross?"

"Yes, I was."

"He conducted a physical exam?"

"Yes."

"Did he do any tests at that time?"

"Yes. He took blood and he did X-rays and a CAT scan of my entire body. And he took a biopsy of my bone marrow."

"How was that done, Mr. Burnet?"

"He stuck a needle in my hipbone, right here. The needle punches through the bone and into the marrow. They suck out the marrow and analyze it."

"And after these tests were concluded, did he tell you his diagnosis?"

"Yes. He said I had acute T-cell lymphoblastic leukemia."

"What did you understand that disease to be?"

"Cancer of the bone marrow."

"Did he propose treatment?"

"Yes. Surgery and then chemotherapy."

"And did he tell you your prognosis? What the outcome of this disease was likely to be?"

"He said that it wasn't good."

"Was he more specific?"

"He said, probably less than a year."

"Did you subsequently get a second opinion from another doctor?"

"Yes, I did."

"With what result?"

"My diagnosis was . . . he, uh . . . he confirmed the diagnosis." Her father paused, bit his lip, fighting emotion. Alex was surprised. He was usually tough and unemotional. She felt a twinge of concern for him, even though she knew this moment would help his case. "I was scared, really scared," her father said. "They all told me . . . I didn't have long to live." He lowered his head.

The courtroom was silent.

"Mr. Burnet, would you like some water?"

"No. I'm fine." He raised his head, passed his hand across his forehead.

"Please continue when you're ready."

"I got a third opinion, too. And everybody said to me that Dr. Gross was the best doctor for this disease."

"So you initiated your therapy with Dr. Gross."

"Yes. I did."

Her father seemed to have recovered. Alex sat back in her chair, took a breath. The testimony unrolled smoothly now, a story her father had told dozens of times before. How he, a scared and frightened man, fearing for his life, had put his faith in Dr. Gross; how he had undergone surgery and chemotherapy under the direction of Dr. Gross; how the symptoms of the disease had slowly faded over the course of the following year; how Dr. Gross had seemed at first to believe that her father was well, his treatment successfully completed.

"You had follow-up examinations with Dr. Gross?"

"Yes. Every three months."

"With what result?"

"Everything was normal. I gained weight, my strength came back, my hair grew back. I felt good."

"And then what happened?"

"About a year later, after one of my checkups, Dr. Gross called to say he needed to do more tests."

"Did he say why?"

"He said some of my blood work didn't look right."

"Did he say which tests, specifically?"

"No."

"Did he say you still had cancer?"

"No, but that's what I was afraid of. He had never repeated any tests before." Her father shifted in his chair. "I asked him if the cancer had come back, and he said, 'Not at this point, but we need to monitor you very closely.' He insisted I needed constant testing."

"How did you react?"

"I was terrified. In a way, it was worse the second time. When I was sick the first time, I made my will, made all the preparations. Then I got well and I got a new lease on life—a chance to start over. Then his phone call came, and I was terrified again."

"You believed you were sick."

"Of course. Why else would he be repeating tests?"

"You were frightened?"

"Terrified."

Watching the questioning, Alex thought, *It's too bad we don't have pictures.* Her father appeared vigorous and hearty. She remembered when he had been frail, gray, and weak. His clothes had hung on his frame; he looked like a dying man. Now he looked strong, like the construction worker he had been all his life. He didn't look like a man who became frightened easily. Alex knew these questions were essential to establish a basis for fraud, and a basis for mental distress. But it had to be done carefully. And their lead lawyer, she knew, had a bad habit of ignoring his own notes once the testimony was rolling.

The lawyer said, "What happened next, Mr. Burnet?"

"I went in for tests. Dr. Gross repeated everything. He even did another liver biopsy."

"With what result?"

"He told me to come back in six months."

"Why?"

"He just said, 'Come back in six months.'"

"How did you feel at this time?"

"I felt healthy. But I figured I'd had a relapse."

"Dr. Gross told you that?"

"No. He never told me anything. Nobody at the hospital ever told me anything. They just said, 'Come back in six months.'"

Naturally enough, her father believed he was still sick. He met a woman he might have married, but didn't because he thought he did not have long to live. He sold his house and moved into a small apartment, so he wouldn't have a mortgage.

"It sounds like you were waiting to die," the attorney said.

"Objection!"

"I'll withdraw the question. But let's move on. Mr. Burnet, how long did you continue going to UCLA for testing?"

"Four years."

"Four years. And when did you first suspect you were not being told the truth about your condition?"

"Well, four years later, I still felt healthy. Nothing had happened. Every day, I was waiting for lightning to strike, but it never did. But Dr. Gross kept saying I had to come back for more tests, more tests. By then I had moved to San Diego, and I wanted to have my tests done there, and sent up to him. But he said no, I had to do the tests at UCLA."

"Why?"

"He said he preferred his own lab. But it didn't make sense. And he was giving me more and more forms to sign."

"What forms?"

"At first, they were just consent forms to acknowledge that I was undertaking a procedure with risk. Those first forms were one or two pages long. Pretty soon there were other forms that said I agreed to be involved in a research project. Each time I went back, there were still more forms. Eventually the forms were ten pages long, a whole document in dense legal language."

"And did you sign them?"

"Toward the end, no."

"Why not?"

"Because some of the forms were releases to permit the commercial use of my tissues."

"That bothered you?"

"Sure. Because I didn't think he was telling me the truth about what he was doing. The reason for all the tests. On one visit, I asked Dr. Gross straight out if he was using my tissues for commercial purposes. He said absolutely not, his interests were purely research. So I said okay, and I signed everything except the forms allowing my tissues to be used for commercial purposes."

"And what happened?"

"He got very angry. He said he would not be able to treat me further unless I signed all the forms, and I was risking my health and my future. He said I was making a big mistake."

"Objection! Hearsay."

"All right. Mr. Burnet, when you refused to sign the consent forms, did Dr. Gross stop treating you?"

"Yes."

"And did you then consult a lawyer?"

"Yes."

"And what did you subsequently discover?"

"That Dr. Gross had sold my cells—the cells he took from my body during all these tests—to a drug company called BioGen."

"And how did you feel when you heard that?"

"I was shocked," her father said. "I had gone to Dr. Gross when I was sick, and scared, and vulnerable. I had trusted my doctor. I had put my life in his hands. I *trusted* him. And then it turned out that he had been lying to me, and scaring me needlessly *for years*, just so he could steal parts of my own body from me and sell them to make a profit. For himself. He never cared about me at all. He just wanted to take my cells."

"Do you know what those cells were worth?"

"The drug company said three billion dollars."

The jury gasped.

CH002

Alex had been watching the jury all during the latest testimony. Their faces were impassive, but nobody moved, nobody shifted. The gasps were involuntary, evidence of how deeply engaged they were with what they were hearing. And the jury remained transfixed as the questions continued:

"Mr. Burnet, did Dr. Gross ever apologize to you for misleading you?"

"No."

"Did he ever offer to share his profit with you?"

"No."

"Did you ask him to?"

"Eventually I did, yes. When I realized what he had already done. They were my cells, from my body. I thought I should have something to say about what was done with them."

"But he refused?"

"Yes. He said it was none of my business what he did with my cells."

The jury reacted to that. Several turned and looked at Dr. Gross. That was a good sign, too, Alex thought.

"One final question, Mr. Burnet. Did you ever sign an authorization for Dr. Gross to use your cells for any commercial purposes?"

"No."

"You never authorized their sale?"

"Never. But he did it anyway."

"No further questions."

The judge called a fifteen-minute recess, and when the court reconvened, the UCLA attorneys began the cross-examination. For this trial, UCLA had hired Raeper and Cross, a downtown firm that specialized in high-stakes corporate litigation. Raeper represented oil companies and major defense contractors. Clearly, UCLA did not regard this trial as a defense of medical research. Three billion dollars were at stake; it was big business, and they hired a big-business firm.

The lead attorney for UCLA was Albert Rodriguez. He had a youthful, easy appearance, a friendly smile, and a disarming sense of seeming new at the job. Actually, Rodriguez was forty-five and had been a successful litigator for twenty years, but he somehow managed to give the impression that this was his first trial, and he subtly appealed to the jury to cut him some slack.

"Now, Mr. Burnet, I imagine it has been taxing for you to go over the emotionally draining experiences of the last few years. I appreciate your telling the jury your experiences, and I won't keep you long. I believe you told the jury that you were very frightened, as anyone would naturally be. By the way, how much weight had you lost, when you first came to Dr. Gross?"

Alex thought, *Uh-oh.* She knew where this was going. They were going to emphasize the dramatic nature of the cure. She glanced at the attorney sitting beside her, who was clearly trying to think of a strategy. She leaned over and whispered, *"Stop it."*

The attorney shook his head, confused.

Her father was saying, "I don't know how much I lost. About forty or fifty pounds."

"So your clothes didn't fit well?"

"Not at all."

"And what was your energy like at that time? Could you climb a flight of stairs?"

"No. I'd go two or three steps, and I'd have to stop."

"From exhaustion?"

Alex nudged the attorney at her side, whispered, *"Asked and answered."* The attorney immediately stood up.

"Objection. Your Honor, Mr. Burnet has already stated he was diagnosed with a terminal condition."

"Yes," Rodriguez said, "and he has said he was frightened. But I think the jury should know just how desperate his condition really was."

"I'll allow it."

"Thank you. Now then, Mr. Burnet. You had lost a quarter of your body weight, you were so weak you couldn't climb more than a couple of stairs, and you had a deadly serious form of leukemia. Is that right?"

"Yes."

Alex gritted her teeth. She wanted desperately to stop this line of questioning, which was clearly prejudicial, and irrelevant to the question of whether her father's doctor had acted improperly after curing him. But the judge had decided to allow it to continue, and there was nothing she could do. And it wasn't egregious enough to provide grounds for appeal.

"And for help in your time of need," Rodriguez said, "you came to the best physician on the West Coast to treat this disease?"

"Yes."

"And he treated you."

"Yes."

"And he cured you. This expert and caring doctor cured you."

"Objection! Your Honor, Dr. Gross is a physician, not a saint."

"Sustained."

"All right," Rodriguez said. "Let me put it this way: Mr. Burnet, how long has it been since you were diagnosed with leukemia?"

"Six years."

"Is it not true that a five-year survival in cancer is considered a cure?"

"Objection, calls for expert conclusion."

"Sustained."

"Your Honor," Rodriguez said, turning to the judge, "I don't know why this is so difficult for Mr. Burnet's attorneys. I am merely trying to establish that Dr. Gross did, in fact, cure the plaintiff of a deadly cancer."

"And I," the judge replied, "don't know why it is so difficult for the defense to ask that question plainly, without objectionable phrasing."

"Yes, Your Honor. Thank you. Mr. Burnet, do you consider yourself cured of leukemia?"

"Yes."

"You are completely healthy at this time?"

"Yes."

"Who in your opinion cured you?"

"Dr. Gross."

"Thank you. Now, I believe you told the court that when Dr. Gross asked you to return for further testing, you thought that meant you were still ill."

"Yes."

"Did Dr. Gross ever tell you that you still had leukemia?"

"No."

"Did anyone in his office, or did any of his staff, ever tell you that?"

"No."

"Then," Rodriguez said, "if I understand your testimony, at no time did you have any specific information that you were still ill?"

"Correct."

"All right. Now let's turn to your treatment. You received surgery and chemotherapy. Do you know if you were given the standard treatment for T-cell leukemia?"

"No, my treatment was not standard."

"It was new?"

"Yes."

"Were you the first patient to receive this treatment protocol?"

"Yes. I was."

"Dr. Gross told you that?"

"Yes."

"And did he tell you how this new treatment protocol was developed?"

"He said it was part of a research program."

"And you agreed to participate in this research program?"

"Yes."

"Along with other patients with the disease?"

"I believe there were others, yes."

"And the research protocol worked in your case?"

"Yes."

"You were cured."

"Yes."

"Thank you. Now, Mr. Burnet, you are aware that in medical research, new drugs to help fight disease are often derived from, or tested on, patient tissues?"

"Yes."

"You knew your tissues would be used in that fashion?"

"Yes, but not for commercial—"

"I'm sorry, just answer yes or no. When you agreed to allow your tissues to be used for research, did you know they might be used to derive or test new drugs?"

"Yes."

"And if a new drug was found, did you expect the drug to be made available to other patients?"

"Yes."

"Did you sign an authorization for that to happen?"

A long pause. Then: "Yes."

"Thank you, Mr. Burnet. I have no further questions."

"How do you think it went?" her father asked as they left the courthouse. Closing arguments were the following day. They walked toward the parking lot in the hazy sunshine of downtown Los Angeles.

"Hard to say," Alex said. "They confused the facts very successfully. We know there's no new drug that emerged from this program, but I doubt the jury understands what really happened. We'll bring in more expert witnesses to explain that UCLA just made a cell line from your tissues and used it to manufacture a cytokine, the way it is manufactured naturally inside your body. There's no 'new drug' here, but that'll probably be lost on the jury. And there's also the fact that Rodriguez is explicitly shaping this case to look exactly like the Moore case, a couple of decades back. Moore was a case very much like yours. Tissues were taken under false pretenses and sold. UCLA won that one easily, though they shouldn't have."

"So, counselor, how does our case stand?"

She smiled at her father, threw her arm around his shoulder, and kissed him on the cheek.

"Truth? It's uphill," she said.

B **arry Sindler,** divorce lawyer to the stars, shifted in his chair. He was trying to pay attention to the client seated across the desk from him, but he was having trouble. The client was a nerd named Diehl who ran some biotech company. The guy talked abstractly, no emotion, practically no expression on his face, even though he was telling how his wife was screwing around on him. Diehl must have been a terrible husband. But Barry wasn't sure how much money there was in this case. It seemed the wife had all the money.

Diehl droned on. How his first suspicions arose when he called her from Las Vegas. How he discovered the charge slips for the hotel that she went to every Wednesday. How he waited in the lobby and caught her checking in with a local tennis pro. Same old California story. Barry had heard it a hundred times. Didn't these people know they were walking clichés? Outraged husband catches wife with the tennis pro. They wouldn't even use that one on *Desperate Housewives*.

Barry gave up trying to listen. He had too much on his mind this morning. He had lost the Kirkorivich case, and it was all over town. Just because DNA tests had shown that it wasn't the billionaire's baby. And then the court wouldn't award him his fees, even though he had cut them to a measly $1.4 mil. The judge gave him a quarter of that. Every damn lawyer in town was gloating, because they all had it in for Barry Sindler. He had heard that *L.A. Magazine* was doing a big story on the case, sure to be unfavorable to Barry. Not that he gave a crap about that. The truth was, the more he got portrayed as an unprincipled,

ruthless prick, the more clients flocked to him. Because when it came
to a divorce, people wanted a ruthless prick. They lined up for one. And
Barry Sindler was without a doubt the most ruthless, unscrupulous,
publicity-hungry, self-aggrandizing, stop-at-nothing son-of-a-bitch
divorce lawyer in Southern California. And proud of it!

No, Barry didn't worry about any of those things. He didn't even
worry about the house he was building in Montana for Denise and her
two rotten kids. He didn't worry about the renovations on their house
in Holmby Hills, even though the kitchen alone was costing $500K,
and Denise kept changing the plans. Denise was a serial renovator. It
was a disease.

No, no, no. Barry Sindler worried about just one thing—the lease.
He had one whole floor in an office building on Wilshire and Doheny,
twenty-three attorneys in his office, none of them worth a shit, but
seeing all of them at their desks impressed the clients. And they could do
the minor stuff, like take depositions and file delaying motions—stuff
Barry didn't want to be bothered with. Barry knew that litigation was a
war of attrition, especially in custody cases. The goal was to run the
costs as high as you could and stretch the proceedings out as long as you
could, because that way Barry earned the largest possible fees, and the
spouse eventually got tired of the endless delays, the new filings, and of
course the spiraling costs. Even the richest of them eventually got tired.

By and large, husbands were sensible. They wanted to get on with
their lives, buy a new house, move in with the new girlfriend, get a nice
blow job. They wanted custody issues settled. But the wives usually
wanted revenge—so Barry kept things from being settled, year after
year, until the husbands caved. Millionaires, billionaires, celebrity
assholes—it didn't matter. They all caved in the end. People said it wasn't
a good strategy for the kids. Well, screw the kids. If the clients cared
anything about the kids, they wouldn't get divorced in the first place.
They'd stay married and miserable like everybody else, because—

The nerd had said something that jogged him back to attention.

"I'm sorry," Barry Sindler said. "Run that by me again, Mr. Diehl.
What did you just say?"

"I said, 'I want my wife tested.'"

"I can assure you, these proceedings will test her to the limit. And of course we'll put a detective on her, see how much she drinks, whether she does drugs, stays out all night, has lesbian affairs, all that. Standard procedure."

"No, no," Diehl said. "I want her tested genetically."

"For what?"

"For everything," he said.

"Ah," Barry said, nodding wisely. What the hell was the guy talking about? Genetic testing? In a custody case? He glanced down at the papers in front of him, and the business card. RICHARD "RICK" DIEHL, PH.D. Barry frowned unhappily. Only assholes put a nickname on the card. The card said he was CEO of BioGen Research Inc., some company out in Westview Village.

"For example," Diehl said, "I'll bet my wife has a genetic predisposition to bipolar illness. She certainly acts erratic. She might have the Alzheimer's gene. If she does, psychological tests could show early signs of Alzheimer's."

"Good, very good." Barry Sindler was nodding vigorously now. This was making him happy. Fresh, new disputed areas. Sindler loved disputed areas. Administer the psychological test. Did the test show early Alzheimer's or not? Who the fuck could say for sure? Wonderful, wonderful—whatever the test results, they would be disputed. More days in court, more expert witnesses to interview, battles of the doctorates, dragging on for days. Days in court were especially lucrative.

And best of all, Barry realized that this genetic testing could become standard procedure for all custody cases. Sindler was breaking new ground here. He'd get publicity for this! He leaned forward eagerly. "Go on, Mr. Diehl . . ."

"Test her for the diabetes gene, breast cancer from the BRCA genes, and all the rest. And," Diehl continued, "my wife might also have the gene for Huntington's disease, which causes fatal nerve degeneration. Her grandfather had Huntington's, so it's in her family. Both her parents are still young, and the disease only shows up when you're older. So my wife could be carrying the gene and that would mean a death sentence from Huntington's."

"Umm, yes," Barry Sindler said, nodding. "That could render her unfit to be the primary caregiver to the children."

"Exactly."

"I'm surprised she hasn't been tested already."

"She doesn't want to know," Diehl said. "There's a fifty-fifty chance she may have the gene. If she does, she'll eventually develop the disease and die writhing in dementia. But she's twenty-eight. The disease might not appear for another twenty years. So if she knew about it now . . . it could ruin the rest of her life."

"But it could also relieve her, if she didn't have the gene."

"Too big a risk. She won't test."

"Any other tests you can think of?"

"Hell yes," Diehl said. "That's just the beginning. I want her tested with all the current panels. There are twelve hundred gene tests now."

Twelve hundred! Sindler licked his lips at the prospect. Excellent! Why had he never heard of this before? He cleared his throat. "But you realize that if you do this, she will demand you be tested, as well."

"No problem," Diehl said.

"You've already been tested?"

"No. I just know how to fake the lab results."

Barry Sindler sat back in his chair.

Perfect.

CH004

Beneath the high canopy of trees, the jungle floor was dark and silent. No breeze stirred the giant ferns at shoulder height. Hagar wiped sweat from his forehead, glanced back at the others, and pushed on. The expedition moved deep into the jungles of central Sumatra. No one spoke, which was the way Hagar liked it.

The river was just ahead. A dugout canoe on the near bank, a rope stretched across the river at shoulder height. They crossed in two groups, Hagar standing up in the dugout, pulling them across on the rope, then going back for the others. It was silent except for the cry of a distant hornbill.

They continued on the opposite bank. The jungle trail grew narrower, and muddy in spots. The team didn't like that; they made a lot of noise trying to scramble around the wet patches. Finally, one said, "How much farther is it?"

It was that kid. The whiny American teenager with spots on his face. He was looking to his mother, a largish matron in a broad straw hat.

"Are we almost there?" the kid whined.

Hagar put his finger to his lips. "Quiet!"

"My feet hurt."

The other tourists were standing around, a cluster of bright-colored clothing. Staring at the kid.

"Look," Hagar whispered, "if you make noise, you won't see them."

"I don't see them anyhow." The kid pouted, but he fell into line as the group moved on. Today they were mostly Americans. Hagar didn't like Americans, but they weren't the worst. The worst, he had to admit, were the—

"*There!*"

"*Look there!*"

The tourists were pointing ahead, excited, chattering. About fifty yards up the trail and off to the right, a juvenile male orangutan stood upright in the branches that swayed gently with his weight. Magnificent creature, reddish fur, roughly forty pounds, distinctive white streak in the fur above his ear. Hagar had not seen him in weeks.

Hagar gestured for the others to be quiet, and moved up the trail. The tourists were close behind him now, stumbling, banging into one another in their excitement.

"Ssssh!" he hissed.

"What's the big deal?" one said. "I thought this was a sanctuary."

"*Ssssh!*"

"But they're protected here—"

"*Ssssh!*"

Hagar needed it quiet. He reached into his shirt pocket and pressed the Record button. He unclipped his lapel mike and held it in his hand.

They were now about thirty yards from the orang. They passed a sign along the trail that said BUKUT ALAM ORANGUTAN SANCTUARY. This was where orphaned orangs were nursed to health, and reintroduced into the wild. There was a veterinary facility, a research station, a team of researchers.

"If it's a sanctuary, I don't understand why—"

"George, you heard what he said. Be quiet."

Twenty yards, now.

"Look, another one! Two! There!"

They were pointing off to the left. High in the canopy, a one-year-old, crashing through branches with an older juvenile. Swinging gracefully. Hagar didn't care. He was focused on the first animal.

The white-streaked orang did not move away. Now he was hanging by one hand, swinging in the air, head cocked to one side as he looked at them. The younger animals in the canopy were gone. White-streak stayed where he was, and stared.

Ten yards. Hagar held his microphone out in front of him. The tourists were pulling out their cameras. The orang stared directly at Hagar and made an odd sound, like a cough. *"Dwaas."*

Hagar repeated the sound back. "Dwaas."

The orang stared at him. The curved lips moved. A sequence of guttural grunts: *"Ooh stomm dwaas, varlaat leanme."*

One of the tourists said, "Is he making those sounds?"

"Yes," Hagar said.

"Is he . . . *talking?*"

"Apes can't talk," another tourist said. "Orangs are silent. It says so in the book."

Several snapped flash pictures of the hanging ape. The juvenile male showed no surprise. But the lips moved: *"Geen lichten dwaas."*

"Does he have a cold?" a woman asked nervously. "Sounds like he's coughing?"

"He's not coughing," another voice said.

Hagar glanced over his shoulder. A heavyset man at the back, a man who had struggled to keep up, red-faced and puffing, now held a tape recorder in his hand, pointing it toward the orang. He had a determined look on his face. He said to Hagar, "Is this some kind of trick you play?"

"No," Hagar said.

The man pointed to the orang. "That's Dutch," he said. "Sumatra used to be a Dutch colony. That's Dutch."

"I wouldn't know," Hagar said.

"I would. The animal said, 'Stupid, leave me alone.' And then it said, 'No lights.' When the camera flashes went off."

"I don't know what those sounds were," Hagar said.

"But you were recording them."

"Just out of curiosity—"

"You had your microphone out long before the sounds began. You knew that animal would speak."

"Orangs can't speak," Hagar said.

"That one can."

They all stared at the orangutan, still swinging from one arm. It scratched itself with the free arm. It was silent.

The heavyset man said loudly, *"Geen lichten."*

The ape just stared, blinked slowly.

"Geen lichten!"

The orang gave no sign of comprehension. After a moment, he swung to a nearby branch, and began to climb into the air, moving easily, arm on arm.

"Geen lichten!"

The ape kept climbing. The woman in the big straw hat said, "I think it was just coughing or something."

"Hey," the heavyset man yelled. *"M'sieu! Comment ça va?"*

The ape continued up through the branches, swinging in an easy rhythm with its long arms. It did not look down.

"I thought maybe it speaks French," the man said. He shrugged. "Guess not."

A light rain began to drip from the canopy. The other tourists put their cameras away. One shrugged on a light, transparent raincoat. Hagar wiped the sweat from his forehead. Up ahead, three young orangs were scampering around a tray of papayas on the ground. The tourists turned their attention to them.

From high in the canopy came a growling sound: *"Espèce de con."* The phrase came to them clearly, surprisingly distinct in the still air.

The heavyset man spun around. *"What?"*

Everyone turned to look upward.

"That was a swear word," the teenager said. "In French. I know it was a swear word. In French."

"Hush," his mother said.

The group stared up at the canopy, searching the dense mass of dark leaves. They could not see the ape up there.

The heavyset man yelled, *"Qu'est-ce que tu dis?"*

There was no answer. Just the crash of an animal moving through branches, and the distant cry of a hornbill.

CHEEKY CHIMP CHEWS OFF TOURISTS
(News of the World)

AFFE SPRICHT IM DSCHUNGEL, FLÜCHE GEORGE BUSH
(Der Spiegel)

ORANG PARLE FRANÇAIS?!!
(Paris Match, beneath a picture of Jacques Derrida)

MUSLIM MONKEY BERATES WESTERNERS
(Weekly Standard)

MONKEY MOUTHS OFF, WITNESSES AGAPE
(National Enquirer)

TALKING CHIMPANZEE REPORTED IN JAVA
(New York Times, subsequent correction printed)

POLYGLOT PRIMATES SIGHTED IN SUMATRA
(Los Angeles Times)

"And, finally, a group of tourists in Indonesia swear they were abused by an orangutan in the jungles of Borneo. According to the tourists, the ape swore at them in Dutch and French, which means it was probably a lot smarter than they were. But no recordings of the cursing chimp have turned up, leading us to conclude that if you believe this story, we have a job for you in the current administration. Plenty of talking apes there!"

(Countdown with Keith Olbermann, MSNBC News, no correction)

CH005

"**G et this,**" Charlie Huggins said, looking at the television in the kitchen of his house in San Diego. The sound was turned off, but he was reading the crawl beneath. "It says, 'Talking Ape Cited in Sumatra.'"

"You mean it got a speeding ticket?" his wife said, glancing at the screen. She was making breakfast.

"No," Huggins said. "They must mean the ape was 'sighted.' With an 's.'"

"The ape was sighted? Meaning the ape could see?" His wife was a high school English teacher. She liked these jokes.

"No, honey. The story says . . . some people in Sumatra encountered an ape in the jungle that talked."

"I thought apes can't talk," his wife said.

"Well, that's what the story says."

"So it has to be a lie."

"You think? Uh, now . . . Britney Spears is not getting divorced. I'm relieved. She may be pregnant again. From the pictures it looks like it. And Posh Spice wore a nice green dress to a gala. And Sting says he can have sex for eight hours without stopping."

"Scrambled or over easy?" his wife said.

"Tantric, apparently."

"I mean your eggs."

"Scrambled."

"Call the kids, will you?" she said. "Everything's almost ready."

"Okay." Charlie got up from the table and headed for the stairs. When he got to the living room, the phone rang. It was the lab.

In the laboratories of Radial Genomics Inc., in the eucalyptus groves of the University of California at San Diego, Henry Kendall drummed his fingers on the countertop while he waited for Charlie to pick up. The phone rang three times. Where the fuck was he? Finally, Charlie's voice: "Hello?"

"Charlie," Henry said. "Did you hear the news?"

"What news?"

"The ape in Sumatra, for Christ's sake."

"That has to be bullshit," Charlie said.

"Why?"

"Come on, Henry. You know it's bullshit."

"They said the ape spoke Dutch."

"It's bullshit."

"It might have been Uttenbroek's team," Kendall said.

"Nah. The ape was big, two or three years old."

"So? Uttenbroek could have done it a few years ago. His team's advanced enough. Besides, those guys from Utrecht are all liars."

Charlie Huggins sighed. "It's illegal in the Netherlands to do that research."

"Right. Which is why they would go to Sumatra to do it."

"Henry, the technology's much too difficult. We're years away from making a transgenic ape. You know that."

"I don't know that. You hear what Utrecht announced yesterday? They harvested bull stem cells and cultured them in mouse testicles. I would say *that* is difficult. I would say that is fucking cutting edge."

"Especially for the bulls."

"I don't see anything funny here."

"Can't you imagine the poor mice, dragging around giant purple bulls' balls?"

"Still not laughing . . ."

"Henry," Charlie said. "Are you telling me you see one report on television about a talking ape, and you actually believe it?"

"I'm afraid I do."

"Henry." Charlie sounded exasperated. "It's television. This story's right up there with the two-headed snake. Pull yourself together."

"The two-headed snake was real."

"I have to get the kids to school. I'll talk to you later." And Charlie hung up.

Fucker. His wife always took the kids to school.

He's avoiding me.

Henry Kendall walked around the lab, stared out the window, paced some more. He took a deep breath. Of course he knew Charlie was right. It had to be a fake story.

But . . . what if it wasn't?

It was true that Henry Kendall had a tendency to be high-strung; his hands sometimes shook when he spoke, especially when he was excited. And he was a bit of a klutz, always stumbling, banging into things at the lab. He had a nervous stomach. He was a worrier.

But what Henry couldn't tell Charlie was that the real reason he was worried now had to do with a conversation that had taken place a week ago. It seemed meaningless at the time.

Now it took on a more ominous quality.

Some ditsy secretary from the National Institutes of Health had called the lab and asked for Dr. Kendall. When he answered the phone, she said, "Are you Dr. Henry A. Kendall?"

"Yes . . ."

"Is it correct that you came to the NIH on a six-month sabbatical four years ago?"

"Yes, I did."

"Was that from May until October?"

"I think it was. What's this about?"

"And did you conduct part of your research at the primate facility in Maryland?"

"Yes."

"And is it correct that when you came to the NIH in May of that year, you underwent the usual testing for communicable diseases, because you were going to do primate research?"

"Yes," Henry said. They had done a battery of tests, everything from HIV to hepatitis to flu. They'd drawn a lot of blood. "May I ask what this is about?"

"I am just filling out some additional paperwork," she said, "for Dr. Bellarmino."

Henry felt a chill.

Rob Bellarmino was the head of the genetics section of NIH. He hadn't been there four years before, when Henry was there, but he was in charge of things now. And he was no particular friend of either Henry or Charlie.

"Is there some problem?" Henry asked. He had the distinct feeling there was.

"No, no," she said. "We've just misplaced some of our paperwork, and Dr. Bellarmino is a stickler about records. While you were at the primate facility, did you do any research involving a female chimpanzee named Mary? Her lab number was F-402."

"You know, I don't remember," Henry said. "It's a long time back. I worked with several chimps. I don't recall specifically."

"She was pregnant during that summer."

"I'm sorry, I just don't remember."

"That was the summer we had an outbreak of encephalitis, and they had to quarantine most of the chimps. Is that right?"

"Yes, I remember the quarantine. They sent chimps all around the country to different facilities."

"Thank you, Dr. Kendall. Oh—while I have you on the phone, can I verify your address? We have 348 Marbury Madison Drive, La Jolla?"

"Yes, it is."

"Thanks for your time, Dr. Kendall."

That was the entire conversation. All Henry really thought, at the time, was that Bellarmino was a tricky son of a bitch; you never knew what he was up to.

But now . . . with this primate in Sumatra . . .

Henry shook his head.

Charlie Huggins could argue all he wanted, but it was a fact that scientists had already made a transgenic monkey. They'd done it years ago. There were all kinds of transgenic mammals these days—dogs, cats, everything. It was not out of the question that the talking orang was a transgenic animal.

Henry's work at NIH had been concerned with the genetic basis of autism. He'd gone to the primate facility because he wanted to know which genes accounted for the differences in communication abilities between humans and apes. And he had done some work with chimp embryos. It didn't lead anywhere. In fact, he had hardly gotten started before the encephalitis outbreak halted his research. He ended up back at Bethesda and working in a lab for the duration of his sabbatical.

That was all he knew.

At least, all he knew for sure.

HUMANS AND CHIMPS INTERBRED UNTIL RECENTLY

Species Split Did Not End Sex, Researchers Find a Controversial Result from Genetics

Researchers at Harvard and MIT have concluded that the split between humans and chimpanzees occurred more recently than previously thought. Gene investigators had long known that apes and human beings both derived from a common ancestor, who walked the earth some 18 million years ago. Gibbons split off first, 16 million years ago. Orangutans split about 12 million years ago. Gorillas split 10 million years ago. Chimpanzees and human beings were the last to split, about 9 million years ago.

However, after decoding the human genome in 2001, geneticists discovered that human beings and chimps differed in only 1.5% of their genes—about 500 genes in all. This was far fewer than expected. By 2003, scientists had begun to catalog precisely which genes differed between the species. It is now clear that many structural proteins, including hemoglobin and cytochrome c proteins, are identical in chimps and humans. Human and chimp blood are identical. If the species split 9 million years ago, why are they still so alike?

Harvard geneticists believe humans and chimpanzees continued to interbreed long after the species split. Such interbreeding, or hybridization, puts evolutionary pressure on the X chromosome, causing it to change more rapidly than normal. The researchers found that the newest genes on the human genome appear on the X chromosome.

From this, researchers argue that ancestral humans continued to breed with chimps until 5.4 million years ago, when the split became permanent. This new view stands in sharp contrast to the consensus view that once speciation occurs, hybridization is "a negligible influence." But according to Dr. David Reich of Harvard, the fact that hybridization has rarely been seen in other species "may simply be due to the fact that we have not been looking for it."

The Harvard researchers caution that interbreeding of humans and chimpanzees is not possible in the present day. They point out that press reports of hybrid "humanzees" have invariably proven false.

BioGen Research Inc. was housed in a titanium-skinned cube in an industrial park outside Westview Village in Southern California. Majestically situated above the traffic on the 101 Freeway, the cube had been the idea of BioGen's president, Rick Diehl, who insisted on calling it a hexahedron. The cube looked impressive and high-tech while revealing absolutely nothing about what went on inside—which is exactly how Diehl wanted it.

In addition, BioGen maintained forty thousand square feet of nondescript shed space in an industrial park two miles away. It was there that the animal storage facilities were located, along with the more dangerous labs. Josh Winkler, an up-and-coming young researcher, picked up rubber gloves and a surgical mask from a shelf by the door to the animal quarters. His assistant, Tom Weller, was reading a news clipping taped to the wall.

"Let's go, Tom," Josh said.

"Diehl must be crapping in his pants," Weller said, pointing to the article. "Have you read this?"

Josh turned to look. It was an article from the *Wall Street Journal*:

SCIENTISTS ISOLATE "MASTER" GENE

A Genetic Basis for Controlling Other People?

TOULOUSE, FRANCE—A team of French biologists have isolated the gene that drives certain people to attempt to control others. Geneticists at the Biochemical Institute of Toulouse University, headed by Dr. Michel Narcejac-Boileau, announced the discovery at a press conference today. "The gene," Dr. Narcejac-Boileau said, "is associated with social dominance and strong control over other people. We have isolated it in sports leaders, CEOs, and heads of state. We believe the gene is found in all dictators throughout history."

Dr. Narcejac-Boileau explained that while the strong form of the gene produced dictators, the milder heterozygous form produced a "moderate, quasi-totalitarian urge" to tell other people how to run their lives, generally for their own good or for their own safety.

"Significantly, on psychological testing, individuals with the mild form will express the view that other people need their insights, and are unable to manage their own lives without their guidance. This form of the gene exists among politicians, policy advocates, religious fundamentalists, and celebrities. The belief complex is manifested by a strong feeling of certainty, coupled with a powerful sense of entitlement—and a carefully nurtured sense of resentment toward those who don't listen to them."

At the same time, he urged caution in interpreting the results. "Many people who are driven to control others merely want everybody to be the same as they are. They can't tolerate difference."

This explained the team's paradoxical finding that individuals with the mild form of the gene were also the most tolerant of authoritarian environments with strict and invasive social rules. "Our study shows that the gene produces not only a bossy person, but also a person willing to be bossed. They have a distinct attraction to totalitarian states." He noted that these people are especially responsive to fashions of all kinds, and suppress opinions and preferences not shared by their group.

Josh said, "'Especially responsive to fashions' . . . Is this a joke?"

"No, they're serious. It's marketing," Tom Weller said. "Today everything is marketing. Read the rest."

Although the French team stopped short of claiming that the mild form of the master gene represented a genetic disease—an "addiction to belonging," as Narcejac-Boileau phrased it—they nevertheless suggested that evolutionary pressures were moving the human race toward ever-greater conformity.

"Unbelievable," Josh said. "These guys in Toulouse hold a press conference and the whole world runs their story about the 'master gene'? Have they published in a journal anywhere?"

"Nope, they just held a press conference. No publication, and no mention of publication."

"What's next, the slave gene? Looks like crap to me," Josh said. He glanced at his watch.

"You mean, we hope it's crap."

"Yeah, that's what I mean. We hope it's crap. Because it gets in the way of what BioGen's announcing, that's for sure."

"You think Diehl will delay the announcement?" Tom Weller asked.

"Maybe. But Diehl doesn't like waiting. And he's been nervous ever since he got back from Vegas."

Josh tugged on his rubber gloves, put on safety goggles and his paper face-mask, then picked up the six-inch-long compressed-air cylinder, and screwed on the vial of retrovirus. The whole apparatus was the size of a cigar tube. Next, he fitted a tiny plastic cone on top of that, pushing it in place with his thumb. "Grab your PDA."

And they pushed through the swinging door, into the animal quarters.

The strong, slightly sweet odor of the rats was a familiar smell. There were five or six hundred rats here, all neatly labeled in cages stacked six feet high, on both sides of an aisle that ran down the center of the room.

"What're we dosing today?" Tom Weller said.

Josh read off a string of numbers. Tom checked his PDA listing of numerical locations. They walked down the aisle until they found the cages with that day's numbers. Five rats in five cages. The animals were white, plump, moving normally. "They look okay. This is the second dose?"

"Right."

"Okay, boys," Josh said. "Let's be nice for Daddy." He opened the first cage, and quickly grabbed the rat inside. He held the animal by the body, forefingers expertly gripping the neck, and quickly fitted the small plastic cone over the rat's snout. The animal's breath clouded the cone. A brief hiss as the virus was released; Josh held the mask in place for ten seconds, while the rat inhaled. Then he released the animal back into the cage.

"One down."

Tom Weller tapped his stylus on the PDA, then moved to the next cage.

The retrovirus had been bioengineered to carry a gene known as ACMPD3N7, one of the family of genes controlling aminocarboxymuconate paraldehyde decarboxylase. Within BioGen they called it the maturity gene. When activated, ACMPD3N7 seemed to modify responses of the amygdala and cingulate gyrus in the brain. The result was an acceleration of maturational behavior—at least in rats. Infant female rats, for example, would show precursors of maternal behavior, such as rolling feces in their cages, far earlier than usual. And BioGen had preliminary evidence for the maturational gene action in rhesus monkeys, as well.

Interest in the gene centered on a potential link to neurodegenerative disease. One school of thought argued that neurodegenerative illnesses were a result of disruptions of maturational pathways in the brain.

If that were true—if ACMPD3N7 were involved in, say, Alzheimer's disease, or another form of senility—then the commercial value of the gene would be enormous.

Josh had moved on to the next cage and was holding the mask over the second rat when his cell phone went off. He gestured for Tom to pull it from his shirt pocket.

Weller looked at the screen. "It's your mother," he said.

"Ah hell," Josh said. "Take over for a minute, would you?"

"Joshua, what are you doing?"

"I'm working, Mom."

"Well, can you stop?"

"Not really—"

"Because we have an emergency."

Josh sighed. "What did he do this time, Mom?"

"I don't know," she said, "but he's in jail, downtown."

"Well, let Charles get him out." Charles Silverberg was the family lawyer.

"Charles is getting him out right now," his mother said. "But Adam has to appear in court. Somebody has to drive him home after the hearing."

"I can't. I'm at work."

"He's your brother, Josh."

"He's also thirty years old," Josh said. This had been going on for years. His brother Adam was an investment banker who had been in and out of rehab a dozen times. "Can't he take a taxi?"

"I don't think that's wise, under the circumstances."

Josh sighed. "What'd he do, Mom?"

"Apparently he bought cocaine from a woman who worked for the DEA."

"Again?"

"Joshua. Are you going to go downtown and pick him up or not?"

Long sigh. "Yes, Mom. I'll go."

"Now? Will you go now?"

"Yes, Mom. I'll go now."

He flipped the phone shut and turned to Weller. "What do you say we finish this in a couple of hours?"

"No problem," Tom said. "I have some notes to write up back in the office, anyway."

Joshua turned, stripping off his gloves as he left the room. He stuck his cylinder, goggles, and paper mask into the pocket of his lab coat, unclipped his radiation tag, and hurried to his car.

Driving downtown, he glanced at the cylinder protruding from the lab coat, which he had tossed onto the passenger seat. To stay within the protocol, Josh had to return to the lab and expose the remaining rats before five p.m. That kind of schedule and the need to keep to it seemed to represent everything that separated Josh from his older brother.

Once, Adam had had everything—looks, popularity, athletic prowess. His high school days at the elite Westfield School had consisted of one triumph after another—editor of the newspaper, soccer team captain, president of the debating team, National Merit Scholar. Josh, in contrast, had been a nerd. He was chubby, short, ungainly. He walked with a kind of waddle; he couldn't help it. The orthopedic shoes his mother insisted he wear did not help. Girls disdained him. He heard them giggle as he passed them in the hallways. High school was torture for Josh. He did not do well. Adam went to Yale. Josh barely got into Emerson State.

How times had changed.

A year ago, Adam had been fired from his job at Deutsche Bank. His drug troubles were endless. Meanwhile, Josh had started at BioGen as a lowly assistant, but had quickly moved up as the company began to recognize his hard work and his inventive approach. Josh had stock in the company, and if any of the current projects, including the maturity gene, proved out commercially, then he would be rich.

And Adam . . .

Josh pulled up in front of the courthouse. Adam was sitting on the steps, staring fixedly at the ground. His ratty suit was streaked with grime and he had a day's growth of beard. Charles Silverberg was standing over him, talking on his cell phone.

Josh honked the horn. Charles waved, and headed off. Adam trudged over and got in the car.

"Thanks, bro." He slammed the door shut. "Appreciate it."

"No problem."

Josh pulled into traffic, glancing at his watch. He had enough time to take Adam back to their mother's house and get back to the lab by five.

"Did I interrupt something?" Adam asked.

That was the annoying thing about his brother. He liked to mess up everyone else's life, too. He seemed to take pleasure in it.

"Yes, actually. You did."

"Sorry."

"Sorry? If you were sorry, you'd stop doing this shit."

"Hey, man," Adam said. "How the fuck was I supposed to know? It was entrapment, man. Even Charles said so. The bitch entrapped me. Charles said he would get me off easy."

"There wouldn't be any entrapment," Josh said, "if you weren't using."

"Oh, go fuck yourself! Don't lecture me."

Josh said nothing. Why did he even bring it up? After all these years, he knew nothing he said mattered. Nothing made a difference. There was a long silence as he drove.

"I'm sorry," Adam said.

"You're not sorry."

"Yeah, you're right," Adam said. "You're right." He hung his head. He sighed theatrically. "I fucked up again."

The repentant Adam.

Josh had seen it dozens of times before. The belligerent Adam, the repentant Adam, the logical Adam, the denying Adam. Meanwhile his brother always tested positive. Every time.

An orange light came on on the dashboard. Gas was low. He saw a station up ahead. "I need gas."

"Good. I got to take a leak."

"You stay in the car."

"I got to take a leak, man."

"Stay in the fucking car." Josh pulled up alongside the pump and got out. "Stay where I can fucking see you."

"I don't want to pee in your car, man . . ."

"You better not."

"But—"

"Just hold it, Adam!"

Josh put a credit card in the slot and started pumping gas. He glanced at his brother through the rear windshield, then looked back at the spinning numbers. Gas was so damn expensive now. He probably should buy a car that was cheaper to run.

He finished and got back in the car. He glanced at Adam. His brother had a funny look on his face. There was a faint odor in the car.

"Adam?"

"What."

"What did you do?"

"Nothing."

He started the engine. That smell . . . Something silver caught his eye. He looked at the floor between his brother's feet and saw the silver cylinder. He leaned over, picked up the cylinder. It was light in his hand.

"Adam . . ."

"I didn't do anything!"

Josh shook the cylinder. It was empty.

"I thought it was nitrous or something," his brother said.

"You asshole."

"Why? It didn't do anything."

"It's for a rat, Adam. You just inhaled virus for a rat."

Adam slumped back. "Is that bad?"

"It ain't good."

By the time Josh pulled up in front of his mother's house in Beverly Hills, he had thought it through and concluded that there was no danger to Adam. The retrovirus was a mouse-infective strain, and while it might also infect human beings, the dose had been calculated for an animal weighing eight hundred grams. His brother weighed a hundred times as much. The genetic exposure was subclinical.

"So, I'm okay?" Adam said.

"Yeah."

"Sure?"

"Yeah."

"Sorry about that," Adam said, getting out of the car. "But thanks for picking me up. See you, bro."

"I'll wait until you get inside," Josh said. He watched as his brother walked up the drive and knocked on the door. His mother opened it. Adam stepped inside, and she shut the door.

She never even looked at Josh.

He started the engine and drove away.

CH007

At noon, Alex Burnet left her office in her Century City law firm and went home. She didn't have far to go; she lived in an apartment on Roxbury Park with her eight-year-old son, Jamie. Jamie had a cold and had stayed home from school. Her father was looking after him for her.

She found her dad in the kitchen, making macaroni and cheese. It was the only thing Jamie would eat these days. "How is he?" she said.

"Fever's down. Still got a runny nose and a cough."

"Is he hungry?"

"He wasn't earlier. But he asked for macaroni."

"That's a good sign," she said. "Should I take over?"

Her father shook his head. "I've got it handled. You didn't have to come home, you know."

"I know." She paused. "The judge issued his ruling, Dad."

"When?"

"This morning."

"And?"

"We lost."

Her father continued to stir. "We lost everything?"

"Yes," she said. "We lost on every point. You have no rights to your own tissue. He ruled them 'material waste' that you allowed the university to dispose of for you. The court says you have no rights to any of your tissue once it has left your body. The university can do what it wants with it."

"But they brought me back—"

"He said a reasonable person would have realized the tissues were being collected for commercial use. Therefore you tacitly accepted it."

"But they told me I was sick."

"He rejected all our arguments, Dad."

"They lied to me."

"I know, but according to the judge, good social policy promotes medical research. Granting you rights now would have a chilling effect on future research. That's the thinking behind the ruling—the common good."

"This wasn't about the common good. It was about getting rich," her father said. "Jesus, three billion dollars . . ."

"I know, Dad. Universities want money. And basically, this judge held what California judges have held for the last twenty-five years, ever since the Moore decision in 1980. Just like your case, the court found that Moore's tissues were waste materials to which he had no right. And they haven't revisited that question in more than two decades."

"So what happens now?"

"We appeal," she said. "I don't think we have good grounds, but we have to do it before we can go to the California Supreme Court."

"And when will that be?"

"A year from now."

"Do we have a chance?" her father said.

"Absolutely not," Albert Rodriguez said, turning in his chair toward her father. Rodriguez and the other UCLA attorneys had come to Alex's law offices in the aftermath of the judge's ruling. "You have no chance on further appeal, Mr. Burnet."

"I'm surprised," Alex said, "that you're so confident about how the California Supreme Court will rule."

"Oh, we have no idea how they will rule," Rodriguez said. "I simply mean that you will lose this case no matter what the court holds."

"How is that?" Alex said.

"UCLA is a state university. The Board of Regents is prepared, on behalf of the state of California, to take your father's cells by right of eminent domain."

She blinked: *"What?"*

"Should the Supreme Court rule that your father's cells *are* his property—which we think is unlikely—the state will take ownership of his property by eminent domain."

Eminent domain referred to the right of the state to take private property without the owner's consent. It was almost always invoked for public uses. "But eminent domain is intended for schools or highways . . ."

"The state can do it in this case," Rodriguez said. "And it will."

Her father stared at them, thunderstruck. "Are you joking?"

"No, Mr. Burnet. It's a legitimate taking, and the state will exercise its right."

Alex said, "Then what is the purpose of this meeting?"

"We thought it appropriate to inform you of the situation, in case you wanted to drop further litigation."

"You're suggesting we end litigation?" she said.

"I would advise it," Rodriguez said to her, "if this were my client."

"Ending litigation saves the state considerable expense."

"It saves everyone expense," Rodriguez said.

"So what are you proposing as a settlement, for us to drop the case?"

"Nothing whatever, Ms. Burnet. I'm sorry if you misunderstood me. This is not a negotiation. We're simply here to explain our position, so that you can make an informed decision in your best interest."

Her father cleared his throat. "You're telling us that you're taking my cells, no matter what. You've sold them for three billion dollars, no matter what. And you're keeping all of that money, no matter what."

"Bluntly put," Rodriguez said, "but not inaccurate."

The meeting ended. Rodriguez and his team thanked them for their time, said their good-byes, and left the room. Alex nodded to her father and then followed the other attorneys outside. Through the glass, Frank Burnet watched as they talked further.

"Those fuckers," he said. "What kind of world do we live in?"

"My sentiments exactly," said a voice from behind him. Burnet turned.

A young man wearing horn-rimmed glasses was sitting in the far corner of the conference room. Burnet remembered him; he had come in during the meeting, bringing coffee and mugs, which he had put on the sideboard. Then he had sat down in the corner for the rest of the meeting. Burnet had assumed he was a junior member of the firm, but now the young man was speaking with confidence.

"Let's face it, Mr. Burnet," he said, "you've been screwed. It turns out your cells are very rare and valuable. They're efficient manufacturers of cytokines, chemicals that fight cancer. That's the real reason you survived your disease. As a matter of fact, your cells churn out cytokines more efficiently than any commercial process. That's why those cells are worth so much money. The UCLA doctors didn't create anything or invent anything. They didn't genetically modify anything. They just took your cells, grew them in a dish, and sold the dish to BioGen. And you, my friend, were *screwed*."

"Who are you?" Burnet said.

"And you have no hope of justice," the young man continued, "because the courts are totally incompetent. The courts don't realize how fast things are changing. They don't understand we are *already* in a new world. They don't get the new issues. And because they are technically illiterate, they don't understand what procedures are done—or in this case, not done. Your cells were stolen and sold. Plain and simple. And the court decided that was just fine."

Burnet gave a long sigh.

"But," the man continued, "thieves can still get their comeuppance."

"How's that?"

"Because UCLA did nothing to change your cells, another company could take those same cells, make minor genetic modifications, and sell them as a new product."

"But BioGen already has my cells."

"True. But cell lines are fragile. Things happen to them."

"What do you mean?"

"Cultures are vulnerable to fungus, bacterial infection, contamination, mutation. All kinds of things can go wrong."

"BioGen must take precautions . . ."

"Of course. But sometimes the precautions are inadequate," the man said.

"Who are you?" Burnet said again. He was looking around, through the glass walls of the conference room, at the larger office outside. He saw people walking back and forth. He wondered where his daughter had gone.

"I'm nobody," the young man said. "You never met me."

"You have a business card?"

The man shook his head. "I'm not here, Mr. Burnet."

Burnet frowned. "And my daughter—"

"Has no idea. Never met her. This is between us."

"But you're talking about illegal activity."

"I'm not talking at all, because you and I have never met," the man said. "But let's consider how this might work."

"Okay . . ."

"You can't *legally* sell your cells at this point, because the court has ruled you no longer own them—BioGen does. But your cells could be obtained from other places. Over the course of your life, you've given blood many times in many places. You went to Vietnam forty years ago. The army took your blood. You had knee surgery twenty years ago in San Diego. The hospital took your blood, and kept your cartilage. You've consulted various doctors over the years. They ran blood tests. The labs kept the blood. So your blood can be found, no problem. And it can be acquired from publicly available databases—if, for example, another company wanted to use your cells."

"And what about BioGen?"

The young man shrugged. "Biotechnology is a difficult business. Contaminations happen every day. If something goes wrong in their labs, that's not your problem, is it?"

"But how could—"

"I have no idea. So many things can happen."

There was a short silence. "And why should I do this?" Burnet said.

"You'll get a hundred million dollars."

"For what?"

"Punch biopsies of six organ systems."

"I thought you could get my blood elsewhere."

"In theory. If it came to litigation, that would be claimed. But, in practice, any company would want fresh cells."

"I don't know what to say."

"No problem. Think it over, Mr. Burnet." The young man stood, pushed his glasses up his nose. "You may have been screwed. But there's no reason to bend over for it."

From Beaumont College *Alumni News*

STEM CELL DEBATE RAGES

Effective Treatments "Decades Away"
Prof. McKeown Shocks Audience

———

By Max Thaler

Speaking to a packed audience in Beaumont Hall, famed biology professor Kevin McKeown shocked listeners by calling stem cell research "a cruel fraud."

"What you have been told is nothing more than a myth," he said, "intended to ensure funding for researchers, at the expense of false hopes for the seriously ill. So let's get to the truth."

Stem cells, he explained, are cells that have the ability to turn themselves into other kinds of cells. There are two kinds of stem cells. Adult stem cells are found throughout the body. They are found in muscle, brain, and liver tissue, and so on. Adult stem cells can generate new cells, but only of the tissue in which they are found. They are important because the human body replaces all its cells every seven years.

Research involving adult stem cells is for the most part not controversial. But there is another kind of stem cell, the embryonic stem cell, that is highly controversial. It is found in umbilical cord blood, or derived from young embryos. Embryonic stem cells are pluripotent, meaning they can develop into any kind of tissue. But the research is controversial because it involves the use of human embryos, which many people feel, for religious and other reasons, have the rights of human beings. This is an old debate not likely to be resolved soon.

SCIENTISTS SEE A BAN ON RESEARCH

The current American administration has said that embryonic stem cells can be taken from existing research lines, but not from new embryos. Scientists regard existing lines as inadequate, and thus view the ruling a de facto ban on research. That's why they are going to private centers to carry out their research, without federal grants.

But in the end, the real problem isn't simply a lack of stem cells. It's the fact that in order to produce therapeutic effects, scientists need each person to have his or her own pluripotent stem cells. This would allow us to regrow an organ, or to repair damage from injury or disease, or to undo paralysis. This represents the great dream. No one is able to perform these therapeutic miracles now. No one even has an inkling how it might be done. But it requires the cells.

Now, for newborns, you can collect umbilical cord blood and freeze it, and people are doing that with their newborns. But what about adults? Where will we get pluripotent stem cells?

That's the big question.

TOWARD THE THERAPEUTIC DREAM

All we adults have left is adult stem cells, which can make only one kind of tissue. But what if there were a way to convert adult stem cells back into embryonic stem cells? Such a procedure would enable every adult to have a ready source of his or her own embryonic stem cells. That would make the therapeutic dream possible.

Well, it turns out that you *can* reverse adult stem cells, but only if you insert them into an egg. Something within the egg unwinds the differentiation and converts the adult stem cell back into an embryonic stem cell. This is good news, but it is vastly more difficult to do with human cells. And if the method could be made to work in human beings, it would require an enormous supply of human egg cells. That makes the procedure controversial again.

So scientists are looking for other ways to make adult cells pluripotent. It is a worldwide effort. A researcher in Shanghai has been injecting human stem cells into chicken eggs, with mixed results—while others cluck in disapproval. It's not clear now whether such procedures will work.

It's equally unclear whether the stem cell dream—transplants without rejection, spinal cord injuries repaired, and so on—will come true. Advocates have made dishonest claims, and media speculation has been fantastical for years. People with serious illnesses have been led to believe a cure is just around the corner. Sadly, this is not true. Working therapeutic approaches lie many years in the future, perhaps decades. Many thoughtful scientists have said, in private, that we won't know whether stem cell therapy will work until 2050. They point out that it took forty years from the time Watson and Crick decoded the gene until human gene therapy began.

A SCANDAL SHOCKS THE WORLD

It was in the context of feverish hope and hype that Korean biochemist Hwang Woo-Suk announced in 2004 that he had successfully created a human embryonic stem cell from an adult cell by somatic nuclear transfer—injection into a human egg. Hwang was a famous workaholic, spending eighteen hours a day, seven days a week, in the lab. Hwang's exciting report was published in March 2005 in *Science* magazine. Researchers from around the world flocked to Korea. Human stem cell treatment seemed suddenly on the verge of reality. Hwang was a hero in Korea, and appointed to head a new World Stem Cell Hub, financed by the Korean government.

But in November 2005, an American collaborator in Pittsburgh announced that he was ending his association with Hwang. And then one of Hwang's co-workers revealed that Hwang had obtained eggs illegally, from women who worked in his lab.

By December 2005, Seoul National University announced that Hwang's cell lines were a fabrication, as were his papers in *Science*. *Science* retracted the papers. Hwang now faces criminal charges. There the matter stands.

PERILS OF "MEDIA HYPE"

"What lessons can be drawn from this?" asked Professor McKeown. "First, in a media-saturated world, persistent hype lends unwarranted credulity to the wildest claims. For years the media have touted stem cell research as the coming miracle. So when somebody announced that the miracle had arrived, he was believed. Does that imply there is a danger in media hype? You bet. Because not only does it raise cruel hopes among the ill, it affects scientists, too. They start to believe the miracle is around the corner—even though they should know better.

"What can we do about media hype? It would stop in a week, if scientific institutions wanted that. They don't. They love the hype. They know it brings grants. So that won't change. Yale, Stanford, and Johns Hopkins promote hype just as much as Exxon or Ford. So do individual researchers at those institutions. And increasingly, researchers and universities are all commercially motivated, just like corporations. So whenever you hear a scientist claim that his statements have been exaggerated, or taken out of context, just ask him if he has written a letter of protest to the editor. Ninety-nine times out of a hundred, he hasn't.

"Next lesson: Peer review. All of Hwang's papers in *Science* were peer-reviewed. If we ever needed evidence that peer review is an empty ritual, this episode provides it. Hwang made extraordinary claims. He did not provide extraordinary evidence. Many studies have shown that peer review does not improve the quality of scientific papers. Scientists themselves know it doesn't work. Yet the public still regards it as a sign of quality, and says, 'This paper was peer-reviewed,' or 'This paper was not peer-reviewed,' as if that meant something. It doesn't.

"Next, the journals themselves. Where was the firm hand of the editor of *Science*? Remember that the journal *Science* is a big enterprise—115 people work on that magazine. Yet gross fraud, including photographs altered with Adobe Photoshop, were not detected. And Photoshop is widely known as a major tool of scientific fraud. Yet the magazine had no way to detect it.

"Not that *Science* is unique in being fooled. Fraudulent research has been published in the *New England Journal of Medicine*, where authors withheld critical information about Vioxx heart attacks; in the *Lancet*, where a report about drugs and oral cancer was entirely fabricated—in that one, 250 people in the patient database had the same birth date! That might have been a clue. Medical fraud is more than a scandal, it's a public health threat. Yet it continues."

THE COST OF FRAUD

"The cost of such fraud is enormous," McKeown said, "estimated at thirty billion dollars annually, probably three times that. Fraud in science is not rare, and it's not limited to fringe players. The most respected researchers and institutions have been caught with faked data. Even Francis Collins, the head of NIH's Human Genome Project, was listed as co-author on five faked papers that had to be withdrawn.

"The ultimate lesson is that science isn't special—at least not anymore. Maybe back when Einstein talked to Niels Bohr, and there were only a few dozen important workers in every field. But there are now three million researchers in America. It's no longer a calling, it's a career. Science is as corruptible a human activity as any other. Its practitioners aren't saints, they're human beings, and they do what human beings do—lie, cheat, steal from one another, sue, hide data, fake data, overstate their own importance, and denigrate opposing views unfairly. That's human nature. It isn't going to change."

CH008

In the BioGen animal lab, Tom Weller was going down the line of cages with Josh Winkler, who was dispensing doses of gene-laced virus to the rats. It was their daily routine. Tom's cell phone rang.

Josh gave him a look. Josh was his senior. Josh could take calls at work, but Tom couldn't. Weller stripped off one rubber glove and pulled the phone from his pocket.

"Hello?"

"Tom."

It was his mother. "Hi, Mom. I'm at work now."

Josh gave him another look.

"Can I call you back?"

"Your dad had a car accident last night," she said. "And . . . he died."

"What?" He felt suddenly dizzy. Tom leaned against the rat cages, took a shallow breath. Now Josh was giving him a concerned look. "What happened?"

"His car hit an overpass around midnight," his mother said. "They took him to Long Beach Memorial Hospital, but he died early this morning."

"Oh God. Are you at home?" Tom said. "You want me to come over? Does Rachel know?"

"I just got off the phone."

"Okay, I'll come over," he said.

"Tom, I hate to ask you this," she said, "but . . ."

"You want me to tell Lisa?"

"I'm sorry. I can't seem to reach her." Lisa was the black sheep of the family. The youngest child, just turned twenty. Lisa hadn't talked to her mother in years. "Do you know where she is these days, Tom?"

"I think so," he said. "She called a few weeks ago."

"To ask for money?"

"No, just to give me her address. She's in Torrance."

"I can't reach her," his mother said.

"I'll go," he said.

"Tell her the funeral is Thursday, if she wants to come."

"I'll tell her."

He flipped the phone shut and turned to Josh. Josh was looking concerned and sympathetic. "What was it?"

"My father died."

"I'm really sorry . . ."

"Car crash, last night. I need to go tell my sister."

"You have to leave now?"

"I'll stop by the office on my way out and send Sandy in."

"Sandy can't do this. He doesn't know the routine—"

"Josh," he said, "I have to go."

Traffic was heavy on the 405. It took almost an hour before he found himself in front of a ratty apartment building on South Acre in Torrance, pushing the buzzer for apartment 38. The building stood close to the freeway; the roar of traffic was constant.

He knew Lisa worked nights, but it was now ten o'clock in the morning. She might be awake. Sure enough, the buzzer sounded, and he opened the door. The lobby smelled strongly of cat piss. The elevator didn't work, so he took the stairs to the third floor, stepping around plastic sacks of garbage. A dog had broken one sack open, and the contents spilled down a couple of steps.

He stopped in front of apartment 38, pushed the doorbell. "Just a fucking minute," his sister called. He waited. Eventually, she opened the door.

She was wearing a bathrobe. Her short black hair was pulled back. She looked upset. "The bitch called," she said.

"Mom?"

"She woke me up, the bitch." She turned, went back into the apartment. He followed her. "I thought you were the liquor delivery."

The apartment was a mess. Lisa padded into the kitchen, and poked around the pans and dishes stacked in the sink, found a coffee cup. She rinsed it out. "You want coffee?"

He shook his head. "Shit, Lise," he said. "This place is a pigsty."

"I work nights, you know that."

She had never cared about her surroundings. Even as a child, her room was always a mess. She just didn't seem to notice. Now Tom looked through the greasy drapes of the kitchen window at the traffic crawling past on the 405. "So. How's work going?"

"It's House of Pancakes. How do you think it's going? Same every fucking night."

"What did Mom say?"

"She wanted to know if I was coming to the funeral."

"What'd you say?"

"I told her to fuck off. Why should I go? He wasn't my father."

Tom sighed. This was a long-standing argument within the family. Lisa believed she was not John Weller's daughter. "You don't think so, either," she said to Tom.

"Yeah, I do."

"You just say whatever Mom wants you to say." She fished out a cigarette butt from a heaping ashtray, and bent over the stove to light it from the burner. "Was he drunk when he crashed?"

"I don't know."

"I bet he was shitfaced. Or on those steroids he used, for his bodybuilding."

Tom's father had been a bodybuilder. He took it up later in life, and even competed in amateur contests. "Dad didn't use steroids."

"Oh sure, Tom. I used to look in his bathroom. He had needles."

"Okay, so you didn't like him."

"It doesn't matter anymore," she said. "He wasn't my father. I don't care about any of it."

"Mom always said that he was your father, that you were just saying it, because you didn't like him."

"Well, guess what? We can settle it, once and for all."

"How do you mean?"

"I mean, a paternity test."

"Lisa," he said. "Don't start this."

"I'm not starting. I'm finishing."

"Don't. Promise me you won't do this. Come on. Dad's dead, Mom's upset, promise me."

"You are a chickenshit pussy, you know that?" That was when he saw she was near tears.

He put his arms around her, and she began to cry. He just held her, feeling her body shake. "I'm sorry," she said. "I'm so sorry."

After her brother had gone, she heated a cup of coffee in the microwave, then sat down at the kitchenette table by the phone. She dialed Information. She got the number for the hospital. A moment later, she heard the receptionist say, "Long Beach Memorial."

"I want to talk to the morgue," she said.

"I'm sorry. The morgue is at the County Coroner's Office. Would you like that number?"

"Someone in my family just died at your hospital. Where would his body be now?"

"One moment please, I will connect you to pathology."

Four days later, her mother called back. "What the hell do you think you're doing?"

"What do you mean?"

"I mean, going down to the hospital and asking for blood from your father."

"He's not my father."

"Lisa. Don't you ever get tired of this game?"

"No, and he's not my father, because the genetic tests came back negative. It says right here"—she reached for the printed sheet—"that there is less than one chance in 2.9 million that John J. Weller is my father."

"What genetic test?"

"I had a genetic test done."

"You're so full of shit."

"No, Mom. You're the one who's full of shit. John Weller's not my father, and the test proves it. *I always knew it.*"

"We'll see about that," her mother said, and hung up.

About half an hour after that, her brother, Tom, called. "Hey, Lise." Real casual, laid-back.

"Just got a call from Mom."

"Yeah?"

"She said something about a test?"

"Yeah. I did a test, Tommy. And guess what?"

"I heard. Who did this test, Lise?"

"A lab here in Long Beach."

"What's it called?"

"BioRad Testing."

"Uh-huh," her brother said. "You know, these labs that advertise on the Internet aren't very reliable. You know that, don't you?"

"They guaranteed it."

"Mom's all upset."

"Too bad," she said.

"You know she'll do her own test now? And there's going to be lawsuits? Because you're accusing her of infidelity."

"Gee, Tommy, I don't really give a damn. You know that?"

"Lise, I think this is causing a lot of needless trouble around Dad's death."

"Your dad," she said. *"Not mine."*

CH009

Kevin McCormick, chief administrator of Long Beach Memorial, looked up at the chubby figure coming into his office, and said, "How the hell did this happen?" He pushed a sheaf of papers across his desk.

Marty Roberts, the chief of pathology, glanced quickly through the document. "I have no idea," he said.

"The wife of the deceased, Mr. John J. Weller, is suing us for unauthorized release of tissue to the daughter."

"What's the legal situation?" Marty Roberts said.

"Unclear," McCormick said. "Legal says the daughter is a family member and has a clear right to be given tissues to test for diseases that may affect her. Problem is, she did a paternity test and it came back negative. So she's *not* his daughter. Arguably that makes our release of tissues unauthorized."

"We couldn't have known that at the time—"

"Of course not. But we're talking about the law. The only important question is, can the family sue? The answer is yes, they have grounds to bring a suit, and they are."

"Where's the body now?" Marty said.

"Buried. Eight days ago."

"I see." Marty flipped through the pages. "And they are asking for . . ."

"Besides unspecified damages, they're asking for blood and tissue samples to conduct further testing," McCormick said. "Do we have blood or tissue samples from the deceased?"

"I'd have to check," Marty said. "But I'd presume that we do, yes."

"We do?"

"Sure. We keep a lot of tissue these days, Kevin. I mean, everybody that comes into the hospital, we collect as much as we possibly can legally . . ."

"That's the wrong answer," McCormick said, glowering.

"Okay. What's the right answer?"

"That we don't have any tissues from this guy."

"But they'll know that we do. At the very least, we did a tox screen on the guy because of the accident, so we have his blood—"

"That sample was lost."

"Okay. It was lost. But what good does that do? They can always dig up the body and get all the tissues they want."

"Correct."

"So?"

"So let them do that. That's Legal's advice. Exhumation takes time, permits, and money. We're guessing they won't have the time or the money—and this thing will go away."

"Okay," Marty said. "And I am here because?"

"Because I need you to go back to pathology and confirm for me that, unfortunately, we have no more samples from the deceased, and that everything not given to the daughter has been lost or misplaced."

"Got it."

"Call me within the hour," McCormick said, and turned away.

Marty Roberts entered the basement pathology lab. His diener, Raza Rashad, a handsome, dark-eyed man of twenty-seven, was scrubbing the stainless steel tables for the next post. If truth be told, Raza really ran the path lab. Marty felt himself burdened by a heavy administrative load, managing the senior pathologists, the residents, the medical student rotations, and all the rest. He'd come to rely on Raza, who was highly intelligent and ambitious.

"Hey, Raza. You remember that forty-six-year-old white guy with crush injuries, a week back? Drove himself into an overpass?"

"Yeah. I remember. Heller, or Weller."

"The daughter asked for blood?"

"Yeah. We gave her blood."

"Well, she ran a paternity test, and it came back negative. Guy was not her father."

Raza stared blankly. "That right?"

"Yeah. Now the mother's all upset. Wants more tissues. What've we got?"

"I'd have to check. Probably the usual. All major organs."

Marty said, "Any chance that material got misplaced? So we couldn't find it?"

Raza nodded slowly, staring at Marty. "Maybe so. Always possible it could be mislabeled. Then it would be hard to find."

"Might take months?"

"Or years. Maybe never."

"That'd be a shame," Marty said. "Now, what about the blood from the tox screen?"

Raza frowned. "Lab keeps that. We wouldn't have access to their storage facility."

"So they still have that blood sample?"

"Yeah. They do."

"And we have no access?"

Raza smiled. "It might take me a couple of days."

"Okay. Do it."

Marty Roberts went to the phone and dialed the administrator's office. When McCormick came on the line, he said, "I have some bad news, Kevin. Unfortunately, all the tissues have been lost or misplaced."

"Sorry to hear that," McCormick said, and hung up.

"Marty," Raza said, coming into the office, "is there a problem with this Weller guy?"

"No," Marty said. "Not anymore. And I told you before—don't call me Marty. My name is Dr. Roberts."

CH010

At the Radial Genomics lab in La Jolla, Charlie Huggins twisted his flat-panel screen around to show Henry Kendall the headline: TALKING APE CLAIMED FRAUD. "What'd I tell you?" Charlie said. "A week later, and we learn the story's a fake."

"Okay, okay. I was wrong," Henry said. "I admit it, I was worried about nothing."

"Very worried . . ."

"It's in the past. Can we talk about something important?"

"What's that?"

"The novelty-seeking gene. Our grant application was denied." He began typing at the keyboard. "Once again, we've been screwed—by your personal favorite, the Pope of Dopamine, Dr. Robert A. Bellarmino of the NIH."

For the last ten years, brain studies had increasingly focused on a neurochemical called dopamine. Levels of dopamine seemed to be important in maintaining health as well as in diseases such as Parkinsonism and schizophrenia. From work in Charlie Huggins's lab, it appeared that dopamine receptors in the brain were controlled by the gene D4DR, among others. Charlie's lab stood at the forefront of this research, until a rival scientist named Robert Bellarmino from the National Institutes of Health began referring to D4DR as the "novelty gene," the gene that supposedly controlled the urge to take risks, seek new sex partners, or engage in thrill-seeking behavior.

As Bellarmino explained it, the fact that dopamine levels were higher in men than women was the reason for the greater recklessness of men, and their attraction to everything from mountain climbing to infidelity.

Bellarmino was an evangelical Christian and a leading researcher at the NIH. Politically skilled, he was the very model of an up-to-date scientist, neatly blending a modest scientific talent with true media savvy. His laboratory was the first to hire its own publicity firm, and as a result, his ideas invariably got plenty of press coverage. (Which in turn attracted the brightest and most ambitious postdocs, who did brilliant work for him, thus adding to his prestige.)

In the case of D4DR, Bellarmino was able to tailor his comments to the beliefs of his audience, either speaking enthusiastically about the new gene to progressive groups, or disparaging it to conservatives. He was colorful, future-oriented, and uninhibited in his predictions. He went so far as to suggest that there might one day be a vaccine to prevent infidelity.

The absurdity of such comments so annoyed Charlie and Henry that six months before, they had applied for a grant to test the prevalence of the "novelty gene."

Their proposal was simplicity itself. They would send research teams to amusement parks to draw blood samples from individuals who rode roller coasters time and again during the day. In theory these "repeat coasters" would be more likely to carry the gene.

The only problem with applying to the NSF was that their proposal would be read by anonymous reviewers. And one of the reviewers was likely to be Robert Bellarmino. And Bellarmino had a reputation for what was politely termed "appropriation."

"Anyway," Henry said, "the NSF turned us down. The reviewers didn't think our idea was worthy. One said it was too 'jokey.'"

"Uh-huh," Charlie said. "What does this have to do with Robbin' Rob?"

"Remember where we proposed to conduct our study?"

"Of course," Charlie said. "At two of the biggest amusement parks in the world, in two different countries. Sandusky in the U.S., and Blackpool in England."

"Well, guess who's out of town?" Henry said.

He hit his e-mail button.

> From: Rob Bellarmino, NIH
> Subject: Out of Office AutoReply: Travel
>
> I will be out of the office for the next two weeks. If you need immediate assistance please contact my office by phone . . .

"I called his office, and guess what? Bellarmino is going to Sandusky, Ohio—and then to Blackpool, England."

"That bastard," Charlie said. "If you're going to steal somebody else's research proposal, you should at least have the courtesy to change it a little."

"Bellarmino obviously doesn't care if we know he stole it," Henry said. "Doesn't that piss you off? What do you say we go for it? Put him up for ethical violations?"

"I'd like nothing better," Charlie said, "but, no. If we formally charge misconduct, it means a lot of time and a lot of paperwork. Our grants could dry up. And in the end, the complaint goes nowhere. Rob's a major player at NIH. He's got huge research facilities and he dispenses millions in grants. He holds prayer breakfasts with congressmen. He's a scientist who believes in God. They love him on the Hill. He'd never be charged with misconduct. Even if we caught him buggering a lab assistant, he wouldn't be charged."

"So we just let him do it?"

"It's not a perfect world," Charlie said. "We have plenty to do. Walk away."

CH011

Barry Sindler was bored. The woman before him yammered on. She was an obvious type—the rich-bitch Eastern broad who wore pants, Katharine Hepburn with an attitude, a trust fund, a nasal Newport accent. But despite her aristocratic airs, the best she could manage was to hump the tennis pro, just like every L.A. fake-tit dimwit in this town.

But she was perfectly suited to the dumb-ass attorney by her side—that Ivy League jackoff Bob Wilson, wearing a pinstripe suit and a button-down shirt with a rep tie and those stupid lace-up wingtips with the little perforations in the toes. No wonder everyone called him Whitey Wilson. Wilson never tired of reminding everyone he was a Harvard-trained lawyer—as if anybody gave a shit. Certainly Barry Sindler didn't. Because he knew Wilson was a gentleman. Which really meant he was chickenshit. He wouldn't go for the throat.

And Sindler always went for the throat.

The woman, Karen Diehl, was still talking. Jesus, these rich bitches could talk. Sindler didn't interrupt her because he didn't want Whitey to state on the record that Sindler was badgering the woman. Wilson had said that four times already. So, fine. Let the bitch talk. Let her tell in full, exhausting, incredibly stupefyingly boring detail why her husband was a lousy father and a total shit heel. Because the truth was, *she* was the one who'd had the affair.

Not that that could ever come out in court. California had no-fault divorce, which meant there were no specific grounds for divorce, just "irreconcilable differences." But a woman's infidelity always colored the proceedings. Because in skilled hands—Barry's hands—that fact could easily be turned into the insinuation that this woman had more important priorities than her darling children. She was a neglectful parent, an unreliable custodian, a selfish woman who sought her own pleasure while she left the kids all day with the Spanish-speaking maid.

And she was good-looking at twenty-eight, he thought. That worked against her, too. Indeed, Barry Sindler could see his central theme shaping up quite nicely. And Whitey Wilson looked a bit anxious. He probably knew where Sindler would take this.

Or maybe Whitey was troubled by the fact that Sindler was attending the depo at all. Because ordinarily Barry Sindler didn't conduct spousal depos. He left those to the jerkoff peons in his office, while he spent his days downtown, racking up expensive courtroom hours.

Finally, the woman stopped to catch her breath. Sindler moved in. "Mrs. Diehl, I would like to hold this line of questioning and go on to another issue. We are formally requesting that you undergo a full battery of genetic tests at a reputable facility, preferably UCLA, and—"

The woman sat bolt upright. Her face colored swiftly. "No!"

"Let's not be hasty," Whitey said, putting his hand on his client's arm. She angrily pushed him away.

"No! Absolutely not! I refuse!"

How wonderful. How unexpected and *wonderful.*

"In anticipation of your possible refusal," Sindler continued, "we have drafted a request that the court order these tests"—he passed a document to Whitey—"and we fully expect the judge to agree."

"I've never heard of such a thing," Whitey said, thumbing through the pages. "Genetic testing in a custody case . . ."

By now Mrs. Diehl was full-bore hysterical. "No! No! I will not! It's *his* idea, isn't it? That prick! How dare he! That sneaking son of a bitch!"

Whitey was looking at his client with a puzzled expression. "Mrs. Diehl," he said, "I think it's best if we discuss this in private—"

"No! No discussion! No test! That's it! No!"

"In that case," Sindler said, with a little shrug, "we have no choice but to go to the judge . . ."

"Fuck you! Fuck him! Fuck all of you! *No fucking test!*"

And she stood up, grabbed her purse, and stomped out of the room, slamming the door behind her.

There was a moment of silence. Sindler said, "Let the record show that at three forty-five p.m. the witness left the room, thus ending the deposition."

He began to put his papers into his briefcase.

Whitey Wilson said, "I've never heard of this, Barry. What's genetic testing got to do with child custody?"

"That's what the tests are intended to find out," Sindler said. "This is a new procedure, but I think you'll find it's the coming thing." He snapped his briefcase shut, shook Whitey's limp hand, and left the office.

CH012

Josh Winkler closed the door to his office and started toward the cafeteria when his phone rang. It was his mother. She was being pleasant, always a danger sign. "Josh, dear, I want you to tell me, what have you done to your brother?"

"What do you mean, done to him? I haven't done anything. I haven't seen him in two weeks, since I picked him up from jail."

"Adam had his arraignment today," she said. "And Charles was there, representing him."

"Uh-huh . . ." Waiting for the other shoe to drop. "And?"

"Adam came to court on time, in a clean shirt and tie, clean suit, hair cut, even his shoes polished. He pleaded guilty, asked to be put in a drug program, said he had not used in two weeks, said he had gotten a job—"

"*What?*"

"Yes, he's got a job, apparently as a limo driver for his old company. Been working there steadily for the last two weeks. Charles says he's gained weight—"

"I don't believe this," Josh said.

"I know," she said. "Charles didn't either, but he swears it's all true. Adam's like a new man. He's acquired a newfound maturity. It's like he suddenly grew up. It's a miracle, don't you think? Joshua? Are you there?"

"I'm here," he said, after a pause.

"Isn't it a miracle?"

"Yes, Mom. A miracle."

"I called Adam. He has a cell phone now, and he answered right away. And he says you did something to help him. What did you do?"

"Nothing, Mom. We just had a talk."

"He said you gave him some genetic thing. An inhaler."

Oh Jesus, he thought. *There are rules against this kind of thing. Serious rules.* Human experimentation without formal application, meetings of the approvals board, following the federal guidelines. Josh would be fired in an instant. "No, Mom, I think he must be misremembering. He was pretty whacked out at the time."

"He said there was a spray."

"No, Mom."

"He inhaled some mouse spray."

"No, Mom."

"He said he did."

"No, Mom."

"Well, don't be so defensive," she said. "I thought you would be pleased. I mean, you're always looking for new drugs, Joshua. Big commercial applications. I mean, what if this spray gets people off drugs? What if it breaks their addiction?"

Joshua was shaking his head. "Mom, really, nothing happened."

"Okay, fine, you don't want to tell me the truth, I get it. Was it something experimental? Is that what your spray is?"

"Mom—"

"Because the thing is, Josh, I told Lois Graham about it because her Eric dropped out of USC. He's on crack or smack or—"

"Mom—"

"And she wants to try this spray on him."

Oh Jesus. "Mom, you can't talk about this."

"And Helen Stern, her daughter is on sleeping pills; she crashed her car; they're talking about putting her baby in foster care. And Helen wants—"

"Mom, please! You can't talk about it *anymore!*"

"Are you crazy? I *have* to talk about it," she said. "You gave me my son back. It's a miracle. Don't you realize, Joshua? You have performed a miracle. The whole world is going to talk about what you have done—whether you like it or not."

He was beginning to sweat, to feel dizzy, but suddenly his vision became clear and calm. *The whole world is going to talk about it.*

Of course, that was true. If you could get people off drugs? It would be the most valuable pharmaceutical in the last decade. Everybody would want it. And what if it did more? Could it cure obsessive-compulsive disorders? Could it cure attention-deficit disorders? The maturity gene had behavioral effects. They already knew that. Adam sniffing that aerosol was a gift from God.

And his next thought was: What's the state of the patent application on ACMPD3N7?

He decided to skip lunch and head back to the office.

"Mom?"

"Yes, Josh."

"I need your help."

"Of course, dear. Anything."

"I need you to do something for me and not to talk about it to anyone, ever."

"Well, that's difficult—"

"Yes or no, Mom."

"Well, all right, dear."

"You said that Lois Graham's son is on smack, and dropped out of college?"

"Yes."

"Where is he now?"

"Apparently," she said, "he's downtown in some godawful flophouse off campus—"

"Do you know where?"

"No, but Lois went to see him. She told me it was squalid. It's on East Thirty-eighth, some old frame house with faded blue shutters. Eight or nine addicts are there sleeping on the floor, but I can call Lois and ask her—"

"No," he said quickly. "Don't do anything, Mom."

"But you said you needed my help—"

"That's for later, Mom. For now, everything is fine. I'll call you in a day or so."

He scribbled on a pad:

> Eric Graham
> E 38th Street
> Frame hse blue shutters

He reached for his car keys.

Rachel Allen, who worked in the dispensary, said, "You still haven't signed back in one oxygen canister from two weeks ago, Josh. Or the virus vial that was with it." The company measured remaining virus in returned vials, as a way of keeping a rough track of dosages to the rats.

"Yes," he said, "I know, uh, I keep forgetting."

"Where is it?"

"It's in my car."

"In your car? Josh, that's a contagious retrovirus."

"Yeah, for mice."

"Even so. It must remain in a negative-pressure laboratory environment at all times." Rachel was a stickler for the rules. Nobody really paid attention to her.

"I know, Rach," he said, "but I had a family emergency. I had to get my brother"—he dropped his voice—"out of jail."

"*Really.*"

"Yes."

"For what?"

He hesitated. "Armed robbery."

"*Really.*"

"Liquor store. Mom is crushed. Anyway, I'll bring the canister back to you. Meanwhile, can I have one more?"

"We only sign out one at a time."

"I need one more now. Please? I'm under a lot of pressure."

Light rain was falling. The streets were slick with oil and shimmered in rainbow patterns. Beneath low, angry clouds, he drove down East Thirty-eighth Street. It was an old section of town, bypassed by modern rebuilding farther north. Here houses built in the 1920s and 1930s were still standing. Josh drove past several wood-frame houses, in various states of disrepair. One had a blue door. None had blue shutters.

He ended up in the warehouse district, the street lined with loading docks. He turned around and headed back. He drove as slowly as he could, and finally he saw the house. It was not actually on Thirty-eighth but on the corner of Thirty-eighth and Alameda, tucked back behind high weeds and ratty bushes. An old mattress streaked with rust lay on the sidewalk in front of the house. There was a truck tire on the front lawn. A battered VW bus was pulled up to the curb.

Josh parked across the street. He watched the house. And waited.

The coffin rose into sunlight. It looked the same as it had when buried a week earlier, except for the clumps of dirt that dropped from the underside.

"This is all so undignified," Emily Weller said. She stood stiffly at the graveside, accompanied by her son, Tom, and her daughter Rachel. Of course, Lisa was not there. She was the *cause* of all this, but she could not be bothered to see what she had done to her poor father.

The coffin swung slowly in the air as the graveside workers guided it to the far side of the pit under the direction of the hospital pathologist, a nervous little man named Marty Roberts. He should be nervous, Emily thought, if he was the one who had given the blood to Lisa without anybody's permission.

"What happens now?" Emily said, turning to her son. Tom was twenty-six, dressed in a sharp suit and tie. He had a master's degree in microbiology and worked for a big biotech company in Los Angeles. Tom had turned out good, as had her daughter Rachel. Rachel was a senior at USC, studying business administration. "Will they take Jack's blood here?"

"Oh, they'll take more than blood," Tom said.

Emily said, "What do you mean?"

"You see," Tom said, "for a genetic test like this, where there is a dispute, they ordinarily take tissues from several organ systems."

"I didn't realize," Emily said, frowning. She felt her heart pounding, thumping in her chest. She hated that feeling. Soon there was a squeezing feeling in her throat. It was painful. She bit her lip.

"You all right, Mom?"

"I should have taken my anxiety pills."

Rachel said, "Will this take long?"

"No," Tom said, "it should be only a few minutes. The pathologist will open the casket, to confirm the identity of the body. Then he'll take it back to the hospital to remove the tissues for genetic analysis. He'll return the body for reburial tomorrow or the next day."

"Tomorrow or the next day?" Emily said. She sniffled, wiped her eyes. "You mean we have to come back here? We have to bury Jack again? This is all so . . . so . . ."

"I know, Mom." He patted her arm. "I'm sorry. But there is no other way. You see, they have to check for something called a chimera—"

"Oh, don't tell me," she said, waving her hand. "I won't know what you're talking about."

"Okay, Mom." He put his arm around her shoulder.

In ancient mythology, chimeras were monsters composed of different animal parts. The original Chimera had the head of a lion, the body of a goat, and a serpent's tail. Some chimeras were part human, like the Egyptian Sphinx, with the body of a lion, the wings of a bird, and the head of a woman.

But true human chimeras—meaning people with two sets of DNA—had been discovered only recently. A woman needing a kidney transplant had tested her own children as possible donors, only to discover that they did not share her DNA. She was told the children weren't hers, and was asked to prove she had actually given birth to them. A lawsuit ensued. After considerable study, doctors realized that her body contained two different strands of DNA. In her ovaries, they found eggs with two kinds of DNA. The skin cells of her abdomen had her children's DNA. The skin of her shoulders did not. She was a mosaic. In every organ of her body.

It turned out that the woman had originally been one of a pair of fraternal twins, but early in development, her sister's embryo had fused with hers. So she was now literally herself and her own twin.

More than fifty chimeras had since been reported. Scientists now suspected that chimerism was not as rare as they had once thought. Certainly, whenever there was a difficult question of paternity, chimerism had to be considered. It was possible that Lisa's father might be a chimera. But to determine that, they would need tissues from every organ of his body, and preferably from several different places on each organ.

That was why Dr. Roberts was required to take so many tissue samples, and why it would have to be done at the hospital, not at the grave site.

Dr. Roberts raised the lid and turned to the family on the opposite side of the grave. "Would one of you make the identification, please?"

"I will," Tom said. He walked around the grave and looked into the coffin. His father appeared surprisingly unchanged, except the skin was much grayer, a dark gray now, and the limbs seemed to have shrunk, to have lost mass, especially the legs inside the trousers.

In a formal voice, the pathologist said, "Is this your father, John J. Weller?"

"Yes. He is, yes."

"All right. Thank you."

Tom said, "Dr. Roberts, I know you have your procedures, but . . . if there is any way you can take the tissues here . . . so my mother doesn't have to go through another day and another burial . . ."

"I'm sorry," Marty Roberts said. "My actions are governed by state law. We're required to take the body to the hospital for examination."

"If you could . . . just this once . . . bend . . ."

"I'm sorry. I wish I could."

Tom nodded and walked back to his mother and sister.

His mother said, "What was all that about?"

"Just asking a question."

Tom looked back and saw that Dr. Roberts was now bent over, his body half inside the casket. Abruptly the pathologist rose up. He walked over to speak in Tom's ear, so no one else could hear.

"Mr. Weller, perhaps we should spare your family's feelings. If we can keep this between us . . ."

"Of course. Then you'll . . . ?"

"Yes, we'll do everything here. It should take only a few moments. Let me get my kit." He hurried off to a nearby SUV.

Emily bit her lip. "What's he doing?"

"I asked him to do all the tests here, Mom."

"And he said yes? Thank you, dear," she said, and kissed her son. "Will he do all the tests that he would do at the hospital?"

"No, but it should be enough to answer your questions."

Twenty minutes later, the tissue samples had been taken and placed in a series of glass tubes. The tubes were placed in slots in a metal refrigeration case. The casket was returned to the grave, disappearing into shadow.

"Come on," Emily Weller said to her children, "let's get out of here. I need a damn drink."

As they drove away, she said to Tom, "I'm sorry you had to do that. Was Jack's poor body very decayed, dear?"

"No," Tom said. "Not much, no."

"Oh, that's good," Emily said. "That's very good."

Marty Roberts was sweating by the time he got back to Long Beach Memorial Hospital. Because of what he had done at the cemetery, he could lose his license, no problem. One of those gravediggers could pick up the phone and call the county. The county could wonder why Marty had broken protocol, especially with a lawsuit pending. When you take tissues in the field, you risk contamination. Everybody knew that. So the county might start wondering why Marty Roberts would risk that. And before long, they might be wondering . . .

Shit. Shit, shit, *shit!*

He pulled into the emergency parking, next to the ambulances, and hurried down the basement hallway to Pathology. It was lunchtime; almost nobody was there. The rows of stainless steel tables stood empty.

Raza was washing up.

"You dumb fuck," Marty said, "are you *trying* to get us both in jail?"

Raza turned slowly. "What is the problem?" he said quietly.

"The problem," Marty said, "is that I told you, take the bones only on the *cremations*. Not the burials. The *cremations*. Is that so fucking hard to understand?"

"Yeah, well. That's what I do," Raza said.

"No, that's *not* what you do. Because I just came from an exhumation, and you know what I saw when I dug the guy up? Very fucking skinny legs, Raza. Very skinny arms. In a *burial*."

"No," Raza said, "that's not what I do."

"Well, *somebody* took the bones."

Raza headed to the office. "What's the name of this guy?"

"Weller."

"What, that guy again? He's the guy we lost the tissues for, right?"

"Right. So the family exhumed him. Because he was *buried*."

Raza leaned over the desk, keyed in the patient name. He stared at the screen. "Oh yeah. You're right. It was a burial. But I didn't do that one."

Marty said, "You didn't do that one? Who the fuck did?"

Raza shrugged. "My brother came in, that's all. I had an appointment that night."

"Your brother? What brother? Nobody else is supposed to be—"

"Don't sweat it, Marty," Raza said. "My brother comes in from time to time. He knows what to do. He works at Hilldale Mortuary."

Marty wiped sweat from his forehead. "Jesus. How long has this been going on?"

"Maybe a year."

"A year!"

"Only at night, Marty. Late night only. He wears my lab coat, looks like me . . . We look the same."

"Wait a minute," Marty said. "Who gave that girl the blood sample? That girl Lisa Weller."

"Okay," Raza said. "So sometimes he makes mistakes."

"And sometimes he works afternoons?"

"Only Sundays, Marty. If I have appointments, is all."

Marty gripped the edge of the desk to steady himself. He leaned over and breathed deeply. "Some fucking guy who doesn't even work for the hospital gave unauthorized blood to a woman because she asked for it? Is that what you're telling me?"

"Not some fucking guy. My brother."

"Jesus."

"He said she was cute."

"That explains everything."

"Come on, Marty," Raza said, in a soothing tone. "I'm sorry about the Weller guy, I really am, but anybody could have made the switch. Fucking cemetery could have dug him up and taken the long bones. Gravediggers working as independent contractors could have done it. You know it happens all over. They got those guys in Phoenix. And the ones in Minnesota. And now Brooklyn."

"And they're all in jail now, Raza."

"Okay," Raza said. "That's true. The thing is, I told my brother to do it."

"You did . . ."

"Yeah. That particular night, the Weller body came in, we had a stat call for bone, and the Weller guy typed right. So do we fill the order or what? Because you know those bone guys can take their business elsewhere. To them, now means *now*. Supply or die."

Marty sighed. "Yeah, when they call stat, you should fill it."

"Okay, then."

Marty slid into the chair and began typing at the keyboard himself. "However," he said, "if you extracted those long bones eight days ago, I don't see any payment transfer to me."

"Don't worry. It's coming."

"The check is in the mail?"

"Hey, I forgot. You'll get your taste."

"Make sure of it," Marty said. He turned to go. "And keep your fucking brother out of the hospital from now on. You understand me?"

"Sure, Marty. Sure."

Marty Roberts went outside to move his car from the emergency space. He backed out and drove to the Doctors Only section of the parking garage. Then he sat in his car for a long time. Thinking about Raza.

You'll get your taste.

It seemed that Raza was starting to believe that this was his program, and that Marty Roberts worked for him. Raza was handing out the payments. Raza was deciding who should come in to help. Raza was not behaving like an employee; he was starting to behave like he was in charge, and that was dangerous for all sorts of reasons.

Marty had to do something about it.

And he had to do it soon.

Or losing his medical license would be the least of his problems.

CH015

At sunset, the titanium cube that housed BioGen Research shimmered with a blinding red glare, and bathed the adjacent parking lot in a dark orange color. As president Rick Diehl stepped out of the building, he paused to put on his sunglasses, then walked toward his brand-new silver Porsche Carrera SC. He loved this car, which he had bought the week before in celebration of his impending divorce—

"Fuck!"

He couldn't believe his eyes.

"Fuck! Fuck! *Fuck!*"

His parking spot was empty. The car was gone.

That bitch!

He didn't know how she had done it, but he was sure she had taken his car. Probably got her boyfriend to arrange it. After all, the new boyfriend *was* a car dealer. Moving up from a tennis pro. Bitch!

He stomped back inside. Bradley Gordon, his chief of security, stood in the lobby's waiting area, leaning over the counter, talking to Lisa, the receptionist. Lisa was cute. That was why Rick had hired her.

"Goddamn it, Brad," Rick Diehl said. "We need to review security tapes of the parking lot."

Brad turned. "Why? What is it?"

"Somebody stole my Porsche."

"No shit," Brad said. "When did that happen?"

And Rick thought, *Wrong guy for this job.* It wasn't the first time he had thought it.

"Let's check the security tapes, Brad."

"Yeah, sure, of course," Brad said. He winked at Lisa, and then headed back through the keycard-swipe door, into a secure area. Rick followed, fuming.

At one of the two desks in the little glass-walled security office, a kid was minutely examining the palm of his left hand. He ignored the bank of monitors before him.

"Jason," Brad said, in a warning tone, "Mr. Diehl is here."

"Oh shit." The kid snapped upright in the chair. "Sorry. Got a rash. I didn't know if—"

"Mr. Diehl wants to review the security cameras. Which cameras are they exactly, Mr. Diehl?"

Oh Jesus. Rick said, "The parking lot cameras."

"The parking lot, right. Jason, let's start forty-eight hours back, and—"

"I drove the car to work this morning," Diehl said.

"Right, what time was that?"

"I got here at seven."

"Right. Jason, let's go back to seven this morning."

The kid shifted in his chair. "Uh, Mr. Gordon, the parking lot cameras are out."

"Oh, that's right." Brad turned to Rick. "The parking lot cameras are out."

"Why?"

"Not sure. We think there's a cable problem."

"How long have they been out?"

"Well—"

"Two months," the kid said.

"Two months!"

Brad said, "We had to order parts."

"What parts?"

"From Germany."

"What parts?"

"I'd have to look it up."

The kid said, "We can still use the roof cameras."

"Well, then show me the roof cameras," Diehl said.

"Right. Jason, bring up the roof cameras."

It took them fifteen minutes to rewind the digital storage and begin to run it forward. Rick watched his Porsche pull in. He watched himself get out and enter the building. What happened next surprised him. Within two minutes, another car pulled up, two men jumped out, broke into his car quickly, and drove it away.

"They were waiting for you," Brad said. "Or following you."

"Looks like it," Rick said. "Call the police, report it, and tell Lisa I want her to drive me home."

Brad blinked at that.

The problem, Rick reflected, as Lisa drove him home, was that Brad Gordon was an idiot, but Rick couldn't fire him. Brad Gordon, surf bum, ski bum, travel bum, recovering alky and college dropout, was the nephew of Jack Watson, a principal investor in BioGen. Jack Watson had always looked after Brad, had always seen that he had a job. And Brad invariably got into trouble. It was even rumored that Brad had been fucking the wife of the vice president of GeneSystems up in Palo Alto—for which he was duly fired—but not without a big stink from his uncle, who saw no reason why Brad should be let go. "It's the vice president's own fault," Watson famously said.

But now: No security cameras in the parking lot. For two months. It made Rick wonder what else was wrong with security at BioGen.

He glanced over at Lisa, who drove serenely. Rick had hired her to be the receptionist soon after he discovered his wife's affair. Lisa had a beautiful profile; she could have been a model. Whoever had refined her nose and chin was a genius. And she had a lovely body, with a narrow waist and perfectly enhanced breasts. She was twenty, on her summer break from Crestview State, and she radiated healthy, all-American sexiness. Everyone in the company had the hots for her.

So it was surprising that whenever they made love, Lisa just lay there. After a few minutes she seemed to notice his frustration and would begin to move mechanically, and make little panting sounds, as if she had been told that was what people did in bed. Sometimes, when Rick was worried and preoccupied, she would talk to him, "Oh baby, yes, baby, do it, baby," as if that was supposed to move things along. But it was only too obvious that she was unmoved.

Rick had done a little research and discovered a syndrome called anhedonia, the inability to feel pleasure. Anhedonics exhibited a flat affect, which certainly described Lisa in bed. Interestingly, anhedonia appeared to have a genetic component. It seemed to involve the limbic system of the brain. So there might be a gene for the condition. Rick intended to do a full panel on Lisa one of these days. Just to check.

Meanwhile, the nights he spent with her might have made him insecure, if it were not for Greta, the Austrian postdoc in the microbiology lab. Greta was chunky and had glasses and short, mannish hair, but she fucked like a mink, leaving them both gasping for breath and covered in sweat. Greta was a screamer and a writher and a howler. He felt great afterward.

The car pulled up at his new condo. Rick checked for his keys in his pocket. Lisa said matter-of-factly, "You want me to come up?"

She had beautiful blue eyes, with long lashes. Beautiful lush lips.

He thought, what the hell. "Sure," he said. "Come on up."

He called his lawyer, Barry Sindler, to report that his wife had stolen his car.

"You think so?" Sindler said. He sounded doubtful.

"Yeah, I do. She hired some guys. I have it on security tape."

"You have her on tape?"

"No, the guys. But she's behind it."

"I'm not so sure," Sindler said. "Usually women trash a husband's car, not steal it."

"I'm telling you—"

"Okay, I'll check into it. But right now, there are a few things I want to go over with you. About the litigation."

Across the room, Lisa was stepping out of her clothes. She folded each item of clothing and placed it on the back of the chair. She was wearing a pink bra and pink briefs that skimmed her pubic bone. No lace, just stretchy fabric that molded smoothly to her smooth body. She reached behind her back to release the bra.

"I'll have to call you back," Rick said.

BLONDES BECOMING EXTINCT

Endangered Species To "Die Out in 200 Years"

According to the BBC, "a study by experts in Germany suggests people with blonde hair are an endangered species and will become extinct by 2202." Researchers predicted that the last truly natural blonde would be born in Finland, a country that boasts the highest proportion of blondes. But the scientists say too few people now carry the gene for blondes to last much longer. The researchers hinted that so-called bottle blondes "may be to blame for the demise of their natural rivals."

Not every scientist agrees with the prediction of impending extinction. But a study by the World Health Organization does indicate that natural blondes are likely to become extinct within the next two centuries.

More recently, the probability of extinction was reviewed by *The Times* of London, in light of new data about the evolution of the MC1R gene for blondeness.

CH016

The jungle was completely silent. Not a buzzing cicada, not a hornbill cry, nor a distant chattering monkey. Utterly silent—and no wonder, Hagar thought. He shook his head as he looked at the ten camera crews from around the world now clustered in little groups on the jungle floor, protecting their lenses from the dripping moisture as they peered upward into the trees overhead. He had told them to be silent, and indeed nobody was actually talking. The French crew smoked cigarettes. Although the German crew maintained silence, the cameraman kept snapping his fingers imperiously as he gestured to his assistant to do this and that. The Japanese crew from NHK was quiet, but beside them, the CNN crew out of Singapore whispered and murmured and changed lenses, clanking metal boxes. The British Sky TV crew from Hong Kong had come inappropriately dressed. They now had their running shoes off and were plucking leeches from between their toes, swearing as they did so.

Hopeless.

Hagar had warned the companies about conditions in Sumatra and the difficulty of filming there. He had recommended that they send wildlife photography teams experienced in fieldwork. No one had listened. Instead, they had rushed the nearest available crews to Berastagi, and as a result half the teams had talent standing by, microphones held ready, as if they were waiting to ambush a head of state.

They had been waiting for three hours.

So far, the talking orangutan had failed to make an appearance, and

Hagar was prepared to bet he never would. Hagar caught the eye of one of the French team and gestured for him to put out his cigarette. The guy shrugged and turned his back to Hagar. He continued smoking.

One of the Japanese team slipped through the group and stood beside Hagar. He whispered, "When does the animal come?"

"When it's silent."

"So, you mean not today?"

Hagar made a helpless gesture, palms upward.

"We are too many?"

Hagar nodded.

"Perhaps tomorrow, we will come alone."

"All right," Hagar said.

Just then a ripple of excitement ran through the crews; they jumped to their cameras, adjusted their tripods, and began to film. Hagar heard the soft murmur of voices in many languages. Nearby, the Sky TV man held his microphone close to his lips and spoke in a stage whisper: "We are standing here deep in the remote jungles of Sumatra, and there, just across the way, we see the creature that has aroused the speculation of the entire world—the chimpanzee that is said to talk and, yes, even to swear."

Christ, Hagar thought. He turned to see what they were filming. He caught a glimpse of brownish fur and a dark head. The animal was clearly no larger than two feet tall, and almost immediately gave the low moaning call of the pig-tailed macaque.

The camera crews were electrified. Microphones pointed like so many gun barrels toward the quick-moving animal. They heard more moans from the distant foliage. Obviously a good-size troop was here.

The Germans recognized it first. *"Nein, nein, nein!"* The cameraman stepped irritably away from the camera. *"Es ist ein macaque."*

Soon the canopy overhead was thrashing as a dozen macaques swung through the area and headed north.

One of the Brits turned to Hagar. "Where's the chimp, then?"

"Orangutan," Hagar said.

"Whatever. Where is he?" His voice was impatient.

"He doesn't keep an appointment calendar," Hagar said.

"Is this where he's usually found? Yes? Can we put some food out for him, something to attract him? Make some mating call?"

"No," Hagar said.

"No way to attract him, is that it?"

"That's it."

"We just sit here and hope for the best?" The journalist glanced at his watch. "They want tape by noon."

"Unfortunately," Hagar said, "we're in the jungle. It happens when it happens. It's the natural world."

"Not if it talks, it's not natural," the cameraman said. "And I haven't got all fucking day."

"I don't know what to tell you," Hagar said.

"Find me the fucking monkey!" the guy yelled. His shout agitated the macaques in the trees, made them scamper and moan.

Hagar looked at the others. The French cameraman said, "Perhaps quieter? For everybody."

"Bugger off, you miserable fuckwit," the Brit said.

"Easy, mate." A huge man from the Australian crew stepped forward and put his hand on the Brit, who swung a roundhouse to his jaw. The Australian caught his hand, twisted it, and shoved him into his tripod. The tripod went down, the cameraman sprawling. The rest of the British crew jumped the Aussie, whose teammates rushed to his defense. So did the Germans. Soon three crews were swinging wildly. When the French tripod fell, and their camera was splattered with mud, other crews began to fight as well.

Hagar just stared.

No orang today, he thought.

Rick **Diehl** of BioGen was changing in the locker room of the Bel Air Country Club. He had gone there to play a foursome with some investors who might be interested in BioGen. One guy from Merrill Lynch, his boyfriend, and a guy from Citibank. Rick tried to play it casual, but he felt some urgency because ever since he watched his wife walk through the lobby with that asshole in white tennis togs, he had been in a panic. Without Karen's financial backing, Rick was exposed to the untender mercies of his other major investor, Jack Watson. And that wasn't comfortable. He needed fresh money.

Out there on the golf course, with the sun shining and a soft breeze blowing, he fed them his little speeches about the emerging wonders of biotech, and the power of the cytokines manufactured by the Burnet cell line BioGen had acquired. It was a real opportunity to get in on a company that was about to grow fast.

They didn't see it that way. The Merrill Lynch guy said, "Aren't lymphokines the same as cytokines? Haven't there been some unexplained deaths from cytokines?"

Rick explained that there had been a few deaths, some years back, because a handful of physicians had jumped the gun on therapy.

The Merrill Lynch guy said, "I was in lymphokines five years ago. Never made a dime."

Then the Citibank guy said, "What about cytokine storms?"

Cytokine storms. Christ, Rick thought. He blew his putt. "Well," he said, "cytokine storms are really just a speculative concept. The idea is that in certain rare circumstances, the immune system overreacts and attacks the body, causing multiple organ systems to fail—"

"Isn't that what happened in the influenza epidemic of 1918?"

"A few academics have said so, but they all work for drug companies that market competing products."

"You're saying it might not be true?"

"You have to be very careful about what universities tell you, nowadays."

"Even about 1918?"

"Disinformation takes many forms," Rick said, picking up his ball. "The truth is cytokines are the wave of the future, they are fast-tracked for clinical testing and product development, and they offer the fastest return on investment of all the product lines out there today. That's why I made cytokines my first acquisition at BioGen. And we have just won the litigation that surrounded—"

"They won't appeal? I heard they were."

"The judge's ruling took the fight out of them."

"But haven't people died from gene transfers that provoked a cytokine storm? Haven't a *lot* of people died?"

Rick sighed. "Not so many . . ."

"What? Fifty, a hundred, something like that?"

"I don't know the exact number," Rick said, now realizing that this was not going to be a good day. And that was an hour before one of them finally said that in his opinion only an idiot would invest in cytokines.

Nice.

And so he felt exhausted and defeated, sitting slumped in the locker room afterward, when Jack Watson, suntanned and resplendent in tennis whites, dropped onto the bench beside him and said, "So. Useful game?"

He was the last person Diehl wanted to see. "Not bad."

"Any of those guys going to come in?"

"Maybe. We'll wait and see."

Watson said, "Those Merrill Lynch guys have no balls. Their idea of taking a risk is peeing in the shower. I wouldn't hold my breath. What do you think about the Radial Genomics business?"

"What Radial Genomics business?"

"I guess word hasn't gotten around. I figured you'd know about it." He bent over, began to unlace his shoes. "I just thought you'd be concerned," he said. "Didn't you have a robbery recently?"

"Yes. My car was stolen from the parking lot," Diehl said. "But I'm going through a divorce, and it's pretty bitter just now."

"So you assume your wife took your car?"

"Well, yes . . ."

"Do you know that for a fact?"

"No," Diehl said, frowning. "I just assumed . . ."

"Because that's how it started at Radial Genomics. Minor thefts of physical property. A lab assistant's car from the lot, a purse from the company dining room. An ID card from the bathroom. Nobody thought much about it—although in retrospect, it was someone probing the system for weaknesses. They understood that, after the massive databank theft."

"Databank theft?" Diehl said, frowning. That was potentially very serious. He knew Charlie Huggins down at Genomics. He'd call him and get the full story.

"Of course," Watson said, "Huggins's not admitting anything happened. They've got an IPO in June, and he knows it'd kill the offering. But the story is, last month they had four cell lines taken from their labs, and fifty terabytes of network data removed, including backups of that data from offsite storage. Very professional job. Really set them back."

"No kidding. I'm sorry to hear that."

"Of course I put Charlie in contact with BDG, Biological Data Group. It's a security outfit. I'm sure you know them."

"BDG?" Diehl couldn't remember that name, but it seemed he ought to know it. "Of course I know BDG."

"Right. They've done security for Genentech, Wyeth, BioSyn, a

dozen other places. Not that any of those guys will ever talk about
what happened, but BDG is unquestionably the best when you have
problems. They come in, analyze your security setup, ID your vulner-
abilities, and close the network holes. Quiet, fast, confidential."

Diehl was thinking the only security problem he had was Jack
Watson's nephew. But what he said was, "Maybe I should talk to
them."

Which was how Rick Diehl found himself sitting in a restaurant across
from an elegant blonde in a dark business suit. She had introduced herself as Jacqueline Maurer. She had short hair and a brisk manner. She
shook hands firmly and handed him her business card. She couldn't
have been more than thirty. She had the tight body of a gymnast. She
looked him in the eye when she spoke and was very direct.

Rick glanced at the card. It had BDG in blue, and beneath, in small
lettering, was her name and a phone number. Nothing else. He said,
"BDG has its offices where?"

"Many cities around the world."

"And you?"

"I am based in San Francisco at the moment. Before that, Zurich."

He was listening to her accent. He had thought it was French, but it
was probably German. "You are from Zurich?"

"No. I was born in Tokyo. My father was in the diplomatic corps.
I traveled a lot when I was young. I attended school in Paris and Cam-
bridge. I worked first for Crédit Lyonnais in Hong Kong, because
I speak Mandarin and Cantonese. Then I went to Lombard Odier in
Geneva. Private bank." The waiter came. She ordered mineral water, a
brand he did not know.

"What is that?" he said.

"It's Norwegian. Very good."

He ordered the same.

"And how did you get to BDG?" he asked.

"Two years ago. In Zurich."

Rick said, "What were the circumstances?"

"I'm sorry, I can't say. A company had a problem. BDG was brought in to solve it. I was asked to help—some technical issues. I subsequently joined them."

"A company in Zurich had a problem?"

She smiled. "I'm sorry."

"What companies have you worked with, since joining BDG?"

"I'm not free to say."

Rick frowned. He was thinking this was going to be a very weird interview, if she couldn't tell him anything.

"You realize," she said, "that data theft is a global concern. It affects companies around the world. Estimated losses of one trillion euros annually. No company wishes its problems made public. So we respect the privacy of our clients."

Rick said, "What exactly *can* you tell me?"

"Think of any large banking or scientific or pharmaceutical firm. We have probably done work for them."

"Very discreet."

"As we will be discreet with you. We will send only three persons to your company, including me. We will identify ourselves as due-diligence accountants for a VC firm that is thinking of investing. We will spend one week reviewing your status, and then report to you."

Very straightforward, very direct. He tried to focus on what she was saying, but he found her beauty distracting. She did not make the slightest sexual gesture—not a glance, not a body movement, not a touch—yet she was immensely sexy. No bra, he could see that, firm breasts beneath a silk blouse . . .

"Mr. Diehl?" she said. She was staring at him. He must have drifted off.

"I'm sorry." He shook his head. "It's been a very difficult time . . ."

"We are aware of your personal stresses," she said. "And also of your security issues. I mean, the political aspects of your security."

"Yes," he said, "we have a head of security, a man named Bradley—"

"He must be replaced immediately," she said.

"I know," he said, "but his uncle—"

"Leave all that to us," she said. The waiter came back, and she ordered lunch.

As the conversation continued, he felt more and more drawn to her. Jacqueline Maurer had an exotic quality, and a personal reserve that he found challenging. It was not difficult to decide to hire her. He wanted to see her again.

At the end of the meal, they walked outside. She shook hands firmly.

"When will you start?" he said.

"Immediately. Today, if you like."

"Yes, good," he said.

"All right, then. We will visit your headquarters in four days."

"Not today?"

"Oh no. We start today, but we must address your political problem first. Then we will come."

A black town car pulled up. The driver came around to open the door for her.

"Oh, and by the way," she said. "Your Porsche has been located in Houston. We are quite certain your wife did not take it." She slipped into the town car, her skirt riding up. She didn't pull it down. She waved to Rick as the driver closed the door.

As the limousine pulled away, Rick realized he was breathless.

CH018

It was just his way of relaxing, Brad Gordon knew, but try explaining that to anyone else. A single guy had to be careful these days. That was why he always brought a PDA and a cell phone whenever he sat in the school bleachers. He'd pretend to send messages and talk on the cell phone, like a busy parent. Maybe an uncle. And he didn't come all the time, just once or twice a week during soccer season. When he didn't have anything else to do.

In the afternoon sun, the girls running around in their shorts and knee socks looked lovely. Seventh-graders—coltish legs, budding breasts that hardly bounced as they ran. Some of them had real racks on them, and butts that were developed, but most retained an endearing, child-like quality. Not yet women, but no longer girls. Innocent, at least for a while.

Brad took his usual seat, halfway up the bleachers and over to one side, as if he were keeping some distance for his private business calls. He nodded to the other regulars, grandparents and Hispanic maids, as he took out his PDA and set his cell phone on his knee. He got his stylus and began to peck at the PDA, acting as if he were too busy to look at the girls.

"Excuse me."

He looked up. An Asian girl was sitting down next to him. He had never seen her before, but she was cute. Maybe eighteen or so.

"I'm really, *really* sorry," she said, "but I have to call Emily's parents" —she nodded toward one of the girls on the field—"and my battery died. Could I possibly use your phone? Just for a minute?"

"Uh, sure," he said, handing her the phone.

"It's just a local call."

"No problem."

She called quickly, saying something about it being the third quarter and they could come and pick her up soon. He pretended not to listen. She handed the phone back to him, her hand touching his. "Hey, thanks."

"You're welcome."

"I haven't seen you at any of the games before," she said. "Do you come a lot?"

"Not as often as I'd like. Work, you know." Bradley pointed to the field. "Which one is Emily?"

"The center forward." She pointed to a black girl, on the other side of the field.

"I'm her friend. Kelly." She extended her hand, shook his.

"Brad," he said.

"Nice to meet you, Brad. And you're here with . . . ?"

"Oh, my niece is at the dentist today," he said. "I didn't find out until I was already here." He shrugged.

"Nice uncle. She must really appreciate you coming. But you don't seem old enough to be the uncle of one of the girls."

He smiled. For some reason he felt nervous. Kelly was sitting very close, her thigh almost touching his. He couldn't use his PDA or his phone. Nobody ever sat close like that.

"My parents are so old," Kelly said. "My dad was fifty when I was born." She stared out at the field. "I guess that's why I like older guys."

He thought, *How old is she?* But he couldn't think of a way to ask her without being obvious.

She held her hands up, scrutinized them, fingers spread wide. "I just got my nails done," she said. "You like this color?"

"Yes. Very good color."

"My dad hates it when I get my nails done. He thinks it makes me look too mature. But I think it's a good color. Hot love. That's the name of the color."

"Yes . . ."

"Anyway, all the girls get their nails done. I mean, come *on*. I was getting my nails done in seventh grade. And besides, I graduated."

"Oh, you graduated?"

"Yes. Last year." She had opened her purse and was rummaging around inside it. Along with the lipstick, car keys, iPod, and makeup cases, he noticed a couple of joints wrapped in plastic and a ribbon of colored condoms that made a crackling sound when she pushed them around.

He looked away. "So, are you in college now?"

"No," she said. "I took a year off." She smiled at him. "My grades weren't too good. Having too much fun." She pulled out a small plastic bottle of orange juice. "Do you have any vodka?"

"Not on me," he said, surprised.

"Gin?"

"Uh, no . . ."

"But you could get some, right?" She smiled at him.

"I suppose I could," he said.

"I promise I'd pay you back," she said, still smiling.

That was how it started.

They left the playing field separately, several minutes apart. Bradley went first, and he waited in his car in the parking lot, watching her walk toward him. She was wearing flip-flops, a short skirt, and a lacy top that looked like something you would wear to bed. But all the girls dressed that way these days. Her huge bag banged against her side as she walked. She lit a cigarette and then climbed into her car. She was driving a black Mustang. She waved to him.

He started his engine, pulled out, and she followed him.

He thought, *Don't get your hopes up.* But the truth was, he already had.

CH019

Marilee Hunter, the pedantic director of the Long Beach Memorial genetics lab, liked to hear herself talk. Marty Roberts did his best to appear interested. Marilee had a fussy, pinched demeanor, like a librarian in an old forties movie. She delighted in catching errors among hospital staff. She had called Marty to say she needed to see him, right away.

"Correct me if I'm wrong on the basics," Marliee Hunter said. "Mr. Weller's daughter obtains a postmortem paternity test that indicates she and her father do not share DNA. Nevertheless, the widow insists Weller *is* the father, and demands further testing. You provide me samples of blood, spleen, liver, kidney, and testes, although all have been compromised from funeral home infusation. You are looking for a chimera, obviously."

"Yes. Or an error in the original test," Marty said. "We don't know where the daughter took the blood for testing."

"Paternity tests have a nontrivial error rate," Marilee said. "Especially in online establishments. My lab does not make errors. We will test all these tissues, Marty—as soon as you provide buccal cells from the daughter."

"Right, right." He had forgotten all about that. They needed cheek cells from the daughter to compare DNA. "She may not cooperate."

"In that case," Marilee said, "we will test the son and the other daughter. But you realize these tissue tests take time. Weeks."

"Of course, yes."

Marilee opened the Weller patient file, which was stamped DECEASED. She thumbed through the pages. "Meanwhile, I can't help but wonder about your original autopsy."

Marty jerked his head up. "What about it?"

"It shows here you ran a tox screen that came back negative."

"We do a tox screen in every automobile fatality. It's routine."

"Umm," Hunter said, pursing her lips. "The thing is, we repeated the tox screen in our lab. And the result is not negative."

"Oh?" he said, controlling his voice. Thinking: *What the fuck?*

"It's difficult to run a tox panel after all the funeral preservatives have been infused, but we have experience dealing with that. And we determined that the deceased Mr. Weller had elevated intracellular levels of calcium and magnesium . . ."

Marty thought, *Oh boy . . .*

" . . . along with significant hepatic elevation of ethanol dehydrogenase, implying a high blood-alcohol level at the time of the accident . . ."

Marty groaned inwardly. Who had done the original tox screen? Had fucking Raza sent it out? Or only *said* that he had?

" . . . and finally," Marilee said, "we found trace levels of ethacrynic acid."

"Ethacrynic acid?" Marty was shaking his head. "That makes no sense at all. That's an oral diuretic."

"Correct."

"The guy was forty-six years old. His injuries were severe, but even so, I could tell he had been in fantastic physical shape—like he was a bodybuilder or something. Bodybuilders take those drugs. If he was taking an oral diuretic, that was probably why."

"You're assuming that he knew he was taking it," Hunter said. "Possibly he didn't know."

"You think somebody poisoned him?" Marty said.

She shrugged. "Toxic reactions include shock, hypotension, and coma. It could have contributed to his death."

"I don't know how you would determine that."

"You did the post," she reminded him, thumbing through the chart.

"Yes, I did. Weller's injuries were massive. Crush trauma to face and chest, pericardial rupture, fracture of hip and femur. His air bag didn't open."

"The car was checked, of course?"

Marty sighed. "Ask the cops. Not my job."

"It should have been checked."

"Look," Marty said, "this was a single-car fatality. There were witnesses. The guy is not drunk or in a coma. He drives straight into a freeway overpass at ninety miles an hour. Nearly all single-car fatalities are suicides. No surprise the victim turned off the air bag first."

"But you didn't check, Marty."

"No. Because we had no reason. The guy's tox screen was negative and his electrolytes were essentially normal, given his injuries and time of death."

"Except they weren't normal, Marty."

"Our tests came back normal."

"Umm," she said. "Are you sure the tests were actually done?"

And that was when Marty Roberts began to think seriously about Raza. Raza had said there was a rush order from the bone bank that night. Raza wanted to fill the order. So Raza would not have wanted Weller's body to lie in a locker for four or six days while the abnormal tox findings were analyzed.

"I'll have to check," Marty said, "to make sure the tests were done."

"I think we ought to," Marilee said. "Because according to the hospital file, the deceased's son works for a biotech company, and the wife works in a pediatrician's office. I assume both have access to biologicals. At this point, we can't be certain that Mr. Weller wasn't poisoned."

"Possible," Marty said. "Though unlikely."

She gave him a frosty look.

"I'll get right on it," Marty Roberts said.

Walking back to the lab, he tried to decide what to do about Raza. The guy was a menace. Marty was certain now that Raza had never ordered the tox screen, which meant that the lab report had been faked. Either Raza had faked it himself, Xeroxing another report and changing the name, or he had an accomplice in the lab who faked it for him. Probably the latter. Dear God, another person involved in all this.

And now Miss Prissypants was on the hunt for wrongdoers because of trace ethacrynic acid. Ethacrynic acid. If John Weller really had been poisoned, Marty had to admit it was a clever choice. The guy was clearly vain about his body. At his age, he had to spend a couple of hours a day in the gym. Probably took a ton of supplements and shit. So it would be hard to prove that he hadn't taken the diuretic himself.

Hard. But not impossible . . . Ethacrynic acid was a prescription drug. There would be paper trails. Even if he got it from somebody, another bodybuilder, or a web site in Australia, all that would take days to check out. It wouldn't be long before somebody decided to take another look at the body and discovered the corpse had no arm and leg bones.

Shit.

Fucking Raza!

Marty started thinking about a forty-six-year-old bodybuilder. Guy that age, grown family—works his ass off to get a body like that, there's only two reasons. He's gay or he's got a girlfriend. Either way he's not humping his wife. So how does she feel about that? Pissed off?

Probably, yeah. Enough to poison the buff hubby? Couldn't rule it out. People killed their spouses for less. Marty found himself thinking hard about Mrs. Weller, recalling everything that had happened at the exhumation. He saw it in his mind: the tearful widow, leaning against her tall son, with the dutiful daughter standing beside, holding tissues for Mom. All very touching.

Except . . .

The minute the casket came out of the ground, Emily Weller got nervous. Suddenly the grieving widow wanted everything done fast. Don't take the body back to the hospital. Don't take too many tissue samples. The woman who had demanded a thorough DNA analysis suddenly seemed to change her mind.

Why, he wondered, had she done that?

He could think of only one possible answer: Mrs. Weller wanted her paternity test, but she never imagined the body would be taken back to the hospital for examination. She never thought they would take tissues from multiple organs. She thought they would just grab a blood sample, put the body back in the ground, and go home.

Anything more than that seemed to make Mrs. Weller nervous.

Maybe there was hope, after all.

He went into his office and closed the door. He needed to call Mrs. Weller. It was a delicate call. There would be a hospital record of the date and time of the call. So, why was he calling her? He frowned.

Oh, yes: Because he had to collect her DNA, and that of her children.

Okay, fine. But why hadn't he collected the DNA from the family at the grave site? It was just a matter of cheek swabs. It would have taken only a moment.

Answer: Because he thought the DNA had already been collected by Miss Prissypants's lab.

Marty considered that. Rolled it over in his mind.

He could find nothing wrong with it. He had a perfectly good reason to call.

He picked up the phone and dialed.

"Mrs. Weller, this is Dr. Roberts at Memorial Hospital. Marty Roberts."

"Yes, Dr. Roberts." A pause. "Is everything all right?"

"Yes, Mrs. Weller. I just want to schedule you and your children to come in and give us blood and cheek tissue samples. For the DNA test."

"We already did that. For that woman at the lab."

"Oh, I see. You mean Dr. Hunter? I'm sorry, I didn't know."

There was a pause. Emily said, "Are you, uh, doing the tests on Jack now?"

"Yes. We do some of the tests here, and the lab does some."

"Have you found anything yet? I mean, are you finding what you expected?"

Marty smiled as he listened. She wasn't asking about paternity. She was worried about something else they might find. "Well actually, Mrs. Weller . . ."

"Yes?"

"There does seem to be a slight complication. Nothing important."

"What kind of a complication?"

"The genetics lab found traces of an unusual chemical in Mr. Weller's tissues. It's probably a lab error, contamination."

"What kind of a chemical?"

"I only mention it because I know you wanted your husband to have his final rest as soon as possible."

"That's right. I want him left undisturbed," she said.

"Of course. I would hate to see his final rest delayed for days, or even weeks," Marty said, "while questions were asked about this chemical and how it came to be found in his body. Because even if it is a lab error, everything from this point on is required as a matter of law, Mrs. Weller. I shouldn't even be making this call to you. But I . . . I guess I feel responsible. As I say, I'd hate to see your husband's final rest delayed for something like a coroner's inquest."

"I understand," she said.

"Of course I would never advise you to do anything but follow the law, Mrs. Weller. But I sensed that disinterment of your husband was an emotionally exhausting experience for you . . ."

"Yes . . . yes . . ."

"And if you didn't want the further emotional exhaustion of reinterment—to say nothing of the expense—you might elect a less emotional solution. And less expensive, if you were short of funds . . . You have the right to order the body cremated."

"I didn't realize that," she said.

"I'm sure you never imagined that taking your husband's body out of the ground would be so traumatic."

"No, I didn't."

"You might decide not to put yourself through it again."

"That's just how I feel," she said.

Marty thought, *I'll bet you do.* "Of course, if you knew there was going to be an investigation, you would not be permitted to cremate the body. Certainly I would never suggest you cremate. But you might decide on cremation yourself, for your own reasons. And if that happened soon—later today, or tomorrow morning—then it would just be one of those things. The body was unfortunately cremated before the inquest was called."

"I understand."

"I have to go," he said.

"I appreciate your taking the time to call me," she said. "Was there anything else?"

"No, that's everything," he said. "Thank you, Mrs. Weller."

"You're welcome, Dr. Roberts."

Click.

Marty Roberts leaned back in his chair. He was very pleased with how that call had gone. Very pleased indeed.

Just one more thing, for the moment, remained to be done.

"Fifth-Floor Lab. This is Jennie."

"Jennie, this is Dr. Roberts down in Pathology. I need you to check on a lab result for me."

"Is it stat, Dr. Roberts?"

"No, it's an old test. Tox screen that was ordered eight days ago. Patient name is Weller." He read off the serial number.

There was a brief pause. He heard the clicking of keys. "John J. Weller? White male, age forty-six?"

"Yes."

"We did a full-panel tox screen at three thirty-seven a.m. on Sunday, May eighth. Tox screen and, uh, nine other tests."

"And you kept the blood sample?"

"Yes, I'm sure we did. We keep all tissues these days."

"Would you check for me?"

"Dr. Roberts, these days we keep everything. We even keep the heel stick cards whenever a child is born. It's PKU testing required by law, but we keep the cards anyway. We keep cord blood. We keep placenta tissue. We keep surgical excisions. We keep everything—"

"I understand, but would you mind checking?"

"I can see it's registered right here on my screen," she said. "We have the frozen sample stored in freezer locker B-7. It'll be taken to the off-site storage at the end of the month."

"I'm sorry," Marty said. "But this involves a potential legal issue. Would you physically check to make sure the sample is where it's supposed to be?"

"Of course. I'll send somebody down there and call you back."

"Thank you, Jennie."

He hung up and leaned back in his chair again. Through the glass wall, he watched Raza scrubbing down a steel table, in preparation for the next autopsy. Raza did a thorough job of cleaning. Marty gave him that: The guy was thorough. He paid attention to details.

Which meant that he was not above changing the hospital database to indicate the storage of a nonexistent sample. Either he did it, or he had someone do it for him.

The phone rang. "Dr. Roberts? It's Jennie."

"Yes, Jennie."

"I'm afraid I spoke too soon. The sample for Weller is thirty cc's of venous blood, frozen. But it's not in B-7; it seems to have been misplaced. I have a trace on it now. I will let you know as soon as it's found. Was there anything else?"

"No," Marty said. "Thank you very much, Jennie."

CH020

Finally!

Ellis Levine found his mother on the second floor of the Polo Ralph Lauren store on Madison and Seventy-second, just as she came out of the dressing room. She was wearing white linen pants and a colorful wraparound top. She stepped in front of the mirror, turning this way and that. Then she saw him.

"Hello, dear," she said. "What do you think?"

"Mom," he said. "What are you doing here?"

"Buying my cruise wardrobe, dear."

"But you're not going on a cruise," Ellis said.

"Oh yes," his mother said. "We take a cruise every year. Do you like the cuffs on the trousers?"

"Mom . . ."

She frowned and fluffed her white hair absently. "And I'm not sure about this top," she said. "Does it make me look like a fruit salad?"

"We have to talk," Ellis said.

"Good. Do you have time for lunch?"

"No, Mom. I have to get back to the office." Ellis was an accountant for an advertising agency. He had left the office and hurried uptown because he had gotten a panic call from his brother.

He walked over to his mother and said quietly, "Mom, you can't shop now."

"Don't be silly, dear."

"Mom, we had a family meeting . . ." Ellis and his two brothers had met with his parents the weekend before. A difficult, painful meeting at the house in Scarsdale. His father was sixty-three. His mother fifty-nine. The brothers had gone over the finances with them.

"You can't be serious," she said to him now.

"I am." He squeezed her arm.

"Ellis Jacob Levine," she said, "you are being inappropriate."

"Mom, Dad lost his job."

"I know, but we have plenty—"

"And his pension tanked."

"It's only temporary."

"No, Mom, it is *not* temporary."

"But we have always had plenty of—"

"*Not anymore.* You don't. Not anymore."

She glared at him. "Your father and I talked, after you boys left. He said we would be fine. All that business about selling the house and the Jag. That's all ridiculous."

"Dad said that?"

"He certainly did."

Ellis sighed. "He was trying to keep you from worrying."

"I'm not worried. And he loves that Jag. Your father always gets a new Jag every year. Ever since you were babies."

The salespeople were staring at them. Ellis steered his mother off to one side. "Mom, things have changed."

"Oh, *please.*"

Ellis looked away from his mother's face. He could not meet her eyes. All his life he had looked up to his parents: they were successful, stable, solid. He and his brothers had their ups and downs—his older brother was already divorced, for God's sake—but his parents were from an earlier generation that was stable. You could count on them.

Even when his father lost his job, nobody worried. True, at his age, there was no chance he would get another. But they had investments, stocks, land in Montana and the Caribbean, an ample pension. There was no reason to worry. His parents did not change their lifestyle. They continued to entertain, travel, spend.

But now he and his brothers were paying the mortgage in Scarsdale. And trying to sell the condo in Charlotte Amalie, and the town house in Vail.

"Mom," he said, "I've got two kids in preschool. Jeff has one in first grade. You know what it costs, private school in the city? Aaron has alimony. We have lives of our own. We can't keep paying for yours."

"You are *not paying for me or your father*," she snapped.

"Yes, we are, Mom. And I am telling you that you cannot buy these clothes. Please. Go back and take them off."

Suddenly, to his horror, she burst into tears, throwing her hands over her face. "I'm *so afraid*," she said. "What will happen to us?" Her body shook. He put his arm around her.

"It'll be fine," he said gently. "Go get dressed. I'll take you to lunch."

"But you *don't have time*." She was sobbing now. "You said so your-self."

"It's okay. We'll have lunch, Mom. We'll go to the Carlyle. It'll be fine."

She sniffled and wiped her eyes. She headed back to the dressing room, head high.

Ellis flipped open his phone, called his office to say he would be late.

At the Congressional Biotechnology Prayer Breakfast in Washington, Dr. Robert Bellarmino waited impatiently for his introduction to end. Congressman Henry Waters, famously long-winded, droned on. "Dr. Bellarmino is known to all of us," he said, "as a physician with a conscience, a man of science and a man of God, a man of principle in an age of expediency, a man of rectitude in a hedonistic era where anything goes, especially on MTV. Dr. Bellarmino is not only a director of the National Institutes of Health, but also a lay pastor of the Thomas Field Baptist Church of Houston and the author of *Turning Points*, his book of spiritual awakening to the healing message of Jesus Christ Our Lord. And I know— well, he's looking at me, and he has to be at the congressional hearing room in one hour, so let me present, our man of God and science, Dr. Robert A. Bellarmino."

Handsome and assured, Bellarmino stepped to the lectern. His topic, according to the printed schedule, was "God's Plan for Mankind in Genetic Science."

"My thanks to Congressman Waters, and to all of you for coming today. Some of you may wonder how a scientist—especially a genetic scientist—can reconcile his work with the word of God. But as Denis Alexander points out, the Bible reminds us that God, the Universal Creator, is separate from His creation but that He also actively sustains it moment to moment. Thus God is the creator of DNA, which underlies the biodiversity of our planet. That may be why some critics

of genetic engineering say we shouldn't do it, because it involves playing God. Some ecological doctrines hold a similar view, that nature is
sacred and inviolable. Such beliefs are of course *pagan*."

Bellarmino paused, letting his audience savor the word. He considered saying more about pagan beliefs, particularly the pantheistic
nature worship that some called "California cosmology." But not today,
he thought. Press on.

"The Bible tells us clearly, in Genesis 1:28 and 2:15, that God has
given human beings the task, the responsibility to care for the earth
and all the creatures on it. We are not playing God. We are answerable
to God if we are not responsible stewards of what God has given us in
all its majesty and biodiversity. This is our God-given assignment. We
are the stewards of the planet.

"Genetic engineering uses the tools the Creator has given us to carry
out good works on the planet. Unprotected crops are eaten by pests, or
die of frost and drought. Genetic modification can prevent that, use less
crop acreage, leave more untouched wilderness, and still feed the hungry. Genetic engineering allows us to distribute the munificence of God
to all His creatures as He would want. Genetically modified organisms
make pure insulin for diabetics, pure clotting factors for hemophiliacs.
Previously these patients often died of contamination. Surely for us to
create this purity is God's work. Who will say it is not?

"Critics charge that genetic engineering is unnatural, because it
changes the very essence of an organism, its deep and profound nature.
That idea is Greek and pagan. But the plain fact is that domestication
of plants and animals, as practiced for thousands of years, does change
the deep and profound nature of an organism. A domestic dog is no longer a wolf. Corn is no longer a stunted, largely inedible weed. Genetic
engineering is simply another step in this long-accepted tradition. It
does not mark a radical departure from the past.

"Sometimes we hear that we shouldn't change DNA, period. But
why not? DNA is not fixed. DNA changes over time. And DNA inter-
acts constantly with our daily existence. Should we tell athletes not to
lift weights, because it will change the size of their muscles? Should we

tell students not to read books, because that will change the structure of their developing minds? Of course not. Our bodies are constantly changing, and our DNA with them.

"But more directly—there are five hundred genetic diseases that can, potentially, be cured by gene therapy. Many of these diseases cause terrible suffering in children, early and agonizing death. Other diseases hang over a person's life like a prison sentence; the person must wait for the disease to come and strike him down. Should we not cure these diseases if we can? Should we not alleviate suffering whenever we can? If so, we must change DNA. Simple as that.

"So do we modify DNA or not? Is this God's work or man's hubris? These are not decisions to be taken lightly. And so it is with that most sensitive subject, the use of germ cells and embryos. Many in the Judeo-Christian tradition are unequivocally opposed to embryo use. But such views will, eventually, conflict with the goal of healing the sick and alleviating suffering. Not this year, not next year, but the time will come. Careful thought and much prayer are needed to arrive at our answer. Our Lord Jesus made men walk again. Does that mean we should not do likewise, if we can? It is most difficult, for we know man's hubris takes many forms—not only over-reaching, but also stubbornly holding back. We are put here to reflect the glory of God in all His works, and not the willful ego of man. I, myself, have no answer as I stand before you today. I confess I am troubled in my heart.

"But I have faith that God shall lead us, in the end, to the world that He wants for us. I have faith that we shall be guided to wisdom, that we shall be cautious, and that we shall not be willful in tending His works, His suffering children, and all the creatures in His creation. And for this I pray, most humbly, in the name of God. Amen."

The speech worked, of course—it always worked. Bellarmino had been giving it in various versions for a decade, and each time, he pushed forward a little harder, spoke a little more firmly. Five years ago, he did not use the word *embryo*. Now he did, cautiously and briefly. He was laying the groundwork. He was getting them thinking. The thought of suffering made them uneasy. So did the thought of enabling the crippled to walk again.

Of course, no one knew whether that would ever happen. Personally, Bellarmino doubted it ever would. But let them think it was coming. Let them worry. They should: the stakes were high and the pace of advance rocket-fast. Any research that Washington blocked would take place in Shanghai, or Seoul, or São Paulo. And Bellarmino, skilled and sanctimonious, intended to make sure that never occurred. Nothing, in short, that would interfere with his lab, his research, and his reputation. He was very good at protecting all three.

An hour later, in the wood-paneled hearing room, Bellarmino gave testimony before the House Select Committee on Genetics and Health. The hearing had been called to consider whether it was appropriate for the patent office to grant patents for human genes. Thousands of such patents had already been issued. Was this a good idea?

"There is no question we have a problem," Dr. Bellarmino said, not looking at his notes. He had memorized his testimony so he could deliver it while facing the television cameras, for greater impact. "Gene patents *by industry* pose a significant problem for future research. On the other hand, gene patenting by academic researchers causes far less concern, since the work is freely shared."

Of course this was nonsense. Dr. Bellarmino did not mention that the distinction between academic and industry workers had long since been blurred. Twenty percent of academic researchers were paid by industry. Ten percent of academics did drug development. More than 10 percent had a product already on the market. More than 40 percent had applied for patents in the course of their careers.

Nor did Bellarmino mention that he, too, pursued gene patents aggressively. In the last four years, his laboratory had filed 572 patent applications covering a wide spectrum of conditions, from Alzheimer's and schizophrenia to manic depression, anxiety, and attention-deficit disorders. He had secured patents for dozens of genes for specific metabolic disorders, ranging from deficiency of l-thyroxy-hydrocambrine (associated with restless leg disorder of sleep) to an excess of para-amino-2, 4-dihydroxybenthamine (causing urinary frequency in sleep).

"However," Dr. Bellarmino said, "I can assure this committee that gene patenting in general is a system that serves the common good. Our procedures to protect intellectual property work well. Important research is protected, and the consumer, the American patient, is the beneficiary of our efforts."

He did not tell them that more than four thousand DNA-based patents were granted each year—two every hour of each working day. Since there were only thirty-five thousand genes in the human genome, most experts estimated that more than 20 percent of the genome was already privately owned.

Bellarmino did not point out that the biggest patent owner was not some industrial giant but the University of California. UC owned more gene patents than Pfizer, Merck, Lilly, and Wyeth combined. They owned more patents than the U.S. government.

"The notion that someone owns part of the human genome strikes some people as unusual," Bellarmino said. "But it's what makes America great and keeps our innovation strong. True, it causes the occasional glitch, but over time, all that will get resolved. Gene patenting is the way to go."

At the conclusion of his testimony, Dr. Bellarmino left the hearing and headed for Reagan Airport, where he would fly back to Ohio, to resume his research on the "novelty gene," research being conducted at an amusement park there. Bellarmino had a film crew from *60 Minutes* following him around, putting together a segment that would show his varied and important genetic research, and also tell his personal story. Time spent in Ohio was a significant part of the final film. Because there he interacted with ordinary people, and as the filmmakers said, the human touch was what was really important, especially with a man of science, and especially on television.

Massachusetts Office of University Technology Transfer

GOVERNMENT CENTER, BOSTON

SCIENTISTS GROW MINIATURE EAR IN LAB
First "Partial Life Form" at MIT
Possible Applications in Hearing Technology

MIT scientists have grown a human ear in tissue culture for the first time.

Australian performance artist Stelarc collaborated with labs at the Massachusetts Institute of Technology to produce an extra ear for himself. The ear was one-quarter scale, slightly larger than a bottle cap. The tissue taken from Stelarc was cultured in a rotating micro-gravity bioreactor while growing.

MIT issued a statement that the extra ear could be considered "a partial life form—partly constructed and partly grown." The ear fits comfortably in the palm of the hand.

Last year, the same MIT lab made steaks of frog tissue grown over bio-polymer mesh. They had also grown steak from the cells of an unborn sheep. And they created what they referred to as "victimless leather." This was skin that had been artificially grown in the laboratory and was suitable for shoes, purses, belts, and other leather goods—presumably with an eye to the robust vegan market.

Several hearing-aid companies have opened talks with MIT about licensing their ear-making technology. According to geneticist Zack Rabi, "As the American population ages, many senior citizens may prefer to grow slightly enlarged, genetically modified ears, rather than rely on hearing-aid technology. A spokesperson for Audion, the hearing-aid company, noted, "We're not talking about Dumbo ears. Just a small increase of 20 percent in pinna size would double auditory efficiency. We think the market for enlarged ears is huge. When lots of people have them, no one will notice anymore. We believe big ears will become the new standard, like silicon breast implants."

CH022

It was a bad day for Marty Roberts, made much worse by a phone call from Emily Weller:

"Dr. Roberts, I'm calling you from the mortuary. It seems there's a problem with my husband's cremation."

"What kind of problem?" Marty Roberts said, sitting in his office in the pathology lab.

"They're saying they can't cremate my Jack if he contains metal."

"Metal? What do you mean, metal? Your husband didn't have any hip replacements or war injuries, did he?"

"No, no. They are saying that his arms and legs have metal pipes in them. And the bones have been removed."

"Really." Marty stood up in his chair and snapped his fingers in the air, getting Raza's attention in the autopsy room outside. "I wonder how that could have happened."

"I was calling to ask you the same thing."

"I don't know what to say. It's quite beyond me, Mrs. Weller. I must say, I'm shocked."

By then Raza had come in the room.

"I'm going to put you on speaker, Mrs. Weller, so I can make some notes as we speak. Are you with your husband at the crematorium now?"

"Yes," she said. "And they are saying he has lead pipes in his arms and legs, so they can't cremate him."

"I see," Marty said, looking at Raza.

Raza shook his head. He scrawled on a pad, *We just took one leg. Put in wood dowel.*

Marty said, "Mrs. Weller, I can't imagine how this might have happened. There may have to be an inquiry. I am concerned that the funeral home, or perhaps the cemetery, may have done something improper."

"Well," she said, "they say he has to be reburied. But they also say maybe I should call the police, because it looks like his bones were stolen. But I don't want to go through the ordeal of the police and everything." A long, pregnant pause. "What do you think, Dr. Roberts?"

"Mrs. Weller," he said, "let me call you right back."

Marty Roberts hung up the phone. "You dumb fuck! I told you: Wood, always wood!"

"I know it," Raza said. "We didn't do that lead job. I swear we didn't. We always use wood."

"Lead pipe . . ." Marty said, shaking his head. "That's crazy."

"It wasn't us, Marty. I swear it wasn't us. Must have been those bastards at the cemetery. You know how easy it is. They hold the ceremony, the family shovels a little dirt, and everybody goes home. Coffin isn't buried. They don't do the actual burial sometimes for a day or so. That night, they come in, take the bones. You know how it works."

"How do *you* know?" Marty said, glaring at him.

"Because, one time last year, woman calls, her husband is buried with the wedding ring, and she wants the ring. Wants to know if we took it off him for the autopsy. I said we didn't have any effects, but I would call the cemetery. And they hadn't buried him yet, and she got the ring back."

Marty Roberts sat down. "Look," he said, "if there is an investigation, if they start looking at bank accounts . . ."

"No, no. Trust me."

"That's a laugh."

"Marty, I'm telling you. *We didn't do it.* No metal pipe. No."

"Okay. I heard you. I just don't believe you."

Raza tapped the desk. "You'd better use the prescription with her."

"I will. Now get out of here while I call her back."

Raza crossed the autopsy room and went into the changing room. No one was there. He dialed his cell phone. "Jesu," he said. "What the fuck you doing, man? You put lead pipes in that car crash guy. Shit, Marty's mad. They're trying to cremate the dude, he's got lead pipes in him . . . Man, how many times do I have to tell you? Use wood!"

"Mrs. Weller," Marty Roberts said, "I think you better rebury your husband. That seems to be your only option."

"You mean, unless I go to the police. About the stolen bones."

"I can't tell you what to do," he said. "You'll have to decide the best course of action. But I'm sure a prolonged police investigation will turn up a prescription in your name for ethacrynic acid from Longwood Pharmacy, on Motor Drive."

"That was for my personal use."

"Oh, I know that. It's just a question of how ethacrynic acid happened to end up in your husband's body. That could be awkward."

"Your hospital lab has found traces of that?"

"Yes, but I am sure the hospital would stop the lab work as soon as you dropped your lawsuit against them. Let me know what you decide to do, Mrs. Weller. Good-bye for now."

He hung up and looked at the thermometer in the autopsy room. The temperature was 59 degrees. But Marty was sweating.

"I was wondering when you'd show up," Marilee Hunter said, in the genetics lab. She didn't look happy. "I'd like to know exactly what part you played in all this."

"In all what?" he said.

"Kevin McCormick called today. There's another lawsuit from that Weller family. This time it's the son of the deceased, Tom Weller. The one who works for a biotech company."

"What's his suit about?"

"I was only following protocol," Marilee said.

"Uh-huh . . . What's the suit about?"

"Apparently his health insurance was canceled."

"Because?"

"His father has the BNB71 gene for heart disease."

"He does? That makes no sense. The guy was a health nut."

"He had the gene. Doesn't mean it was expressed. We found it in the tissues. And that fact was duly noted. The insurance company picked it up and canceled the son as 'pre-ill.'"

"How did they get the information?"

"It's online," she said.

"It's *online?*"

"This is a legal inquiry," she said. "Under state law it's all discoverable. We're required to post all lab findings to an FTP address. In theory it's password-protected, but anyone can get to it."

"You put genetic data *online?*"

"Not everyone's data. Just the lawsuits. Anyway, the son is saying he did not authorize the release of genetic information about himself, which is true. But if we release the father's information, as we're required by state law to do, we also release the son's, which we're required by law *not* to do. Because his children share half the same genes as the father. One way or another, we break the law." She sighed. "Tom Weller wants his insurance back, but he won't get it."

Marty Roberts leaned against the desk. "So where does it stand?"

"Mr. Weller sued me along with the hospital. Legal is insisting this lab no longer touches any material from the Wellers." Marilee Hunter sniffed. "We're off the case."

Off the case! No more investigation, no digging up the body! Marty Roberts felt nothing but relief, although he did his best to appear distressed. "It's so unfair," he said, "the way lawyers just run our society."

"Doesn't matter. It's over, Marty," she said. "It's done."

Marty went back to the pathology lab later that day. "Raza," he said, "one of us has to leave this lab."

"I know," Raza said. "And I'm going to miss you, Marty."

"What do you mean?"

"I got a new job," he said, smiling. "Hamilton Hospital in San Francisco. Their diener just had a heart attack. I start day after tomorrow. So with packing and everything, this is my last day on the job."

Marty Roberts stared. "Well," he said. He didn't know what else to say.

"I know you get two weeks," Raza said, "but I told the hospital this was a special case and you would understand. By the way, I have a guy who would be a good replacement. He's a friend of mine, Jesu. Very good guy. Works in a funeral home right now, so it would not be a big transition."

"I'll meet with him," Marty said. "But I think maybe I will pick my own guy."

"Hey, sure, no problem," Raza said. He shook hands with Marty. "Thanks for everything, Dr. Roberts."

"You remembered." Marty smiled.

Raza turned and left the lab.

CH023

Josh Winkler was staring out his office window that overlooked the reception area at BioGen. Things were up in the air. Josh's assistant, Tom Weller, had taken the week off because his father had died in a car crash in Long Beach. And now there was a problem with his health insurance, as well. Which meant Josh had to work with another assistant, who didn't know the routines. Outside, repair crews were fixing the surveillance cameras in the parking lot. At the reception desk below, Brad Gordon was again chatting up the beautiful Lisa. Josh sighed. What kind of juice did Brad have, that he could do whatever he wanted, including chasing the boss's trim? Because Brad was clearly never going to be fired.

Lisa had beautiful breasts.

"Josh? Are you listening to me?"

"Yes, Mom."

"Is something on your mind?"

"No, Mom."

From above, he could look down at Lisa's scoop-neck blouse, which revealed the smooth contours of her firm breasts. Undoubtedly too firm, but that didn't bother Josh. Everybody and everything was surgically enhanced these days. Including guys. Even guys in their twenties were getting face-lifts and penile implants.

"Then what about it?" his mother said.

"What? Sorry, Mom. What were you saying?"

"About the Levines. My cousins."

"I don't know. Where do they live again?"

"Scarsdale, dear."

He remembered now. The Levine family had parents that spent too much. "Mom, this is not legal."

"You went and did it to Lois's boy. You did it yourself."

"That's true." But he had only done it because he thought nobody would ever catch him.

"And now that boy has quit drugs and is working. *At a bank*, Josh. A *bank*."

"As what?"

"I don't know, a teller or something."

"That's great, Mom."

"It's more than great," his mother said. "This spray of yours could be a real moneymaker, Josh. It's the drug everybody wants. You could finally make something of yourself."

"Nice, Mom."

"You know what I mean. The spray could be great." She paused. "But you need to know how it affects older people, don't you."

He sighed. It was true. "Yes . . ."

"That's why the Levines might work out for you."

"Okay," he said, "I'll try to get a canister."

"For both parents?"

"Yes, Mom. For both."

He flipped the phone shut. He was contemplating what, exactly, he should do about this—and deciding to do something else entirely—when he heard the sound of sirens. A moment later two black-and-white police cars pulled up in front of the building. Four cops piled out of the cars, entered the building, and walked right up to Brad, who still leaned on the counter talking to Lisa.

"Are you Bradley A. Gordon?"

A moment later, one spun him around, pulled his arms back, and handcuffed him.

Holy shit, Josh thought.

Brad was bellowing. "What the hell is this? What the *hell* is this!"

"Mr. Gordon, you are under arrest for aggravated assault and rape of a minor."

"*What?*"

"You have the right to remain silent—"

"*What?*" He was shouting. "What minor? Goddamn it, I don't know any fucking minor."

The cop stared at him.

"Okay, wait—wrong word! I don't know any minor!"

"I think you do, sir."

"You guys are making one big-ass mistake!" Brad said, as they started to lead him away.

"Just come with us, sir."

"I'm going to sue your freaking asses off!"

"This way, sir," they said.

And he went through the doors to the sunlight outside.

When Brad had gone, Josh looked over at the other people standing at the railing. Half the office was looking down, talking, whispering. And at the far end of the balcony, he saw Rick Diehl, the head of the company.

Just standing there, with his hands in his pockets. Watching the whole thing play out.

If Diehl was upset, he certainly didn't show it.

Brad Gordon frowned unhappily at the toilet in his jail cell. A strip of damp toilet paper clung to the side of the metal bowl. There was a puddle of brownish liquid in front of the seat. It had flecks of stuff floating in it. Brad wanted to pee, but he wasn't going to step in that liquid, whatever the hell it was. He didn't even like to think about it.

A key turned in the lock behind him. He stood. The door swung open.

"Gordon? Let's go."

"What is it?"

"Attorney's here."

The cop pushed Brad down a hallway and into a small room. There was an older man in a pinstripe suit and a younger kid in a Dodgers jacket, sitting at a table with a laptop. The kid had thick horn-rim glasses, which made him look like an owl, or Harry Potter or something. They both stood up, shook his hand. He didn't catch their names. But he knew they were from his uncle's law firm.

"What's going on here?" he said.

The older lawyer opened a folder. "Her name is Kelly Chin," he said. "You met her at a soccer game, you came on to her—"

"*I* came on to *her*?"

"And then you took her to the Westview Plaza Hotel, room four-thirteen . . ."

"You don't have this story right . . ."

"And once in the room you had oral, genital, and anal sex with her. And she's sixteen."

"Christ," he said. "It never happened."

The older attorney just stared at him. "You're in very deep shit, my friend."

"I'm telling you it *never happened*."

"I see. The two of you were photographed on hotel security cameras in the lobby and again in the elevator. Hallway cameras on the fourth floor recorded you with Miss Chin as you entered room four-thirteen. You were there one hour and seven minutes. Then she left by herself."

"Yeah, sure, but—"

"She was crying in the elevator."

"What?"

"She drove to the Westview Community Hospital and reported she had been assaulted and raped. She was examined at that time, and photographs were taken. She had vaginal tears and contusions, and anal tears. Semen was obtained from her rectum. It is being analyzed now, but she says it's yours. Is it?"

"Oh shit," Brad said softly.

"It's best to come clean," the attorney said. "Tell me exactly what happened."

"That little bitch."

"Let's begin with the soccer game where you met her. Witnesses say that you have been seen at girls' soccer games before. What are you doing at those games, Mr. Gordon?"

"Oh Jesus," he said.

Brad told the story, but the older man interrupted a lot. It took nearly half an hour to explain exactly what had happened. And to get to the hotel room.

"You say this girl was turned on to you," the attorney said.

"Yeah, she sure was."

"There was no kissing or signs of affection in the elevator, going up."

"No, she had that reserved exterior. You know, the Asian thing."

"I see. The Asian thing. Unfortunately, on the cameras it doesn't appear that she was an entirely willing participant."

"I think she got cold feet," he said.

"When was that?"

"Well, we were in the bedroom making out, and she was kind of hot, but also a little weird, you know, backing off. Like she'd want to do it, and then not want to. But mostly she was going for it. I mean, she put the rubber on me. I was ready, and she lies back with her legs open and suddenly she goes, 'No, I don't want to do it.' I'm beside her with my pecker sticking up, and I started to get peeved. So she says she's really sorry and she goes down on me, and I come in the rubber. She was as good as a pro, but you know young chicks today. Anyway, she takes it off me, carries it into the bathroom, and I hear her flushing the toilet. She comes back with a hot washcloth, wipes me down, says she's sorry, but she thinks she needs to go home now.

"I'm like, hey, whatever. Because by now I figure something's wrong with this chick. She's kinky or something, maybe she's a tease, I seen that before—or mentally disturbed, in which case I want her the hell out of my room. So I say, 'Sure, go, sorry it wasn't comfortable for you.' And she tells me maybe I should wait a while before I leave. I say, 'Sure, okay.' She leaves. I wait. Then I left, too. And I swear," he said, "that's all there was to it."

"She never told you her age?"

"No."

"You never asked?"

"No. She said she was out of high school."

"She's not. She's a sophomore."

"Oh fuck."

A silence. The attorney thumbed through the pages of the folder in front of him. "So your story is, this girl seduced you at the soccer game, you took her to a hotel room, she collected your sperm in a condom, left you, gave herself self-inflicted genital injuries, put your sperm up her rectum, drove to the hospital, and reported a rape. Is that it?"

"It had to be that way," Brad said.

"That's a difficult story, Mr. Gordon."

"But it had to be that way."

"Do you have any proof at all that your story is true?"

Brad fell silent. Thinking.

"No," he said finally. "I don't have anything."

"That's going to be a problem," the attorney said.

After Brad was taken back to his cell, the attorney turned to the young man in the Dodgers jacket and horn-rim glasses. "You have anything to contribute here?"

"Yes." He flipped his screen around so the senior man could see a series of jagged black lines. "Audio stress meters remained in the normal range. Hesitation patterns that indicate prefrontal interference with cognition were absent at all times. The guy isn't lying. Or at least, he's convinced it happened his way."

"Interesting," the attorney said. "But it doesn't matter. There's not a chance in hell we'll ever get this guy off."

CH025

Henry Kendall parked in the Long Beach Memorial parking lot, and walked into the side door of the hospital, carrying a tissue container. He went down to the basement to the pathology lab and asked to see Marty Roberts. They had been high school friends in Marin County. Marty came out at once.

"Oh my God," he said, "I heard your name and I thought you were dead!"

"Not yet," Henry said, shaking his hand. "You look good."

"I look fat. You look good. How's Lynn?"

"Good. Kids are good. How's Janice?"

"She took off with a cardiac surgeon a couple of years ago."

"Sorry, I didn't know."

"I'm over it," Marty Roberts said. "Life is good. Been hectic around here, but things are good now." He smiled. "Anyway, aren't you a ways from La Jolla? Isn't that where you are now?"

"Right, right. Radial Genomics."

Marty nodded. "So. Uh . . . what's up?"

"I want you to look at something," Henry Kendall said. "Some blood."

"Okay, no problem. Can I ask whose it is?"

"You can ask," Henry said. "But I don't know. I mean, I'm not sure." He handed Marty the tissue container. It was a small styrofoam case, lined with insulation. In the center was a tube of blood. Marty slid the tube out.

"Packing label says, 'From the Laboratory of Robert A. Bellarmino.' Hey, the big time, Henry." He peeled it back, looked closely at the older label beneath. "And what's this? A number? Looks like F-102. I can't quite make it out."

"I think that's right."

Marty stared at his old friend. "Okay, level with me. What is this?"

"I want you to tell me," Henry said.

"Well, let me tell you straight off," Marty said, "I won't do anything illegal. We just don't do things like that here."

"It's not illegal . . ."

"Uh-huh. You just don't want to analyze it at your lab."

"That's right."

"So you drive two hours up here to see me."

"Marty," he said, "just do it. Please."

Marty Roberts peered through the microscope, then adjusted the video screen so they could both look. "Okay," he said. "Red cell morphology, hemoglobin, protein fractions, all completely normal. It's just blood. Whose is it?"

"Is it human blood?"

"Hell yes," Marty said. "What, you think it's animal blood?"

"I'm just asking."

"Well, if it's certain kinds of ape blood, we can't distinguish it," Marty said. "Chimps and people, we can't tell the difference. Blood's identical. I remember cops arrested a guy worked in the San Diego zoo, covered in blood. They thought he was a murderer. Turned out to be menstrual blood from a female chimpanzee. I had that one when I was a resident."

"You can't tell? What about sialic acid?"

"Sialic acid's a marker for chimp blood . . . So *you* think this is chimp blood?"

"I don't know, Marty."

"We can't do sialic acid at our lab. No call for it. I think Radial Genomics in San Diego can do it, though."

"Very funny."

"You want to tell me what this is, Henry?"

"No," he said. "But I want you to do a DNA test on it. And on me."

Marty Roberts sat back. "You're making me nervous," he said. "You getting into anything kinky?"

"No, no, nothing like that. It was a research project. From a few years ago."

"So you think this might be chimp blood. Or your blood?"

"Yeah."

"Or both?"

"Will you do the DNA test for me?"

"Sure. I'll take a buccal swab, and get back to you in a few weeks."

"Thanks. Can we keep this between us?"

"Jesus," Marty Roberts said, "you're scaring me again. Sure. We can keep it between us." He smiled. "I'll call you when it's done."

We're talking submarines," the patent attorney said to Josh Winkler. "Significant submarines."

"Go on," Josh said, smiling. They were in a Mc-Donald's outside town. Everyone else in the place was under seventeen. No chance that word of their meeting would get back to the company.

The attorney said, "You had me search for patents or patent applications related to your so-called maturity gene. I found five, going back to 1990."

"Uh-huh."

"Two are submarines. That's what we call vague patents that are applied for with the intention of letting them lie dormant until somebody else makes a discovery that activates them. The classic being COX-2—"

"Got it," Josh said. "Old news."

The COX-2 inhibitor patent fight was famous. In 2000 the University of Rochester was granted a patent for a gene called COX-2, which produced an enzyme that caused pain. The university promptly sued the pharmaceutical giant Searle, which marketed a successful arthritis drug, Celebrex, that blocked the COX-2 enzyme. Rochester said Celebrex had infringed on its gene patent, even though their patent only claimed general uses of the gene to fight pain. The university had not claimed a patent on any specific drug.

And that was what the judge pointed out, four years later, when Rochester lost. The court ruled that Rochester's patent was "little more than a research plan," and ruled that its claim against Searle was invalid.

But such rulings did not alter the long-standing behavior of the patent office. They continued to grant gene patents that included lists of vague claims. A patent might claim all uses of a gene to control heart disease or pain, or to fight infection. Even though the courts ruled that these claims were meaningless, the patent office granted them anyway. Indeed, the grants accelerated. Your tax dollars at work.

"Get to the point," Josh said.

The attorney consulted a notepad. "Your best candidate is a patent application from 1998 for aminocarboxymuconate methaldehyde dehydrogenase, or ACMMD. The patent claims effects on neurotransmitter potentials in the cingulate gyrus."

"That's the mode of action," Josh said, "for our maturity gene."

"Exactly. So if you owned ACMMD, you would effectively control the maturity gene because you would control its expression. Nice, huh?"

Josh said, "Who owns the ACMMD patent?"

The attorney flipped pages. "Patent filed by a company called Gen-CoCom, based in Newton, Mass. Filed for Chapter 11 in 1995. As part of the settlement, all patent apps went to the principal investor, Carl Weigand, who died in 2000. Patents passed to his widow. She is ill with terminal cancer and intends to give all the patents to Boston Memorial Hospital."

"Can you do anything about that?"

"Just say the word," he said.

"Do it," Josh said, rubbing his hands.

CH027

Rick Diehl approached the whole thing like a research project. He read a book on the female orgasm. Two books, actually. One with pictures. And he watched a video. He ran it three times, and even took notes. Because, one way or another, he had sworn he would get a reaction from Lisa.

Now he was down there between her legs, hard at work for the last half hour, his fingers stiff, tongue aching, knees sore—but Lisa's body remained completely relaxed, indifferent to his every attention. Nothing the books predicted had occurred. No labial tumescence. No perineal engorgement. No retraction of the clitoral hood. No change in breathing, abdominal tension, moans or groans . . .

Nothing.

He was exhausting himself, while Lisa stared at the ceiling, zoned out like she was at the dentist's. Like a person waiting for something vaguely unpleasant to be over.

And then . . . wait a minute . . . her breathing changed. Only slightly at first, but then distinctly. Sighing. And her stomach was tensing, rhythmically tensing. She began to squeeze her breasts and moan softly.

It was working.

Rick redoubled his efforts. She responded strongly. It certainly was working . . . working . . . she was grunting now . . . gasping, writhing, building strongly . . . her back arched . . . And suddenly she heaved and screamed, *"Yes! Yes! Brad! Yessss!"*

Rick rocked back on his heels as if he had been hit. Lisa threw her hand over her mouth and twisted away from him on the bed. She shuddered briefly, then sat up, pushed the hair out of her eyes, looked down at him. Her cheeks were flushed, her eyes dark with arousal. "Gee," she said. "I'm really sorry."

At this awkward moment, Rick's phone rang. Lisa lunged for it on the bedside table and handed it to him quickly.

"Yes, what is it?" Rick snapped. He was angry.

"Mr. Diehl? It's Barry Sindler here."

"Oh. Hi, Barry."

"Something wrong?"

"No, no." Lisa was off the bed, getting dressed, her back to him.

"Well, I have good news for you."

"What's that?"

"As you know, last week your wife refused to undergo genetic testing. So we got a court order. Came through yesterday."

"Yes . . ."

"And confronted with the order, your wife fled rather than submit to testing."

"What do you mean?" Rick said.

"She's gone. Left town. No one knows where."

"What about the kids?"

"She abandoned them."

"Well, who's taking care of them?"

"The housekeeper. Don't you call your kids every day?"

"Yeah, usually I do, but it's been busy at work—"

"When was the last time you called them?"

"I don't know, maybe three days ago."

"You better get your ass over to your house right now," Sindler said. "You wanted custody of your kids, and you got it. You'd better show the court some parental responsibility."

And he hung up. He'd sounded pissed.

Rick Diehl leaned back on his knees and looked at Lisa. "I gotta go," he said.

"Okay," she said. "I'm sorry. See you."

Bail was set at half a million dollars. Brad Gordon's attorney paid it. Brad knew it was his uncle's money, but at least he was free to go. As he was leaving the courtroom, the funny-looking kid in the Dodgers jacket sidled up to him and said, "We need to talk."

"About what?"

"You were set up. I know exactly what happened."

"Oh yeah?"

"Yeah. We need to talk."

The kid had booked an interview room in another part of the courthouse. It was just Brad and him. The kid shut the door, flipped open his laptop, and waved Brad into a chair. He turned the laptop so Brad could see it.

"Someone accessed your phone records."

"How do you know?"

"We have contacts with the carrier."

"And?"

"They accessed your cell-phone records when you were *off* work."

"Why?"

"As you probably know, your phone contains GPS technology. That means your location is recorded whenever you make a call." He tapped a key. "Graphing your locations over a thirty-day period, we find this." The map showed red dots all over town, but a cluster of dots in one part of Westview. The kid zoomed in. "That's the soccer field."

"You mean they knew I went there?"

"Yeah. Tuesdays and Thursdays. Somebody knew that two weeks ago."

"So this *was* a setup," Brad said.

"That's what I have been telling you, yes."

"What about the girl?"

"We're working on her. She's no ordinary teenager. We think she's a Philippine national. She's appeared on a webcam, masturbating for money. Anyway, what's relevant now are the inconsistencies in her story. If you look at the hotel security camera"—he tapped another key—"you see here that she turns her body away from the camera while waiting for the elevator, opens her purse, and touches her face. We think she is putting drops, or some irritant, in her eyes. When she gets in the elevator a moment later she is visibly crying. But notice: as a supposed rape victim, crying in the elevator, apparently very upset, she doesn't go right to the hotel desk to report that she has been raped. You have to wonder why not."

"Uh-huh," Brad said, eyes narrowing.

"Instead, she goes straight through the lobby to her car. Security camera in the parking lot shows her driving away at five-seventeen p.m. Depending on traffic, the drive from the hotel to the hospital is between eleven and seventeen minutes. She doesn't show up until six-oh-five p.m. Forty-five minutes later. What was she doing during that time?"

"Injuring herself?"

"No. We've had several experts look at the pictures from the hospital, and the nurse who examined her was an experienced trauma nurse. The pictures are very clear. We think she met an accomplice who produced the injuries for her."

"You mean, some guy . . ."

"Yes."

"Then he would have left his DNA, right?"

"He wore a condom."

"So at least two people were involved in this."

"Actually, we think a whole team was involved," the kid said. "You were very professionally set up. Who would do this to you?"

Brad had been thinking about that while he sat in his jail cell. And he knew there was only one answer: "Rick. The boss. He's wanted me out of there ever since I started."

"And you were trying to boff his girl . . ."

"Hey. I wasn't trying. I was doing it."

"And now you're suspended from your job, you've got nine months, minimum, before you go to trial, and you're looking at ten to twenty if you lose in court. Nice." The kid flipped his laptop shut, and stood.

"So what happens now?"

"We'll work on the girl. If we can get a prior history, maybe some video of her on the Internet, we can press the DA to drop the charges. But if this thing goes to trial, it's not good."

"Fucking Rick."

"Yeah. You owe him, buddy." He headed for the door. "Just do yourself a favor, okay? Stay away from that soccer field."

From *Science* magazine's "News of the Week":

Neanderthal Man: Too Cautious to Survive?
Scientist Finds a "Species Death Gene"

An anthropologist has extracted a gene from Neanderthal skeletons that he says explains the disappearance of this subspecies. "People don't realize that Neanderthals actually had larger brains than the modern Cro-Magnon men. They were stronger and tougher than Cro-Magnons, and they made excellent tools. They survived several ice ages before the Cro-Magnons came on the scene. Why, then, did Neanderthals die out?"

The answer, according to Professor Sheldon Harmon of the University of Wisconsin, was that the Neanderthals carried a gene that led them to resist change. "Neanderthals were the first environmentalists. They created a lifestyle in harmony with nature. They limited game hunting, and they controlled tool use. But this same ethos also made them intensely conservative and resistant to change. They disapproved of the newcomer Cro-Magnons, who painted caves, made elaborately decorated tools, and who drove whole herds of animals over cliffs, causing species extinction. Today we consider the cave paintings a wondrous development. But the Neanderthals regarded them as so much graffiti. They saw it as prehistoric tagging. And they viewed the elaborate Cro-Magnon tools as wasteful and destructive of the environment. They disapproved of these innovations, and they stuck to the old ways. Eventually, they died out as a species."

However, Harmon insists that the Neanderthals bred with the modern Cro-Magnons. "They unquestionably did, because we have identified this same gene in modern human beings. This gene is clearly a Neanderthal remnant, and it promotes cautious or reactionary behavior. Many of the people who today wish to return to the glorious past, or at the very least to keep things as they are, are driven by this same Neanderthal gene." Harmon described the gene as modifying dopamine receptors in the lateral posterior cingulate gyrus and in the right frontal lobe. "There's no question about its mode of action," he said.

Harmon's claim has provoked a firestorm of criticism from academic colleagues. Not since E. O. Wilson published his sociobiology thesis two decades ago has such furious controversy erupted. According to Columbia University geneticist Vartan Gorvald, Harmon was injecting politics into what should be a purely scientific inquiry.

"Not at all," Harmon said. "The gene is present in both Neanderthals and modern humans. Its action has been confirmed in scans of brain activity. The correlation between this gene and reactionary behavior is indisputable. It's not a matter of politics, of left or right. It's a question of basic attitude—whether you are open to the future, or fearful of it. Whether you see the world as emergent, or deteriorating. We have long known that some people favor innovation and look positively toward the future, while others are frightened of change and want to halt innovation. The dividing line is genetic, and represents the presence or absence of the Neanderthal gene."

The story was picked up in the *New York Times* the next day:

NEANDERTHAL GENE PROVES ENVIRONMENTAL AGENDA

Fears of 'Rampant Technology' Justified

STUTTGART, Germany – Anthropologist Sheldon Harmon's discovery of a Neanderthal gene which promotes environmental preservation "proves the need for sound environmental policy," said Greenpeace spokesperson Marsha Madsden. "The fact that Neanderthals lost the battle for the environment should serve as a warning to us all. Like the Neanderthals, we will not survive unless we take radical global action now."

And in the *Wall Street Journal*:

CAUTION KILLED THE NEANDERTHALS

Is the 'Precautionary Principle' Lethal?

Oppose Free Markets at Your Peril,
Club for Growth Notes

BY STEVE WEINBERG

An American anthropologist has concluded that Neanderthals died from a genetic predisposition to resist change. In other words, "Neanderthals applied the Precautionary Principle so dear to illiberal, reactionary environmentalists." That was the view of Jack Smythe of the American Competitive Institute, a progressive Washington think tank. Smythe said, "The extinction of Neanderthals serves as a warning to those who would halt progress and take us back to a life that is nasty, brutish, and short."

CH029

In the corner of the office, the TV showed Sheldon Harmon, professor of anthropology and self-proclaimed discoverer of the "Neanderthal gene," being assaulted during a lecture with a bucket of water poured over his head.

On-screen, the event was shown repeatedly in slow motion, the water sloshing over a skinny, bald guy who looked oddly amused. "See? He's smiling," Rick Diehl said. "This is all a publicity stunt to promote the gene."

"Probably," Josh Winkler said. "They had cameras there to catch it."

"Exactly," Diehl said. "And aside from the publicity this guy is getting for his damn Neanderthal gene, he is claiming a mode of action closely related to our maturity gene. Activation of the cingulate gyrus and so on. Could steal our thunder."

"I doubt it," Josh said. "Dozens of genes work in the cingulate gyrus."

"Even so," Rick said, "I think we ought to announce. Soon. I want to get the maturity gene out there."

Josh said, "With all due respect, Rick, we'd be premature."

"You've tested the gene in rats. That's gone well."

"Yes, but it's not exactly newsworthy. Showing baby rats pushing turds in a cage—that won't make the evening news."

Diehl nodded slowly. "Yeah. True. We need something better."

Josh said, "What's the urgency?"

"The board. Ever since Brad got arrested, his uncle has been pissed.

Seems to think Brad's problems are *our* fault. Anyway, he's pressing us to put the company on the map with a big announcement."

"Fine, but we're not there yet."

"I know. But what if we just . . . what if we just *say* that we're ready to start human testing?"

Josh shivered. "I wouldn't," he said. "I mean, we haven't even applied to the FDA for—"

"I know. Stage one. So let's make the application."

"Rick, you know what a stage-one application requires. It's a stack of research data and forms ten feet high. That's just to *start* the process. And we would have to lay out a timetable of milestones—"

Rick waved his hand impatiently. "I know. I'm saying we just *announce* it."

"You mean, announce it when we're not doing it?"

"No, announce that we're *going* to do it."

"But that's my point," Josh said. "It'd be months before we could even file."

"Reporters don't care. We just say that BioGen Research in Westview Village is ready to begin stage-one testing, and is in the process of making an application to the FDA."

"For the maturity gene . . ."

"Yes. To be inserted with a retrovirus vector."

"And what will we say the maturity gene does?" Josh said.

"I don't know. We could say that . . . it cures drug addiction."

Josh felt a chill. "Why would we say something like that?"

"Well, it makes sense, don't you think?" Rick Diehl said. "The maturity gene promotes balanced, mature behavior, which is by definition addiction-free behavior."

"I guess . . ."

"You *guess*?" Diehl turned to face him. "Let's show a little enthusiasm here, Josh. I'm telling you, this is a great idea. What's the recidivism rate in addiction-treatment programs today? Eighty percent? Ninety percent? A hundred percent? Most rehab doesn't work for most people. That's a fact. How many addicts are there in this country? Christ, we got more than a million in prisons. So how many are on the streets? Twenty million? Thirty million?"

Josh was beginning to sweat. "That would be like, eight or ten percent of the population."

"Sounds about right. I'd bet ten percent of the American population is addicted to drugs, when you include alcohol. Ten percent, easy. Which makes the maturity gene a hell of a product!"

Josh was silent.

"What do you have to say, Josh?"

"Uh, I guess it's a good idea . . ."

"You wouldn't be fucking with me, would you?"

"No," Josh said. "Of course not."

"You wouldn't be holding out on me. Striking out on your own?"

"No," he said. "Why would you say that?"

"Your mother called today," Diehl said.

Oh shit.

"She's very proud of what you've done, and doesn't understand why I haven't given you a promotion."

Josh sank into a chair. He felt drenched in cold sweat. "So, what are you going to do?" he said.

Rick Diehl smiled. "Give you a promotion, of course," he said. "Did you keep records of the dosages you administered?"

CH030

In a glass-walled conference room on Madison Avenue, the marketing firm of Watson & Naeme was engaged in naming a new product. The room was packed with hip young people in their teens and twenties, all casually dressed, as if they were attending a rock concert instead of a dry lecture from a professor standing at a lectern wearing a bowtie and talking about a gene called A58799-6B. The professor was now showing graphs of enzymatic action, black squiggly lines on white. The kids sagged, slumped in their seats, thumbed their BlackBerrys. Only a few tried to focus on the material.

Sitting in the back of the room, the team leader, a psychologist named Paul Gode, spun his finger in the air, signaling the professor to wind it up. Bowtie looked surprised, but he concluded smoothly.

"In summary," the professor said, "our team at Columbia University has isolated a gene that promotes social harmony and group cohesion. It does this by activating the prefrontal cortex of the brain, an area known to be important in determining belief and credence. We have demonstrated this gene action by exposing experimental subjects to both conventional and controversial ideas. Controversial ideas produce a distinctive prefrontal signature, whereas conventional ideas create a diffused activation—what you might call a warm glow. Thus subjects with the gene show a marked preference for conventional thinking and familiar ideas. They also show a preference for group thinking of all kinds. They like television. They like Wikipedia. They like cocktail parties. They like small talk. They like to be in agreement with people around them. Our gene is an important force for social stability and civilization. Since it's the gene that promotes conventional wisdom, we call it the conventional gene."

The audience sat silent. Stunned. Finally one of them said, "You call it *what*?"

"The conventional gene."

"Jesus, that's terrible!"

"Suicide."

"Forget it."

"Or," the professor said quickly, "we call it the civilizing gene."

Groans in the room. "The *civilizing* gene? That's worse! Worse!"

"Horrible."

"Argh!"

"Jump off a bridge!"

The professor looked nonplussed. "What's wrong with that name? Civilization is a good thing, isn't it?"

"Of course," said the team leader, coming forward from the back. Paul Gode stepped up to the lectern. "The only trouble is, nobody in this country wants to think of themselves as joiners or civilizers. Just the opposite—we're all rugged individualists. We're all rebels. We're antiestablishment. We stand out, we strike out, we do our own thing, go our own way. The herd of independent minds, somebody called it. Nobody wants to feel they're *not* a rebel. Nobody wants to admit that they just want to fit in."

"But in truth, everybody *does* want to fit in," the professor said. "At least, almost everybody. About ninety-two percent of people have the conventional-wisdom gene. The real rebels lack it, and they are—"

"Stop right there," the team leader said, holding up his hand. "Just stop. You want to make your gene valuable. That means your gene creates something people *want* to possess—something exciting and desirable. Conventional wisdom is not exciting or desirable. It's mundane. It's buttered toast with grape jelly. That's what the group is telling you." He gestured to a chair. "You might want to take a seat, professor."

Gode turned to the group, which now looked slightly more alert. "All right. People? BlackBerrys away. Let's hear it."

"How about the smart gene?" someone said.

"Good, but inaccurate."

"Simplicity gene."

"Good direction . . ."

"Social gene."

"Oversell."

"Socializing gene."

"Therapeutic."

"Wisdom gene. Wise gene."

"Wise gene. Good, very good."

"Right-thinking gene."

"Too Maoist. Or Buddhist. Come on, wake up here!"

"Party gene."

"Fun gene."

"Stone-washed genes. Hip-hugger genes."

"Happy gene."

"Live-it-up gene."

Gode was frowning, and held up his hand again. "Redirect," he said. "Back up. Rewind. Rethink. What's our problem? This gene is really the gene for conventional wisdom—the conventional-wisdom gene—but we don't want to say that. So. What's *good* about conventional wisdom? What does embracing conventional wisdom do for a person? Quickly, now."

"Makes you belong."

"You don't stand out."

"You think like everybody else."

"Reduces friction."

"You fit in."

"Means you read the *Times*."

"Nobody looks at you funny."

"Makes your life simpler."

"No arguments."

"Feel safe expressing an opinion."

"Everybody agrees with you."

"You're a good person."

"You feel good."

"Makes you comfortable."

Gode snapped his fingers and pointed. "*Good.* Conventional thinking makes us *comfortable* . . . Yes! No surprises, no distress. In the world out there, everything is constantly changing, every minute. It's not a comfortable place. And everybody wants to feel comfortable, right? Old pair of shoes, comfortable sweats, favorite chair . . ."

"Comfortable gene?"

"Comfy gene."

"Comfort gene. The comfort gene."

"Warm and fuzzy gene. Warm gene?"

"Happy gene."

"Friendly gene? Easy gene?"

"Soothing gene. Smooth gene."

"Calm gene. Balm gene."

This went on for a while, until finally there were nine candidates scrawled on the whiteboard. A furious argument ensued as names were deleted, though of course all the names would be concept-tested with focus groups. In the end, everybody agreed the winner would be the comfort gene.

"Let's test it in the field," Gode said. "Professor? Tell us: Where is this gene going, commercially?"

It was too early to say, the professor explained. They had isolated the gene, but they didn't yet know the full range of diseases associated with it. However, since nearly everybody in the world carried the comfort gene, they believed that many people probably suffered from genetic anomalies involving the gene. For example: People who were overly desirous of joining the majority—that might prove to be a genetic disorder. And people who felt depressed when they were alone, by themselves—conceivably, another disorder. People who joined protest marches, went to sports games, who sought out situations where they would be surrounded by lots of like-minded people—a potential genetic disorder. Then there were people who felt obliged to agree with whomever they were with, no matter what was said—yet another disorder. And what about people who were afraid to think for themselves? Fear of independence from the surrounding group?

"Let's face it, that's a lot of people," the professor said. "Nobody thinks for themselves if they can help it."

"You mean all this behavior is going to be considered pathological?" someone asked.

"Any compulsive behavior is pathological," the professor answered.

"But positive behavior? Protest marches?"

"Our position," the professor said, "is that we are on the verge of identifying a range of disease states all related to sociability." These genetic anomalies involving the comfort gene had not yet been definitively established, but Columbia University had applied for a patent on the gene itself, meaning that the gene would have increasing value as disorders involving it were identified with certainty.

Gode coughed. "We've made a mistake. These are all disorders of sociability. This needs to be the sociability gene."

And so it was.

From *Business Online*:

SCIENTISTS FIND GENE FOR SOCIABILITY

Is the tendency to sociability inherited? Scientists at the Morecomb Laboratories, at Columbia University, believe that it is. They report they have found the gene that regulates it, and they have applied for a patent on the gene . . .

Op-Ed Commentary from the *New York Times*:

A "SOCIABILITY GENE"? WHEN WILL THIS NONSENSE STOP?

Columbia University researchers now claim to have found a sociability gene. What's next? The shyness gene? The reclusive gene? The monastic gene? How about the get-off-my-back gene?

In truth, researchers are taking advantage of the public's lack of knowledge about how genes actually operate. No single gene controls any behavioral trait. Unfortunately, the public doesn't know that. They think there's a gene for eye color, for height, and for hair curliness, so why not one for sociability? Geneticists will not speak out. They all sit on the boards of private companies, and are in a race to identify genes they can patent for their own profit.

Will this ever stop? Evidently not.

From *Grist* online:

FEELING SOCIABLE? THAT'S PATENTED

The research office of Columbia University has applied for a patent on a gene that it says controls sociability. Does this mean that one day everyone on antidepressants, or ADD medications, or anxiety medications, will have to pay a royalty to Columbia? Reportedly, pharmaceutical giants in Switzerland are bidding frantically to license the gene.

The fact-finding hearing of the Bioethics Review Panel at the National Institutes of Health in Bethesda was carefully structured to feel collegial and unintimidating. Everyone sat at the same long table in the third-floor conference room of the main building, a familiar setting, with notices for upcoming seminars tacked on the walls and the aging coffeemaker sputtering in the corner. The coffee was notoriously awful; nobody drank it.

The six scientists on the review panel dressed a little more formally for this meeting. Most had put on jackets; one even wore a tie. But they sat slouched and relaxed as they talked to the person being investigated, Dr. Ronald Marsh, forty-one, who sat at the same table with them.

"And how, exactly, did this twelve-year-old girl die?"

Dr. Marsh was a professor of medicine at the University of Texas in Austin. "She suffered from congenital transport factor deficiency." CTFD was a fatal genetic deficiency. "This girl was treated with diet and renal dialysis from the age of nine months. She showed some stunting of growth but no mental retardation. She and her family both wanted this procedure, in the hope that she could have a normal life. Not be tied to a machine forever. As you know, it's not much of a life, especially for a young kid."

Those around the table listened impassively.

"And looking to the future," Marsh continued, "we all recognized that she could not be maintained through adolescence. Hormonal changes were already affecting her metabolism. She was certain to die in the next three to four years. It was on that basis that we undertook the procedure to insert the gene into her body." He paused. "The risks were known."

One of the scientists said, "These risks were discussed with the family?"

"Of course. In detail."

"And with the patient?"

"Yes. She was a bright girl. She was the one who first proposed the procedure. She read about it on the Internet. She understood that the risks were enormous."

"Did you give the family an estimate of those risks?"

"We did. We told them the chances of success were on the order of three percent."

"And they went ahead anyway?"

"Yes. The daughter pushed them. She felt that if she was going to die anyway, she might as well take the chance."

"She was a minor . . ."

"Yes," Marsh said. "But she was also the one with the disease."

"You got signed releases?"

"Yes."

"We've read those releases. Some of us felt the releases struck an unrealistic positive tone, minimizing risks."

"The releases were prepared by the hospital's legal department," Marsh said. "And you will notice the family signed off on a statement that they had been fully informed of the risks. What they were told is also noted in the patient's charts. We would not have proceeded without fully informed consent."

During that speech, the head of the panel, Dr. Robert Bellarmino, slipped into the room and eased into a seat at the end of the table.

"So you did the procedure?" Dr. Marsh was asked.

"We did."

"What vector was used?"

"Modified adenovirus infusion, in combination with standard Barlow immunosuppression protocols."

"And the outcome?"

"She spiked a fever almost at once. It ran to 107 degrees. She had signs of multiple organ system failure on the second day. Liver and kidney function did not recover. She died on the third day."

There was a short silence.

"If I may make a personal comment," Marsh said, "this has been a shattering experience for all of us at the hospital, and shattering for me personally. We had cared for this girl since infancy. She was . . . beloved by everyone on the staff. She was a little ray of sunshine, whenever she came into the clinic. We attempted this risky procedure because she wanted it. But at night I ask myself, was it the right thing to do? And I always feel I had an obligation to take that risk with the patient, if that was what she wanted. She wanted life. How could I deny her that chance?"

A cough. "But, uh, your team had no experience with gene transplantation."

"No. We considered sending her to another team."

"Why didn't you?"

"No one else would do the procedure."

"What did that tell you?"

Marsh sighed. "Have any of you seen a patient die of CTFD? Their kidneys necrose. Their livers shut down. Their bodies swell, turn a purple-gray color. They can't breathe. They're in agony. They take days to die. Should I have waited for that to happen to this lovely girl? I didn't think so."

There was another moment of silence at the table. The mood was distinctly disapproving. "Why is the family suing now?"

Marsh shook his head. "I haven't been able to speak to them."

"They have stated in court documents that they weren't informed."

"They were," Marsh said. "Look: we all hoped it would work. Everybody was optimistic. And parents can't really accept the truth— that a three percent success rate means ninety-seven percent of the patients die. Ninety-seven percent. It's almost certain death. They knew that, and when their hopes were dashed, they felt cheated. But we never misled them."

After Dr. Marsh left the room, the panel met in closed session. Of the seven members on the panel, six were outraged. They argued that Marsh was not telling the truth now, and had not told the truth before. They said he was reckless. They said that he gave genetics a bad name, which the field now had to overcome. They spoke of the Wild West, of his going off half-cocked.

They were clearly moving toward censure of Marsh, and recommending that he lose his license and his ability to apply for government grants.

The head of the panel, Rob Bellarmino, said nothing for a long time. Finally, he cleared his throat. "I can't help but reflect," he said, "that these arguments were exactly the same as those first voiced when Christiaan Barnard did the first heart transplant."

"But this isn't the first of anything—"

"Going off half-cocked. Not seeking proper authorization. Liable to lawsuits. Let me remind you," Bellarmino said, "what Barnard's original statistics were. His first seventeen patients died almost immediately. He was called a killer and a charlatan. But now, more than two thousand heart transplants are performed every year in this country. Most live five to fifteen years. Kidney transplants are routine. Lung and liver transplants that were considered outrageous a few years ago are accepted now. Every new therapy passes through a hazardous, pioneering stage. And we will always rely on courageous individuals, such as Dr. Marsh, to take risks."

"But so many rules were broken—"

"What would you do to Dr. Marsh?" Bellarmino said. "The man can't sleep at night. You see it in his face. His beloved patient died under his care. What greater punishment will you inflict? And who are you to tell him he did the wrong thing?"

"The ethics rules—"

"None of us looked in that little girl's eyes. None of us knew her life, her pain, her hopes. Marsh did. He knew her for years. Will we now stand in judgment of him?"

The room was quiet.

In the end, they voted to censure the University of Texas legal staff, with no penalty for Dr. Marsh. Bellarmino had turned them around, one of the panel said later. "It was classic Rob Bellarmino. Talking like a preacher, subtly invoking God, and somehow getting everyone to push the envelope, no matter who got hurt, no matter what happened. Rob can justify anything. He's brilliant at it."

But in fact, before the final vote was taken, Bellarmino had left the room, because he was late for his next meeting.

From the bioethics panel meeting, Bellarmino returned to his lab, where he was meeting with one of his postdocs. The kid had come to him from Cornell Medical Center, where he had done remarkable work on the mechanisms that controlled chromatin formation.

Normally, the DNA of a cell was found inside the nucleus. Most people imagined DNA in the form of a double helix, the famous twisting staircase discovered by Watson and Crick. But that staircase was only one of three forms that DNA might take within the cell. DNA could also form a single strand, or a more condensed structure called a centromere. The particular form was dependent on the proteins associated with the DNA.

This was important because when DNA was compressed, its genes were unavailable to the cell. One way to control genes was to change the chromatin of various sections of DNA.

So, for example, when genes were injected into new cells, steps also had to be taken to keep the chromatin in an available form, through the use of added chemicals.

Bellarmino's new postdoc had done breakthrough research on methylation by certain proteins, and their effect on chromatin structure. The kid's paper, "Genome-Protein Accessibility Control and Adenine Methyltransferase," was a model of clear writing. It was bound to be important, and would make the kid's reputation.

Bellarmino was sitting in his office with the kid, who was looking eager as Bellarmino scanned the paper. "Excellent, just excellent." He tapped the paper. "I think this work does great credit to the lab. And of course to you."

"Thank you, Rob," the kid said.

"And you have the seven co-authors in place, and I am appropriately high on the list," Bellarmino said.

"Third," the kid said, "but if you felt second position was warranted—"

"Actually, I am remembering a conversation we had a few months back, in which we discussed possible methylation mechanisms, and I suggested to you—"

"Yes, I remember . . ."

"The very mechanisms you elucidate here. I feel rather strongly that I should be the lead author."

The kid blinked. "Umm . . ." He swallowed.

"That ensures the paper will be cited more often," Bellarmino said, "which is important for a contribution of this magnitude. And of course the exact listing is just a formality. As second author you will be understood to have done the footwork here, the fill-in-the-gaps labor. From your standpoint, it's really a win-win. You will get greater citations, and you will see much larger grants coming your way." He smiled. "I can assure you of that. Your next work will be entirely independent. And in a year or two, I'll be supporting you for a lab of your own."

"I, uh . . ." The kid gulped. "I understand."

"Good, good. Make these changes, shoot it back to me, and I'll submit it to *Nature*. I think this deserves a better platform than *Science*, which is a little down at the heels these days. I'll call over to *Nature* and make sure the editor understands the importance of this paper, and see that we get immediate publication."

"Thanks, Rob," the kid said.

"Anytime," Rob Bellarmino said.

"wet art" on display

Transgenic Organisms in Galleries
Living Creatures for Sale

In London, South African artist Laura Cinti displayed a transgenic cactus that contained human genetic material, and grew human hairs. Cinti said, "The cactus with all its hairs coming out is showing all the desires, all the signs of sexuality. It doesn't want to be trapped. It wants to be released."

When asked about the public reaction to the cactus, Cinti said, "Bald men are particularly interested."

Artist Marta de Menezes created modified butterflies where one wing was different from the other. She said, "People were very shocked at first. They didn't think it was a good idea." She said that, next, she would make the stripes of zebra fish vertical instead of horizontal so the fish would look more like zebras. These changes would be inherited.

Finnish artist Oron Catts grew pig wings in culture from pig bone marrow stem cells. He said the artist's team played music to the pig cells to make them grow. "We downloaded lots of pig songs . . . and played them to the cells." He said the cells seemed to do better with music.

Chicago-based artist Eduardo Kac created a transgenic rabbit called Alba that glowed green. The fertilized egg of an albino rabbit was injected with GPF, the gene for green fluorescent protein from a Pacific Northwest jellyfish. The animal that grew from the egg now glows. A furor resulted. Kac observed that "[the rabbit] does make some people uncomfortable," but noted that GPF is a common research tool and has been injected into yeast, molds, plants, fruit flies, mice, and cow embryos. Kac said he was looking forward to making a fluorescent dog.

Alba died prematurely of unknown causes. So did the transgenic cactuses.

In 2003 the first transgenic pet was offered for sale to the public. A red-fluorescing zebra fish, it was created by Dr. Zhiyuan Gong in Singapore, and licensed to a company in Austin, Texas. It was marketed under the name GloFish, after two years of review by federal and state agencies, which concluded the fish were safe, so long as they were not eaten.

CH032

"**M adame Bond,**" the first-grade teacher said, "your son is a delightful boy, but he is having trouble with his math. Addition comes slowly to him; subtraction is even more difficult. However, his French is much improved."

"I am glad to know that," Gail Bond said. "The move here from London was hard for him. But I must admit, I'm surprised about his difficulty with math."

"Because you are a scientist, you mean?"

"I suppose so, yes. I work at the Institut National here in Paris," she said, "and Evan's father is an investment banker; he works all day with numbers."

"Well," the teacher replied, "as you are a geneticist, I am sure you know everything is not in the genes. Sometimes the child of a great artist cannot draw. But I must tell you that it does your son no good if you do his homework for him."

"Sorry?" Gail Bond said. "Do his homework?"

"Well, this must be the case," the teacher said. "You or someone else in the household."

"I don't understand."

"Evan's homework is always perfect. But when there is a quiz in class, he does poorly. Evidently, someone is doing his homework for him."

Gail Bond shook her head. "But I don't know who it could be," she said. "My son comes home from school and only the housekeeper is there when he does his homework. She doesn't speak much French.

I return at five, and by then his homework is finished. Or so he tells me."

"You do not review it?"

"No. Never. He says there is no need."

"Well," the teacher said, "he is getting help from somewhere." She took out the homework sheets and spread them on the desk. "You see? Every problem, on every sheet. Perfect."

"I see," Gail said, staring at the papers. "And these stains . . ." There were small green and white stains on the paper, droplets.

"Often these marks are present. Usually at the bottom of the sheet. As if something were spilled."

"I think I know who is helping him," Gail Bond said.

"Who?"

"It's someone from the lab."

She unlocked the door to the apartment and heard Gerard call, "Hello, sweetheart," exactly as her husband did.

"Hi, Gerard," she said. "What's new with you?"

"I need a bath."

"I'll see that you get one," she said. She walked into the hallway where Gerard was standing on his perch. He was a transgenic African grey parrot, now two years old. While he was a chick, he had received a variety of human genes, so far with no noticeable effect.

"You look good, baby, I've missed you," Gerard said, again imitating her husband's voice.

"Thank you," she said. "I have a question for you, Gerard."

"Okay, if you insist."

"Tell me. What is the answer to thirteen minus seven?"

"I don't know."

She hesitated. "What is the answer to thirteen take away seven?" That was how Evan would phrase it.

Promptly, the bird said, "Six."

"Eleven take away four?"

"Seven."

"Twelve take away two?"

"Ten."

She frowned. "Twenty-four take away eleven?"

"Oh. Oh. Oh," the parrot said, moving on the perch. "You try to trick me. Thirteen."

"What's one-oh-one take away seventy?"

"Thirty-one. But we never get so many numbers. Most is two numbers."

"We?"

Gerard said nothing. He ducked his head rhythmically. He began to sing, "I love a parade . . ."

"Gerard," Gail said, "does Evan ask you for help?"

"Oh sure." And then a perfect imitation of Evan: "Hey, Gerrie, come and help me. It's too hard for me." Then a whine: "It's too *haaard* . . ."

Gail said, "I have to get the video camera."

"Am I a star? Am I a star?"

"Yes," she said, "you are a star."

He spoke in an American drawl: "We're sorry we're late but we had to pick up our son Hank."

"What movie is that?" she said.

The same drawl: "Now Jo, just take it easy."

"You're not going to tell me, are you?" she said.

"I need a bath," Gerard said, "before any filming. You promised me a bath."

Gail Bond hurried off to get the camera.

During his first year of life, Gerard showed little effect from the human transgenes that had been injected into him as a chick by Yoshi Tomizu and Gail Bond in the laboratory of Maurice Grolier at the Institut National in Paris. This was not surprising. The successful injection of transgenes was a tricky business, and required dozens, even hundreds, of attempts before it worked properly. That was because multiple conditions had to be fulfilled for the gene to work in a new environment.

First, the gene had to be incorporated correctly into the existing

genetic material of the animal. Sometimes the new gene was incorporated backward, which had a negative effect, or none at all. Sometimes
it was inserted into an unstable region of the genome, and triggered
lethal cancer in the animal. That was rather common.

Furthermore, transgenics was never a matter of inserting a single
gene. Researchers also had to insert the associated genes necessary for
the primary gene to function. For example, most genes had insulators
and promoters. The promoters might make proteins that switched off
the animal's own genes, to allow the new addition to take over. Or they
might enhance the workings of the injected gene itself. The insulators
kept the new gene separated from the genes around it. They also made
sure the new genetic material remained available within the cell.

Complex as they were, these considerations didn't take into account
the further intricacies that might arise from messenger RNAs within
the cell. Or from the genes that controlled translation. And so on.

In reality, the task of injecting a gene into an animal and making
it work more closely resembled debugging a computer program than it
did any biological process. You had to keep fixing the errors, making
adjustments, eliminating unwanted effects, until you got the thing
working. And then you had to wait for downstream effects to show up,
sometimes years later.

That was why the lab felt that Gail Bond should take Gerard
home, and keep him as a pet for a while. To see if any positive or
untoward effects showed up. Home rearing was especially important
because African greys were highly intelligent—generally considered
as intelligent as chimpanzees—and with a far greater capacity for
language. Using sign language or computer keyboards, a few non-
human primates had mastered about 150 words. But that was merely
average for a grey parrot. Some grey parrots had as many as a thousand words. So they needed the kind of interaction and stimulation
found in a human environment. They couldn't be left in an animal
holding facility, around mice and hamsters, or they would go mad
from lack of stimulation.

Indeed, animal activists believed that many grey parrot pets were mentally disturbed as a result of insufficient interaction. It was as if they had been held in solitary confinement, year after year. A grey parrot required at least as much interaction as a human being. More, some scientists argued.

Gerard was finger-trained as a chick, and began talking early. He already had quite a vocabulary when Gail, who was thirty-one and married to an investment banker, brought him home to her apartment. As Gerard came into the living room, he said, "Hey, nice place, Gail. Way to go." (He had unfortunately picked up bits of American slang from watching television at the lab.)

"I'm glad you like it, Gerard," she said.

"I was just saying that," the parrot said.

"You mean you don't like it?"

"I mean I was just saying that."

"Okay."

"Just an observation."

"Right. Fine."

She immediately made notations in a logbook. Gerard's speech might prove highly significant. One of the goals of the transgenic experiment was to see to what extent scientists could modify the intelligent behavior of non-human animals. Primates were off-limits—too many rules and regulations—but people weren't so sensitive about parrots. There were no ethics committees to supervise parrot experimentation. So the Grolier lab worked with African greys.

Among the things they were looking for was evidence of self-awareness in the parrot's speech. Parrots were known to be self-aware. They recognized themselves in mirrors. But speech was different. Parrots did not reliably use the word *I* when referring to themselves. Generally, when they used the personal pronoun it was to quote someone else.

The question was whether a transgenic parrot would ever use the word *I* unambiguously. And it seemed to Gail Bond that Gerard had just done exactly that.

It was a good start.

Her husband, Richard, showed little interest in the new arrival. His sole reaction was to shrug and say, "Don't look for me to clean that cage." Gail said she would not. Her son was more enthusiastic. Evan immediately began to play with Gerard, putting him on his finger, and later on his shoulder. As the weeks went on, it was Evan who spent time with the bird, who bonded with it, who kept it on his shoulder much of the time.

And, it seemed, who got help from the bird.

Gail set up the video camera on a tripod, adjusted the frame, and turned the camera on. Some grey parrots were able to count, and there were claims that some had a rudimentary understanding of the concept of zero. But none was able to do arithmetic.

Except Gerard.

She had to work very hard to conceal her excitement. "Gerard," she said, in her calmest voice, "I am going to show you a picture and I want you to tell me what it says." She showed him one sheet from her son's homework, folding it to reveal a single problem. She covered the answer with her thumb.

"I did that already."

"But what does this say?" Gail asked, pointing to the problem. It was fifteen minus seven.

"You have to say it."

"Can you look at this paper and tell me the answer?" she said.

"You have to say it," Gerard repeated. He was hopping from one leg to the other on his perch, getting irritable. He kept glancing at the camera. Gerard didn't like to be embarrassed.

Gail said, "It says fifteen take away seven."

"Eight," the parrot replied, at once.

Gail resisted the temptation to turn to the camera and shriek with delight. Instead, she calmly turned the page to reveal another problem. "Now. What is twenty-three take away nine?"

"Fourteen."

"Very good. And now . . ."

"You promised me," Gerard said.

"I promised you?"

"Yes, you promised me," he said. "You know . . ."

He meant the bath.

"I'll do that later," she said. "For now . . ."

"You promised me." Sulky tone. "My bath."

"Gerard, I am going to show you this next problem. And ask you: What is twenty-nine take away eight?"

"I hope they are watching," he said, in an odd voice. "They'll see. They'll see and they'll know and they'll say, 'Why, she wouldn't even harm a fly.'"

"Gerard. Now, please pay attention. What is twenty-nine take away eight?"

Gerard opened his mouth. The front doorbell rang. Gail was close enough to the bird to know that Gerard himself had made the sound. He could imitate all sorts of sounds perfectly—doorbells, phone rings, toilet flushes.

"Gerard, please . . ."

The sound of footsteps. A click, and a creak as the front door opened.

"You look good, baby, I've missed you," Gerard said, imitating her husband's voice.

"Gerard," she began.

A woman's voice: "Oh Richard, it's been so long . . ."

Silence. Sound of kissing.

Gail froze, watching Gerard. The parrot continued, his beak hardly moving. He was like a tape recorder.

The woman's voice: "Are we alone?"

"Yes," her husband said. "Kid doesn't come back until three."

"And what about, uh . . ."

"Gail is at a conference in Geneva."

"Oh, so we have all day. Oh, God . . ."

More kissing.

Two pairs of footsteps. Crossing the room.

Her husband: "You want something to drink?"

"Maybe later, baby. Right now, all I want is *you*."

Gail turned, and switched the video off.

Gerard said, "Now will you give me my bath?"

She glared at him.

The bedroom door slammed shut.

Creaking of the bedsprings. A woman squealing, laughing. More creaking springs.

"Stop it, Gerard," Gail said.

"I knew you would want to know," he said.

"I hate that fucking bird," her husband said, later that night. They were in the bedroom.

"That's not the point," she said. "You'll do what you want, Richard. But not in my house. Not in our bed." She had already changed the sheets, but even so, she didn't want to sit on the bed. Or go near it. She was standing on the other side of the room, by the window. Paris traffic outside.

"It was just that one time," he said.

She hated it when he lied to her. "When I was in Geneva," she said. "Do you want me to ask Gerard if there were other times?"

"No. Leave the bird out of it."

"There were other times," she said.

"What do you want me to say, Gail. I'm sorry, all right? I'm sorry."

"I don't want you to say anything," she said. "I want you not to do it again. I want you to keep your fucking women out of this house."

"Right. Fine. I will do that. Can we drop it now?"

"Yes," she said. "We can drop it now."

"I hate that fucking bird."

She walked out of the room. "If you touch him," she said, "I'll kill you."

"Where are you going?"

"Out."

She met Yoshi Tomizu at his apartment. They had begun their affair a year before and had resumed it again in Geneva. Yoshi had a wife and child in Tokyo, and he would be returning there in the fall. So it was just a friendship with privileges.

"You feel tense," he said, stroking her back. He had wonderful hands. "Did you argue with Richard?"

"Not really. A bit." She looked at the moonlight coming in through the window, surprisingly bright.

"Then what is it?" Yoshi asked.

"I'm worried about Gerard."

"Why?"

"Richard hates him. Really hates him."

"Oh, he wouldn't do anything. It's such a valuable animal."

"He might," she said. She sat up in bed. "Maybe I should go back." Yoshi shrugged. "If you think . . ."

"I'm sorry," she said.

He kissed her lightly. "Do what you think is best."

Gail sighed. "You're right," she said. "I'm being silly." She slid back down under the covers. "Tell me I am being silly. Please."

Brad Gordon clicked off the TV and yelled, "It's open. Come in."

It was noon. He was lounging in his third-floor apartment in Sherman Oaks, watching the ball game and waiting for the pizza delivery guy. But to his surprise, the door opened and in walked the best-looking woman he had ever seen in his life. She had elegance written all over her—thirtyish, tall, slim, European clothing, heels that were not too high. Sexy, but in control. Brad sat forward in his lounger chair and ran his hand over his chin, feeling the stubble.

"I'm sorry," he said. "I didn't expect any visitors—"

"Your uncle, Mr. Watson, sent me," the woman said, walking directly toward him. He hastened to stand. "My name is Maria Gonzales." She had a slight accent, but it didn't sound Spanish. More German. "I'm involved with the firm that does your uncle's investment work," she said, shaking his hand.

Brad nodded, inhaling her light perfume. He wasn't surprised to hear she worked for Uncle Jack: the old guy surrounded himself with good-looking, extremely competent businesswomen. He said, "What can I do for you, Ms. Gonzales?"

"Nothing for me," she answered smoothly, looking around the apartment for a place to sit. She decided to remain standing. "But you can do something for your uncle."

"Well, sure. Anything."

"I don't need to remind you that your uncle has paid your bail, and will be assuming the cost of your legal defense. Since the charge involves sex with a minor, the defense will be difficult."

"But I was set up—"

She raised her hand. "It's none of my affair. The point is this: your uncle has helped you many times over the years. Now he needs your help—confidentially—in return."

"Uncle Jack needs *my* help?"

"He does."

"Okay. Sure."

"In *strict* confidence."

"Right. Yes."

"You will discuss this with no one. Ever."

"Right. Understood."

"Word of this must never get out. If it did, you would lose your legal defense funding. You'd spend twenty years in prison as a child molester. You know what that means."

"Yes." He wiped his hands on his trousers. "I understand."

"No screwups this time, Brad."

"Okay, okay. Just tell me what you want me to do."

"Your favorite company, BioGen, is about to announce an important new discovery—a gene that cures drug addiction. It's the first step toward a huge commercial product, and it will attract a lot of financing. Your uncle currently holds a large position in the company, and he does not want his position diluted by additional investors. He wants them scared off."

"Yes . . ."

"By some bad news coming out of BioGen."

"What kind of bad news?"

"At the moment," Maria Gonzales said, "BioGen's most important commercial product consists of a cell line, the Burnet line, which the company bought from UCLA. The cell line produces cytokines, important in cancer treatment."

"Yeah . . ."

"Contamination of those cell lines would be disastrous."

She reached into her purse and brought out a small plastic bottle of a well-known brand of eye drops. The bottle contained clear liquid. She unscrewed the cap and put a single drop of liquid on the tip of each finger of her other hand. "Got it?"

"Yes," he said.

"One drop on each finger. Let it dry."

"Okay."

"Go into BioGen. Your swipe cards still work. Check the database for storage locations and research lockers containing the Burnet line. The storage number is on this card." She handed him a small card with the number BGOX6178990QD. "There are frozen samples and there are live in-vitro incubators. You go to each one and . . . just touch them."

"Just touch them?" Brad looked at the bottle. "What is that stuff?"

"Nothing that will hurt you. But the cells won't like it."

"The security cameras will record me. Card swipes are recorded. They'll know who did it."

"Not if you go in between one and two a.m. The systems are down for backup."

"No, they're not."

"Yes, they are. This week only."

Brad took the plastic bottle from her and turned it over in his hand.

"You realize," he said, "they have off-site storage for that cell line, too."

"Just do what your uncle asks," she said. "And leave the rest to him." She closed her purse. "And one final thing. Do not call or contact your uncle about this or any other matter. He wants no record of *any* contact with you. Clear?"

"Clear."

"Good luck. And on behalf of your uncle, thank you." She shook his hand again and left.

NO BLONDE EXTINCTION, AFTER ALL

BBC Reported False Story Absent Fact Check
No WHO Study, No German Study
A Bad Blonde Joke for 150 Years

The World Health Organization (WHO) today denied it had ever conducted or published any study predicting the extinction of the blonde hair gene. According to the UN group spokesman, "WHO has no knowledge of how these news reports originated but would like to stress that we have no opinion on the future existence of blondes."

According to the *Washington Post,* the BBC story stemmed from a German wire service account. That story, in turn, was based on an article published two years before in the German women's magazine *Allegra,* which cited a WHO anthropologist as its source. But no record of the anthropologist exists.

The story would never have run, said Georgetown media professor Len Euler, if even minimal fact-checking had been done by BBC editors. Some media observers noted that news organizations no longer check anything. "We just publish the press release and move on," one reporter observed. Another reporter, speaking on condition of anonymity, said, "Let's face it, it's a good story. Accuracy would kill it."

Further inquiry by the urban legend site Snopes.com uncovered multiple versions of the extinct blonde story going back 150 years, to the time of Abraham Lincoln. In every instance, scientific validity was claimed to bolster the story's credibility. A typical example dates from 1906:

• BLONDES DOOMED TO VANISH FROM EARTH •
Major Woodruff Sounds Their Deathknell—It's Science

The girl with the golden tresses is doomed, and within six hundred years blondes will be extinct. The fate of the blonde was foretold today by Major C. E. Woodruff in a lecture at the Association for the Advancement of Science at Columbia University . . .

Clearly, blondes will not become extinct, but neither will the news stories that predict their demise, since the stories have been repeated for a century and a half with no basis whatsoever, said Professor Euler.

enry Kendall's wife, Lynn, designed web sites for a living, so she was usually at home during the day. Around three in the afternoon, she got an odd call. "This is Dr. Marty Roberts at Long Beach Memorial," a voice said. "Is Henry there?"

"He's at a soccer game," she said. "Can I take a message?"

"I called his office, and I called his cell, but there was no answer." Dr. Roberts's tone made it sound urgent.

"I'll see Henry in an hour," Lynn said. "Is he all right, Dr. Roberts?"

"Oh sure, he's fine. *He's* perfectly fine. Just ask him to call me, would you?"

Lynn said she would.

Later, when Henry came home, she went into the kitchen, where he was getting cookies and milk for their eight-year-old son, Jamie. Lynn said, "Do you know somebody at Long Beach Memorial Hospital?"

Henry blinked. "Did he call?"

"This afternoon. Who is he?"

"He's a friend of mine from school. A pathologist. What did he say?"

"Nothing. He wanted you to call him back." She somehow managed not to ask her husband what it was all about.

"Okay," he said. "Thanks."

She saw Henry glance at the phone in the kitchen, then turn on his heel and walk into the little study that they both shared. He closed the

door. She heard him speaking softly on the phone. She couldn't make
out the words.

Jamie was eating his snack. Tracy, their thirteen-year-old, was playing her music very loud upstairs. Lynn yelled up the stairwell: "A little
less noise, please!" Tracy didn't hear her. There was nothing to do but
go upstairs and tell her.

When she came back down, Henry was in the living room, pacing.
"I have to take a trip," he said.

"Okay. Where?"

"I have to go to Bethesda."

"Something at the NIH?" The National Institutes of Health were
in Bethesda. Henry went there a couple of times a year, for conferences.

"Yes."

She watched him pace. "Henry," she said, "are you going to tell me
what this is about?"

"I just have some research—I just have to check on something—
I just—I'm not sure."

"You have to go to Bethesda but you're not sure why?"

"Well, of course I'm sure. It's, um, it's to do with Bellarmino."

Robert Bellarmino was the head of genetics at NIH, and no friend
of her husband. "What about him?"

"I have to, uh, deal with something he has done."

She sat down in a chair. "Henry," she said, "I love you but I am really
confused here. Why aren't you telling me—"

"Look," he said, "I don't want to talk about it. I just have to go back
there, that's all. Just for a day."

"Are you in trouble?"

"I said I don't want to talk about it, Lynn. I have to go back."

"Okay . . . when?"

"Tomorrow."

She nodded slowly. "All right. Do you want me to book—"

"I've already done it. I have it handled." He stopped pacing and went
over to her. "Look," he said, "I don't want you to worry."

"That's pretty hard, under the circumstances."

"It's fine," he said. "It's just something I have to take care of, and then it'll be taken care of."

And that was all he would say.

Lynn had been married to Henry for fifteen years. They had two children together. She knew better than anyone that Henry was prone to nervous tics and flights of fancy. The same imaginative leaps that made him such a good researcher also made him a bit of a hysteric. He was inclined to frequent self-diagnoses of dreaded diseases. He visited his doctor every couple of weeks, and telephoned more often than that. He was plagued by aches, itches, rashes, and sudden fears that woke him in the middle of the night. He dramatized small concerns. A minor accident was a brush with death, the way Henry told it.

So even though his behavior about a trip to Bethesda was odd, she was inclined to regard it as probably minor. She glanced at her watch and decided it was time to defrost the spaghetti sauce for dinner. She didn't want Jamie eating too many cookies or it would spoil his appetite. Tracy had turned her music up louder again.

In short, daily events took over, and pushed Henry and his odd trip from her mind. She had other things to do, and she did them.

CH035

Henry Kendall left Dulles Airport and drove north on 267, heading toward the Primate Facility in Lambertville. It was almost an hour before he saw the chain-link fence and the guardhouse behind the double gates. Beyond the gates he saw huge maple trees that obscured the complex of buildings farther back. Lambertville was one of the largest primate-research facilities in the world, but the National Institutes did not publicize that fact, or its location. Partly because primate research was so politically charged, and partly out of concern for vandalism by activists. Henry pulled up at the outer gate, pushed the button, and said, "Henry Kendall," and gave his code number. He hadn't been here for four years, but the code was still good. He leaned out of the car so the camera could see his face clearly.

"Thank you, Dr. Kendall." The gate opened. He pulled through to the second gate. The first closed behind him. A guard came out and checked his ID. He vaguely remembered the guy. "Didn't expect you today, Dr. Kendall." He handed him a temporary swipe card.

"They want me to clear out some things from my storage locker."

"Yeah, I'll bet. Things are getting tighter around here, since, you know."

"Yeah, I know." He meant Bellarmino.

The inner gate opened and Henry drove through. He passed the admin building and went straight to the holding facilities. The chimps were formerly in Building B. He assumed they still were.

He opened the outer door and swiped his card on the inner door.

He went down a corridor to the B Monitor Room. It was a room filled with display screens, showing all the chimpanzees on two floors of the facility. There were about eighty animals of various ages and sexes.

The on-duty veterinary assistant was there, in khaki uniform. But also there was Rovak, the head of the facility. He must have been notified by the front gate. Rovak was fifty, steel gray hair, military bearing. But he was a good scientist.

"I wondered when you'd show up," Rovak said. He shook hands. He seemed friendly. "You got the blood?"

"Yes." Henry nodded.

"Fucking Bellarmino had a cow," Rovak said. "He hasn't been out here yet, and we think we know why."

"What do you mean?" Henry said.

"Let's take a walk," Rovak said.

Henry consulted his paper. "I'm looking for female F-402."

"No," Rovak said. "You're looking for the offspring of female F-402. He's this way."

They started down a side corridor. This led to a small training facility that was used for short-term teaching experiments with animals. "You keep him here?"

"Have to. You'll see."

They came into the training facility. At first glance, it looked like a kindergarten play room, brightly colored toys scattered around, blue carpet on the floor. A casual visitor might not notice that the toys were all made of high-impact, durable plastic. There were observation glass walls on one side. Mozart was playing over the speakers.

"Likes Mozart," Rovak said, shrugging. They went into a smaller room, off to the side. A shaft of sunlight came down from the ceiling. There was a five-by-five cage in the center. Inside sat a young chimpanzee, about the size of a four-year-old child. The chimp's face was flatter than usual, and the skin was pale, but it was clearly a chimp.

"Hello, Dave," Rovak said.

"Hello," the chimp said. His voice was raspy. He turned to Henry. "Are you my mother?" he said.

Henry Kendall could not speak. His jaw moved, but no words came out. Rovak said, "Yes, he is, Dave." He turned to Kendall. "His name is Dave."

The chimp was staring at Henry. Just staring silently, sitting there in the cage, holding his toes in his fingers.

"I know it's a shock," Rovak said. "Think how people here felt, when they found out. Vet almost passed out. Nobody had any idea he was different until out of the blue; he came up negative on a sialic acid test. They repeated it because they assumed it was an error. But it wasn't an error. And then he started talking about three months ago."

Henry sighed.

"He speaks well," Rovak said. "Has a little trouble with verb tenses. But nobody has been instructing him. In fact, he's been kept away from everybody around here. You want to let him out?"

Kendall hesitated. "Is he, uh . . ." Chimps could be nasty and aggressive; even small ones might be dangerous.

"Oh sure, he's very docile. He's not a chimp, right?" He opened the cage. "Come on out, Dave."

Dave came out hesitantly, like a man released from jail. He seemed frightened to be outside the cage. He looked at Henry. "Am I going to live with you?"

"I don't know," Henry said.

"I don't like the cage."

He reached out and took Henry's hand. "Can we go play?"

They went into the playroom. Dave led.

Henry said, "Is this his routine?"

"Right. He gets about an hour a day. Mostly with the vet. Sometimes me."

Dave went over to the toys and began to arrange them into shapes. A circle, then a square.

"I'm glad you came to see him," Rovak said. "I think it's important."

"What's going to happen to him?"

"What do you think? This is illegal as shit, Henry. A transgender higher primate? You know Hitler tried to cross a human and a chimp.

And Stalin tried. You might say they defined the field. Let's see, Hitler, Stalin, and now an American researcher at the NIH? No way, my friend."

"So what are you . . ."

"This represents an unauthorized experiment. It has to be terminated."

"Are you kidding?"

"You're in Washington," Rovak said, "and you're looking at political dynamite. NIH funding is already flat from the current administration. It'd be cut to a tenth, if word of this got out."

"But this animal is extraordinary," Henry said.

"But unauthorized. That's all anybody cares about." Rovak shook his head. "Don't get sentimental. You have a transgenic experiment that was never authorized and the rules state explicitly that any experiment not approved by the boards will be terminated and there will be no exceptions."

"What will you, uh . . ."

"Morphine drip intravenously. Won't feel a thing." Rovak said. "You don't need to worry. We'll take good care of him. And after incineration, there will be no evidence at all that it ever happened." He nodded to Dave. "Why don't you go play with him for a while? He'd like the company. He's bored with all of us."

They played a sort of impromptu game of checkers, using toy blocks, jumping over each other while they both sat on the floor. Henry noticed details—Dave's hands, which were the proportion of human hands; his feet, which were prehensile like a chimp's; his eyes, which had flecks of blue; and his smile, which was not quite human, not quite ape-like.

"This is fun," Dave said.

"That's because you are winning." Henry didn't really understand the rules, but he thought he should let Dave win. That's what he had done with his own kids.

And then he thought, *This is my own kid.*

He wasn't thinking clearly, he knew that. He was acting by instinct. He was aware of watching intently as Dave was returned to his cage, of the way he was locked in with a keypress padlock, of the way—

"Let me shake his hand again," Henry said. "Open it up again."

"Look," Rovak said, "don't do this to yourself. Or him."

"I just want to shake his hand."

Rovak sighed, unlocked the lock. Henry watched. 01-05-04.

He shook Dave's hand and said good-bye.

"Are you coming tomorrow?" Dave said.

"Soon," Henry said.

Dave turned away, not looking at him as Henry left the room and closed the door.

"Listen," Rovak said, "you ought to be grateful you're not being prosecuted and thrown into jail. Now don't be foolish about this. We'll handle it. You go on about your business."

"Okay," Henry said. "Thank you."

He asked to stay at the facility until it was time for his plane home; they put him in a room with a terminal for researchers. He spent the afternoon reading about Dave and all the annotations in his file. He printed the entire file out. He walked around the facility, went to the bathroom several times, so that the guards would be accustomed to seeing him on the monitors.

Rovak went home at four, stopping in to say good-bye on his way out. The vets and guards changed shifts at six. At five-thirty p.m., Henry went back into the training facility and headed straight for Dave's room.

He unlocked the cage.

"Hello, Mother," Dave said.

"Hi, Dave. Would you like to take a trip?"

"Yes," Dave said.

"Okay. Do exactly what I say."

Researchers frequently walked with the tamer chimps, sometimes holding their hands. Henry walked with Dave down the training corridor, moving at a casual pace, ignoring the cameras. They turned left into the main corridor and headed for the exterior door. He swiped the inner door, led Dave through, and opened the outer door. As he expected, there were no alarms.

The Lambertville facility had been designed to keep intruders out, and to keep animals from escaping, but not to prevent researchers from removing animals. Indeed, for a variety of reasons, researchers sometimes needed to remove animals without going through extensive red tape. And so it was that Henry put Dave on the floor of the backseat of his car and drove to the exit gate.

It was now shift change, with a lot of cars coming and going. Henry turned in his swipe card and his badge. The guard on duty said, "Thanks, Dr. Kendall," and Henry drove out into the rolling green hills of western Maryland.

"You're driving back?" Lynn said. "Why?"

"It's a long story."

"Why, Henry?"

"I have no choice. I have to drive."

"Henry," she said, "you're behaving very strangely, you know that."

"It was a moral issue."

"What moral issue?"

"I have a responsibility."

"What responsibility? Goddamn it, Henry—"

"Honey," he said, "it's a long story."

"You said that."

"Believe me, I want to tell you everything," he said, "I really do. But it'll have to wait until I get home."

Dave said, "Is that your mother?"

Lynn said, "Who's in the car with you?"

"Nobody."

"Who was talking? That raspy voice."

"I really can't explain it," he said. "You'll just have to wait until I get home, and then you'll understand."

"Henry—"

"Gotta go, Lynn. Love to the kids." He hung up.

Dave was watching him with patient eyes. "Was that your mother?"

"No. Somebody else."

"Is she angry?"

"No, no. Are you hungry, Dave?"

"Soon."

"Okay, we'll find a drive-in. But meantime, you have to wear your seat belt."

Dave looked puzzled. Henry pulled over, and clipped the seat belt around him. It didn't really fit; he was only slightly larger than a child.

"I don't like it." He started to tug at the harness.

"You have to wear it."

"No."

"Sorry."

"I want to go back."

"Can't go back, Dave."

Dave stopped struggling. He stared out the window. "It's dark."

Henry ran his hand over the animal's head, feeling the short fur. He could feel Dave relax when he did it. "It's okay, Dave. Everything is going to be fine, now."

Henry pulled back onto the road, and headed west.

CH036

"**W**hat are you talking about?" Lynn Kendall said, staring at Dave, who sat quietly on the living room couch. "This monkey is your *son?*"

"Well, not exactly . . ."

"Not *exactly?*" She paced around the living room. "What the hell does *that* mean, Henry?"

It had been a normal Saturday afternoon. Their teenage daughter, Tracy, was in the backyard, sunbathing and talking on the telephone, and not doing her homework. Her brother, Jamie, was splashing in the wading pool. Lynn had spent the day inside the house, finishing a job on a tight deadline. She'd been working hard on it for the last three days, so she was surprised when she opened the front door and her husband had walked in, leading a chimpanzee by the hand.

"Henry? Is he your son or not?"

"He is, in a way."

"In a way. That's clear. I'm glad you cleared that up." She spun, glared at him. An awful thought occurred to her. "Wait a minute. Wait just a minute. Are you trying to tell me that you had sex with a—"

"No, no," her husband said, holding up his hands. "No, honey. Nothing like that. It was just an experiment."

"Just an experiment. Jesus. An experiment? What kind of experiment, Henry?"

The monkey sat curled up, holding his toes in his hand. Looking up at the two adults.

"Try to keep your voice down," Henry said. "You're upsetting him."

"I'm upsetting him? I'm upsetting him? He's a fucking monkey, Henry!"

"Ape."

"Ape, monkey . . . Henry, what is he doing here? Why is he in our house?"

"Well . . . I'm not . . . Actually, he's come to live with us."

"He's come to live with us. Out of the blue. You have a monkey son and you never knew about it. He just suddenly arrives with you. Great. That makes sense. That makes perfect sense. Anybody can understand that. Why didn't you tell me, Henry? Oh, never mind, let it be a surprise. I'm driving home with my monkey son but I'll tell you about it when I walk in the door. That's great, Henry. I'm glad we had all those therapy sessions about intimacy and communications."

"Lynn, I'm sorry—"

"You're always sorry. Henry: what are you going to do with him? Are you going to take him to the zoo, or what?"

"I don't like the zoo," Dave said, speaking for the first time.

"I didn't ask you," Lynn said. "You keep out of this."

And then she froze.

She turned.

She stared.

"He talks?"

"Yes," Dave said. "Are you my mother?"

Lynn Kendall didn't actually pass out, but she began to tremble, and when her knees buckled Henry caught her and helped her to sit in her favorite chair, facing the coffee table, next to the couch. Dave didn't move. He just stared with wide eyes. Henry went into the kitchen and got his wife some lemonade, and brought it back to her.

"Here," he said. "Drink this."

"I want a damn martini."

"Honey, those days are over." Lynn was AA.

"I don't know what days are what," she said. She was staring at Dave. "He talks. The monkey talks."

"Ape."

"I'm sorry I upsetted you," Dave said to her.

"Thank you, uh . . ."

"His name is Dave," Henry said. "He doesn't always get his tenses right."

Dave said, "Sometimes people get upsetted by me. They feel bad."

"Dave," she said. "This is not about you, honey. You seem to be very nice. This is about him." She jerked her thumb toward Henry. "The asshole."

"What is ah-sole?"

"He's probably never heard swearing," Henry said. "You need to watch your language."

"How do you watch language?" Dave said. "It's noises. You can't watch noises."

"I'm very confused," Lynn said, sinking into her chair.

"It's an expression," Henry said. "A figure of speech."

"Oh, I see," Dave said.

There was a silence. His wife sighed. Henry patted her arm.

"Do you have any trees?" Dave said. "I like to climb trees."

At that moment Jamie came into the house. "Hey, Mom, I need a towel—" He broke off and stared at the chimp.

"Hello," Dave said.

Jamie blinked, recovered fast. "Hey, neat!" he said. "I'm Jamie."

"My name is Dave. Do you have any trees to climb?"

"Sure! A big one! Come on!"

Jamie headed for the door. Dave looked questioningly at Lynn and Henry.

"Go ahead," Henry said. "It's okay."

Dave leapt off the couch, and scampered to the door, following Jamie.

"How do you know he won't run away?" Lynn said.

"I don't think he will."

"Because he's your son . . ."

The door banged shut. Outside, they heard their daughter screaming and shrieking, "What is that?"

They heard Jamie say, "He's a chimp, and we're climbing trees."

"Where'd you get him, Jamie?"

"He's Dad's."

"Does he bite?"

They couldn't make out Jamie's answer, but through the window they saw the tree branches swaying and moving. Giggles and laughter from outside.

"What are you going to do with him?" Lynn said.

"I don't know," Henry said.

"Well, he can't stay here."

"I know that."

"I won't have a dog in the house. I certainly won't have an ape."

"I know."

"And besides there's no room for him."

"I know."

"This is really a mess," she said.

He said nothing, just nodded.

"How the hell did this happen, Henry?" she said.

"It's a long story," he said.

"I'm listening."

When the human genome was decoded, he explained, scientists discovered that the genome of a chimpanzee was nearly identical to that of a man. "All that separates our two species," he said, "is five hundred genes."

Of course, that number was deceptive, because human beings and sea urchins also shared a lot of genes. In fact, nearly every creature on the planet shared tens of thousands of the same genes. There was a great underlying unity of all life, genetically speaking.

So that created a lot of interest in what had caused the differences in different species. Five hundred genes weren't a lot, yet a great chasm seemed to separate chimps from human beings.

"Many species can crossbreed to produce hybrids—lions and tigers, leopards and jaguars, dolphins and whales, buffalo and cattle, zebras and horses, camels and llamas. Grizzlies and polar bears sometimes mate in the wild, producing grolars. So there was a question of whether chimps and humans could hybridize to make a humanzee. The answer seems to be no."

"Somebody has tried?"

"Many times. Starting back to the 1920s."

But even if hybridization were impossible, Henry explained, one might still insert human genes directly into a chimp embryo to create a transgenic animal. Four years back, when Henry was on sabbatical at the National Institutes of Health, he was studying autism, and he wanted to know which genes might account for the difference in communication abilities between people and apes. "Because chimps can communicate," he said. "They have a range of cries and hand gestures; they can organize themselves into very effective hunting parties to kill small animals. So they have communication, but no language. Like severe autistics. That's what interested me."

"And what did you do?" his wife asked.

In the laboratory, under a microscope, he inserted human genes into a chimpanzee embryo. His own genes.

"Including the genes for speech?" she asked.

"Actually, all of them."

"You inserted all your genes."

"Look, I never expected the experiment to go to term," he said. "I was looking to retrieve a fetus."

"A fetus, not an animal?"

If the transgenic fetus survived eight or nine weeks before it spontaneously aborted, there would be enough differentiation that he could dissect the fetus and advance his understanding of speech in apes.

"You expected the fetus to die?"

"Yes. I was just hoping that it would carry long enough—"

"And then you were going to cut the fetus up?"

"Dissect it, yes."

"Your own genes, your own fetus—you did this in order to have something to dissect?" She was looking at him like he was a monster.

"Lynn, it was an experiment. We do this kind of thing all the—" He broke off. No point going there. "Look," he said, "the genes were close at hand. I didn't have to get anybody's permission to use them. It was an experiment. It wasn't about me."

"It is now," she said.

The question Henry was trying to answer was fundamental. Chimps and humans had split from a common ancestor six million years ago. And scientists had long ago noticed that chimpanzees most closely resemble human beings at their fetal stage. This suggested that human beings differed from chimps in part because of difference in intrauterine development. Human development could be thought of as having been arrested at the chimp fetal stage. Some scientists felt it was related to the eventual growth of the human brain, which doubled in the first year after birth. But Henry's interest was in speech, and for speech to occur, the vocal cords had to move down the throat from the mouth, creating a voice box. That happened in humans, but not in chimps. The entire developmental sequence was immensely complicated.

Henry hoped to harvest a transgenic fetus, and from that to gain some knowledge of what drove the change in human development that made speech possible. At least, that was his original experimental plan.

"Why didn't you remove the fetus as you intended?" she asked him.

Because that summer, several chimps contracted viral encephalitis, and the healthy chimps had to be moved away for quarantine. They were taken to different labs around the East Coast. "I never heard anything about the embryo I implanted. I just assumed that the female had spontaneously aborted in a quarantine facility somewhere, and the fetal material was discarded. I couldn't inquire too closely . . ."

"Because what you did was illegal."

"Well. That's a strong word. I assumed the experiment had failed, and it was over."

"Guess not."

"No," he said. "I guess not."

What happened was that the female gave birth to a full-term infant, and the two were returned to Bethesda. The infant chimp appeared to be normal in every respect. Its skin was somewhat pale, especially around the mouth, where there was no hair. But chimps varied widely in the amount of pigmentation they showed. No one thought anything of it.

As the infant grew, it appeared less normal. The face, which was originally flat, did not bulge outward with age. The facial features remained rather infantile. Still, nobody thought to question the baby's appearance—until they discovered on a routine blood exam that the infant tested negative for the Gc sialic acid enzyme. Since all apes carry this enzyme, the test was obviously wrong, and repeated. It again came back negative. The infant chimp did not have the enzyme.

"Absence of that enzyme is a human trait," Henry said. "Sialic acid is a kind of sugar. No humans have the Gc form of sialic acid. All apes have it."

"But this infant didn't."

"Right. So they did a DNA panel, and quickly realized that the infant didn't have the usual 1.5 percent difference in genes from a human being. It had many fewer differences. And they started to put it all together."

"And tested the chimp's DNA against everybody who had worked in the lab."

"Yes."

"And found he matched your DNA."

"Yes. Bellarmino's office sent me a sample a few weeks ago. I guess to give me a heads-up."

"What'd you do?"

"Took it to a friend for analysis."

"Your friend in Long Beach?"

"Yes."

"And Bellarmino?"

"He just doesn't want to be responsible, when word gets out." He shook his head. "I was driving home, and I was just west of Chicago when I got a call from this guy Rovak, at the animal lab. And he says, you're on your own with this one, pal. That's their attitude. My problem, not theirs."

Lynn frowned. "Why isn't this a major discovery? Shouldn't this make you famous around the world? You've created the first transgenic ape."

"The problem," Henry said, "is that I can be censured for it, or even put in jail. Because I didn't have permission from the committees that oversee primate research. Because the NIH now forbids transgenic work on any animal other than rats. Because all the anti-GM whackos and Frankenfood nuts will be up in arms over this. Because the NIH doesn't want any involvement in this and will deny any knowledge of it."

"So you can't tell anyone where Dave came from? That's a problem, Henry, because you'll never keep him a secret."

"I know," he said miserably.

"Tracy's on the phone right now, telling all her friends about the cute little ape in her backyard."

"Yes . . ."

"Her girlfriends will be over here in a few minutes. How are you going to explain Dave to them? Because after the girls will come the reporters." Lynn glanced at her watch. "In one, two hours, max. What'll you say?"

"I don't know. Maybe . . . I'll say the work was done in another country. In China. Or in South Korea. And they sent him here."

"And what will Dave say, when the reporters talk to him?"

"I'll ask him not to talk to them."

"Reporters won't leave this alone, Henry. They'll be camped outside the house with long lenses; they'll be circling in helicopters overhead. They'll be on the next plane to China or Korea to talk to the person who did this. And when they don't find that person . . . then what?"

She stared at him, then walked to the door. She looked into the backyard, where Dave was playing with Jamie. The two of them yelling and swinging through the trees. She was silent for a moment. Then she said, "You know, his skin really is quite pale."

"I know."

"His face is flat, almost human. What would he look like with a haircut?"

And so was born Gandler-Kreukheim syndrome, a rare genetic mutation causing short stature, excessive body hair, and facial deformities that yielded a rather ape-like appearance. The syndrome was so rare, it had only been documented four times in the last century. First, in an aristocratic Hungarian family in Budapest in 1923. Two children were born with the syndrome, described in the medical literature by an Austrian physician, Dr. Emil Kreukheim. The second appearance occurred in an Inuit child born in northern Alaska in 1944. A third child, a girl, was born in São Paulo in 1957, but she died of infection a few weeks after birth. A fourth child, in Bruges, Belgium, in 1988, was briefly seen by media but subsequently vanished. His whereabouts were now unknown.

"I like this," Lynn said. She was typing on her portable. "What's the name of that hairy syndrome? Excessive familial hairiness?"

"Hypertrichosis," Henry said.

"Right." She kept typing. "So Gandler-Kreukheim is related . . . to hypertrichosis. Actually . . . congenital hypertrichosis langinosa. And there've only been fifty cases reported in the last four hundred years."

"Are you writing that, or reading that?"

"Both." She sat back. "Okay," she said, "that's all I need for now. You better go tell Dave."

"Tell him what?"

"That he's human. He probably thinks he is, anyway."

"Okay." As Henry walked to the door, he said, "You really think this will work?"

"I know it will," Lynn said. "California has laws against invading the privacy of special children. Many of these kids have serious deformities. They've got enough challenges growing up and going to school without the added burden of media exposure. Big fines if the media do it. They won't."

"Maybe," he said.

"It's the best we can do for now," she said. She was typing again.

He paused at the door. "If Dave is a human being," he said, "we can't very well send him to a circus."

"Oh no," Lynn said. "No, no. Dave lives with us. He's part of our family now—thanks to you. We have no choice."

Henry went outside. Tracy and her friends were standing beneath the tree, pointing into the branches. "Look at the monkey! Look at him!"

"No," Henry said to them. "He's not a monkey. And please don't embarrass him. Dave suffers from a rare genetic syndrome . . ." And he explained it to them, as they listened wide-eyed.

Jamie had a trundle bed that he used when friends slept over. Lynn pulled it out, and Dave slept on it, alongside Jamie. His last words were "It's very soft," and almost immediately he was asleep, while Lynn ran her hands soothingly through his hair. Jamie said, "This is so neat, Mom. It's like having a brother."

"It is, isn't it," she said.

She turned out the light and closed the door. When she looked back in on them later, she found that Dave had twisted his sheets into a circle around him, making a kind of nest in the middle of the bed.

"No," Tracy said, standing in the kitchen, hands on hips. "No, he cannot live in our house. How could you do this to me, Dad?"

"Do what?"

"You know what the other kids are going to say. He's a monkey that looks like a person, Dad. And he sounds like you with a stuffy nose." She was near tears. "He's related to you, isn't he? He has your genes."

"Now, Tracy . . ."

"I am *so* embarrassed." She started to sob. "I had a chance to be a freshman cheerleader."

"Tracy," he said, "I'm sure you will—"

"This was my year, Dad!"

"It's still your year."

"Not if I have a monkey in my house!"

She went to the refrigerator for a Coke, came back, still sobbing. That was when her mother walked in. "He's not a monkey," Lynn said firmly. "He is an unfortunate young boy who suffers from a serious disease."

"Oh, sure, Mom."

"Go look it up yourself. Google it."

"I will!" Still sobbing, she walked over to the computer. Henry glanced at Lynn, then moved to look over his daughter's shoulder.

Hypertrichosis Variant Disorder Reported 1923 (Hungary)
Gandler-Kreukheim Syndrome on Monday 01/Jan/06@5:05pm Doubtless the hirsuitism is secondary to QT/TD. The Hungarian cases showed no induration, according to 1923 . . .
Dot.gks.org/9872767/9877676/490056 – 22K – Cached – Similar pages

Gandler-Kreukheim Syndrome – Inuit Lawsuit (1944)
In the hectic days of World War II, the young Inuit boy suffering from **Gandler-Kreukheim** in the northern Alaska town of Sanduk was treated by a local . . .
dot.gks.org/FAQ_G-K_S/7844908Inuit 41K – Cached – Similar pages

Prostitute Gives Birth to Ape Child in Beijing
New China Post reports an infant with chimp-like hair and large hands and feet, born to a Mongolian prostitute who claims to have mated with a Russian ape for money. Question whether this is **Gandler-Kreukheim syndrome,** extremely rare condition . . .
Dot.gks.org/4577878/9877676/490056 – 66K – Cached – Similar pages

The Delhi "Monkey Man" – A New Case of **Gandler-Kreukheim?**
Hindustan Times reports a man with the appearance and agility of a monkey, able to leap from rooftop to rooftop, frightening local residents. 3,000 police called out to . . .
Dot.gks.org/4577878/9877676/490056 – 66K – Cached – Similar pages

Gandler-Kreukheim Syndrome – From Belgium

Looking like a monkey, the young boy's picture appeared widely in the
Brussels press as well as publications in Paris and Bonn. After 1989 the child,
whose name was Gilles, disappeared from public view . . . (Translated)
Dot.gks.org/4577878/9877676/490056 – 52K – Cached – Similar pages

Syndrome Gandler-Kreukheim – De la Belgique

Ressemblant à un singe, l'image du jeune garçon est apparue partout dans la
presse de Bruxelles comme les publications dispersées à Paris et à Bonn.
Après 1989, l'enfant dont le nom était Gilles, est disparu de la vue publique . . .
Dot.gks.fr/4577878/77676/0056/9923.shmtl – 36K – Cached – Similar pages

---

"I had no idea," Tracy said, staring at the screen. "There have only
been four or five cases in all of history. That poor kid!"

"He's very special," Henry said. "I hope you will treat him better
now." He put his hand on Tracy's shoulder and glanced back at his wife.
"All this in a couple of hours?"

"I've been busy," she said.

CH037

here were fifty reporters in the conference room of Shanghai's Hua Ting Hotel, sitting at row after row of green felt–covered tables. The TV cameras were all at the back of the room, and sitting on the floor up front were the cameramen, with their bulky telephoto lenses.

Strobes flashed as Professor Shen Zhihong, head of the Institute of Biochemistry and Cell Biology, in Shanghai, stepped up to the microphones. Wearing a black suit, Shen was a distinguished-looking man, and his English was excellent. Before becoming the head of IBCB, he had spent ten years in Cambridge, Massachusetts, as a professor of cell biology at MIT.

"I do not know whether I am telling you good news or bad news," he said. "But I suspect it may be disappointing news. Nevertheless, I will set certain rumors finally to rest."

For some reason, he explained, rumors of unethical research in China began to circulate after the 12th East Asia Joint Symposium on Biomedical Research at Shaoxing City, in Zhejiang Province. "I have no idea why," Shen said. "The conference was quite ordinary, and technical in nature." However, at the next conference, in Seoul, reporters from Taiwan and Tokyo were asking pointed questions.

"I was therefore advised by Byeong Jae Lee, the head of molecular biology at Seoul National University, to address this matter directly. He has some experience with the power of rumors."

There were knowing chuckles in the audience. Shen was referring,

of course, to the worldwide scandal that had erupted around the eminent Korean geneticist Hwang Woo-Suk.

"Therefore, I shall come directly to the point," he said. "For many
years there have been rumors that Chinese scientists were attempting to
create a hybrid of human and chimpanzee. According to the story, back
in 1967, a surgeon named Ji Yongxiang fertilized a female chimpanzee
with human sperm. The chimp was in the third month of pregnancy
when outraged citizens stormed his lab and ended the experiment.
The chimpanzee later died, but researchers at the Chinese Academy of
Science supposedly said they would continue the research."

Shen paused. "That is the first story. It is entirely untrue. No chimpanzee was ever impregnated by Dr. Yongxiang or anyone else in China.
Nor has a chimpanzee been impregnated anywhere in the world. If it
had happened, you would know about it.

"Then, in 1980, a new story circulated that Italian researchers had
seen human-chimp embryos in a Beijing laboratory. I heard this story
when I was a professor at MIT. I asked to meet the Italian researchers
in question. They could never be found. They were always the friend
of a friend."

Shen waited while strobes flashed again. The cameramen crawling
around at his feet were annoying. After a moment, he continued. "Next,
a few years ago, was the story that a Mongolian prostitute gave birth
to a baby with the features of a chimpanzee. This chimp-man was said
to look like a human being, but was very hairy, with large hands and
feet. The chimp-man drank whiskey and spoke in sentences. According
to the story, this chimp is now at the Chinese Space Agency headquarters in Chao Yang District. He can sometimes be seen at the windows,
reading a newspaper and smoking a cigar. Supposedly he will be sent to
the moon because it is too dangerous to send a human.

"This story, too, is false. All the stories are false. I know these stories
are tantalizing, or amusing. But they are not true. Why they should
be located in China, I am not sure. Especially since the country with
the least regulation of genetic experiments is the United States. You
can do almost anything there. It was there that a gibbon was success-

fully mated with a siamang—primates that are genetically more distant than a human and chimp. Several live births resulted. This happened at Georgia State University. Almost thirty years ago."

He then opened the floor to questions. According to the transcript:

QUESTION: Dr. Shen, is the U.S. working on a chimp hybrid?
DR. SHEN: I have no reason to think so. I am merely observing that the U.S. has the fewest rules.

QUESTION: Is it possible to fertilize a chimpanzee with human sperm?
DR. SHEN: I would say no. That has been tried for nearly a century. Going back to the 1920s, when Stalin ordered the most famous animal breeder in Russia to do it, to make a new race of soldiers for him. His name was Ivanov, and he failed, and was thrown in jail. A few years later, Hitler's scientists tried it, and also failed. Today we know that the genomes of humans and chimps are very close, but the uterine conditions are considerably different. So, I would say no.

QUESTION: Could it be done with genetic engineering?
DR. SHEN: That is difficult to say. It would be extremely difficult from a technical standpoint. From an ethical standpoint, I would say it is impossible.

QUESTION: But an American scientist already applied to patent a human hybrid.
DR. SHEN: Professor Stuart Newman of New York was refused a patent on a part-human hybrid. But he did not make a hybrid. Dr. Newman said he applied for the patent to draw attention to the ethical issues involved. The ethical issues remain unresolved.

QUESTION: Dr. Shen, do you think a hybrid will eventually be created?
DR. SHEN: I called this press conference to end speculation, not to increase it. But if you ask my personal opinion, I think, yes—it will eventually be done.

CH038

The memory haunted Mark Sanger—the image burned in his mind of that poor animal, stranded on the beach at night in Costa Rica, helpless as the jaguar pounced, bit off her head, and proceeded to eat the flesh while her legs still kicked feebly. And all with the sound of crunching bones. The bones of her head.

Mark Sanger had not expected to see anything so horrific. He had come to the beach at Tortuguero to witness the giant leatherback turtles crawling out of the ocean to lay their eggs in the sand. As a biologist, he knew this was a great migration the planet had witnessed for countless eons. The female turtles were engaged in one of the great demonstrations of maternal caring, crawling high onto the beach, depositing their eggs deep in the ground, covering them with exhausted flippers, then carefully sweeping the sand clean, obliterating any trace of the eggs beneath. It was a slow, gentle ceremony, directed by genes that survived from millennia past.

Then came the jaguar, a black streak in the night. And suddenly last summer everything changed for Mark Sanger. The brutality of the attack, its speed and viciousness, shocked him profoundly. It confirmed his suspicion that the natural world had gone badly wrong. Everything that mankind was doing on the planet had upset the delicate balance of nature. The pollution, the rampant industrialization, the loss of habitat—when animals were squeezed and cornered, they behaved viciously, in a desperate effort to survive.

That was the explanation for the ghastly attack he had witnessed.

The natural world was in collapse. He mentioned this to the very hand-some naturalist Ramon Valdez, who had accompanied him. Valdez shook his head. "No, Señor Sanger, this is always the way it has been since my father and grandfather, and grandfather before. They always spoke of the jaguar attacks in the night. It is part of the cycle of life."

"But there are more attacks now," Sanger said. "Because of all the pollution . . . "

"No, señor. There is no change. Every month, the jaguars take two to four turtles. We have records going back many years."

"The violence we see here is *not* normal."

A short distance away, the jaguar was still eating the mother. Bones still crunching.

"But it *is* normal," Ramon Valdez said. "It is the way things are."

Sanger did not want to talk about it anymore. Clearly, Valdez was an apologist for the industrialists and polluters, the big American compa-nies that dominated Costa Rica and other Latin American countries. Not surprising to find such a person here, since the CIA had controlled Costa Rica for decades. This wasn't a country; it was a subsidiary of American business interests. And American businesses did not give a damn for the environment.

Ramon Valdez said, "The jaguars must eat, too. I think better a turtle than to take a human baby."

That, Mark Sanger thought, was a matter of opinion.

Back at home in Berkeley, Sanger sat in his loft and pondered what to do. Although Sanger told people he was a biologist, he had no formal training in the field. He had attended one year of college before drop-ping out to work briefly for a landscape architecture firm, Cather and Holly; the only biology he had taken was a course in high school. The son of a banker, Sanger possessed a substantial trust fund and did not need to work to support himself. He did, however, need a purpose in life. Wealth, in his experience, made the quest for self-identity even more difficult. And the older he got, the harder it was to think about going back and finishing college.

Recently, he had started to define himself as an artist, and artists did not need formal training. In fact, formal education interfered with the artist's ability to feel the zeitgeist, to ride the waves of change rolling through society, and to formulate a response to them. Sanger was very well informed in his opinion. He read the Berkeley papers, and sometimes magazines like *Mother Jones*, and several of the environmental magazines. Not every month, but sometimes. True, he often just looked at the pictures, skimming the stories. But that was all that was necessary to track the zeitgeist.

Art was about *feeling*. About how it *felt* to live in this materialistic world, with its gaudy luxuries, false promises, and profound disappointments. What was wrong with people today was that they ignored their feelings.

It was the job of art to bring true feelings alive. To shock people into awareness. That was why so many young artists were using genetic techniques and living material to create art. Wet art, they called it. Tissue art. Many artists now worked full-time in science labs, and the art that resulted was distinctly scientific. One artist had grown steaks in a Petri dish, and then ate them in public, as a performance. (Supposedly they tasted awful. Anyway, they were genetically modified. Ugh.) An artist in France had made a glowing bunny rabbit by inserting luminescent genes from a firefly or something. And still other artists had changed the hair color of animals, giving them rainbow hues, and had grown porcupine quills on the head of a cute puppy.

These works of art provoked strong feelings. Many people were disgusted. But, then, Sanger thought, they should be disgusted. They should feel the same revulsion that he himself had felt watching the slaughter of a mother turtle by a jaguar on a beach in Costa Rica. That horrid perversion of nature, that repellent savagery that he could not put out of his mind.

And that, of course, was the reason to make art.

Not art for art's sake. Rather, art to benefit the world, art to help the environment. That was Mark Sanger's goal, and he set about to attain it.

LOCAL DOCTOR ARRESTED FOR ORGAN THEFT

Long Beach Memorial Hospital Staffer Implicated; Thieves Sold Bones, Blood, Organs

A prominent Long Beach physician has been arrested for selling organs illegally removed from dead bodies at Long Beach Memorial Hospital. Dr. Martin Roberts, chief administrator of the pathology laboratory, which conducts autopsies at the hospital, was charged on 143 counts of illegally harvesting body parts from cadavers, and selling the contraband to tissue banks.

Said Long Beach District Attorney Barbara Bates, "This indictment reads like a B-movie horror story." Bates also alleged in her indictment that Dr. Roberts forged death certificates, falsified lab results, and colluded with local funeral homes and cemeteries to conceal his reign of error.

The case is only the most recent episode in a nationwide pandemic of modern-day bodysnatching. Other cases include "Dr. Mike" Mastromarino, a millionaire Brooklyn, N.Y., dentist who, over a five-year period, purportedly stole organs from thousands of cadavers, including bones from the 95-year-old Alastair Cooke; a Fort Lee, N.J., biomedical firm that sold Mastromarino's body parts to tissue banks across the United States; a crematorium in San Diego alleged to have stolen body parts from the cadavers entrusted to it; another in Lake Elsinore, California, where body parts were kept in huge freezers prior to sale; and UCLA Medical Center, where 500 bodies were cut up and sold for $700,000, some to the firm of Johnson & Johnson.

"The problem is worldwide," said DA Bates. "Tissue theft has been reported in England, Canada, Australia, Russia, Germany, and France. We believe such thefts now occur everywhere in the world," Bates added. "Patients are very concerned."

Dr. Roberts pleaded innocent to all charges in Superior Court and was released on a $1 million bond. Also indicted were four other Long Beach Memorial Hospital staffers, including Marilee Hunter, the head of the hospital genetics lab.

Long Beach Memorial administrator Kevin McCormick expressed shock at the indictments, and said that "Dr. Roberts's behavior contravenes everything that our institution stands for." He said he had ordered a thorough review of hospital procedures and would make the report public when it was completed.

Prosecutors say the events were brought to their attention by a whistleblower, Raza Rashad. Mr. Rashad is a first-year medical student in San Francisco who had previously worked in Dr. Roberts's pathology lab, where he had witnessed firsthand numerous illegal activities there. "Mr. Rashad's testimony was vital to building the prosecutor's case," Bates said.

CH039

J **osh Winkler** hurried into the animal facility to see what Tom Weller was talking about. "How many rats died?" he said.
"Nine."

The stiff bodies of nine dead rats lying on their sides in nine successive cages made Josh Winkler start to sweat. "We'll have to dissect them," he said. "When did they die?"

"Must have been during the night," Tom said. "They were fed at six; no notation of problems then." Tom was looking at a clipboard.

"What study group were they in?" Josh said. Fearing he already knew the answer.

"A-7," Tom said. "The maturity gene study."

Jesus.

Josh tried to remain calm. "And how old were they?"

"Ummm . . . let's see. Thirty-eight weeks and four days."

Oh God.

The average life span of a lab rat was 160 weeks—a little over three years. These rats had died in a quarter of that time. He took a deep breath. "And what about the others in the cohort?"

"There were twenty in the original study group," Tom said. "All identical, all the same age. Two of them died a few days ago, of respiratory infection. I didn't think much about it at the time. As for the others . . . well, you better see for yourself." He led Josh down the row of cages to the other rats. It was immediately clear what their condition was.

"Ragged coats, inactive, excessive sleeping, trouble standing on their hind legs, muscle wasting, hind leg paralysis in four of them . . ."

Josh stared. "They're *old*," he said. "They're all *old*."

"Yes," Tom said. "It's unmistakable: premature aging. I went back and checked the dead rats from two days ago. One had a pituitary adenoma and the other had spinal cord degeneration."

"Signs of age . . ."

"Right," Tom said. "Signs of age. Maybe this gene won't be the wonder product Rick is counting on after all. Not if it causes early death. It'd be a disaster."

"How am I feeling?" Adam said, as they sat together at lunch. "I feel fine, Josh, thanks to you. I'm a little tired sometimes. And my skin is dry. I'm getting a few wrinkles. But I feel okay. Why?"

"Just wondered," Josh said, as casually as he could. He tried not to stare at his older brother. In fact, Adam's appearance had changed dramatically. Where he once had a touch of gray at the temples, he now had a full head of salt-and-pepper hair. His hairline had receded. The skin around his eyes and lips was noticeably wrinkled. His forehead was deeply creased. He looked much older.

Adam was thirty-two.

Jesus.

"No, uh, drugs?" Josh asked.

"No, no. That's over, thank God," Adam said. He had ordered a hamburger, but he put it down after a few bites.

"Doesn't taste good?"

"Got a sore tooth. I need to see the dentist." Adam touched his cheek. "I hate complaining. Actually, I was thinking I'd better get some exercise. I need exercise. Sometimes I get constipated."

"You going to join your old b-ball group?" Josh said brightly. His brother used to play basketball twice a week with the investment bankers.

"Uh, no," Adam said. "I was thinking doubles tennis, or maybe golf."

"Good idea," Josh said.

A silence fell over the table. Adam pushed his plate aside. "I know I look older," he said. "You don't need to pretend you haven't noticed. Everybody's noticed it. I asked Mom, and she said that Dad was the same way; he just suddenly looked older in his thirties. Almost over-night. So maybe it's genetic."

"Yeah, could be."

"Why?" Adam said. "Do you know something?"

"Me? No."

"You just suddenly wanted to have lunch, urgently, today? Couldn't wait?"

"I hadn't seen you in a while, that's all."

"Cut the crap, Josh," he said. "You were always a shitty liar."

Josh sighed. "Adam," he said, "I think we should do some tests."

"For what?"

"Bone density, lung capacity. And an MRI."

"For what? What are these tests for?" He stared at Josh. "For aging?"

"Yes."

"I'm aging too fast? Is it that gene spray?"

"We need to find out," Josh said. "I want to call Ernie." Ernie Lawrence was the family physician.

"Okay, set it up."

CH040

S peaking in Washington at a noon briefing for congressmen, Professor William Garfield of the University of Minnesota said, "Despite what you hear, nobody has ever proven a single gene causes a single human behavioral trait. Some of my colleagues believe such associations may eventually be found. Others don't think it will ever happen, that the interaction of genes and environment is just too complex. But, in any case, we see reports of new 'genes for' this or that in the papers every day, and none of them has ever proven true in the end."

"What are you talking about?" said the aide to Senator Wilson. "What about the gay gene, that causes gayness?"

"A statistical association. Not causal. No gene causes sexual orientation."

"What about the violence gene?"

"Not verified in later research."

"A sleep gene was reported . . ."

"In rats."

"The gene for alcoholism?"

"Didn't hold up."

"What about the diabetes gene?"

"So far," he said, "we've identified ninety-six genes involved in diabetes. We'll undoubtedly find more."

There was a stunned silence. Finally, one aide said, "If no gene has been shown to cause behavior, what is all the fuss about?"

Professor Garfield shrugged. "Call it an urban legend. Call it a media myth. Blame public education in science. Because the public certainly believes that genes cause behavior. It seems to make sense. In reality, even hair color and height are not simple traits fixed by genes. And conditions like alcoholism certainly aren't."

"Wait a minute. Height isn't genetic?"

"For individuals, yes. If you're taller than your friend, it's probably because your parents are taller. But for populations, height is a function of environment. In the last fifty years, Europeans have grown an inch every decade. So have the Japanese. That's too fast for a genetic change. It's entirely an effect of environment—better prenatal care, nutrition, health care, and so on. Americans, by the way, haven't grown at all in this period. They've shrunk slightly, possibly because of poor prenatal care and junk food diets. The point is that the actual relationship of genes and environment is very complicated. Scientists don't yet have a good understanding of how genes work. In fact, there's no general agreement about what a gene *is*."

"Say that again?"

"Among scientists," Garfield said, "there is no single agreed-upon definition of what a gene is. There are four or five different definitions."

"I thought a gene was a section of the genome," someone said. "A sequence of base pairs, ATGC, that codes for a protein."

"That's one definition," Garfield said. "But it's inadequate. Because a single ATGC sequence can code for multiple proteins. Some sections of code are basically switches that turn other sections on and off. Some sections lie silent unless activated by specific environmental stimuli. Some sections are active only during a period of development, and never again. Others turn on and off constantly throughout an individual's life. As I said, it's complicated."

A hand went up. An aide for Senator Mooney, who received substantial contributions from drug companies, had a question. "Professor, I gather yours is a minority opinion. Most scientists wouldn't agree with your view of the gene."

"Actually, most scientists do agree," Garfield said. "And with good reason."

When the human genome was decoded, scientists were startled to find that it contained only about thirty-five thousand genes. They had expected far more. After all, a lowly earthworm had twenty thousand genes. That meant that the difference between a human being and a worm might be only fifteen thousand genes. How, then, could you explain the huge difference in complexity between the two?

That problem vanished as scientists began to study the interactions among genes. For example, one gene might make a protein, and another gene could make an enzyme that snipped out part of the protein and thus changed it. Some genes contained multiple coding sequences separated by regions of meaningless code. That gene could use any of its multiple sequences to make a protein. Some genes were activated only if several other genes were activated first, or when a number of environmental changes occurred. This meant that genes were far more responsive to the environment, both inside and outside the human being, than any-one had anticipated. And the fact of multiple gene interactions meant there were billions of possible outcomes.

"It's not surprising," Garfield said, "that researchers are moving toward what we call 'epigenetic studies,' which look at exactly how genes interact with the environment to produce the individual we see. This is an extremely active area." He started to explain the intricacies.

One by one, the congressional aides finished eating and left. Only a handful remained, and they were checking messages on their cell phones.

Neanderthals Were the First Blondes

Stronger, Bigger-Brained, Smarter Than Us

Genetic mutations for hair color indicate that the first blondes were Neanderthals, not Homo sapiens. The blonde gene emerged sometime in the Würm glaciation, perhaps in response to the relative lack of sunlight in the ice age. The gene spread among Neanderthals, who were mostly blonde, researchers say.

"Neanderthals had brains one-fifth larger than ours. They were taller than we were, and stronger. They were undoubtedly smarter, too," says Marco Svabo, of the Helsinki Genetics Institute. "In fact, there is little doubt that modern man is a domesticated version of the Neanderthal, as the modern dog is a domesticated version of the stronger and more intelligent wolf. Modern man is a degraded, inferior creature. Neanderthals were intellectually superior, and better looking. With blonde hair, high cheekbones, and strong features, they would have appeared as a race of supermodels.

"Homo sapiens—skinnier and uglier than Neanderthals—would naturally have been attracted to the beauty, strength, and intelligence of blondes. Apparently a few Neanderthal women took pity on the puny Cro-Magnons and bred with them. It's a good thing for us. We are lucky that we carry blonde Neanderthal genes to prevent our species from becoming hopelessly stupid. Although, we demonstrate plenty of stupidity anyway." He said that pretending blondes were stupid was "a dark-haired prejudice designed to deflect attention from the real problem of the world, which is dark-haired shortcomings." He added, "Make a list of the stupidest people in history. You will find they are all dark-haired."

Dr. Evard Nilsson, a spokesperson for the Marburg Institute in Germany, which has been sequencing the entire Neanderthal genome, said the blonde theory was interesting. Nilsson said, "My wife is a blonde, and I always do what she tells me to do, and our children are blonde, and quite intelligent. So I agree there is something to this theory."

Dave's first few days in the Kendall household went surprisingly well. When he went outside, he wore a baseball cap, which helped his appearance a lot. With his hair trimmed, wearing jeans and sneakers and a Quicksilver shirt, he looked much like any other kid. And he learned quickly. He had good coordination, and writing his name proved easy under Lynn's instruction. Reading was harder for him.

Dave did well at weekend sports, though sometimes it was disconcerting. At a Little League game, a high pop fly flew off the field toward the two-story school building; Dave ran over, scaled the wall, and caught the ball at the second-story window. The kids viewed this accomplishment with a mixture of admiration and resentment. It wasn't fair, and they had wanted to see the window shatter. On the other hand, everybody wanted Dave on their team.

So Lynn was surprised when, one Saturday afternoon, Dave came home early. He looked sad.

"What is it?" she said.

"I don't fit."

"Everybody feels that way, sometimes," she said.

He shook his head. "They look at me."

She paused. "You're not the same as the other kids."

"Yes."

"Do they make fun of you?"

He nodded. "Sometimes."

"What do they do?"

"Throw things. Call me names."

"What names?"

He bit his broad lip. "Monkeyboy." He was on the verge of tears.

"That feels bad," she said. "I'm sorry." She took his baseball cap off and began to stroke his head, the back of his neck. "Kids can be mean."

"Sometimes my feelings hurt," he said. Sad, he turned his back to her. He pulled his shirt off. She ran her fingers through his hair, looking for bruises and other signs of injury. As she did so, she felt him relax. His breathing slowed. His mood seemed to improve.

Only later did she realize she was grooming him, like monkeys in the wild. One turned its back to the other, while the other picked through the fur.

She decided she would do it every day. Just to make Dave more comfortable.

Since Dave's arrival, everything in Lynn's life had changed. Although Dave was clearly Henry's responsibility, the chimp showed little interest in him. He was immediately drawn to her, and something about his manner, or his appearance—the soulful eyes? the childish demeanor?—tugged at her heart. She'd started reading about chimps, and learned that because chimpanzee females took multiple sexual partners, they did not know which male fathered their infant, and thus chimpanzees showed no notion of fatherhood or fathers. Chimps had only mothers. Dave seemed to have been an abused child, uncared for by his actual chimp mother. He looked to Lynn with open longing, and she responded. It was all deeply emotional, and entirely unexpected.

"Mom, he's not your kid," Tracy had snapped. Tracy was at the age when she craved her parents' attention. She was jealous of any distraction.

"I know, Trace," Lynn said. "But he needs me."

"Mom! He's not your responsibility!" She threw up her hands in a theatrical gesture.

"I know."

"Well, can you leave him alone?"

"Is he getting too much attention?"

"Well, duh! Yes."

"I'm sorry, I didn't realize." She put her arm around her daughter, gave her a hug.

"Don't treat *me* like a monkey," Tracy said, and pushed her away.

But they were, after all, primates. Human beings were apes. Her experience with Dave was giving Lynn an uncomfortable awareness of what humans shared with other apes: Grooming, touching, physical attention as a source of relaxation. Eyes lowered under threat, or displeasure, or as a sign of submission. (Tracy around her boy friends, flirting with downcast eyes.) Direct eye contact meant intimidation, a sign of anger. Goose bumps for fear and anger—those same skin muscles made a primate's hair fluff up, to create a bigger appearance in the presence of threat. Sleeping communally, curling up in a kind of nest . . .

On and on.

Apes.

They were all apes.

More and more, the biggest difference seemed to be hair. Dave was hairy; those around him weren't. According to her reading, the loss of hair had occurred after human beings separated from chimps. The usual explanation was that human beings had become for a time swamp creatures, or water creatures. Because most mammals were hairy—their coats of fur were necessary to help maintain their internal temperature. But water mammals, such as dolphins and whales, had lost their hair in order to be streamlined. And people, too, had lost their hair.

But for Lynn the strangest thing was the persistent sense that Dave was both human and not human. She didn't quite know how to deal with that feeling. And as the days passed, it did not get any easier.

CANAVAN GENE LITIGATION ENDS
ETHICS OF GENE PATENTING DISPUTED

Canavan disease is an inherited genetic disorder that is fatal to children in the first years of life. In 1987 Dan Greenberg and his wife learned their nine-month-old son had the disease. Since no genetic test was available, the Greenbergs had another child, a daughter, who also was diagnosed with the disease.

The Greenbergs wanted to make sure other families were spared this heartbreak, and so they convinced Reuben Matalon, a geneticist, to work on a prenatal test for Canavan disease. The Greenbergs donated their own tissues, the tissues of their dead children, and they worked to obtain tissues from other families with Canavan disease around the world. Finally in 1993 the gene for Canavan disease was discovered. A free prenatal test was at last made available for families worldwide.

Unknown to the Greenbergs, Dr. Matalon patented the gene, and then demanded high fees for further tests. Many families that had contributed tissues and money to help discover the gene now could not afford the test. In 2003 the Greenbergs and other concerned parties sued Matalon and Miami Children's Hospital, claiming breach of informed consent, unjust enrichment, fraudulent concealment, and misappropriation of trade secrets. The suit was settled out of court. As a result, the test is more widely available, although fees must still be paid to Miami Children's Hospital. The ethics of the behavior of physicians and institutions involved in this case are still hotly debated.

Psychology News

ADULTS DON'T GROW UP ANYMORE

British Researcher Blames Formal Education
Professors, Scientists "Strikingly Immature"

If you believe the adults around you are acting like children, you're probably right. In technical terms, it is called "psychological neoteny," the persistence of childhood behavior into adulthood. And it's on the rise.

According to Dr. Bruce Charlton, evolutionary psychiatrist at Newcastle upon Tyne, human beings now take longer to reach mental maturity—and many never do so at all.

Charlton believes this is an accidental by-product of formal education that lasts well into the twenties. "Formal education requires a child-like stance of receptivity," which "counteracts the attainment of psychological maturity" that would normally occur in the late teens or early twenties.

He notes that "academics, teachers, scientists and many other professionals are often strikingly immature." He calls them "unpredictable, unbalanced in priorities, and tending to overreact."

Earlier human societies, such as hunter-gatherers, were more stable and thus adulthood was attained in the teen years. Now, however, with rapid social change and less reliance on physical strength, maturity is more often postponed. He notes that markers of maturity such as graduation from college, marriage, and first child formerly occurred at fixed ages, but now may happen over a span of decades.

Thus, he says, "in an important psychological sense, some modern people never actually become adults."

Charlton thinks this may be adaptive. "A child-like flexibility of attitudes, behaviors and knowledge" may be useful in navigating the increased instability of the modern world, he says, where people are more likely to change jobs, learn new skills, move to new places. But this comes at the cost of "short attention span, frenetic novelty-seeking, ever shorter cycles of arbitrary fashion, and . . . a pervasive emotional and spiritual shallowness." He added that modern people "lack a profundity of character which seemed commoner in the past." ▶

E llis," Mrs. Levine said, "what is that tube?"
Her son was holding a silver canister with a little plastic cup at the tip. They were in the living room of his parents' house in Scarsdale. Outside, workmen were hammering on the garage. Making repairs: getting the house ready to sell.

"What's in the tube?" she said again.

"It's a new genetic treatment, Mom."

"I don't need it."

"It rejuvenates your skin. Makes it young."

"That's not what you told your father," she said. "You told your father that it would improve his sex life."

"Well . . ."

"He put you up to this, didn't he?"

"No, Mom."

"Listen to me," she said. "I don't want to improve my sex life. I have never been happier than I am right now."

"The two of you sleep in separate rooms."

"Because he snores."

"Mom, this spray will help you."

"I don't want any help."

"It will make you happier, I promise . . ."

"You never did listen, even as a child."

"Now, Mom . . ."

"And you never got any better, your whole adult life."

"Mom, please . . ." Ellis was starting to get angry. He wasn't supposed to be the one doing this to her, anyway. His brother Aaron was supposed to do it. Aaron was his mother's favorite. But Aaron had a court date, he'd said. So Ellis was stuck with it.

He moved toward her with the canister.

"Get away from me, Ellis."

He continued to approach.

"I am *your mother*, Ellis."

She stamped on his toe. He howled in pain, and in the next moment grabbed her by the back of the head, pushed the canister over her nose, and squeezed. She writhed and twisted.

"I will not! I will not!"

But she was breathing it in. Even as she protested.

"No, no, *no!*"

He held it there for a while. It was as if he were strangling her, the same sort of grip, the same sensation, as she struggled in his arms. It made him incredibly uncomfortable. The flesh of her cheeks against his fingers as she twisted and protested. He smelled the powder of her makeup.

Finally Ellis stepped away from her.

"How dare you!" she said. "How *dare* you!" She hurried from the room, swearing.

Ellis leaned against the wall. He felt dizzy, to have physically accosted his mother like that. But it had to be done, he told himself. *It had to be done.*

CH043

Things were not going well, Rick Diehl thought, as he wiped puréed green peas off his face and paused to clean his glasses. It was five in the afternoon. The kitchen was hot. His three kids were sitting at the kitchen table screaming and hitting one another. They were throwing hot dog relish and mustard. The mustard stained everything.

The baby, in the high chair, refused to eat and spat her food right back out. Conchita should have been feeding her, but Conchita had vanished that afternoon. She had become increasingly unreliable ever since Rick's wife left. Broads stick together. Probably he would have to replace Conchita, which was a big pain in the neck, to hire somebody new, and of course she would sue him. Maybe he could negotiate a settlement with her before she went to court.

"You want it? Take it!" Jason, his oldest, mashed the hot dog with the bun into Sam's face. Sam howled and acted like he was choking. Now they were rolling on the floor.

"Dad! Dad! Stop him! He's choking me."

"Jason, don't choke your brother."

Jason paid no attention. Rick grabbed him by the collar and pulled him off Sam. "I said, don't choke him."

"I wasn't. He asked for it."

"You want to lose TV tonight? No? Then eat your own hot dog and let your brother eat his."

Rick picked up the spoon to feed the baby, but she closed her mouth stubbornly, staring at him with beady little hostile eyes. He sighed. What was it that made kids in high chairs refuse to eat, and throw all their toys on the floor? Maybe it wasn't such a good idea for his wife to have gone away, he thought.

As for the office, the situation was even worse. His ex–security guy had been humping Lisa, and now that he was out of jail, he was undoubtedly humping her again. That girl had zero taste. If Brad was convicted of pedophilia, that would be bad publicity for the company, but even so, Rick hoped for it. Josh Winkler's wonder drug was apparently killing people. Josh had gone way out on a limb, doing his own unauthorized human testing, but if he were sent to jail, that would reflect badly on the company, too.

He was poking at his daughter with the spoon when the phone rang. And things became much, much worse.

"Son of a bitch!"

Rick Diehl turned away from the banks of security screens. "I can't believe it," he said. On the screens, the hated Brad Gordon was swiping open doors to the labs, touching Petri dishes everywhere, and moving on. Brad had been recorded as he went methodically through all the labs in the building. Rick bunched his fists.

"He came into the building at one in the morning," the security temp said. "He must have had an admin card we didn't know about, because his was disabled. He went to all the storage points, and he contaminated every single culture in the Burnet cell line."

Rick Diehl said, "He's an asshole, but there's no problem. We have off-site bio-storage in San Jose, London, and Singapore."

"Actually, those samples were removed yesterday," the security temp said. "Someone picked up the cell lines and left. They had proper authorization. Secure e-transmission of codes."

"Who authorized it?"

"You did. It came from your secure account."

"Oh Christ." He spun. "How did *that* happen?"

"We're working on it."

"But the cell line," Rick said, "we have other sites—"

"Unfortunately, it seems . . ."

"Well, then we have customers who have leased—"

"I'm afraid we don't."

"What are you saying?" Rick said. He was starting to scream. "Are you saying every fucking Burnet culture is gone? In the entire fucking world? Gone?"

"As far as we know. Yes."

"This is a goddamn *disaster.*"

"Evidently."

"This could be the end of my company! That was our safety net, those cells. We paid a fortune to UCLA for them. You're saying they're gone?" Rick frowned angrily, as the reality hit him. "This is an organized, coordinated attack on my company. They had people in London and Singapore; they had everything arranged."

"Yes. We believe so."

"To destroy my company."

"Possibly."

"I need to get those cell lines back. Now."

"No one has them. Except, of course, Frank Burnet."

"Then let's get Burnet."

"Unfortunately, Mr. Burnet seems to have vanished, too. We can't seem to locate him."

"Great," Rick said. "Just great." He turned and yelled to his assistant, "Get the fucking lawyers, get fucking UCLA here, and get everybody here by eight o'clock tonight!"

"I don't know if—"

"Do it!"

Gail Bond fell into a routine. She would spend the night with Yoshi, then come home at six in the morning to wake up Evan, give him breakfast, and see him off to school. One morning, as soon as she unlocked the door, she saw that Gerard was gone. His cage stood uncovered in the hallway, his perch unoccupied. Gail swore. She went into the bedroom, where Richard was still sleeping. She shook him awake.

"Richard. Where's Gerard?"

He yawned. "What?"

"Gerard. Where's Gerard?"

"I'm afraid there's been an accident."

"What accident? What have you done?"

"The cage was being cleaned in the kitchen, and the window was open. He flew out."

"He did not. His wings were clipped."

"I know that," Richard said, yawning again.

"He did not fly out."

"All I can tell you is that I heard Nadezhda shriek, and when I came to the kitchen, she was pointing out the window, and when I looked, the bird was fluttering awkwardly to the ground. Of course I ran downstairs to the street at once, but he was gone."

The bastard was trying not to smile.

"Richard, this is very serious. That is a transgenic animal. If he escapes he may transmit his genes to other parrots."

"I am telling you, it was an accident."

"Where is Nadezhda?"

"She comes in at noon now. I thought I would cut back."

"Does she have a cell?"

"You hired her, pet."

"Don't call me pet. I don't know what you have done with that grey, but this is extremely serious, Richard."

He shrugged. "I don't know what to tell you."

Of course it ruined all her plans. They had intended to publish online the following month, and inevitably there would be cries from around the world that their claim was untrue. Scientists would call it the Clever Hans effect, mere mimicry, God knows what else. Everyone would demand to see the bird. And now the bird was gone.

"I could kill Richard," she said to Maurice, the head of the lab.

"And I will hire the best *avocat* for your defense," he said, not smiling. "Do you think he knows where the bird is?"

"Probably. But he'll never tell me. He hated Gerard."

"You're having a custody fight over a bird."

"I'll talk to Nadezhda. But he has probably paid her off."

"Did the bird know your name? The name of the lab? Phone numbers?"

"No, but he memorized the tones for my cellular phone. He used to make them as a sequence of sounds."

"Then perhaps he will call us, one day."

Gail sighed. "Perhaps."

CH045

Alex Burnet was in the middle of the most difficult trial of her career, a rape case involving the sexual assault of a two-year-old boy in Malibu. The defendant, thirty-year-old Mick Crowley, was a Washington-based political columnist who was visiting his sister-in-law when he experienced an overwhelming urge to have anal sex with her young son, still in diapers. Crowley was a wealthy, spoiled Yale graduate and heir to a pharmaceutical fortune. He hired notorious D.C. attorney Abe ("It Ain't There") Ganzler to defend him.

It turned out that Crowley's taste in love objects was well known in Washington, but Ganzler—as was his custom—tried the case vigorously in the press months before the trial, repeatedly characterizing Alex and the child's mother as "fantasizing feminist fundamentalists" who had made up the whole thing from "their sick, twisted imaginations." This, despite a well-documented hospital examination of the child. (Crowley's penis was small, but he had still caused significant tears to the toddler's rectum.)

It was in the midst of frantic preparation for the third day of the trial that Amy, Alex's assistant, buzzed her to say that her father was on the phone. Alex picked up. "Pretty busy, Dad."

"I won't take long. I'm going away for a couple of weeks."

"Okay, fine." One of the other lawyers came in and dropped the latest newspapers on her desk. The *Star* was running photographs of the raped child, the hospital in Malibu, and unflattering pictures of

Alex and the kid's mother, squinting in hard sunlight. "Where are you going, Dad?"

"Don't know yet," her father said, "but I need some time alone. Cell phone probably won't work. I'll send you a note when I get there. And a box of some stuff. In case you need it."

"Okay, Dad, have fun." She thumbed through the *L.A. Times* as she talked to him. For years the *Times* had fought for the right to access and print all court documents, however preliminary, private, or speculative. California judges were extremely reluctant to seal even those documents that involved the home addresses of women being stalked or the anatomical details of children who had been raped. The *Times'* policy of publishing everything also meant that attorneys could put gross and unfounded allegations in their pretrial filings, knowing the *Times* would print them. And it invariably did. The public's right to know. Yes, the public really needed to know exactly how long the tear was in the poor little boy's—

"You holding up all right?" her father said.

"Yeah, Dad, I'm okay."

"They're not getting to you?"

"No. I'm waiting for help from the child welfare organizations, but they're not issuing any statements. Strangely silent."

"I'm sure you're shocked by that," he said. "The weasel is politically connected, right? Little dickhead. Gotta go, Lexie."

"Bye, Dad."

She turned away. The DNA matches were due today, but they hadn't arrived yet. The samples obtained had been small, and she was worried about what they would show.

CH046

The lights dimmed smoothly in the plush presentation room at Selat, Anney, Koss Ltd., the preeminent London advertising agency. On the screen, an image of an American strip mall, blurred traffic rushing past a wretched cluster of signs. Gavin Koss knew from experience this image was an immediate rapport-builder. Anything critical of America was surefire.

"American businesses spend more on advertising than any other country in the world," Koss said. "Of course, they must do, given the quality of American products . . ."

Snickers floated through the darkness.

"And the intelligence of the American audience . . ."

Mild, muted laughter.

"As one of our columnists recently noted, the great majority of Americans couldn't find their own behinds with both hands."

Open laughter. They were warming to him.

"A crude, cultureless people, slapping each other on the back as they drift ever deeper into debt." That should suffice, he thought. He changed his tone: "But what I wish to draw to your attention is the sheer volume of commercial messages, as you see them here, arranged in space along the motorway. And every vehicle driving past has its radio on, sending out even more commercial messages. In point of fact, it's estimated that Americans listen to three thousand messages every day—or what is more probable, they don't listen to them. Psychologists have determined that the sheer volume of messages creates a kind of anesthesia, which becomes ingrained over time. In a saturated media environment, all messages lose impact."

The image changed to Times Square at night, then Shinjuku, in Tokyo, then Piccadilly, in London. "The saturation today is global. Huge messages, including large-screen video, appear in public squares, along motorways, in tube stations, train depots. We place videos at point-of-sale in retail stores. In toilets. In waiting rooms, pubs, and restaurants. In airport lounges and aboard aircraft.

"Furthermore, we have conquered personal space. Logos, brands, and slogans appear on ordinary objects from knives to tableware to computers. They appear on all our possessions. Consumers wear logos on their clothing, handbags, shoes, jewelry. Indeed, it is rare for a person to appear in public without them. Thirty years ago, if anyone predicted that the entire global public would turn themselves into sandwich boards, walking about advertising products, the idea would have seemed fantastical. Yet it has happened.

"The result is an imagistic glut, sensory exhaustion, and a diminution of impact. What can we do now? How can we move forward in the new era of technology? The answer may be heretical, but it is *this*."

The screen changed dramatically, to a forest image. Huge trees rising toward the sky, shade beneath. Then a snowy mountain peak. A tropical island, an arc of sand, crystalline water, palm trees. And, finally, an underwater reef, with fish swimming among coral heads and sponges.

"The natural world," Koss intoned, "is entirely without advertising. The natural world has yet to be tamed. Colonized by commerce. It remains virgin."

From the darkness: "Isn't that rather the point?"

"Conventional wisdom would put it so. Yes. But conventional wisdom is invariably out of date. Because in the time it has taken to become conventional—to become what everyone believes—the world has moved on. Conventional wisdom is a remnant of the past. And so it is in this case."

On the screen, the reef scene was suddenly branded. Coral branches had lettering that read BP CLEAN. A school of small fish wriggled by, each winking VODAFONE, VODAFONE. A slithering shark with CADBURY curving across the snout. A puffer fish with LLOYDS TSB GROUP in black lettering swam over convoluted heads of brain coral, with SCOTTISH POWER printed along the ridges in orange. And, finally, a moray eel poked its head out of a hole. Its greenish skin pattern said MARKS & SPENCER.

"Think of the possibilities," Koss said.

The audience was stunned—as he had expected it would be. He pressed on with the argument.

The slide now showed a desert scene, with spires of red rock rising against a blue sky laced with clouds. After a moment, the clouds coalesced into a larger, misty cloud that hung above the landscape and said:

BP MEANS CLEAN POWER.

"Those letters," Koss said, "are nine hundred feet high. They stand a quarter of a mile above the landscape. They are clear to the naked eye, and they photograph well. At sunset, they become quite beautiful." The image changed. "Here, you see their appearance as the sun goes down—the lettering changes from white to pink, to red, and finally deep indigo. So it has the quality, the feeling, of being a natural element within the natural landscape."

He returned to the original cloud image in daylight. "These letters are generated by a marriage of nanoparticles and genetically modified clostridium perfringens bacteria. The image is, in effect, a nanoswarm, and it will remain visible in the air for a variable period of time, depending on conditions—just as any cloud would. It may appear for only a few minutes. At other times, it may appear for an hour. It may appear in multiples . . ."

On the screen, the fluffy clouds became the BP slogan, repeated infinitely in cloud after cloud, stretching away to the horizon. "I think everyone will recognize the impact of this new medium. The *natural* medium."

He had expected spontaneous applause for this dramatic visual, but there was still only silence in the darkness. Yet surely they would be experiencing some sort of reaction by now. An infinitely repeated advert hanging in the sky? Surely it must arouse them.

"But these clouds are a special case," he said.

He returned to the underwater image, fishes moving over the coral reef. "In this case," he said, "signage and adverts are borne by the living creatures themselves, through direct genetic modification of each species. We call this genomic advertising. To capture this new medium, speed is of the utmost importance. There are only a limited number of reef fishes common to tourist waters. Some fish are more incandescent than others. Many are a bit drab. So we want to choose the best. And the genetic modifications will require patenting the marine animal in each case. Thus we will patent the Cadbury clown fish, the British Petroleum stag coral, the Marks and Spencer moray eel, the Royal Bank of Scotland angelfish, and gliding silently overhead, the British Airways manta ray."

Koss cleared his throat. "Speed matters because we are entering a competitive situation. We want our Cadbury clown fish out there, before the clown fish is patented by Hershey's or McDonald's. And we want a strong creature, since in the natural environment the Cadbury clown fish will compete against ordinary clown fish, and hopefully triumph over them. The more successful our patented fish, the more frequently our message shall be seen, and the more completely the original, messageless fish will be driven to extinction. We are entering the era of Darwinian advertising! May the best advert win!"

A cough from the audience. "Gavin, forgive me," came a voice, "but this appears to be an environmental nightmare. Brand names on fish? Slogans in clouds? And what else? Rhinos in Africa that carry the Land Rover logo? If you go about branding animal species, every environmentalist in the world will oppose you."

"Actually, they will not," Koss said, "because we're not suggesting that corporations *brand* species. We ask corporations to *sponsor* species. As a public service." He paused. "Think how many museum exhibitions, theater companies, and symphony orchestras are entirely dependent on corporate sponsorship. Even sections of roadway are sponsored, today. Why shouldn't the same philanthropic spirit be directed toward the natural world—which surely would benefit far more than our roads? Endangered species could be attractively sponsored. Corporations can stake their reputations on the survival of animal species, as they once staked their reputations on the quality of dull television programs. And it is the same for other animals that are not yet endangered. For all the fish in the sea. We are talking about an era of magnificent corporate philanthropy—on a global scale."

"So, this is the black rhino, brought to you by Land Rover? The jaguar, brought to you by Jaguar?"

"I shouldn't put it so crudely, but, yes, that's what we are proposing. The point," he continued, "is that this is a win-win situation. A win for the environment. For corporations. And for advertising."

Gavin Koss had done hundreds of presentations in his career, and his feeling for the audience had never failed him. He could feel now that this group was not buying it. It was time to bring the lights up and take questions.

He stared at the rows of frowning faces. "I admit my notion is radical," he said. "But the world is changing rapidly. Someone is going to do this. This colonization of nature *will* happen—the only question is, by whom. I urge you to consider this opportunity with the greatest care, and then decide if you want to be a part of it."

From the back, Garth Baker, the head of Midlands Media Associates Ltd., stood. "It's quite a novel idea, Gavin," he said. "But I must tell you with some assurance that it will not work."

"Oh? Why is that?"

"Because someone has already done it."

There was no moon and no sound, except the booming of the surf in the darkness and the whine of the damp wind. Tortuguero beach extended for more than a mile along the rough Atlantic coast of Costa Rica, but tonight it was no more than a dark strip that merged with a black, starry sky. Julio Manarez paused, waiting for his eyes to adjust to the dark. A man can see by starlight, if he takes the time.

Soon he could make out the palm trunks and debris scattered over the dark sand, and the low, scrubby plants whipped by the wind off the ocean. He could just see whitecaps in the churning seas. The ocean, he knew, was filled with sharks. This stretch of the Atlantic coast was bleak and inhospitable.

A quarter mile down the beach he saw Manuel, a dark shape hunched beneath the mangroves. He was keeping out of the wind. There was no one else on the beach.

Julio started toward him, passing the deep pits dug by the turtles in previous days. This beach was one of the breeding grounds for leatherback turtles, which came up from the ocean in darkness to lay their eggs. The process took most of the night, and the turtles were vulnerable— in the old days, to poachers, and now mostly to the jaguars that roamed the beach, black as the night itself. As the newly appointed conservation chief of the region, Julio was well aware that turtles were killed every week along this coast.

Tourists helped prevent this; if tourists were walking the beach, the jaguars stayed away. But often the cats came after midnight, when the tourists had gone home to their hotels.

It was possible to imagine an evolutionary selection pressure producing some defense against the jaguar. When he was in graduate school, in San Juan, he and the other students used to joke about it. Were tourists agents of evolution? Tourists changed everything else about a country, why not its wildlife? Because if a turtle happened to possess some quality—perhaps a tolerance for flashlights, or the ability to make a plaintive, pained mothering sound—if they had something that drew tourists and kept them hanging around into the night, then those turtles would be more likely to survive, and their eggs more likely to survive, and their offspring more likely to survive.

Differential survival that resulted from being a tourist attraction. That had been the joke, in school. But, of course, it was theoretically possible. And if what Manuel was telling him was true . . .

Manuel saw him and waved. He stood as Julio approached. "This way," he said, and started down the beach.

"You find more than one tonight, Julio?"

"Just one. Of that kind I was speaking of."

"*Muy bien.*"

They walked down the beach in silence. But they had not gone far— perhaps a hundred yards or so—when Julio saw the faint purple glow, low to the sand, and pulsing slightly.

"That's it?"

"That's it," Manuel said.

She was a female of perhaps one hundred kilos, a meter and a quarter long. She had characteristic shell plates, about the size of his palm. Brownish, streaked with black. She was half buried in the sand, digging a pit at the rear with her flippers.

Julio stood over her and watched.

"It starts and stops," Manuel said.

And then it began again. A purple glow that seemed to emanate from within the individual plates of the shell. Some plates did not have the glow and were dark. Some glowed only occasionally. Others glowed each time. Each pulse seemed to last about a second, rising quickly, fading slowly.

"So how many turtles like this have you seen?" Julio said.

"This is the third."

"And this light keeps the jaguars away?" He continued to watch the soft pulsing. He felt that the quality of the glow was oddly familiar. Almost like a firefly. Or a glowing bacterium in the surf. Something he had seen before.

"Yes, the jaguars keep their distance."

"Wait a minute," Julio said. "What is this?" He pointed to the shell, where a pattern of light and dark plates emerged.

"It only happens sometimes."

"But you see it?"

"Yes, I see it."

"It looks like a hexagon."

"I don't know . . ."

"But it is like a symbol, wouldn't you say? Of a corporation?"

"Perhaps, yes. It is possible."

"What about the other turtles? They show this pattern?"

"No, each one is different."

"So this might be a random pattern that just happens to look like a hexagon?"

"Yes. Julio, I believe it is. Because you see the image on the shell is not so good, it is not symmetrical . . ." Even as he spoke, the image faded. The turtle was dark again.

"Can you photograph this pattern?"

"I already have. It is a time exposure, without the flash, so there is some blurring. But, yes, I have it."

"Good," Julio said. "Because this is a genetic change. Let's review the visitor log, and see who might have done this."

osh." It was his mother, on the phone.

"Yes, Mom."

"I thought you should know. You remember Lois Graham's son, Eric, who was on heroin? There's been a terrible tragedy. He died."

Josh gave a long sigh. He leaned back in his chair and closed his eyes. "How?"

"In a car crash. But then they did the autopsy or whatever. Eric had a fatal heart attack. He was twenty-one, Josh."

"Was it in the family? Some congenital thing?"

"No. Eric's father lives in Switzerland; he's sixty-four. He climbs mountains. And Lois is fine. Of course she's crushed. We're all crushed."

Josh said nothing.

"Things were going so well for Eric. He was off drugs, he had a new job, he'd applied to go back to school in the fall . . . he was getting bald, was the only thing. People thought he'd had chemo. He'd lost so much hair. And he walked stooped over. Josh? Are you there?"

"I'm here."

"I saw him last week. He looked like an old man."

Josh said nothing.

"The family's sitting. You ought to go."

"I'll try."

"Josh. Your brother looks old, too."

"I know."

"I tried to tell him it was like his father. To cheer him up. But Adam just looks *so old*."

"I know."

"What's going on?" she said. "What have you done to him?"

"What have *I* done?"

"Yes, Josh. You gave these people some gene. Or whatever that spray was. And they're getting old."

"Mom. Adam did it to himself. He sucked down the spray himself because he thought it'd get him high. I wasn't even with him at the time. And you asked me to give the spray to Lois Graham's son."

"I don't know how you could think such a thing."

"You called me up."

"Josh, you're being ridiculous. Why would I call? I don't know anything about your work. *You* called *me*, and asked where Eric lived. And you asked me not to tell his mother. That's what I remember."

Josh said nothing. He pressed the tips of his fingers against his closed eyes until he saw bright patterns. He wanted to escape. He wanted to leave this office, this company. He wanted none of this to be true.

"Mom," he said finally. "This could be very serious." He was thinking that he could go to jail.

"Of course it's serious. I'm very frightened now, Josh. What's going to happen? Am I going to lose my son?"

"I don't know, Mom. I hope not."

"I think there's a chance," she said. "Because I called up the Levines in Scarsdale. They're already old, the two of them. Past sixty. And they sounded just fine. Helen said she was never better. George is playing a lot of golf."

"That's good," he said.

"So maybe they're okay."

"I think so."

"Then maybe Adam will be okay, too."

"I really hope so, Mom. I really do."

He got off the phone. Of course the Levines were fine. He had sent sterile saline in the spray tubes. They hadn't gotten the gene. He wasn't about to send his experimental genes to some people in New York he didn't know.

And if this gave his mother hope, then fine. Keep it that way.

Because right now, Josh didn't hold out much hope. Not for his brother. And ultimately not for himself.

He was going to have to tell Rick Diehl. But not now. Not right now.

CH049

Gail Bond's husband, Richard, the investment banker, often worked late entertaining important clients. And none was more important than the American sitting across the table from him now: Barton Williams, the famous Cleveland investor.

"You want a surprise for your wife, Barton?" Richard Bond said. "I believe I have just the thing."

Hunched down over the dinner table, Williams looked up with only slight interest. Barton Williams was seventy-five, and closely resembled a toad. He had a jowly, droopy face with large pores, a broad, flat nose, and bug eyes. His habit of placing his arms flat on the table and resting his chin on his fingers made him look even more like a toad. In fact, he was resting an arthritic neck, since he disliked wearing a brace. He felt it made him look old.

He could lie flat on the table, as far as Richard Bond was concerned. Williams was old enough and rich enough to do whatever he wanted, and what he had always wanted, all his life, was women. Despite age and appearance, he continued to have them in prodigious quantities, at all times of day. Richard had arranged for several women to drop by the table at the end of the meal. They would be members of his staff, dropping off papers for him. Or old girlfriends, coming by for a kiss and an introduction. A few would be other diners, admirers of the great investor, and so dazzled they had to come and meet him.

None of this fooled Barton Williams, but it amused him, and he expected his business partners to go to a little trouble for him. When you were worth ten billion dollars, people made an effort to keep you happy. That was how it worked. He viewed it as a tribute.

Yet at this particular moment, more than anything else, Barton Williams wanted to placate his wife of forty years. For inexplicable reasons, Evelyn, at age sixty, was suddenly dissatisfied with her marriage and with Barton's endless escapades, as she referred to them.

A present would help. "But it better be damn good," Barton said. "She's accustomed to everything. Villas in France, yachts in Sardinia, jewelry from Winston, chefs flown in from Rome for her dog's birthday. That's the problem. I can't buy her off anymore. She's sixty and jaded."

"I promise you, this present is unique in the world," Richard said. "Your wife loves animals, does she not?"

"Has her own damn zoo, right on the property."

"And she keeps birds?"

"Christ. Must be a hundred. We got finches in the damn sun room. Chitter all day. She breeds 'em."

"And parrots?"

"Every kind. None talk, thank God. She never had much luck with parrots."

"Her luck is about to change."

Barton sighed. "She doesn't want another damn parrot."

"She wants this one," Richard said. "It's the only one like it in the world."

"I'm leaving at six tomorrow morning," Barton grumbled.

"It'll be waiting on your plane," Richard said.

CH050

Rob Bellarmino smiled reassuringly. "Just ignore the cameras," he said to the kids. They had set up in the school library of George Washington High in Silver Spring, Maryland. Three semicircles of chairs around a central chair, where Dr. Bellarmino sat while he talked to the students about the ethical issues of genetics.

The TV people had three cameras going, one at the back of the room, one at the side, close on Bellarmino, and one facing the kids, to record their expressions of fascination as they heard about the life of a working geneticist at the NIH. According to the show's producer, it was important to show Bellarmino's interaction with the community, and he could not have agreed more. The kids were specially picked to be bright and knowledgeable.

He thought it would be fun.

He spoke about his background and training for a few minutes, and then took questions. The first one made him pause. "Dr. Bellarmino," a young Asian girl asked, "what is your opinion of that woman in Texas who cloned her dead cat?"

In fact, Bellarmino thought the whole dead-cat business was ridiculous. He thought it diminished the important work he and others were doing. But he couldn't say that.

"Of course, this is a difficult, emotional situation," Bellarmino said diplomatically. "We are all fond of our pets, but . . ." He hesitated. "This work was done by a California company called Genetic Savings and Clone, and it was reported that the cost was fifty thousand dollars."

"Do you think it's ethical to clone a pet cat?" the girl asked.

"As you know," he said, "quite a few animals have now been cloned, including sheep, mice, dogs, and cats. So it has become rather unremarkable . . . One concern is that a cloned animal does not have the same life span as a normal animal. "

Another student said, "Is it ethical to pay fifty thousand dollars to clone a pet, when so many people are starving in the world?"

Bellarmino groaned inwardly. How was he going to change the subject? "I am not enthusiastic about this procedure," he said. "But I would not go so far as to call it unethical."

"Isn't it unethical because it makes a climate of normality to clone a human being?"

"I don't think cloning a pet has any effect on the issues concerning human cloning."

"Would it be ethical to clone a human being?"

"Fortunately," Bellarmino said, "that issue is quite far in the future. Today, I hope we might consider real contemporary issues. We have people who express concerns about genetically modified foods; we have concerns about gene therapy, and stem cells; and these are real issues. Do any of you share that concern?" A young boy in the back raised his hand. "Yes?"

"Do you think it is possible to clone a human being?" the boy asked.

"Yes, I think it is possible. Not now, but eventually."

"When?"

"I wouldn't want to guess when. Are there questions on a different subject?" Another hand. "Yes?"

"In your opinion, is human cloning unethical?"

Again, Bellarmino hesitated. He was acutely aware his response was going to be broadcast on television. And who could know how the network would edit his remarks? They'd probably do their best to make him look as bad as possible. Reporters had a distinct prejudice against people of faith. And his words also carried professional weight, because he ran a division of NIH.

"You've probably heard a lot about cloning, and most of it is untrue. Speaking as a scientist, I must admit I see nothing inherently wrong with cloning. I see no moral issue. It is just another genetic procedure. We already have done it with a variety of animals, as I have mentioned. However, I also know that the procedure of cloning has a high failure rate. Many animals die before one is successfully cloned. Clearly that would be unacceptable for human beings. So, for the moment, I regard cloning as a non-problem."

"Isn't cloning playing God?"

"I personally wouldn't define the issue that way," he said. "If God has made human beings, and made the rest of the world, then clearly God has made the tools of genetic engineering. So, in that sense, God has already made genetic modification available. That is the work of God, not man. And, as always, it is up to us to use wisely what God has given us." He felt better after this; it was one of his stock answers.

"So is cloning a wise use of what God has given us?"

Against his every instinct, he wiped his forehead with the sleeve of his jacket. He hoped they wouldn't use that bit of film, although he was sure they would. Young kids sweat the head of NIH. "Some people think they know what God intends," he said. "But I don't believe I know. I don't believe anyone can know that, except God. I think anyone who says he knows God's intention is showing a lot of very human ego."

He wanted to glance at his watch, but he didn't. The kids were looking quizzical, not enraptured, as he had expected.

"There's a great range of genetic issues," he said. "Let's move on."

"Dr. Bellarmino," said a kid to the left, "I wanted to ask about antisocial personality disorder. I've read there is a gene for it, and it's associated with violence and crime, sociopathic behavior . . ."

"Yes, that's true. The gene appears in about two percent of the population around the world."

"What about New Zealand? It is in thirty percent of the white New Zealand population, and sixty percent of the Maori population . . ."

"That's been reported, but you must be careful—"

"But doesn't that mean violence is hereditary? I mean, shouldn't we be trying to get rid of this gene, the way we got rid of smallpox?"

Bellarmino paused. He was starting to wonder how many of these kids had parents who worked in Bethesda. He hadn't thought to ask for the names of the kids in advance. But the questions from these kids were too knowledgeable, too relentless. Was one of his many enemies trying to discredit him, by using these kids? Was the whole network plan a trap to make him look bad? The first step toward pushing him out of NIH? This was the information age; it was how such things were done today. Arrange to make you look bad, make you look weak. Push you to say something foolish, and then watch your words repeated over and over for the next forty-eight hours on every cable news show and in every newspaper column. Next, have congressmen call for you to re-tract your statements. Clucking tongues, shaking heads . . . How could he be so insensitive? Was he really suited for the job? Wasn't he really a liability at his post?

And then you were out.

That was how it was done, these days.

Now Bellarmino was facing a dangerously loaded question about Maori genetics. Should he say what he really believed, and risk being accused of demeaning a downtrodden ethnic minority? Did he mute his comments, but still risk criticism for promoting eugenics? How, actually, could he say anything at all?

He decided he couldn't. "You know," he said, "that's an extremely interesting area of research, but we just don't know enough yet to answer. Next question?"

CH051

t had been raining all day in southern Sumatra. The jungle floor was wet. The leaves were wet. Everything was wet. The video crews from around the world had long since gone on to other assignments. Now Hagar was back with only one client: a man named Gorevitch. A famous wildlife photographer who had flown in from Tanzania.

Gorevitch had set up beneath a large ficus tree, unzipped a duffel bag, and removed a nylon mesh sling, like a hammock. He set this on the ground carefully. Then he brought out a metal case, popped it open, and assembled a rifle.

"You know that's illegal," Hagar said. "This is a preserve."

"No shit."

"If the rangers come through, you better get that stuff out of sight."

"Not a problem." Gorevitch charged the compressor, opened the chamber. "How big is this guy?"

"He's a juvenile, two or three years old. Maybe thirty kilos. Probably less."

"Okay. Ten cc's." Gorevitch pulled a dart out of the case, checked the level, and slipped it into the chamber. Then another. And another. He clicked the chamber closed. He said to Hagar, "When was the last time you saw him?"

"Ten days ago."

"Where?"

"Near here."

"He comes back? This is his home range?"

"Seems to be."

Gorevitch squinted down the telescopic sight. He swung it in an arc, then up to the sky, then back. Satisfied, he put the gun down.

"You got a low enough dose?"

"Don't worry," Gorevitch said.

"Also, if he's high in the canopy, you can't shoot because—"

"I said, don't worry." Gorevitch looked at Hagar. "I know what I'm doing. Dose is just enough to unsteady him. He'll come down by himself, long before he collapses. We may have to track him on the ground for a while."

"You've done this before?"

Gorevitch nodded.

"With orangs?"

"Chimps."

"Chimps are different."

"Really." Sarcastic.

The two men fell into an uneasy silence. Gorevitch got out a video camera and tripod, and set them up. Then a long-range microphone with a one-foot dish, which he clipped to the top of the camera with a mounting pole. It made an ungainly apparatus, but effective, Hagar thought.

Gorevitch squatted on his haunches and stared out at the jungle. The men listened to the sound of the rain, and waited.

In recent weeks, the talking orangutan had faded from the media. The story had gone the way of other animal reports that didn't prove out: that Arkansas woodpecker nobody could find again, and the six-foot Congo ape that nobody could locate despite persistent stories by natives, and the giant bat with the twelve-foot wingspan that was supposedly seen in the jungles of New Guinea.

As far as Gorevitch was concerned, the declining interest was ideal. Because when the ape was finally rediscovered, media attention would be ten times greater than it would have been otherwise.

Especially because Gorevitch intended to do more than record the talking ape. He intended to bring it back alive.

He zipped his jacket collar tight against the dripping rain, and he waited.

It was late in the afternoon, and starting to get dark. Gorevitch was dozing off when he heard a low gravelly voice say, *"Alors. Merde."*

He opened his eyes. He looked at Hagar, sitting nearby.

Hagar shook his head.

"Alors. Comment ça va?"

Gorevitch looked slowly around.

"Merde. Scumbag. Espèce de con." It was a low sound, throaty, like a drunk at a bar. *"Fungele a usted."*

Gorevitch turned on the camera. He couldn't tell where the voice was coming from, but he could at least record it. He swung the lens in a slow arc, while he watched the microphone levels. Because the mike was directional, he was able to determine that the sound was coming from . . . the south.

Nine o'clock from where he was. He squinted through the finder, zoomed in. He could see nothing. The jungle was becoming darker every minute.

Hagar stood motionless nearby, just watching.

Now there was a crashing of branches, and Gorevitch glimpsed a shadow as it streaked across the lens. He looked up and saw the shape moving higher and higher, swinging on branches as it went up into the overhead canopy. In a few moments the orang was seventy feet in the air above them.

"Gods vloek het. Asshole wijkje. Vloek."

He took the camera off the tripod, tried to film. It was black. Nothing. Flicked on night vision. He saw nothing but green streaks as the animal moved in and out of the thick foliage. The orang was moving higher and laterally.

"Vloek het. Moeder fucker."

"Nice mouth on him." But the voice was growing fainter.

Gorevitch realized he had a decision to make, and quickly. He set the camera down and reached for the rifle. He swung it up and sighted down the scope. Military night vision, bright green, very clear. He saw the ape, saw the eyes glowing white dots—

Hagar said, "No!"

The orang jumped to another tree, suspended in space for an instant.

Gorevitch fired.

He heard the hiss of gas and the *thwack* of the dart smacking the leaves.

"Missed him." He raised the rifle again.

"Don't do this—"

"Shut up." Gorevitch sighted, fired.

In the trees above, there was a momentary pause in the thrashing sound.

"You hit him," Hagar said.

Gorevitch waited.

The crashing of leaves and branches began again. The orang was moving, now almost directly overhead.

"No, I didn't." Gorevitch raised the gun once more.

"Yes, you did. If you shoot again—"

Gorevitch fired.

A whoosh of gas near his ear, then silence. Gorevitch lowered the gun and moved to reload it, keeping his eyes on the canopy overhead. He crouched down, flicked open his metal case, and felt for more cartridges. He kept looking upward the whole time.

Silence.

"You hit him," Hagar said.

"Maybe."

"I know you hit him."

"No, you don't." Gorevitch popped three more cartridges into the gun. "You don't know that."

"He's not moving. You hit him."

Gorevitch took his position, raised the rifle, just in time to see a dark shape come plummeting downward. It was the orang, falling straight down from the canopy more than 150 feet above them.

The animal crashed to the ground at Gorevitch's feet, splattering mud. The orang didn't move. Hagar swung a flashlight.

Three darts protruded from the body. One in the leg, two in the chest. The orang was not moving. The animal's eyes were open, staring upward.

"Great," Hagar said. "Great work."

Gorevitch dropped to his knees in the mud, put his mouth over the orang's big lips, and blew air into his lungs, to resuscitate him.

Six attorneys sat at the long table, all shuffling through papers. It sounded like a windstorm. Rick Diehl waited impatiently, biting his lip. Finally Albert Rodriguez, his head attorney, looked up.

"The situation is this," Rodriguez said. "You have good reason—sufficient reason, anyway—to believe that Frank Burnet conspired to destroy the cell lines in your possession, so that he could sell them again to some other company."

"Right," Rick said. "Fucking right."

"Three courts have ruled that Burnet's cells are your property. You therefore have a right to take them."

"You mean, take them *again*."

"Correct."

"Except the guy has gone into hiding."

"That is inconvenient. But it does not change the material facts of the situation. You are the owner of the Burnet cell line," Rodriguez said. "Wherever those cells may occur."

"Meaning . . ."

"His children. His grandchildren. They probably have the same cells."

"You mean, I can take cells from the kids?"

"The cells are your property," Rodriguez said.

"What if the kids don't agree to let me take them?"

"They may very well not agree. But since the cells are your property, the children don't have any say in the matter."

"We're talking punch biopsies of liver and spleen, here," Diehl said. "They're not exactly minor procedures."

"They're not exactly major, either," Rodriguez said. "I believe they are ordinary outpatient procedures. Of course, you would have a duty to make sure that the cell extractions were performed by a competent physician. I assume you would."

Diehl frowned. "Let me see if I understand. You're telling me I can just grab his kids off the street and haul them to a doctor and remove their cells? Whether they like it or not?"

"I am. Yes."

"And how," Rick Diehl said, "can that be legal?"

"Because they are walking around with cells that are legally yours, hence with stolen property. That's felony two. Under the law, if you witness a felony being committed, you are entitled to perform a citizen's arrest, and take the offender into custody. So if you were to see Burnet's children walking on the street, you could legally arrest them."

"Me, personally?"

"No, no," Rodriguez said. "In these circumstances one avails oneself of a trained professional—a fugitive-recovery agent."

"You mean a bounty hunter?"

"They don't like that term, and neither do we."

"All right. Do you know of a good fugitive-recovery agent?"

"We do," Rodriguez said.

"Then get him on the phone," Diehl said. "Right now."

CH053

Vasco Borden faced the mirror and reviewed his appearance with a professional eye, while he brushed mascara into the graying edges of his goatee. Vasco was a big man, six-feet-four and two-forty, all muscle, nine percent body fat. His shaved head and his trimmed, black goatee made him look like the devil. One big mother of a devil. He meant to appear intimidating, and he did.

He turned to the suitcase on the bed. In it he had neatly packed a set of coveralls with a Con Ed logo on the breast; a loud plaid sport coat; a sharp black Italian suit; a motorcycle jacket that read DIE IN HELL on the back; a velour tracksuit; a breakaway plaster leg cast; a short-barrel Mossberg 590 and two black Para .45s. For today, he was dressed in a tweed sport coat, casual slacks, and brown lace-up shoes.

Finally, he laid three photos out on the bed.

First, the guy, Frank Burnet. Fifty-one, fit, ex-Marine.

The guy's daughter, Alex, early thirties, a lawyer.

The guy's grandson, Jamie, now eight.

The old guy had vanished, and Vasco saw no reason to bother finding him. Burnet could be anywhere in the world—Mexico, Costa Rica, Australia. Much easier to get the cells directly from other family members.

He looked at the photo of the daughter, Alex. A lawyer—never good, as a target. Even if you handled them perfect, you still got sued. This gal was blond, looked to be in decent physical shape. Attractive enough, if you liked the type. She was too skinny for Vasco's taste. And she probably took some Israeli defense class on weekends. You never knew. Anyway, she spelled potential trouble.

That left the kid.

Jamie. Eight years old, second grade, local school. Vasco could get down there, pick him up, collect the samples, and be done with this whole thing by the afternoon. Which was fine with him. Vasco had a fifty-thousand-dollar completion bonus if he recovered in the first week. That declined to ten thousand after four weeks. So he had plenty of reason to get it over with.

Do the kid, he thought. Simple and to the point.

Dolly came in, the paper in her hand. Today she was wearing a navy blue suit, low shoes, white shirt. She had a brown leather briefcase. As usual, her bland looks enabled her to move about without attracting notice. "How does this look?" she said, and handed him the paper.

He scanned it quickly. It was a "To Whom It May Concern," signed by Alex Burnet. Allowing the bearer to pick up her son, Jamie, from school and take him to the family doctor for his exam.

"You called the doctor's office?" Vasco said.

"Yeah. Said Jamie had a fever and sore throat, and they said bring him in."

"So if the school calls the doctor . . ."

"We're covered."

"And you're sent from the mother's office?"

"Right."

"Got your card?"

She pulled out a business card, with the logo of the law firm.

"And if they call the mother?"

"Her cell number is listed on the paper, as you see."

"And that's Cindy?"

"Yes." Cindy was their office dispatcher, in Playa del Rey.

"Okay, let's get it done," Vasco said. He put his arm around her shoulder. "You going to be okay, doing this?"

"Sure, why not?"

"You know why not." Dolly had a weakness for kids. Whenever she looked in their eyes she melted. They'd had a fugitive in Canada, ran him down in Vancouver, the kid answered the door and Dolly asked if her father was home. The kid was a little girl about eight, she said no, not there. Dolly said okay and left. Meanwhile the guy was driving up the street, on his way home. His darling kid shut the door, went to the phone, called her old man, and told him to keep going. The kid was experienced. They'd been on the run since she was five. They never got close to the guy again.

"That was just one time," Dolly said.

"There's been more than one."

"Vasco," she said. "Everything's going to be fine today."

"Okay," he said. And he let her kiss him on the cheek.

Out in the driveway, the ambulance was parked, rear doors open. Vasco smelled cigarette smoke. He went around to the back. Nick was sitting there in a white lab coat, smoking.

"Jesus, Nick. What're you doing?"

"Just one," Nick said.

"Put it out," Vasco said. "We're heading off now. You got the stuff?"

"I do." Nick Ramsey was the doc they used on jobs when they needed a doc. He'd worked in emergency rooms until his drug-and-alcohol habit took over. He was out of rehab now, but steady employment was hard to come by.

"They want liver and spleen punch biopsies, and they want blood—"

"I read it. Fine-needle aspirations. I'm ready."

Vasco paused. "You been drinking, Nick?"

"No. Shit no."

"I smell something on your breath."

"No, no. Come on, Vasco, you know I wouldn't—"

"I got a good nose, Nick."

"No."

"Open your mouth." Vasco leaned forward and sniffed.

"I just had a taste is all," Nick said.

Vasco held out his hand. "Bottle."

Nick reached under the gurney, handed him a pint bottle of Jack Daniel's.

"That's great." Vasco moved close, got in his face. "Now listen to me," he said quietly. "You pull any more stunts today, and I'll personally throw you out the back of this ambulance onto the 405. You want to make a tragedy of your life, I'll see that it happens. You got me?"

"Yeah, Vasco."

"Good. I'm glad we have an understanding." He stepped back. "Hold out your hands."

"I'm fine—"

"Hold out your hands." Vasco never raised his voice in moments of tension. He lowered it. Make them listen. Make them worry. "Hold your hands out now, Nick."

Nick Ramsey held out his hands. They weren't shaking.

"Okay. Get in the car."

"I just—"

"Get in the car, Nick. I'm through talking."

Vasco got in the front with Dolly, and started driving. Dolly said, "He okay back there?"

"More or less."

"He won't hurt the kid, right?"

"Nah," Vasco said. "It's just a couple of needles. Few seconds is all."

"He better not hurt that kid."

"Hey," Vasco said. "Are you fine about this, or what?"

"Yeah, I'm fine."

"Okay then. Let's do it."

He drove down the road.

CH054

Brad Gordon had a bad feeling as he walked into the Border Café on Ventura Boulevard and looked at the booths. The place was a greasy spoon, filled with actors. A guy waved from a rear booth. Brad walked back to him.

The guy was wearing a light gray suit. He was short and balding and looked unsure of himself. His handshake was weak. "Willy Johnson," he said, "I'm your new attorney for the upcoming trial."

"I thought my uncle, Jack Watson, was providing the attorney."

"He is," Johnson said. "I'm he. Pederasty is my specialty."

"What's that mean?"

"Sex with a boy. But I have experience with any underage partner."

"I didn't have sex with anybody," Brad said. "Underage or not."

"I've reviewed your file and the police reports," Johnson said, pulling out a legal pad. "I think we have several avenues for your defense."

"What about the girl?"

"She is not available; she left the country. Her mother is ill in the Philippines. But I am told she will return for the trial."

"I thought there wasn't going to be a trial," Brad said. The waitress came over. He waved her away. "Why are we meeting here?"

"I have to be in court in Van Nuys at ten. I thought this would be convenient."

Brad looked around uneasily. "Place is full of people. Actors. They talk a lot."

"We won't discuss the details of the case," Johnson said. "But I want to lay out the structure of your defense. In your case, I am proposing a genetic defense."

"Genetic defense? What's that mean?"

"People with various genetic abnormalities find themselves helpless to suppress certain impulses," Johnson said. "That makes them, in technical terms, not guilty. We will be proposing that as the explanation in your case."

"What genetic disorder? I don't have any genetic disorder."

"Hey, it's not a bad thing," Johnson said. "Think of it as a type of diabetes. You're not responsible for it. You were born that way. In your case, you have an irresistible impulse to engage in sex with attractive young women." He smiled. "It's an impulse that's shared by about ninety percent of the adult male population."

"What kind of a fucking defense is that?" Brad Gordon said.

"A very effective one." Johnson shuffled through papers in a folder. "There have been several recent newspaper reports—"

"You mean to tell me," Brad said, "that there's a gene for sex with young girls?"

Johnson sighed. "I wish it were that simple. Unfortunately, no."

"Then what's the defense?"

"D4DR."

"Which is?"

"It's called the novelty gene. It's the gene that drives us to take risks, engage in thrill-seeking behavior. We will argue that the novelty gene inside your body drove you to risky behavior."

"Sounds like bullshit to me."

"Is it? Let's see. Ever jump out of an airplane?"

"Yeah, in the army. Hated it."

"Scuba diving?"

"Couple of times. Had a hot girlfriend who liked it."

"Mountain climbing?"

"Nope."

"Really? Didn't your high school class climb Mount Rainer?"

"Yeah, but that was—"

"You climbed a major American peak," Johnson said, nodding. "Driving sports cars fast?"

"Not really, no."

"You have five tickets for speeding in your Porsche in the last three years. Under California law, you have been at risk for losing your license all that time."

"Just normal speeding . . ."

"I think not. How about sex with the boss's girlfriend?"

"Well . . ."

"And sex with the boss's wife?"

"Just once, a couple of jobs back. But she was the one who came on to—"

"Those are risky sex partners, Mr. Gordon. Any jury would agree. How about unprotected sex? Venereal diseases?"

"Just a minute, here," Brad said, "I don't want to get into—"

"I'm sure you don't," Johnson said, "and that's not surprising, considering three cases of *pediculosis pubis*—crabs. Two episodes of gonorrhea, one of chlamydia, two episodes of condyloma—or genital warts—including . . . hmm, one near the anus. And that's just the last five years, according to the records of your doctor in Southern California."

"How'd you get those?"

Johnson shrugged. "Sky diving, scuba diving, mountain climbing, reckless driving, high-risk sex partners, unprotected sex. If that doesn't comprise a pattern of high-risk, thrill-seeking behavior, I don't know what does."

Brad Gordon was silent. He had to admit the little guy knew how to make a case. He'd never thought of his life that way before. Like when he was screwing the boss's wife, his uncle just gave him hell about it. Why, his uncle had said, did you make that kind of fucked-up decision? Keep it in your pants, jerkoff! Brad had had no answer at the time. Under his uncle's glare, his actions did seem pretty stupid. The broad wasn't even that good-looking. But now it seemed Brad had an answer to his uncle's question: He couldn't help it. It was his genetic inheritance that was controlling his behavior.

Johnson explained further, giving a lot of detail. According to him, Brad was at the mercy of this D4DR gene, which controlled the chemical levels in the brain. Something called dopamine was driving Brad to take risks, and to enjoy the experience, to crave it. Brain scans and other tests proved that people like Brad could not control the desire to take risks.

"It's the novelty gene," Johnson said, "and it has been named by the most important geneticist in America, Dr. Robert Bellarmino. Dr. Bellarmino is the biggest genetics researcher at the National Institutes of Health. He has a huge lab. He publishes fifty papers a year. No jury can ignore his research."

"Okay, so I have the gene. You really think this will work?"

"Yes, but I want to see some frosting on the cake, before we go to trial."

"Meaning what?"

"Before your trial, you're naturally worried, stressed."

"Yeah . . ."

"So I want you to take a trip, to take your mind off things. I want you to travel around the country, and I want you to take risks wherever you go."

Johnson laid it out: Speeding tickets, amusement parks, getting into fights, roller coasters, climbing expeditions in national parks—always making sure to get into an argument, a dispute about safety, a claim that equipment was faulty. Anything that would get his name recorded in a document that could later be used in trial.

"That's it," Johnson said. "Get going. I'll see you in a few weeks." He gave him a sheet of paper.

"What's this?"

"A list of the biggest roller coasters in the U.S. Make sure you visit the top three."

"Christ. Ohio . . . Indiana . . . Texas . . ."

"I don't want to hear it," Johnson said. "You're facing twenty years in prison, my friend, with some big guy with tattoos who's going to be giving you lots worse than anal warts. So do as I tell you. And leave town today."

Back in his apartment, in Sherman Oaks, he packed a bag. The thought of a big guy with tattoos preoccupied him for a moment. He wondered if he should take his pistol. Going cross-country, to crazy places like Ohio—who knew what he might come across. He put a box of ammo in his bag, and his pistol with the leg holster.

Heading for his car, Brad found that he felt better about everything. It was a sunny day, his Porsche was sparkling clean, and he had a plan.

Road trip!

CH055

lynn Kendall ran into the La Jolla school, arriving out of breath at the principal's office. "I got here as soon as I could," she said. "What's the problem?"

"It's David," the principal said. She was a woman of forty. "The child you are home-schooling. Your son Jamie brought him to school for the day."

"Yes, to see how he did . . ."

"And I am afraid he did not do well. On the playground, he bit another child."

"Oh dear."

"He very nearly drew blood."

"That's terrible."

"We see this in home-schooled children, Mrs. Kendall. They severely lack socialization skills and inner controls. There is no substitute for daily school environment with peers."

"I'm sorry this has happened . . ."

"You need to speak to him," the principal said. "He is in detention, in the next room."

Lynn went into a small room. It was filled with green metal filing cabinets, stacked high. Dave was on a wooden chair, looking very small and brown curled up in the seat.

"Dave. What happened?"

"He hurted Jamie," Dave said.

"Who did?"

"I don't know his name. He bees in six grade."

Lynn thought, sixth grade? Then it would have been a much bigger child.

"And what happened, Dave?"

"He push-ed Jamie on the ground. Hurted him."

"And what did you do?"

"I jump-ed on his back."

"Because you wanted to protect Jamie?"

Dave nodded.

"But you shouldn't bite, Dave."

"He bited me first."

"Did he? Where did he bite you?"

"Here." Dave held up a stubby, muscular finger. The skin was pale and thick. There might be bite marks, but she couldn't be sure.

"Did you tell the principal?"

"She's not with my mother." That, Lynn knew, was Dave's way of saying the principal didn't like him. Young chimps inhabited a matriarchal society where the allegiances of females were very important and constantly tracked.

"Did you show her the finger?"

Dave shook his head. No.

"I'll speak to her," Lynn said.

"That's his story, is it?" the principal said. "Well, I'm not surprised. He jumped on the child's back. What did he expect would happen?"

"Then the other child did bite first?"

"Biting is not allowed, Mrs. Kendall."

"Did the other child bite him?"

"He says no."

"Is the child in sixth grade?"

"Yes. In Miss Fromkin's class."

"I'd like to speak to him," Lynn said.

"We can't permit that," the principal said. "He's not your child."

"But he's accused Dave. And the situation is very serious. If I am going to deal correctly with Dave, I need to know what happened between them."

"I've told you what happened."

"You saw it happen?"

"No, but it was reported by Mr. Arthur, the playground supervisor. He is very accurate in the matter of disputes, I can assure you. The point is, we don't allow biting, Mrs. Kendall."

Lynn was feeling an invisible hand pressing on her. The conversation had a distinct uphill quality. "Perhaps I should talk with my son Jamie," Lynn said.

"Jamie's story will agree with David's, I'm sure. The point is, Mr. Arthur says that it didn't happen that way."

"The bigger boy didn't attack Jamie first?"

The principal stiffened. "Mrs. Kendall," she said, "in cases of disciplinary disputes, we can refer to a security camera on the playground. We can go to that if we need to—now or later. But I would encourage you to stay with the issue of the biting. Which is David. However uncomfortable that may be."

"I see," Lynn said. The situation was clear. "All right, I will deal with Dave, when he comes home from school."

"I think you should take him with you."

"I would prefer he finish the day," she said, "and walk home with Jamie."

"I don't think—"

"Dave has a problem integrating in the classroom, as you explained," Lynn said. "I don't think we help his integration if we pull him out of class now. I will deal with him when he comes home."

The principal nodded reluctantly. "Well . . ."

"I will speak to him now," Lynn said, "and tell him he'll stay here for the rest of the day."

CH056

Alex Burnet jumped out of the cab and ran toward the school. When she saw the ambulance, her heart began to pound.

A few minutes before, she had been with a client—who was sobbing—when the receptionist buzzed to say that Jamie's teacher had called. Something about a doctor's visit for her son. The story was garbled, but Alex didn't wait. She handed the client a box of Kleenex and ran. She'd jumped in a cab downstairs and told the guy to run stoplights.

The ambulance was at the curb, doors open, a white-coated doctor waiting in the back—she wanted to scream. She had never felt like this before. The world was greenish-white; she was sick with fear. She ran past the ambulance and into the school courtyard. The mother at the front desk said, "Can I help—" but Alex knew where Jamie's classroom was, on the ground floor, at the rear courtyard. She headed straight toward it.

Her cell phone rang. It was Jamie's teacher, Miss Holloway. "That woman is waiting outside the class," she whispered. "She gave me a letter with your phone number on it, but I didn't trust that. I used the number we had on your school file and called that . . ."

"Good work," Alex said. "I'm almost there."

"She's outside."

Alex came around the corner and saw a woman in a blue suit, standing outside the classroom. Alex went right up to her. "And who the hell are you?"

The woman smiled calmly, held out her hand. "Hi, Ms. Burnet. Casey Rogers, I'm sorry you had to come all this way."

She was so easy, so relaxed, Alex was disarmed. She put her hands on her hips, breathing deeply, catching her breath. "What seems to be the problem, Casey?"

"There isn't any problem, Ms. Burnet."

"You work in my office?"

"Gosh no. I work in Dr. Hughes's office. Dr. Hughes wanted me to pick up Jamie and bring him in for his tetanus shot. It's not an emergency, but it does need to be done. He cut his ankle a week ago, isn't that right?"

"No . . ."

"No? Well, I can't imagine . . . Do you suppose I was sent for the wrong child? Let me call Dr. Hughes . . ." She took out her cell phone.

"Yes, do that."

Inside the classroom, the kids were looking at them through the glass. She waved to Jamie, who smiled back.

"Perhaps we should move away," Casey Rogers said. "Not disrupt them." Then into the phone: "Dr. Hughes, please. Yes. It's Casey."

Together, they walked back toward the school entrance. Through the entry arch, Alex saw the ambulance. Alex said, "Did you bring an ambulance?"

"Gosh, no. I have no idea why it's here." She pointed to the windshield. "Looks like the driver is eating lunch."

Through the windshield, Alex saw a burly man with a black goatee munching on a submarine sandwich. Had he stopped by the school just to eat lunch? Something about that didn't seem right. She couldn't put her finger on it.

"Dr. Hughes? It's Casey. Yes, I'm with Ms. Burnet right now, and she says her son Jamie did not cut his foot."

"He did not," Alex repeated. They walked through the arch and outside, moving closer to the ambulance. The driver put his sandwich on the dashboard and opened the door on the driver's side. He was getting out.

"Yes, Dr. Hughes," Casey said, "we're leaving the school right now." She held the phone out to Alex. "Would you like to speak to Dr. Hughes?"

"Yes," Alex said. As she put the phone to her ear, she heard a piercing electronic shriek—it disoriented her—she dropped the phone as Casey Rogers grabbed her elbows and yanked her arms back. The driver was coming around the front of the ambulance toward her.

"We don't need the kid," the driver said. "She'll do fine."

It took a moment before she put it together: they were kidnapping her. What happened next was instinct. She slammed her head straight back, hitting Casey in the nose. Casey screamed and let go. Blood gushed down from her nose. Alex grabbed Casey's arm and swung her forward, throwing her at the big man. He sidestepped gracefully as Casey hit the concrete and rolled, howling in pain.

Alex fumbled in her pocket. "Get back," she warned him.

"We're not going to hurt you, Ms. Burnet," the man said. He was a good head and a half taller than she, and big, muscular. Just as he reached for her, she got her finger on the button and sprayed pepper in his face.

"Shit! Goddamn it!" He threw his arm up to protect his eyes, and half turned away from her. She knew that was her one chance—she kicked up, fast and hard, hitting him in the throat with her high heel. He yelled in agony, and she fell backward on the sidewalk, unable to keep her balance. She scrambled back to her feet immediately. The woman was getting to her feet, her blood pouring onto the sidewalk. She ignored Alex and went to comfort the big man, who was leaning against the ambulance, bent over, clutching his throat, moaning in pain.

Alex heard distant sirens—someone had called the police—and now the woman was helping the big man into the ambulance, putting him in the passenger seat. It was happening fast. Alex started to worry that these two would get away before the cops showed up. But there wasn't much she could do. As the woman climbed into the ambulance she screamed at Alex, "We'll arrest you yet!"

"You'll what?" Alex said. The unreality of this whole incident was starting to hit her. *"You'll what?"*

"We'll be back, bitch!" the woman screamed, starting the engine. "You won't get away!" The red flasher came on with the siren. She put the ambulance in gear.

"For what?" Alex yelled again. All she could think was that this entire business had been some dreadful mistake. But Vern Hughes *was* her doctor. They had used her correct name. They had come for Jamie . . .

No. It was not a mistake.

"We'll arrest you yet!"

What could that mean? She turned, and hurried back into the school. Her one thought now was Jamie.

It was snack time. The kids were all sitting at their tables, eating pieces of cut fruit. Some had yogurt. They were quite noisy. Miss Holloway gave her the paper the woman had brought. It appeared to be a Xerox of stationery from Alex's law firm, signed by her. It wasn't a note from the doctor's office.

That meant that the woman in the blue suit was a cool operator. When caught, she instantly changed her story. Smiling, shaking hands with Alex. Smoothly finding an excuse for the two of them to walk back outside . . . Offering her the phone so that when she took it . . .

We don't need the kid, she'll do fine.

They had come to kidnap Jamie. But they were ready to kidnap her, instead. Why? Ransom? She had no money to speak of. Was it some lawsuit she was involved in? She'd had dangerous lawsuits in the past, but there wasn't anything pending at the moment.

She'll do fine.

Either her son or her.

Miss Holloway said, "Is there anything I should know? Or the school should know?"

"No," Alex said. "But I'm going to take Jamie home."

"They've almost finished their snack."

Alex nodded to Jamie, waved for him to come over. He came reluctantly.

"What is it, Mom?" he said.

"We need to go."

"I want to stay here."

Alex sighed. Contrary as ever. "Jamie . . ." she began.

"I missed a lot 'cause I was sick. Ask Miss Holloway. And I didn't get to see my friends. I want to stay. And we have hot dogs for lunch."

"I'm sorry," she said. "Go to your cubby and get your stuff. We have to leave."

In front of the school, two police cars and four police officers were examining the pavement. One of them said, "Are you Ms. Burnet?"

"Yes, I am."

"We have a report from a woman in the principal's office who saw the whole thing," the policeman said, pointing to a nearby window. "But there's a lot of blood here, Ms. Burnet."

"Yes, the woman hurt her nose when she fell."

"Are you divorced, Ms. Burnet?"

"Yes, I am."

"For how long?"

"Five years."

"So it is not recent."

"Not at all."

"Your relations with your ex . . ."

"Very cordial."

She talked to the police for a few minutes more, while Jamie waited impatiently. The police seemed to Alex to be oddly reluctant to become involved; they were detached, and seemed to feel they had come upon a private matter, like a domestic dispute.

"Are you filing a complaint?"

"I would," Alex said, "but I have to take my son home now."

"We can give you the paperwork to take home."

"That will be fine," she said.

One of the cops gave her a business card and said to call if there was anything further she needed. She said she would. Then she and Jamie started home.

Out on the street, the world around her suddenly seemed entirely different. Nothing could be more cheerfully bland than the sunlight of Beverly Hills. But now, Alex saw only menace.

She didn't know where that menace was coming from, or why. She held Jamie's hand. "Are we *walking* home?" he said, sighing.

"Yes, we're walking." But even as he asked, she started to wonder. They lived only a few blocks from the school. But was it safe to go home? Would those people with the ambulance be waiting? Or would they hide themselves better the next time?

"It's too far to walk." Jamie trudged along. "And too hot."

"We're walking. And that's all there is to it." As they walked, she flipped open her cell and dialed the office. Her assistant, Amy, answered.

"Listen, I want you to check recent county filings. Find out if my name comes up as a defendant anywhere."

"Is there something I need to know?" Amy asked, laughing. But it was a nervous laugh. Wrongdoing by an attorney might land their assistants in jail. It had happened a couple of times recently.

"No," Alex said. "But I think I have bounty hunters chasing me."

"You jump bail anywhere?"

"No," Alex said. "That's the point. I don't know what these people think they are doing."

The assistant said she would check. Jamie, walking alongside Alex, said, "What's a bowie hunter? Why is she chasing you, Mom?"

"I'm trying to find out, Jamie. I think it's a mistake."

"Were they trying to *hurt* you?"

"No, no. Nothing like that." There was no reason to make him worry.

The assistant called back.

"Okay, you do have a complaint, all right. In Superior Court, Ventura County."

NEXT   271

That was a good hour from Los Angeles, up past Oxnard. "What's the complaint?"

"It was filed by BioGen Research Incorporated of Westview Village. I can't read the complaint online. But you're showing up as a failure to appear."

"Appear when?"

"Yesterday."

"Was I served?"

"Indicates you were."

"I wasn't," Alex said.

"Shows you were."

"So, is there a contempt citation? A warrant for my arrest?"

"Nothing's showing. But the online lags up to a day, so there might be."

Alex flipped the phone shut.

Jamie said, "Are you going to be arrested?"

"No, honey. I'm not."

"Then can I go back to school after lunch?"

"We'll see."

Her apartment building, on the north side of Roxbury Park, looked quiet in the midday sun. Alex stood on the other side of the park and watched for a while.

"Why are we waiting?" Jamie said.

"Just for a minute."

"It's been a minute already."

"No, it hasn't."

She was watching the man in coveralls, going around the side of the house. He looked like the meter reader for the utility company. Except that he was big, with a bad wig and a trimmed black goatee that she had seen somewhere before. And the meter readers never came to the front. They always entered from the back alley.

She was thinking that if this guy was a bounty hunter, he had the right to enter her property without warning and without a warrant.

He could break down the door, if he wanted to. He had the right to search her apartment, to go through her things, to take her computer and inspect the hard drive. He could do whatever he wanted to do to apprehend a fugitive. But she wasn't a—

"Can we go in, Mom?" Jamie whined. "Please?"

Her son was right about one thing. They couldn't just stand there. There was a sandbox in the middle of the park, several kids, maids, and mothers sitting around.

"Let's go play in the sandbox."

"I don't want to."

"Yes."

"It's for babies."

"Just for a while, James."

He stamped his foot, and sat down on the edge of the sandbox. He kicked sand irritably while Alex dialed her assistant.

"Amy, I am wondering about BioGen, the company that bought my father's cell line. We don't have any motions pending, do we?"

"No. California Supreme Court is a year from now."

So what's going on? she wondered. What kind of suit was BioGen bringing now? "Call the judge's clerk up in Ventura. Find out what this is about."

"Okay."

"Have we heard from my father?"

"Not for a while."

"Okay." It actually wasn't okay, because she was now having the strong feeling that all this had to do with her father. Or at least with her father's cells. The bounty hunters had brought an ambulance—with a doctor in the back—because they were going to take a sample, or do some surgical procedure. Long needles. She'd seen sunlight glint on long needles wrapped in plastic, as the doctor at the back of the ambulance shuffled things about.

Then it hit her: *They wanted to take their cells.*

They wanted cells from her, or from her son. She couldn't imagine why. But they clearly felt entitled to take them. Should she call the police? Not yet, she decided. If there were a warrant for her failure to appear, they'd simply take her into custody. And then what would she do about Jamie? She shook her head.

Right now, she needed time to figure out what was going on. Time to get everything straightened out. What was she supposed to do? She wanted to call her father, but he hadn't been answering for days. If these guys knew where she lived, they would know what kind of car she had, and—

"Amy," she said, "how'd you like to drive my car for a couple of days?"

"The BMW? Sure. But—"

"And I'll drive yours," Alex said. "But you need to bring it over to me. Stop that, Jamie. Stop kicking sand."

"Are you sure? It's a Toyota with a bunch of dents."

"Actually, that sounds perfect. Come to the southwest side of Roxbury Park, and pull over in front of a white Spanish apartment building with wrought-iron gates in front."

Alex was unprepared by temperament and training for the situation in which she now found herself. All her life had been spent in the sunlight. She obeyed the rules. She was an officer of the court. She played the game. She didn't run yellow lights; she didn't park in the red; she didn't cheat on her taxes. At the firm, she was regarded as by-the-book, stodgy. She told clients, "Rules are made to be followed, not twisted." And she meant it.

Five years earlier, when she discovered her husband was screwing around on her, she threw him out within an hour of learning the truth. She packed his bag and put it outside the door, and had the locks changed. When he came back from his "fishing trip," she spoke through the door and told him to get lost. Matt was actually screwing one of her best friends—that was Matt's way—and she never again spoke to that woman.

Of course, Jamie had to see his father, and she made sure that happened. She delivered her son to Matt at the appointed time, on the dot. Not that he ever returned her son on time. But it was Alex's view that the world stabilized one person at a time. If she did her part, she felt eventually others might do theirs.

At work she was called idealistic, impractical, unrealistic. She responded that in lawyer-speak, *realistic* was another word for *dishonest*. She stuck to her guns.

But it was true that sometimes she felt she limited herself to the kinds of cases that did not challenge her illusions. The head of the firm, Robert A. Koch, had said as much. "You're like a conscientious objector, Alex. You let other people do the fighting. But sometimes we have to fight. Sometimes, we can't avoid conflict."

Koch was an ex-Marine, like her father. Same kind of rough-and-tumble talk. Proud of it. She'd always shrugged it off. Now she wasn't shrugging anything off. She didn't know what was going on, but she felt pretty sure she couldn't just talk her way out of it.

She was also sure nobody was going to stick a needle into her, or her son. To prevent that, she would do whatever had to be done.

Whatever had to be done.

She replayed in her mind the incident at the school. She hadn't had a gun. She didn't own a gun. But she wished she had had one. She thought, *If they were trying to do something to my son, could I have killed them?*

And she thought, *Yes. I could have killed them.*

And she knew it was true.

A white Toyota Highlander with a battered front bumper pulled up. She saw Amy sitting in the car. Alex said, "Jamie? Let's go."

"Finally!"

He started toward their apartment, but she steered him in another direction.

"Where're we going?"

"We're taking a little trip," she said.

"Where?" He was suspicious. "I don't want to take a trip."

Without hesitation, she said, "I'll buy you a PSP." She had steadfastly refused for a year to buy him one of those electronic game things. But now she was just saying whatever came to mind.

"For real? Hey, thanks!" More frowns. "But which games? I want Tony Hawk Three, and I want Shrek—"

"Whatever you want," she said. "Let's just get in the car. We're going to drive Amy back to work."

"And then? Where are we going then?"

"Legoland," she said.

The first thing that came into her mind.

Driving back to the office, Amy said, "I brought your father's package. I thought you might want it."

"What package?'

"It came to the office last week. You never opened it. You were at trial with the Mick Crowley rape case. You remember, that political reporter who likes little boys."

It was a small FedEx box. Alex tore it open, dumped the contents on her lap.

A cheap cellular phone, the kind you bought and put a card in.

Two prepaid telephone cards.

A tinfoil-wrapped packet of cash: five thousand in hundred-dollar bills.

And a cryptic note: "In Case of Trouble. Don't use your credit cards. Turn off your cell phone. Don't tell anyone where you are going. Borrow somebody's car. Page me when you are in a motel. Keep Jamie with you."

Alex sighed. "That son of a bitch."

"What is it?"

"Sometimes my father annoys me," she said. Amy didn't need to hear details. "Listen, today's Thursday. Why don't you take a long weekend?"

"That's what my boyfriend wants to do," she said. "He wants to go to Pebble Beach and watch the old car parade."

"That's a great idea," Alex said. "Take my car."

"Really? I don't know . . . what if something happened to it? I got in an accident or something."

"Don't worry about it," Alex said. "Just take the car."

Amy frowned. There was a long silence. "Is it safe?"

"Of course it's safe."

"I don't know what you're involved in," she said.

"It's nothing. It's a mistaken-identity thing. It'll be worked out by Monday, I promise you. Bring the car back Sunday night, and I'll see you in the office Monday."

"For sure?"

"Absolutely."

Amy said, "Can my boyfriend drive?"

"Absolutely."

CH057

Georgia Bellarmino would never have known, if it hadn't been for the cereal box.

Georgia was on the phone with a client in New York, an investment banker who had just gotten a DOE appointment; they were talking about the house he was buying for his family move to Rockville, Maryland. Georgia, who was Best-Selling Realtor of the Year in Rockville for three years running, was busy going over the terms of the purchase when her sixteen-year-old daughter, Jennifer, called from the kitchen, "Mom, I'm late for school. Where's the cereal?"

"On the kitchen table."

"No, it's not."

"Look again."

"Mom, it's empty! Jimmy must have eaten it."

Mrs. Bellarmino covered the phone with her hand. "Then get another box, Jen," she said. "You're sixteen; you're not helpless."

"Where is it?" Jennifer said.

Banging doors in the kitchen.

"Look above the oven," Mrs. Bellarmino said.

"I did. It's not there."

Mrs. Bellarmino told the client she'd call back, and walked into the kitchen. Her daughter was wearing low-cut jeans and a sheer top that looked like something a hooker would wear to work. These days, even junior high girls dressed that way. She sighed.

"Look above the oven, Jen."

"I told you. I did."

"Look again."

"Mom, will you just get it for me? I'm late."

Mrs. Bellarmino stood firm. "Above the oven."

Jennifer reached up, opening the doors, stretching for the cereal box, which was right there, of course. But Mrs. Bellarmino was not looking at the box. She was looking at her daughter's exposed stomach.

"Jen . . . you have those bruises again."

Her daughter brought the box down, tugged at her top, covering her belly. "It's nothing."

"You had them the other day, too."

"Mom, I'm late." She was walking to the table, sitting down.

"Jennifer. *Show me.*"

With an exasperated sigh, her daughter stood and lifted her top, exposing her abdomen. Mrs. Bellarmino saw an inch-long horizontal bruise just above the bikini line. And another one, fainter, on the other side of the belly.

"It's nothing, Mom. I just keep banging into the edge of the desk."

"But you shouldn't bruise . . ."

"It's nothing."

"Are you taking your vitamins?"

"Mom? Can I please just eat?"

"You know you can tell me anything, you know that—"

"Mom, you're making me late for school! I have a French test!"

There was no point in pushing her now. In any case, the phone had started ringing—no doubt the New York client telephoning back. Clients were impatient. They expected realtors to be available every minute of the day. She went into the other room to take the call and opened her documents to review the numbers.

Five minutes later, her daughter yelled, "Bye, Mom!" and Georgia heard the front door slam.

It left her distinctly uneasy.

She just had a *feeling*. She dialed her husband's lab in Bethesda. For once Rob was not in meetings, and she was put right through. She told him the story.

"What do you think we should do?" she asked.

"Search her room," he said promptly. "We have an obligation."

"Okay," she said. "I'll call the office and tell them I'll be late."

"I'm flying later," he said, "but let me know."

CH058

Barton **Williams's** Boeing 737 rolled to a stop at the Hopkins private terminal in Cleveland, Ohio, and the whine of the engines wound down. The interior of the aircraft was luxuriously appointed. There were two bedrooms, two full baths with showers, and a dining room seating eight. But the master bedroom, which took up the entire rear third of the plane, with a king-size bed and a fur throw and mood lighting, was where Barton spent most of the flight. He needed only one flight attendant, but he invariably flew with three. He liked company. He liked laughter and chatter. He liked young, smooth flesh on the fur, with the mood lighting low, warm, reddish, sensual. And, hell, forty thousand feet up in the air was the only place he could be sure he was safe from the wife.

The thought of the wife dampened his mood. He looked at the parrot standing on the perch in the living room of the plane. The parrot said, "You kidnapped me."

"What's your name again?" Barton said.

"Riley. Doghouse Riley." Speaking in a funny voice.

"Don't be smart with me."

"My name is Gerard."

"That's right. Gerard. I don't much like it. Sounds foreign. How about Jerry? That suit you?"

"No," the parrot said. "It doesn't."

"Why not?"

"It's stupid. It's a stupid idea."

There was an uncomfortable silence. "Is it really?" Barton Williams said, with a hint of menace in his voice. Williams knew this was a mere animal, but he was not accustomed to being called stupid—especially by a bird—and no one had done so in many, many years. He felt his enthusiasm for this gift cooling.

"Jerry," he said, "you better be getting along with me, because I own you now."

"People can't be owned."

"And you ain't people, Jerry. You're a damn bird." Barton stepped close to the perch. "Now, let me tell you how it's going to be. I'm going to give you to my wife, and I want you to behave, I want you to be amusing, I want you to compliment and flatter her and make her feel good. Is that clear?"

"Everyone else does," Gerard said. He was mimicking the voice of the pilot, who heard it from the cockpit and snapped his head around to look back. "Jesus, I get sick of the old fart sometimes," Gerard continued.

Barton Williams frowned.

Next he heard a precise imitation of the sound of jet engines in flight, and superimposed on that, a girl's voice, one of the flight attendants: "Jenny, are you going to blow him or am I?"

"Your turn."

Sigh. "Oh-kay . . ."

"Don't forget to take him his drink."

Click of a door opening and closing.

Barton Williams began to turn red. The bird continued:

"Oh, Barton! Oh, give it to me! Oh, you're so big! Oh Barton! Yes, baby. Yes, big boy! Ooh I love it! So big, so big, aaaaaah!"

Barton Williams stared at the bird. "I believe," he said, "that you will not be a welcome addition to my household."

"You're the reason our kids are ugly, little darlin'," Gerard said.

"That's enough from you," Barton said, turning away.

"Oh Barton! Oh, give it to me! Oh, you're so big! Oh—"

Barton Williams threw the cover over the bird's cage.

"Jenny, honey, you've got family in Dayton, don't you?"

"Yes, Mr. Williams."

"You think anybody in your family would enjoy a talking bird?"

"Uh, well, actually—yes, Mr. Williams, I'm sure they would love it."

"Good, good. I would appreciate it if you delivered him down there today."

"Of course, Mr. Williams."

"And if by some chance," he said, "your family is not appreciative of feathered companions, just have them tie very heavy weights to his legs and drop him in the river. Because I never want to see this bird again."

"Yes, Mr. Williams."

"I heard that," said the bird.

"Good," Barton Williams said.

After the old man's limousine had gone, Jenny stood on the tarmac holding the covered cage. "What am I going to do with this thing?" she said. "My daddy hates birds. He shoots 'em."

"Take him to a pet store," the pilot said. "Or give him to somebody who'll ship him to Utah, or Mexico, or someplace like that."

Refreshing Paws was an upscale store in Shaker Heights. There were mostly puppies in the store. The young guy behind the counter was cute, maybe a little younger than Jenny was. He had a good body. She walked in carrying Gerard in his covered cage. "You got any parrots?"

"No. We just have dogs." He smiled at her. "What've you got there? I'm Stan." His name tag said STAN MILGRAM.

"Hi, Stan. I'm Jenny. And this is Gerard. He's an African grey."

"Let's have a look at him," Stan said. "You want to sell him, or what?"

"Or give him away."

"Why? What's the matter?"

"Owner doesn't like him."

Jenny whipped off the cover. Gerard blinked, flapped his feathers. "I've been kidnapped," he said.

"Hey," Stan said, "he talks pretty good."

"Oh, he's a good talker," Jenny said.

"Oh, he's a good talker," Gerard said, mimicking her voice. Then: "Stop patronizing me."

Stan frowned. "What's he mean?"

"I am surrounded by fools," Gerard said.

"He just talks a lot," Jenny said, shrugging.

"Is there anything wrong with him?"

"No, nothing."

Gerard turned to Stan. "I told you," he said, emphatically. "I've been kidnapped. She is involved. She is one of the kidnappers."

"Is he stolen?" Stan asked.

"Not stolen," Gerard said. *"Kidnapped."*

"What kind of accent is that?" Stan asked. He was smiling at Jenny. She turned sideways, to show him her breasts in profile.

"French."

"He sounds British."

"He came from France, is all I know."

"Ooh la la," Gerard said. "Will you please listen to me?"

"He thinks he's a person," Jenny said.

"I *am* a person, you little twit," Gerard said. "And if you want to hump this guy, go on and do it. Just don't make me wait around while you wiggle your assets in front of him."

Jenny turned red. The kid looked away, then smiled back at her.

"He's got a mouth on him," Jenny said, still blushing.

"Does he ever swear?"

"I never heard him do that, no."

"'Cause I know someone who might like him," Stan said, "as long as he doesn't swear."

"What do you mean, someone?"

"My aunt, out in California. She's in Mission Viejo. That's Orange County. She's widowed, lives alone. She likes animals, and she's lonely."

"Oh, okay. That could be okay."

"You are *giving me away*?" Gerard said, in a horrified tone. "This is *slavery*! I am not something you *give away*."

"I have to drive out there," Stan Milgram said, "in a couple of days. I could take him with me. I know she'd like him. But, uh, what're you doing later tonight?"

"I could be free," Jenny said.

CH059

The warehouse was located near the airport in Medan. It had a skylight, so the lighting in the room was good, and the young orang in the cage appeared healthy enough, bright-eyed and alert. He seemed to have recovered completely from the darts.

But Gorevitch paced back and forth, intensely frustrated, glancing at his watch. On the table nearby, his video camera lay on its side, the case cracked, muddy water draining out of it. Gorevitch would have taken it apart to dry it, but he lacked the tools. He lacked . . . he lacked . . .

Off to one side, Zanger, the network representative, said, "What are you going to do now?"

"We're waiting for another bloody camera," Gorevitch said. He turned to the DHL rep, a young Malay man in a bright yellow uniform. "How much longer now?"

"They said within the hour, sir."

Gorevitch snorted. "They said that two hours ago."

"Yes, sir. But the plane has left Bekasi and is on its way to us."

Bekasi was on the north coast of Java. Eight hundred miles away. "And the camera is on the plane?"

"I believe so, yes."

Gorevitch paced, avoiding Zanger's accusatory stare. It was all a comedy of errors. In the jungle, Gorevitch had worked to resuscitate the ape for almost an hour before the animal showed signs of life. Then he had struggled to bind the animal and tranquilize it again—not too much this time—and then monitor the animal with care, to prevent the creature from going into adrenaline shock while Gorevitch brought him north to Medan, the nearest big town with an airport.

The orang survived the journey without incident, ending up in the warehouse, where he cursed like a Dutch sailor. Gorevitch notified Zanger, who immediately flew in from New York.

But by the time Zanger arrived, the ape had developed laryngitis, and no longer spoke, except for a raspy whisper.

"What the hell good is that?" Zanger said. "You can't hear him."

"It won't matter," Gorevitch said. "We'll tape him and then dub in his voice later. You know, lip-synch him."

"You'll dub in his voice?"

"Nobody will know."

"Are you out of your mind? *Everybody* will know. Every lab in the world will go over this video with sophisticated equipment. They'll spot a dub in five minutes."

"All right," Gorevitch said, "then we'll wait until he gets better."

Zanger didn't like that, either. "He sounds quite ill. Did he catch a cold somewhere?"

"Possible," Gorevitch said. In fact, he was almost certain the ape had caught his own cold, during the mouth-to-mouth resuscitation. It was a mild cold for Gorevitch, but appeared to be serious for the orang, who was now bent over in spasms of coughing.

"He needs a vet."

"Can't," Gorevitch said. "He's a protected animal, and we stole him, remember?"

"*You* stole him," Zanger said. "And if you're not careful, you'll kill him as well."

"He's young. He'll recover."

And, indeed, the following day, the ape was talking again, but coughing spasmodically and spitting up ugly, yellow-green gobs. Gorevitch decided he'd better film the animal now, so he went to get his equipment from the car, stumbled, and dropped the camera in a muddy ditch. Cracked the case open. All this not ten feet from the warehouse door.

And of course in the entire city of Medan, they did not seem to be able to lay their hands on a decent video camera. So they had had to fly one in from Java. They were waiting for the camera now, while the ape swore and hacked and coughed and spat at them from inside his cage.

Zanger stood just out of range, shaking his head. "Christ, what a cock-up."

And once again Gorevitch turned to the Malay kid and said, "How much longer?" The kid just shook his head and shrugged.

And inside the cage, the orang coughed and swore.

Georgia Bellarmino opened the door to her daughter's bedroom and began a swift examination. The room was a mess, of course. Crumbs in the creases of the rumpled bedcovers, scratched CDs on the floor, knocked-over Coke cans beneath the bed, along with a dirty hairbrush, a curling iron, and an empty tube of self-tanner. Georgia pulled open the drawers of the bedside table, revealing a clutter of chewing-gum wrappers, balled-up underwear, breath mints, mascara, photos from last year's prom, matches, a calculator, dirty socks, old issues of *Teen Vogue* and *People. And a pack of cigarettes, which didn't make her happy.*

Then to the dresser drawers, riffling through them quickly, feeling all the way to the back; then the closet, which took her quite a while. A jumble of shoes and sneakers at the bottom. The cabinet under the bathroom sink, and even the dirty clothes hamper.

She found nothing to explain the bruises.

Of course, she thought, there was hardly any purpose to putting a hamper in the room, since Jennifer just dropped her clothes all over the bathroom floor. Georgia Bellarmino bent over and picked them up, not really thinking about it. That was when she noticed the streaks on the tile floor of the bathroom. Rubber streaks. Faint. In parallel.

She knew what had caused those streaks: a stepladder.

Looking up at the ceiling she saw a panel that provided an entrance to the attic. There were smudged fingerprints on that panel.

Georgia went to get a stepladder.

She pushed the panel aside, and needles and syringes tumbled out, clattering onto the floor.

Dear God, she thought. She reached up into the attic space, feeling around. Her hand touched a stack of cardboard tubes, like toothpaste. She brought them out; they all bore medical labels: LUPRON, GONAL-F, FOLLESTIM.

Fertility drugs.

What was her daughter doing?

She decided not to call her husband; he would get too upset. Instead, she took out her cell phone and dialed the school.

CH061

I n the Chicago offices of Dr. Martin Bennett, the intercom was buzzing, but Dr. Bennett paid no attention.

The biopsy report was worse than he had expected, much worse. He ran his fingers along the edge of the paper, wondering how he would tell his patient.

Martin Bennett was fifty-five; he had been a practicing internist for nearly a third of a century, and had delivered bad news to many patients in his day. But it never got easier. Especially if they were young, with young children. He glanced at the pictures of his sons on his desk. They were both in college now. Tad was a senior at Stanford; Bill was at Columbia. And Bill was premed.

A knock on the door and his nurse, Beverly, stuck her head in. "I'm sorry, Dr. Bennett, but you weren't answering the intercom. And I thought it was important."

"I know. I was just . . . trying to think how to put it." He stood up behind the desk. "I'll see Andrea now."

Beverly shook her head. "Andrea hasn't arrived," she said. "I'm talking about the other woman."

"What other woman?"

Beverly slipped into the office and closed the door behind her. She lowered her voice. "Your daughter," she said.

"What are you talking about? I don't have a daughter."

"Well, there's a young woman in the waiting room who says she's your daughter."

"That's impossible," Bennett said. "Who is she?"

Beverly glanced at a note card. "Her name is Murphy. She lives in Seattle. Her mother works at the university. She's about twenty-eight and she has a toddler with her, maybe a year and a half. Little girl."

"Murphy? Seattle?" Bennett was thinking back. "Twenty-eight, you say? No, no. Impossible." He had had his share of affairs in college, and even in medical school. But he'd married Emily almost thirty years ago, and since then the only times he had been unfaithful had been at medical conferences. True, that was at least twice a year, in Cancún, in Switzerland, somewhere exotic. But he'd only started that about ten, fifteen years ago. He just didn't think it was possible he'd have a child that old.

Beverly said, "I guess you never know for sure . . . Will you see her?"

"No."

"I'll tell her," Beverly said. She dropped her voice to a whisper. "But we don't want her making a scene in front of the patients. She seems like she might be a little, uh, unstable. And if she's not your daughter, maybe you should set her straight in private."

Bennett nodded slowly. He dropped back into his chair. "Okay," he said. "Show her in."

"Big surprise, huh?" The woman standing in the doorway, bouncing a child in her arms, was an unattractive blonde of medium height, wearing jeans and a T-shirt, grunge clothes. Her baby's face was dirty, dripping snot. "Sorry I didn't dress for the occasion, but you know how it is."

Bennett stood behind his desk. "Please come in, Miss, uh . . ."

"Murphy. Elizabeth Murphy." She nodded to the baby. "This is Bess."

"I'm Dr. Bennett." He waved her to the seat on the other side of the desk. He looked at her closely as she sat down. He saw no resemblance at all, not the slightest. He, himself, was dark-haired, fair-skinned, slightly overweight. She was olive-complexioned, rail-thin, brittle, tense.

"Yeah, I know," she said. "You're thinking I don't look anything like you. But with my natural hair color, and more weight, you can see the family thing."

"I'm sorry," Bennett said, sitting down, "but to be frank, I don't see it."

"That's okay," she said, shrugging. "I figure it must be a shock to you. My showing up at your office like this."

"It's certainly a surprise."

"I wanted to call ahead and warn you, but then I decided I should just come. In case you refused to see me."

"I see. Miss Murphy, what makes you believe you are my daughter?"

"Oh, I'm yours, all right. There's no question about it." She was speaking with an uncanny confidence.

Bennett said, "Your mother says she knows me?"

"No."

"Ever met me?"

"God, no."

He gave a sigh of relief. "Then I'm afraid I don't understand—"

"I'll come right to the point. You did your residency in Dallas. At Southern Memorial."

He frowned. "Yes . . ."

"All the residents had their blood typed, in case they were needed as emergency blood donors."

"That was a long time ago." He was thinking back. About thirty years, now.

"Yeah, well. They kept the blood, Dad."

Again, he heard that conviction in her voice. "Meaning what?"

She shifted in her seat. "You want to hold your granddaughter?"

"Not at the moment, thank you."

She gave a crooked smile. "You're not what I expected. I thought a doctor would be more . . . sympathetic. They've got more sympathetic people at the methadone clinic in Bellevue."

"Miss Murphy," he said, "let me—"

"But when I got off the drugs, and I had this beautiful daughter, I wanted to make sense of my life. I wanted my baby to know her grand-parents. And I wanted to finally meet you."

It was time, Bennett decided, to cut this short. He stood up. "Miss Murphy, you realize that I can have genetic testing done, and it will show—"

"Yes," she said. "I realize that." She tossed a folded sheet of paper onto his desk. He opened it slowly. It was a report from a genetic laboratory in Dallas. He scanned the paragraphs. He felt dizzy.

"It says you are definitely my father," she said. "One chance in four billion that you are not. They tested my genetic material against your stored blood."

"This is crazy," he said, dropping back in his chair.

"I thought you would congratulate me," she said. "It wasn't easy to figure it out. My mom was living in St. Louis twenty-eight years ago; she was married at the time . . ."

Bennett had gone to medical school in St. Louis. "But she doesn't know me?"

"She had artificial insemination from an anonymous donor. Which was you."

Bennett felt dizzy.

"I figured the donor must have been a medical student," she continued, "because she went to the clinic at the medical school. And they had their own sperm bank. Medical students donated sperm for money back then, right?"

"Yes. Twenty-five dollars."

"There you go. Good pocket money in those days. And you could do it, what, once a week? Go in there and pop off?"

"Something like that."

"The clinic burned down fifteen years ago, and all the records were lost. But I got the student yearbooks and searched them. Each year the class was a hundred and twenty students, half female. That means sixty males. Eliminate Asians and other minorities, you have about thirty-five a year. Back then sperm didn't keep for more than a year or so. I ended up with about a hundred and forty names to check. It went faster than I thought."

Bennett slumped down in his chair.

"But you want to know the truth? When I saw your picture in the medical yearbook, I knew immediately. Something about your hair, your eyebrows . . ." She shrugged. "Anyway, here I am."

"But this was never supposed to happen," Bennett said. "We were all anonymous donors. Untraceable. No one would ever know whether we had children or not. And back then, our anonymity was a given."

"Yeah, well. Those days are over."

"But I never agreed to be your parent. That's my point."

She shrugged. "What can I say?"

"I wasn't having a child. I was helping infertile couples so they could have a child."

"Well, I'm your child."

"But you have parents . . ."

"I'm your child, Dr. Bennett. And I can prove it in court."

There was a silence. They stared at each other. The baby drooled and squirmed. Finally, he said, "Why did you come here?"

"I wanted to meet my biological father . . ."

"Well, you've met him."

"And I wanted him to fulfill his duties and obligations. Because of what he did to me."

So there it was. Finally out on the table.

"Miss Murphy," he said slowly, "you'll get nothing from me."

He stood. She stood, too.

"The reason I'm an addict," she said, "is because of your genes."

"Don't be absurd."

"Your father was an alcoholic and you had drug troubles of your own. You carry the genes for addiction."

"What genes?"

"AGS3. Heroin dependence. DAT1. Cocaine addiction. You have those genes, and so do I. You gave me those genes. You never should have donated defective sperm in the first place."

"What are you talking about?" he said, suddenly agitated. This woman was clearly following a memorized script. He felt danger.

"I donated sperm thirty years ago. There were no tests back then . . . and there is no responsibility now . . ."

"You knew," she snapped. "You knew you had a problem with cocaine. You knew it ran in your family. But you sold your sperm anyway. You put your damaged, dangerous sperm on the market. Not caring who you infected."

"Infected?"

"You had no business doing what you did. You're a disgrace to the medical profession. Burdening other people with your genetic diseases. And not giving a damn."

Through his agitation, he somehow found self-control. He reached for the door. "Miss Murphy," he said, "I have nothing more to say to you."

"You're throwing me out? You'll regret this," she said. "You'll regret this very, very much."

And she stormed out of the office.

Feeling suddenly drained, Bennett collapsed into the chair behind his desk. He was in a state of shock. He stared at his desk, at the files for his waiting patients. None of it seemed to matter, now. He dialed his attorney, and explained the situation quickly.

"Does she want money?" the attorney said.

"I assume so."

"Did she tell you how much?"

"Jeff," Bennett said, "you're not taking this seriously?"

"Unfortunately, we have to," the attorney said. "This happened in Missouri, and Missouri had no clear laws regarding paternity from artificial insemination back then. Cases like yours were never a problem until quite recently. But as a rule in paternity disputes, the court orders child support."

"She's twenty-eight."

"Yes, and she has parents. Still, she can make an argument in court. Based on this gene thing, she can claim reckless endangerment, she can claim child abuse, and whatever else she can pull out of a hat. Maybe

she'll get something from a judge, maybe she won't. Remember, paternity rulings are stacked against males. Say you get a woman pregnant
and she decides to have an abortion. She can do that without consulting
you. But if she decides to give birth, you'll pay support, even though
you never agreed to have a child with her. The court will say it's your
responsibility not to have gotten her pregnant in the first place. Or
suppose you do genetic testing on your kids, and discover they're not
yours—your wife cheated on you. The court will still require you to
pay support for kids that aren't yours."

"But she's twenty-eight years old. She's not a child—"

"The question is, does a prominent physician want to go to court on
a case that involves not supporting his own daughter?"

"No," Bennett said.

"That's right, you don't. She knows that. And I assume she knows
Missouri law, too. So wait until she calls back, arrange a meeting, and
call me. If she has an attorney, all the better. Make sure he comes.
Meanwhile, fax me that genetic report she gave you."

"I'm going to have to pay her off?"

"Count on it," the attorney said, and hung up.

CH062

The desk officer at the Rockville Police Station was an attractive, smooth-skinned black woman of twenty-five. The desk plate read OFFICER J. LOWRY. Her uniform was crisp.

Georgia Bellarmino pushed her daughter close to the other side of the desk. She set the paper bag of syringes in front of the policewoman and said, "Officer Lowry, I want to know why my daughter has these things, but she refuses to tell me."

Her daughter glared at her. "I hate you, Mom."

Officer Lowry showed no surprise. She glanced at the syringes. She turned to Georgia's daughter. "Were these prescribed to you by a physician?"

"Yes."

"Do they involve matters of reproduction?"

"Yes."

"How old are you?"

"Sixteen."

"Can I see some ID?"

"She's sixteen, all right," Georgia Bellarmino said, leaning forward. "And I want to know—"

"I'm sorry, ma'am," the policewoman said. "If she is sixteen, and these drugs involve reproductive issues, you have no right to be informed."

"What do you mean I have no right to be informed? She's my *daughter*. She's *sixteen*."

"That's the law, ma'am."

"But that law is for abortions. She isn't having an abortion. I don't know what the hell she is doing. These are fertility drugs. She's *shooting up fertility drugs.*"

"I'm sorry, I can't help you on this."

"You mean my daughter is allowed to inject drugs into her body, and I am not allowed to know what is going on?"

"Not if she won't tell you, no."

"And what about her doctor?"

Officer Lowry shook her head. "He can't tell you, either. Doctor-patient privilege."

Georgia Bellarmino collected the syringes and threw them back in the bag. "This is ridiculous."

"I don't make the laws," the policewoman said. "I just enforce them."

They were driving home. "Honey," Georgia said. "Are you trying to get pregnant?"

"No." Sitting there with her arms folded. Furious.

"I mean, you're sixteen, that shouldn't be a problem . . . So what *are* you doing?"

"You made me feel like an *idiot.*"

"Honey, I'm just concerned."

"No you're not. You're a nosy, evil bitch. I hate you, and I hate this car."

It went on like this for a while, until finally Georgia drove her daughter back to school. Jennifer got out of the car, slamming the door. "*And* you made me late for French!"

It was an exhausting morning, and she had canceled two appointments. Now she had to try and reschedule the clients. Georgia went into the office, set the bag of needles on the floor, and started dialing.

The office manager, Florence, walked by and saw the bag. "Wow," she said. "Aren't you a little old for this?"

"It's not me," Georgia said irritably.

"Then . . . not your daughter?"

Georgia nodded. "Yeah."

"It's that Dr. Vandickien," Florence said.

"Who?"

"Down in Miami. These teenage girls take hormones, pump up their ovaries, sell their eggs to him, and pocket the money."

"And do what?" Georgia said.

"Buy breast implants."

Georgia sighed. "Great," she said. "Just great."

She wanted her husband to talk to Jennifer, but unfortunately, Rob was on a flight to Ohio, where they were making a TV segment about him. That discussion—which was sure to be fiery—would have to wait.

CH063

Riding the underground tram from the Senate Office Building to the Senate Dining Room, Senator Robert Wilson (D-Vermont) turned to Senator Dianne Feinstein (D-California) and said, "I think we ought to be more proactive on this genetic thing. For example, we should consider a law that would prevent young women from selling their eggs for profit."

"Young girls already doing that, Bob," Feinstein said. "They sell their eggs now."

"Why, to pay for college?"

"Maybe a few. Mostly, they do it to buy a new car for their boyfriend, or plastic surgery for themselves."

Senator Wilson looked puzzled. "How long has *that* been going on?" he said.

"A couple of years now," Feinstein said.

"Maybe in California . . ."

"Everywhere, Bob. A teenager in New Hampshire did it to make bail for her boyfriend."

"And this doesn't trouble you?"

"I don't like it," Feinstein said. "I think it's ill-advised. I think medically the procedure has dangers. I think these girls may be risking their reproductive futures. But what would be the basis for banning it? Their bodies, their eggs." Feinstein shrugged. "Anyway, the boat's sailed, Bob. Quite a while ago."

CH064

Not again!

Ellis Levine found his mother on the second floor of the Polo Ralph Lauren store on Madison and Seventy-second. She was standing in front of the mirror, wearing a cream-colored linen suit with a green scarf. She was turning this way and that.

"Hello, dear," she said, when she saw him. "Are you going to make another scene?"

"Mom," he said. "What are you doing?"

"Buying a few things for summer, dear."

"We talked about that," Ellis said.

"Just a few things," his mother said. "For summer. Do you like the cuffs on these pants?"

"Mom, we've been here before."

She frowned, and fluffed her white hair absently. "Do you like the scarf?" she said. "I think it's a bit much."

"We have to talk," Ellis said.

"Are we having lunch?"

"The spray didn't work," he said.

"Oh, I don't know." She brushed her cheek. "I felt a little moisturization. For about a week afterward. But not a great deal, no."

"And you kept shopping."

"I hardly shop at all anymore."

"Three thousand dollars last week."

"Oh, don't worry. I took a lot of those things back." She tugged at the scarf. "I think, that green does a funny thing to my complexion. Makes me look sick. But a pink scarf might be nice. I wonder if they have this in pink."

Ellis was watching her intently, with a growing sense of foreboding. Something was wrong with his mother, he decided. She was standing at the mirror, in exactly the same place she had been weeks before, when she showed a total indifference to him, to his message, to her family situation, to her financial situation. Her attitude was completely inappropriate.

As an accountant, Ellis had a horror of people who were inappropriate about money. Money was real, it was tangible, it was hard facts and spreadsheet figures. Those facts and figures were not a matter of opinion. It didn't depend on how you looked at it. His mother was not recognizing the cold reality of her financial situation.

He watched her smile, asking the salesgirl if the scarf came in pink. No, the salesgirl said, he didn't make pink this year. They only had green, or white. His mother asked to try the white. The salesgirl walked away. His mother smiled at him.

Very inappropriate. Almost as if . . .

It might be early dementia, he thought. *It might be the first sign.*

"Why are you looking at me that way?"

"What way, Mom?"

"I'm not crazy. You're not putting me in a home."

"Why would you even say that?"

"I know you boys want the money. That's why you're selling the condos in Vail and the Virgin Islands. For the money. You're greedy, the bunch of you. You are like vultures waiting for your parents to die. And if we won't die, you'll hurry it up. Put us in a home. Get us out of the way. Get us declared insane. That's your plan, isn't it?"

The salesgirl came back with a white scarf. His mother draped it around her neck, flung it over her shoulder with a flamboyant gesture. "Well, Mr. Smartypants, you're not putting me in any home. You get that through your head right now." She turned to the salesgirl. "I'll take it," she said. Still smiling.

The brothers met that evening. Jeff, who was handsome, and had connections in every restaurant in town, got them a table near the waterfall at Sushi Hana. Even early, the place was packed with models and actresses, and Jeff was making plenty of eye contact. Annoyed, Ellis said, "How're things at home?"

Jeff shrugged. "Fine. Sometimes I have to work late. You know."

"No, I don't. Because I'm not a big investment banker and the girls don't wink at me like they wink at you."

Aaron, the youngest brother, the lawyer, was talking on his cell phone. He finished, flipped it shut. "Knock it off, you two. It's the same conversation you've been having since high school. What about Mom?"

Ellis said, "It's what I told you on the phone. It's spooky. She's smiling and happy. She doesn't care."

"Three grand last week."

"She doesn't care. She's buying more than ever."

"So much for that gene spray," Aaron said. "Where'd you get that, anyway?"

"Some guy works at some company in California. BioGen."

Jeff had been looking over his shoulder. Now he turned back to the table. "Hey, I heard something about BioGen. They've got some problems."

"What do you mean, problems?" Aaron said.

"Some product of theirs is contaminated, earnings are down. Did something sloppy, made a mistake. I can't remember. They got an IPO coming up, but it'll tank for sure."

Aaron turned to Ellis. "You think that spray you got is affecting Mom?"

"No, I don't think so. I think the damn stuff just didn't work."

"But if they had contamination . . ." Aaron said.

"Stop being a lawyer. Some cousin of Mom's, her son sent it as a favor to us."

"But gene therapy is dangerous," Aaron said. "There have been deaths from gene therapy. Lots of them."

Ellis sighed. "Aaron," he said, "we're not suing anybody. I think we're looking at the start of, you know, mental deterioration. Alzheimer's or something."

"She's only sixty-two."

"It can start that early."

Aaron shook his head. "Come on, Ellie. She was in perfect health. She was sharp. Now you're telling me she's losing it. It could be the spray."

"Contamination," Jeff reminded them. He was smiling at a girl.

"Jeff, will you fucking pay attention?"

"I am. Look at the rack on her."

"They're fake."

"You just like to ruin everything."

"And she has a nose job."

"She's beautiful."

"She's paranoid," Ellis said.

"You don't know that."

"I'm talking about Mom," Ellis said. "She thinks we're going to put her in a home."

"And we may have to," Aaron said. "Which will be very expensive. But if we do, it's because of that genetics company. You know the public has no sympathy for these biotech companies. Public opinion polls run ninety-two percent against them. They're perceived as unscrupulous scumbags indifferent to human life. GM crops, trashing the environment. Patenting genes, grabbing up our common heritage while no one is looking. Charging thousands of dollars for drugs that cost pennies. Pretending they do research when they really don't; they just buy other people's work. Pretending they have high research costs when they spend most of their money on advertising. And then lying in the advertising. Sneaky, scummy, sloppy, money-grabbing schmucks. It'd be a slam-dunk case."

"We're not talking about a lawsuit," Ellis said. "We're talking about Mom."

Jeff said, "Dad's fine. Let him deal with her." He got up and left the table, going over to sit with three long-legged girls in short skirts.

"They can't be more than fifteen," Ellis said, wrinkling his nose.

"They've got drinks on the table," Aaron said.

"He has two kids in school."

"How're things at home?" Aaron said.

"Fuck you."

"Let's stay on the topic," Aaron said. "Maybe Mom's losing it and maybe she's not. But we're going to need a lot of money if she goes into a home. I'm not sure we can afford it."

"So what are you saying?"

"I want to know more about BioGen and that gene spray they sent us. A lot more."

"You sound like you're already planning the lawsuit."

"Just thinking ahead," Aaron said.

This is *on,* man!

Riding his skateboard, Billy Cleever, angry sixth-grader, came ripping off the playground with an old-school aerial, came down into a backside three-sixty with a tail grab, then heel-flipped onto the sidewalk. He did it flawlessly, which was good, because he was feeling he'd lost some of his cool today. The four kids following behind were quiet, instead of yelling like usual. And this was the big downhill run to Market Street in San Diego. But they were quiet. Like they had lost confidence in him.

Billy Cleever had been humiliated today. His hand hurt like a mother. He told the stupid nurse just to put a Band-Aid on it, but she insisted on a big white thing. He ripped it off the minute school was out, but still. Looked like crap. He looked like an invalid. Something sick.

Humiliated. At age eleven, Billy Cleever was five-nine and 120 pounds, solid muscle for a kid his age, and a good foot taller than anybody else in the school. He was bigger than most of the teachers, even. Nobody messed with him.

That little skin-shit Jamie, that nimrod doof with buck teeth, he should have stayed out of Billy's way. Markie Lester the Pester was throwing him a football, and when he went back to receive it he tripped over Bucky Beaver and fell, taking Bucky with him. Billy was pissed and embarrassed, sprawling like that in front of everybody, with Sarah Hardy and the others giggling. The kid was still lying on the ground, so Billy gave him a couple of kicks with his Vans—nothing really, just a warning—and when the kid got up he smacked him a little. No biggie.

And the next thing he knows, he's got Monkeyboy jumping on his back, yanking his hair and growling in his ear like a fucking ape, and Billy reached back and grabbed for him and Monkeyboy took a bite like—whoa! Pissing pain! Seeing stars.

Of course the monitor, Mr. Snotty NoseDrip, does nothing, whining, "Break it up, boys. Break it up, boys." They put Monkeyboy in detention, and called his mother to come and pick him up, but his mother obviously didn't take him home, which was too bad for him. Because there they were now, walking along at the bottom of the hill, starting to cross the baseball field.

Jamie and Monkeyboy.

And this is *on*!

Billy hits them side on, moving fast, and the two go flying like bowling pins, right next to the dugout by the side of the field. Jamie skids on his chin on the dirt, raising a cloud of brown dust, and Monkeyboy bangs into the chain-link backstop behind home plate. Off to one side, Billy's buddies are yelling: *Blood! We want blood!*

The little kid, Jamie, is moaning in the dust, so Billy goes right for Monkeyboy. He charges him with his deck, trucks out, swinging the skateboard hard, and catches the little black fucker back of the ear, thinking that'll teach him a lesson. Monkeyboy's legs go out, he flops on the ground like a rag doll, and Billy kicks him a good one, right under the chin, lifts his ass off the dirt a little, that one does. But Billy doesn't want to get that monkey blood on his Vans, so he comes back swinging the deck again, figuring to whack the monkey square in the face, maybe break his nose and jaw, make him even uglier than he is.

But Monkeyboy springs to one side, the deck clangs the fence, *kawang-kawang-kwang*, and Monkeyboy sinks his teeth into Billy's wrist and bites *fucking hard!* Billy screams and drops his deck, and Monkeyboy hangs on. Billy is feeling his hand get numb, there's blood pouring down from the arm, down Monkeyboy's chin, and he's snarling like a dog, and his eyes are popping out, staring at Billy. And it's like his hair is raised or something, and Billy thinks in an instant of pure panic: *Shit, this black fuck's gonna eat me.*

By then his skateneck buddies run up, all swinging their boards at the monkey, four boards whacking him downside the head, while Billy is yelling and the monkey is growling—it takes forever until Monkey-boy drops the hand, springs at Markie Lester, and hits him full in the chest, and the Pester goes down, and the others all chase after them as they roll in the dust, while Billy nurses his bleeding arm.

A few seconds later, when the pain is bearable and Billy looks up, he sees the monkey has scrambled up the chain-link backstop and is maybe fifteen feet in the air above them. Staring down at them. While his buds all stand below and yell and shake their decks at him. But nothing is happening. Billy staggers to his feet and says, "You look like a bunch of monkeys."

"We want him to come down!"

"Well, he won't," Billy said. "He's not stupid. He knows we'll kick the shit out of him if he comes down. Least, I will."

"So how we get him down?"

Billy is feeling mean now, blind mean, he wants to hurt something, so he goes right over to Jamie and starts kicking the kid, trying to hit him in his little nuts, but the kid is rolling and yelling for help, fucking baby that he is. Some of the buds don't like it, "Hey, leave 'im alone, hey, he's a little kid," but Billy is thinking, *Fuck it. I want that monkey down here.* And this will do it, nimrod kid rolling in dust. Kick and kick . . . kick . . . the kid yelling for help . . .

And suddenly the buddies are screaming, "Aw, *shit!*"

"Shit! Shit!"

"*Shit!*"

And they're running away, and then something hot and soft smacks Billy on the back of the neck, he gets the weird smell and he can't believe it, he reaches back and . . . Jesus. He can't believe it.

"Shit! He's throwing shit!"

The Monkeyboy's up there with his pants down, heaving crap down at them. And never missing. Deadly, the kids are all covered in it, and then another one hits Billy right in the face. His mouth is half open.

"Ooo-uk!" He spits and spits, wipes his face, and spits again, trying to get that taste out of his mouth. Monkey shit! Fuck! Shit! Billy raises his fist. "You fucking animal!"

And gets another one right on the forehead. *Splaat!*

He grabs his deck and runs away. Joins his buds. They're spitting, too. It's disgusting. It sticks to their clothes, faces. Shit. They all look to Billy, it's on their faces: *Look what you got us into.* It's the moment to step up. And Billy knows how.

"Guy's an animal," Billy said. "Only one thing to do with animals. My dad's got a gun. I know where it is."

"Big talk," Markie says.

"You're full of shit," Hurley says.

"Yeah? Wait and see. Monkeyboy won't make school tomorrow. Wait and see."

Billy trudges home, carrying his board, and the others drag on after him. And he's thinking, *Oh shit, what did I just promise to do?*

CH066

S tan Milgram had begun the long trip to see his aunt in California, but he had only been driving for an hour before Gerard started to complain.

"It stinks," Gerard said, perched in the backseat. "It stinks to high heaven." He looked out the window. "What hellhole is this?"

"It's Columbus, Ohio," Stan said.

"Disgusting," Gerard said.

"You know what they say," Stan said. "Columbus is Cleveland without the glitter."

The bird said nothing.

"You know what glitter is?"

"Yes. Shut up and drive."

Gerard sounded cranky. And he shouldn't be, Stan felt, considering how well the parrot had been treated the last couple of days. Stan had gone online to find out what greys ate, and had gotten Gerard some delicious apples and special greens. He had left the TV on in the pet shop at night, for Gerard to watch. And after a day, Gerard had stopped nipping at his fingers. He even allowed Stan to put him on his shoulder, without biting his ear.

"Are we almost there?" Gerard said.

"No. We've only been gone an hour."

"How much farther is it?"

"We have to drive three days, Gerard."

"Three days. That is twenty-four times three, that is seventy-two hours."

Stan frowned. He had never heard of a bird that did math. "Where'd you learn that?"

"I am a man of many talents."

"You're not a man at all." He laughed. "Was that from a movie?" Sometimes the bird repeated lines from movies, he was sure of it.

"Dave," Gerard said, in a monotone, "this conversation can serve no purpose anymore. Good-bye."

"Oh, wait, I know that one. It's *Star Wars*."

"Fasten your seat belts, it's going to be a bumpy night." It was a woman's voice.

Stan frowned. "Some airplane movie . . ."

"They seek him here, they seek him there, those Frenchies seek him everywhere—"

"I know, that's not a movie, that's poetry."

"Sink me!" Now he sounded British.

"I give up," Stan said.

"So do I," Gerard said, with an elaborate sigh. "How much farther is it?"

"Three days," Stan said.

The parrot stared out the window at the passing city. "Well, they're saved from the blessings of civilization," he said, in a cowboy drawl. And he began to make the sounds of a plunking banjo.

Later in the day, the parrot began to sing French songs, or maybe they were Arab songs, Stan couldn't be sure. Anyway, some foreign language. It seemed he had gone to a live concert, or at least heard a recording of one, because he mimicked the crowd sounds, and the instruments tuning up, and the cheering as the performers came on, before he sang the song itself. It sounded like he was singing "Didi," or something like that.

It was interesting for a while, kind of like hearing radio from a foreign country, but Gerard tended to repeat himself. On a narrow side road, they were stuck behind a woman driver. Stan tried to pass her once or twice, but never could.

After a while Gerard started to say, *"Le soleil c'est beau,"* and then make a loud sound like a gunshot.

"Is that French?" Stan asked.

More gunshots. *"Le soleil c'est beau."* Bang! *"Le soleil c'est beau."* Bang! *"Le soleil c'est beau."* Bang!

"Gerard . . ."

The bird said, *"Les femmes au volant c'est la lacheté personifié."* He made a rumbling sound. *"Pourquoi elle ne dépasse pas? . . . Oh, oui, merde, des travaux."*

The lady driver finally turned off to the right, but she was slow making the turn, and Stan had to brake slightly as he went past her.

"Il ne faut jamais freiner . . . Comme disait le vieux père Bugatti, les voitures sont faites pour rouler, pas pour s'arrêter."

Stan sighed. "I don't understand a word you are saying, Gerard."

"Merde, les flics arrivent!"

He began to wail like a police siren.

"That's enough," Stan said. He turned on the radio. By now it was late afternoon. They'd passed Maryville and were heading toward St. Louis. Traffic was picking up.

"Are we almost there?" Gerard said.

Stan sighed. "Never mind." It was going to be a long trip.

CH067

Lynn sat on the edge of the tub and used the washcloth gently to clean the gash behind his ear. "Dave," Lynn said. "Tell me what happened." She could see the cut was deep, but he wasn't complaining.

"They came after us, Mom!" Jamie was excited, moving his arms. He was covered in dust and had bruises on his stomach and shoulders, but was otherwise not badly hurt. "We didn't do anything! Sixth-graders! Evil dudes!"

"Jamie," she said, "let Dave tell me. How did you get this cut?"

"Billy swung the board at him," Jamie said. "We didn't do anything!"

"You didn't do anything?" she said, raising an eyebrow. "You mean this happened for no reason at all?"

"Yes, Mom! I swear! We were just walking home! They came after us!"

"Mrs. Lester called," Lynn said quietly. "Her son came home covered in excrement."

"No, it was poo," Jamie said.

"How did that—"

"Dave threw it! He was great! They were beatin' us and he threw it and they ran away! He never missed!"

Lynn continued to clean the cut gently. "Is that true, Dave?"

"They hurted Jamie. They beated him and kicked him."

"So you threw . . . poo at them?"

"They hurted Jamie," he said again, as if it explained everything.

"No kidding," Henry said, when he came home later. "He threw feces? That's classic chimp behavior."

"Maybe, but it's a problem," Lynn said. "They say he's disruptive in class. He's getting into scrapes on the playground. He's bitten other children. Now he's thrown feces . . ." She shook her head. "I don't know how to be a parent to a chimpanzee."

"Half-chimp."

"Even quarter-chimp, Henry. I can't make him understand that he can't behave this way."

"But they pick on him, right?" Henry said. "And these older kids, they were sixth-graders? Skateboarders? Those kids are in and out of reform school. And what're six-graders doing bothering with second-graders, anyway?"

"Jamie says the kids make fun of Dave. They call him Monkey-boy."

"You think Dave picked this fight?"

"I don't know. He's aggressive."

"This happened at the playground. I bet there's a security camera there."

"Henry," she said, "you're not understanding what I am telling you."

"Yes, I am. You believe Dave started this. And I have the feeling some bullying dumb-ass kid—"

That was when they heard the gunshot in the backyard.

CH068

Traffic crawled. The 405 Freeway was a river of red lights in the night. Alex Burnet sighed. Sitting beside her, Jamie said, "How much farther is it?"

"It's going to be a while, Jamie."

"I'm tired."

"See if you can lie back and rest."

"I can't. It's boring."

"It's going to be a while," she said again. She flipped open the new cell phone, found the number she had entered for her old childhood friend. She didn't know whom else to call. Lynn was always there for her. When Alex and her husband were breaking up, she and the baby had gone down to see Lynn and Henry. The little kids, both named Jamie, played together.

Alex had stayed there a week.

But now, she was having trouble getting Lynn on the phone. At first, she worried she didn't have the right number. Then she thought there was something wrong with her cheap cell phone. But then she got the answering machine, and now—

"Hello? Hello, who is this?"

"Lynn, it's Alex. Listen I—"

"Oh, Alex! I'm really sorry, I can't talk now—"

"What?"

"Not now. I'm sorry. Later."

"But what—"

She heard the dial tone.

Lynn had already hung up.

She stared forward at the red lights of the creeping freeway.

"Who's that?" her son asked.

"Aunt Lynn," she said. "But she couldn't talk. They just sounded busy."

"So are we still going there?"

"Maybe tomorrow."

She pulled off the freeway at San Clemente and started to look for a motel. For some reason, she was strangely disoriented by the fact that she could not see Lynn. She hadn't realized that she'd been counting on it.

"Where're we going, Mom?" Jamie sounded anxious.

"We'll stay at a motel."

"What motel?"

"I'm looking."

He stared at her. "Do you know where it is?"

"No, Jamie. I'm looking."

They passed one, a Holiday Inn, but it was too big, and it looked exposed. She found a Best Western, unobtrusive, on Camino Real, and pulled in. She told Jamie to stay in the car while she went into the lobby.

A pimply, gangly kid stood behind the counter. He was tapping his fingers on the polished granite surface, humming a little to himself. He seemed restless. "Hi," Alex said. "Do you have a room for tonight?"

"Yes, ma'am."

"I'd like one."

"Just for yourself?"

"No, for me and my son."

He glanced out the door at Jamie. "He under twelve?" He was still clicking his fingernails.

"Yes, why?"

"If he goes to the pool, you gotta accompany him."

"That's fine."

Still tapping the counter. She gave him a credit card and he swiped it, all the while tapping out a beat with his other hand. It was getting on her nerves. "Can I ask you why you do that?"

He began to sing in a monotone. "Trouble's where I'm going, and trouble's where I've been." He thumped the counter. "'Cause trouble is my middle name and trouble is my sin." He smiled. "It's a song."

"That's very unusual," she said.

"My dad used to sing it."

"I see."

"He's dead now."

"I see."

"Killed himself."

"I'm sorry to hear that."

"Shotgun."

"I'm sorry."

"Want to see it?"

She blinked. "Maybe some other time."

"I keep it right here," he said, nodding to the underside of the counter. "Not loaded, of course." Tapping, singing. "Trouble is the only place I've been . . ."

"I'll just sign in," Alex said. He gave her back her card, and she filled out the form. Still clicking, all the time. She thought about going elsewhere, but she was tired. Jamie was waiting. She had to feed him, buy some new clothes for him, a toothbrush, all that.

"There you go," the kid said, giving her the room keys.

It wasn't until she was back in her car, driving to a parking spot near the room, that she remembered she was not supposed to have used her credit card.

Too late now.

"Mom, I'm hungry."

"I know, honey. We'll get something."

"I want a burger."

"Okay, we can do that."

She drove through the parking lot and back onto the street. Better to get him fed before they went to the room.

CH069

There were two more gunshots as Lynn ran into the backyard. Her daughter, Tracy, was screaming, Dave was up in the tree yelling and shaking the branches, and Jamie lay on the ground with blood pouring from his head. She felt sick. She started forward, and Tracy screamed, "Mom! Stay down!"

The gunshots seemed to be coming from the street. Whoever it was was shooting through their wooden slat fence. There was the sound of distant sirens. She could not take her eyes off Jamie. She started to move toward him.

More gunshots, and snapping of leaves in the tree. They were shooting at Dave. Dave was whooping and growling, shaking the branches angrily. He yelled, "You dead! You dead, boy!"

"Dave, be quiet," she shouted. She started crawling toward Jamie. Tracy was shouting into the cell phone, giving the address to 911. Jamie was moaning on the grass. He was all she saw. She hoped that Henry had gone out the front door and would see who it was, and would not get hurt. It was obviously someone trying to get Dave.

The sirens were louder. She heard shouts and running footsteps on the street. Some car had pulled up, bright lights shining through the slats of the fence, casting streaks of shadow.

Overhead, Dave gave a war whoop and was gone. Tracy was yelling. Lynn got to Jamie. The blood was thick around his head.

"Jamie, Jamie . . ."

She got to her knees, turned him over gently. He had a huge gusher on his forehead. Red blood pouring down one side of his face.

He smiled weakly. "Hi, Mom."

"Jamie, where are you hit?"

"Not . . ."

"Where, Jamie?"

"I fell. From the tree."

She had the edge of her skirt in her hand, was cautiously wiping the wound. She saw no bullet hole. Just a huge abrasion, bleeding profusely.

"Honey, you weren't shot?"

"No, Mom." He shook his head. "It wasn't me, anyway. He was after Dave."

"Who was?"

"Billy."

Lynn looked up at the tree overhead. Branches gently swaying in the light of the headlamps.

Dave was gone.

Dave's first jump landed him on the sidewalk, and he began running after the fleeing Billy Cleever, who was heading down the street, running home. Dave could move swiftly when he wanted to, loping on all fours. He ran parallel to the sidewalk, staying on the grass, because the concrete hurt his knuckles. He was growling continuously, as he closed in on Billy.

At the end of the block, Billy turned and saw Dave bearing down on him. He held his gun in two shaking hands and fired a shot, then another. Dave kept coming. Along the street, people were looking out their windows. All the windows glowed blue from the TV sets inside.

Billy turned to run, and Dave caught him and slammed his head into a traffic signpost. It rang with the impact. Billy tried to turn, but he was terrified. Dave held him firmly and smashed his head into the concrete. He would have killed him for sure, but the sound of approaching sirens made him pause and look up.

In that moment, Billy kicked, scrambled to his feet, and ran up the driveway of the nearest house. He climbed into a car parked in the driveway. Dave chased him. Billy slammed the door and locked it just as Dave landed on the windshield. He slid over the surface of the hood, peering into the interior.

Billy aimed his gun but he was too shaken, too terrified to fire. Dave dropped down to the passenger side, tried the door, yanking again and again at the handle. Billy was gasping for breath, watching him.

Then Dave dropped down again, completely out of sight.

The sirens came closer.

Billy realized his predicament slowly. The police were coming. He was locked in the car with a gun in his hand, his blood and fingerprints smeared all over it. Powder marks and a red cut where the hammer had nipped him. He didn't know how to shoot, not really. He had just wanted to scare them, is all.

The police were going to find him here. Trapped in this car.

Cautiously, he peered out the passenger window, trying to see Dave.

Black and screaming, Dave leapt up and slammed against the window. Billy screamed and jumped back. The gun fired, hitting the dashboard, plastic splinters cutting into his arm, the car filling with smoke. He dropped the gun onto the floorboard, leaned back in the seat. He was gasping for breath.

Sirens. Closer.

Maybe they would find him here, but it was self-defense. That would be obvious. Monkeyboy was a vicious animal. The police would take one look at him and realize that everything Billy had done was self-defense. He had to protect himself. The monkey kid was vicious. He looked like an ape and he acted like an ape. He was a killer. He belonged behind bars in a zoo . . .

Flashing red lights sweeping the roof of the car. The sirens stopped. Billy heard a bullhorn. "This is the police. Come out of the car now. Very slow with your hands where we can see them."

"I can't!" he yelled. "He's out there!"

"Come out of the car now!" the voice boomed. "With your hands up."

Billy waited awhile, then came out, holding his hands high, blinking in the bright spotlight of the police cars. A cop came up and shoved him onto the ground. He snapped handcuffs on him.

"It wasn't my fault," Billy said, his face pushed in the grass. "It was that kid Dave. He's under the car."

"There's nobody under the car, son," the cop said, lifting him to his feet. "Just you. Nobody else. Now: you going to tell us what this is about?"

His father came. Billy knew he was going to get a beating. But his father didn't give any indication of that. He asked to see the gun. He asked Billy where the bullets were. Billy said he was shooting at a vicious kid who was attacking him.

Billy's father just nodded, his face bland. But he said he would follow the cops down to the station, when they took Billy there to book him.

Henry said, "I think we have to admit, it just isn't working."

"What do you mean?" Lynn said, running her fingers through Dave's hair. "This isn't Dave's fault, you said so yourself."

"I know. But there seems to be trouble all the time. Biting, fighting . . . Now gunshots, for God's sake. He's endangering all of us."

"But it's not his fault, Henry."

"I'm worried about what will happen next."

"You could have thought of that earlier," she said, in a sudden burst of anger. "Like four years ago, when you decided to do your experiment. Because now it's a little too late to be having regrets, don't you think? He's our responsibility, and he's staying with us."

"But—"

"We're his family."

"They were shooting at Jamie."

"Jamie's all right."

"But *shooting* . . ."

"It was some crazy kid. Sixth-grader. The police have him."

"Lynn, you're not listening."

She glared at him. "What do you think, that you can quietly get rid of him, like a Petri dish that didn't turn out right? You can't just dump Dave in the biotrash. You're the one who's not listening. Dave is a living, thinking sentient being, and you made him. You are the reason why he exists on this earth. You don't have the right to abandon him just because he's inconvenient or has trouble at school." She paused to catch her breath. She was very angry. "Anyway, I'm not giving him up," she said. "And I don't want to talk about it anymore."

"But—"

"Not now, Henry."

Henry knew that tone. He shrugged and left.

"Thank you," Dave said, bending his head so she could run her fingers through the fur on his neck. "Thank you, Mom."

Alex took her son to an In-N-Out drive-in, and they had burgers and fries and strawberry shakes. It was now dark outside. She thought of calling Lynn again, but Lynn had sounded harried. She decided not to.

She paid for the burgers in cash. Then they drove to a Walston's drugstore, one of those block-long places that had everything. She bought Jamie some underwear and a change of clothes; she did the same for herself. She bought a couple of toothbrushes and toothpaste.

She was heading toward the checkout when she saw the guns for sale, over by the cameras and watches. She went to look. Over the years, she had gone to shooting ranges with her father. She could handle a gun. She told Jamie to go look at the toy aisle, and she went to the gun rack.

"Help you?" It was a wimpy guy with a mustache.

"I'd like to see that Mossberg double-action." She nodded to the wall.

"That's our model 590, twelve-gauge, perfect for home defense. Got a special price this week only."

She hefted it. "Okay, I'll take it."

"I'll need an ID, and a deposit to hold it."

"No," she said, "I mean, I'll buy it now."

"Sorry, ma'am, ten-day waiting period in California."

She handed the gun back. "I'll think it over," she said.

She returned to Jamie, bought the Spider-Man toy he was playing with, and walked out to the parking lot.

A man was standing at the back of her car, bending over the license plate. Writing the number down. He was an older guy, in some kind of uniform. He looked like a security guard from the store.

She thought: *Run. Leave now.*

But that didn't make sense; she needed a car. It was time to think fast. She told Jamie to get in the car, and she walked to the back. "You know he's a damn liar," she said.

"Who's that?" the guard said.

"My ex-husband. He pretends like this car is his, but it isn't. He's just harassing me. I got a court order to stop him, and I got a big judgment against the security guard at Wal-Mart."

"How's that?" he said.

"Don't act dumb," she said. "I know you got a call from him. He pretends to be an attorney, he pretends to be a bail bondsman, or a court agent, and he wants you to check if my car is in the lot. He says it's some pending legal matter."

"Well, yes—"

"He's lying, and you're now liable. Did he tell you I was an attorney?"

"No, he just—"

"Well, I am. And you're an accessory to his breaking the court order. That makes you liable to damages. Invasion of privacy and harassment." She took a pad from her purse. "Now your name is . . ." She squinted at the name tag, began to write.

"I don't want any trouble, ma'am—"

"Then give me that sheet of paper you wrote my license on, and back off," she said. "And when my husband calls again, you damn well tell him you never set eyes on me, or I'll see you in court, and I promise you, you'll be lucky if all you lose is your job."

He nodded, gave her the paper. His hands were shaking. She got in the car and drove off.

As she pulled out of the parking lot, she thought, *Maybe it will work.* Then again, maybe not. Mostly she was stunned by how fast this bounty hunter had located her.

He no doubt had followed her own car north for a couple of hours, and then realized that she had switched cars with her assistant. He and his cohorts knew her assistant's name, and they got her car registration. So now they knew the car Alex was driving.

Then Alex had used her credit card, and within minutes, the bounty hunter had known about it and fixed her position at a motel in San Juan Capistrano. Realizing that she'd need supplies, the hunter had probably called every convenience store within a five-mile radius of the motel, and gave a story to the security people. Be on the lookout for a white Toyota, license so-and-so.

And this guy found her.

Right away.

Unless she missed her bet, the bounty hunter was on his way to Capistrano right now. If he was driving, he would be there in three hours. But if he had access to a helicopter, he might be here already.

Already.

"Mom, can I watch TV when we go back to the motel?"

"Sure, honey."

But, of course, they weren't going back to the motel.

She parked around the corner from the motel. From her position, she could see the lobby, and the kid inside. He was talking on the phone, looking around as he did so.

She turned on her regular cell phone, and dialed the motel.

The kid put the other line on hold, and picked up.

"Best Western."

"Yes, this is Mrs. Colson. I checked in earlier."

"Yes, Mrs. Colson."

It seemed to excite him. He looked around in all directions now, frantic.

"You put me in room 204."

"Yes . . ."

"I think there's someone in my room."

"Mrs. Colson, I can't imagine—"

"I want you to come here and open the door for me."

"If it's anybody, it's probably the maid—"

"I think it's a man."

"Oh no, it couldn't be—"

"Come here and open the door. Or do I have to call the police?"

"No, I'm sure . . . I'll be right there."

"Thank you."

He switched to the other line, spoke quickly, and then left the lobby, running down toward the rooms at the back.

Alex got out of her car and sprinted across the street to the lobby. She moved in quickly, stepped behind the counter, picked up the shotgun, and walked out again. It was a sawed-off twelve-gauge Remington. Not her first choice, but it would do for now. She'd get shells later.

She got back in the car. "What's the gun for?" Jamie said.

"Just in case," she said. She drove off, turning onto Camino Real. Through her rearview mirror, she saw the kid coming back into the lobby, looking puzzled.

"I want to watch TV," Jamie said.

"Not tonight," she said. "Tonight we are going to have an adventure."

"What kind of adventure?"

"You'll see."

She drove east, away from the lights, and into the darkness of the mountains.

Stan Milgram was lost in endless darkness. The road ahead was a strip of light, but on each side he could see no signs of life at all, nothing except pitch-black desert landscape stretching away into the distance. To the north he could just detect the ridge of the mountains, a faint line of black against black. But nothing else—no lights, no towns, no houses, nothing.

It had been that way for an hour.

Where the hell was he?

From the backseat, the bird gave a piercing shriek. Stan jumped; the sound made his eardrums ache. If you ever plan to motor west, he thought, don't take a damn bird on the highway, that's the best. He'd put cloth over the cage hours ago, but the cloth didn't shut the bird up anymore. From St. Louis down through Missouri, and on to Gallup, New Mexico. All the way the bird would not shut up. Stan checked into a Gallup motel, and at around midnight the bird began to scream, ear-splitting shrieks.

There was nothing to do but check out—with all the other motel guests yelling at him—and start driving again. The bird was silent, once they were driving. But he pulled off the road for a few hours during the day to sleep, and later, when he stopped at Flagstaff, Arizona, the bird began to scream again. It started before he even checked into the motel.

He kept driving. Winona, Kingman, Barstow, heading for San Bernardino—San Berdoo, his aunt called it—and all he could think was this trip would be over soon. Please, God. Let it be over before he killed the bird.

But Stan was exhausted, and after driving more than two thousand miles, he had become strangely disoriented. Either he had missed the San Berdoo turnoff or . . . or he wasn't sure.

He was lost.

And the bird still shrieked. "Your heart sweats, your body shakes, another kiss is what it takes . . ."

He pulled the car over. He opened the door to the backseat. He took the cloth off. "Gerard," he said. "Why are you doing this?"

"You can't sleep, you can't eat—"

"Gerard, stop it. Why?"

"I'm afraid."

"Why?"

"It's too far from home." The bird blinked, looked at the darkness outside. "What fresh hell is this?"

"This is the desert."

"It's freezing."

"The desert is cold at night."

"Why are we here?"

"I'm taking you to your new home." Stan stared at the bird. "If I leave your cloth off, will you be quiet?"

"Yes."

"No talking at all?"

"Yes."

"You promise?"

"Yes."

"Okay. I need it quiet so I can find out where we are."

"I don't know why, I love you like I do, after all the changes—"

"Try and help me, Gerard. Please." Stan went around and got in the driver's seat. He pulled out onto the road and started driving. The bird was quiet. The miles rolled by. Then he saw a sign for a town called Earp, three miles ahead.

"Mellow greetings, ukie dukie," Gerard said.

Stan sighed.

He drove forward into the night.

"You remind me of a man," Gerard said.

"You promised," Stan said.

"No, you are supposed to say, 'What man?'"

"Gerard, shut up."

"You remind me of a man," Gerard said.

"What man?"

"The man with the power."

"What power?"

"The power of hoodoo."

"Hoodoo?" Stan said.

"You do."

"Do what?"

"Remind me of a man."

"What man?" Stan said. And then he caught himself. "Gerard, *shut up* or I will put you outside *right now*."

"Ooh, aren't you the twisted bunny."

Stan glanced at his watch.

One more hour, he thought. One more hour, and that bird was out.

CH072

Ellis sat down across from his brother Aaron, in Aaron's office at the law firm. The office window looked south over the city, down toward the Empire State Building. It was a hazy day, but the view was still spectacular, powerful.

"Okay," Ellis said, "I talked to that guy in California, Josh Winkler."

"Uh-huh."

"He says he never gave anything to Mom."

"Uh-huh."

"Says what he sent was water."

"Well, that's what you would expect him to say."

"Aaron," Ellis said, "they gave her water. Winkler said that he was not going to transport anything across state lines. His mother wanted it done, so he sent water, to test the placebo effect."

"And you believe him," Aaron said, shaking his head.

"I think he has documentation."

"Of course he does," Aaron said.

"Sign-outs, lab reports, other documentation maintained by his company."

"Falsified," Aaron said.

"That documentation is required by the FDA. Falsifying it is a federal offense."

"So is giving gene therapy to friends." Aaron pulled out a sheaf of papers. "Do you know the history of gene therapy? It's a horror story,

Ellie. Starting back in the late 1980s, the biotech guys went off half-cocked and killed people right and left. At least six hundred people we know about have been killed. And plenty more we don't know about. You know why we don't know?"

"No, why?"

"Because they claimed—get this—that the deaths couldn't be reported, because they were proprietary information. Killing their patients was a trade secret."

"Did they really say that?"

"Could I make this shit up? And then they bill Medicare for the cost of the experiment that killed the patient. They kill, we pay. And if the universities get caught, they claim they don't have to give informed consent to subjects because they are nonprofit institutions. Duke, Penn, University of Minnesota—big places have been caught. Academics think they're above the law. Six hundred deaths!"

Ellis said, "I don't see what this has to do—"

"You know how gene therapy kills people? All sorts of ways. They don't know what's going to happen. They insert genes into people, and it turns on cancer genes, and the people die of cancer. Or they have huge allergic reactions and die. These goofballs don't know what the hell they are doing. They're reckless and they don't follow the rules. And we," he said, "are going to smack their asses down."

Ellis squirmed in his chair. "But what if Winkler is telling the truth? What if we are wrong?"

"We didn't break the rules," Aaron said. "They did. Now Mom's got Alzheimer's, and they're in deep, deep shit."

When Brad Gordon started the bar fight at the Lucky Lucy Saloon on Pearl Street in Jackson Hole, Wyoming, he hadn't intended to end up in the hospital. The two guys in the tight-fitting plaid shirts with the pointy pearl-button pockets looked like pussies to him, and he figured he could take them easily. There was no way to know they were brothers, not lovers, and they didn't take kindly to his remarks about them.

And there was no way to know that the smaller one taught karate at Wyoming State and had won some kind of championship at a Bruce Lee tournament for martial arts in Hong Kong.

Kickboxing with metal-tipped cowboy boots. Brad lasted all of thirty seconds. And a lot of his teeth were loose. He had been lying in this fucking infirmary for three hours, while they tried to push the teeth back in place. There was one periodontist they kept calling, but he wasn't answering, possibly because (as the intern explained) he was off hunting for the weekend—he liked elk. Tasty eating.

Elk! Brad's fucking mouth was killing him.

So they left him there with icepacks on his face and his jaw shot full of Novocain, and somehow he fell asleep, and the next morning, the swelling had gone down enough that he could talk on the phone, so he called his attorney, Willy Johnson, in Los Angeles, holding the business card between his bruised thumb and forefinger.

The receptionist was cheerful: "Johnson, Baker, and Halloran."

"Willy Johnson, please."

"Hold on, please." The phone clicked, but he wasn't put on hold, and then he heard the woman say, "Faber, Ellis, and Condon."

Brad looked again at the card in his hand. The address was an office building in Encino. He knew what that place was. It was a building where solo attorneys could rent a tiny office and share a receptionist who was trained to answer the phone as if she was working at a big law firm, so clients would not suspect their attorneys were on their own. That building housed only the most unsuccessful sort of attorney. The ones who handled small-time drug dealers. Or who had done jail time themselves.

"Excuse me . . ." he said, into the phone.

"Sorry sir, I am trying to find Mr. Johnson for you." She cupped her hand over the phone. "Anybody seen Willy Johnson?"

And he heard a muffled voice yell back, "Willy Johnson is a dick!"

Sitting there at the entrance to the emergency room, weak and in pain, his jaw aching like hell, Brad did not feel good about what he was hearing. "Did you find Mr. Johnson?"

"One moment sir, we're looking . . ."

He hung up.

He felt like crying.

He went out to get breakfast, but it hurt too much to eat, and people in the coffee shop looked at him oddly. He saw his reflection in the glass and realized his whole jaw was blue and puffy. Still it was better than last night. He wasn't worried about anything except this attorney Johnson. All his initial suspicions about the man were confirmed. Why had they met at a restaurant, instead of his law firm? Because Johnson didn't belong to a law firm.

There was nothing to do but call his uncle Jack.

"John B. Watson Investment Group."

"Mr. Watson, please."

They put him through to the secretary, who put him through to his uncle.

"Hey, Uncle Jack."

"Where the fuck are you?" Watson said. He sounded distinctly unfriendly.

"I'm in Wyoming."

"Staying out of trouble, I hope."

"Actually, my attorney sent me here," he said, "and that's why I am calling you. I'm a little worried, I mean this guy—"

"Look," Watson said, "you're up on a molestation charge, and you've got a molestation expert to handle your case. You don't have to like him. Personally I hear he's a prick."

"Well—"

"But he wins cases. Do what he says. Why are you talking funny?"

"Nothing . . ."

"I'm busy, Brad. And you were told never to call."

Click.

Brad was feeling worse than ever. Back at his motel room, the guy at the desk said someone from the police had come looking for him. Something about a hate crime. Brad decided it was time to leave beautiful Jackson Hole.

He went to his room to pack, watching some true-crime show where the police caught a dangerous fugitive by pretending to put him on television. They staged a fake TV interview setup, and as soon as the guy relaxed, they slapped cuffs on him. And now the guy was on death row.

Police were getting tricky. Brad hastily finished packing, paid his bill, and hurried out to his car.

The self-proclaimed environmental artist Mark Sanger, recently returned from a trip to Costa Rica, looked up from his computer in astonishment as four men broke down the door and burst into his Berkeley apartment. The men were dressed head to foot in blue rubber hazmat suits, with big rubber helmets and big faceplates, rubber gloves, and boots, and they carried evil-looking rifles and big pistols.

He had hardly reacted to the shock when they were on him, grabbing him with their rubber hands and wrestling him away from the keyboard.

"Pigs! Fascists!" Sanger yelled, but suddenly it seemed like everybody was shouting and screaming in the room. "This is an outrage! Fascist pigs!" he shouted as they cuffed him, but he could see their faces behind the masks, and they were afraid. "Jesus, what do you think I'm doing here?" he said, and one of them answered, "We know what you're doing, Mr. Sanger," and spun him away.

"Hey! Hey!" They pulled him—roughly—down the steps from his apartment to the street. Sanger could only hope media would be waiting, cameras ready to film this outrage in broad daylight.

The press, however, was cordoned off across the street. They could hear Sanger as he shouted, and they were filming him, but their distance prevented the up-close, in-your-face confrontation he hoped for. In fact, Sanger suddenly realized how this scene must look through their lenses—policemen dressed in frightening hazmat suits escorting a thirtyish bearded man in jeans and a Che Guevara T-shirt, who struggled in their arms, cursing and shouting.

Sanger knew he must look like a madman. Like one of the Teds: Ted Bundy, Ted Kaczynski, one of those guys. The cops would say that he had microbiology equipment in his apartment, that he had tools for genetic engineering, and he was making a plague, making a virus, making a disease—something horrible. A madman.

"Put me down," he said, forcing himself to be calm. "I can walk. Let me walk."

"All right, sir," one of them said. They let him stand on his feet, and walk.

Sanger walked with as much dignity as he could muster, straightening his shoulders, shaking his long hair, as they led him to a waiting car. Of course it was an unmarked car. He should have expected that. Fucking FBI or CIA or whatever. Secret government organizations, the shadow government. Black helicopters. Unaccountable, the crypto Nazis among us.

Fuming, he wasn't prepared to see Mrs. Malouf, the black lady who lived on the second floor of his building, standing outside with her two young kids. As he passed her, she leaned forward and started yelling at him. "You bastard! You risk my family! You risk my children's lives! You Frankenstein! Frankenstein!"

Sanger was intensely aware of how that moment would play on the evening news. A black mother shouts at him, calls him Frankenstein. And the kids at her side were crying, frightened by everything that was happening around them.

Then the cops shoved Sanger into the unmarked car, with one rubber-gloved hand on his head, easing him into the backseat. And as the door slammed shut, he thought, *I am fucking screwed.*

Sitting in his jail cell, watching the television in the hallway, trying to hear the commentary over the arguments of the other guys in the cell, trying to ignore the faint smell of vomit and the deep sense of despair that settled over him as he watched.

First there was footage of Sanger himself, hair long, dressed like a bum, walking between two guys in hazmat suits. He looked even worse than he had feared. The corporate flunky reading the news was mouthing all the buzzwords: Sanger was *unemployed*. He was an *uneducated* drifter. He was a *fanatic* and a *loner* who had *genetic engineering* materials in his *cramped, filthy apartment,* and he was considered *dangerous* because he fit the classic *bioterrorist profile.*

Next, a bearded San Francisco lawyer from some environmental defense group said Sanger should be prosecuted to the full extent of the law. Sanger had caused irreparable harm to an endangered species, and had jeopardized the very existence of the species by his depredations.

Sanger frowned: what the hell was he talking about?

Next the TV showed a picture of a leatherback turtle and a map of Costa Rica. Now it seemed that authorities had been alerted to Sanger's activities because he had visited Tortuguero, on the Atlantic coast of Costa Rica, sometime before. And because he had made *serious threats to the environment* regarding leatherback turtles.

Sanger couldn't follow this. He had never made any threats. He had wanted to help, that was all. And the fact was, once he got back to his apartment, he had been unable to carry out his plans. He bought stacks of genetics textbooks, but the whole thing was much too complicated. He opened the shortest of the texts and scanned some of the captions to graphics: "A plasmid harboring a normal LoxP has little chance of remaining integrated in a genome at a similar LoxP site since the Cre recombinase will eliminate the integrated DNA fragment . . ." "Lentiviral vectors injected into one-cell embryos or incubated with embryos from which zona pellucida was withdrawn were particularly . . ." "A more efficient way to replace a gene relies on the use of mutant ES cells devoid of the HPRT gene (hypoxanthine phosphoribosyl transferase). These cells cannot survive in the HAT medium, which contains hypoxanthine, aminopterine, and thymidine. The HPRT gene is introduced at the targeted site by a double homologous recombination . . ."

Sanger had stopped reading.

And now the TV screen showed turtles on the beach at night, glowing a weird purple color . . . and they thought that he had done that? The very idea was ridiculous. But a fascist state demanded blood for any transgression, real or imagined. Sanger could foresee himself thrown in jail for a crime he hadn't committed—a crime that he didn't even know *how* to commit.

New Transgenic Pets on Horizon

Giant Cockroaches, Permanent Pups

Artists, Industry Hard at Work

Yale-trained artist Lisa Hensley has joined forces with the genetic firm of Borger and Snodd Ltd. to create giant cockroaches to be sold as pets. The GM cockroaches will be three feet long and stand approximately one foot off the ground. "They will be the size of large dachshunds," says Hensley, "although of course they won't bark."

Hensley regards the pets as works of art, intended to raise human awareness of the insect community. "The overwhelming majority of living matter on our planet consists of insects," she said. "Yet we maintain an irrational prejudice against them. We should embrace our insect brethren. Kiss them. Love them."

She observed that "the real danger of global warming is that we may render so many insects extinct." Hensley acknowledged that she was inspired by the work of artist Catherine Chalmers (B.S. Engineering, Stanford University), whose project American Cockroach first elevated cockroaches to a major theme of contemporary art.

Meanwhile, in suburban New Jersey, the firm of Kumnick Genomics is hard at work creating an animal they believe dog owners really want: permanent puppies. "Kumnick's Perma-Puppies will never grow up," according to spokesperson Lyn Kumnick. "When you buy a PermaPuppy, it stays a puppy forever." The firm is working to eliminate unwanted puppy behavior, such as chewing shoes, which gets on dog owners' nerves. "Once the teeth are in, this behavior stops," Kumnick said. "Unfortunately, at this point our genetic interventions have prevented the growth of teeth altogether, but we'll solve that." She said that rumors they were going to market a toothless animal called a GummyDog were untrue.

Kumnick observes that since adulthood in human beings is being replaced by permanent adolescence, people naturally wish to be accompanied through life by similarly youthful dogs. "Like Peter Pan, we never want to grow up," she says. "Genetics makes it possible!"

Still lost, now driving through very hilly terrain, Stan Milgram squinted at the road sign emerging from the darkness ahead. PALOMAR MOUNTAIN 37 MILES. Where the hell was that? He had never realized California was so big. He had passed through a couple of towns a ways back, but at three in the morning everything was closed, including gas stations. And then he was once more in dark, empty countryside.

He should have brought a map.

Stan was exhausted, irritable, and he needed to pull over and sleep. But the damn bird would start shrieking as soon as he stopped the car.

Gerard had been silent for the last hour, but now, inexplicably, he began to make telephone dial tones. As if he were calling someone.

"Stop it, Gerard," Stan said.

And the bird stopped. At least for a moment. Stan was able to drive in silence. But of course it didn't last.

"I'm hungry," Gerard said.

"You and me both."

"You bring any chips?"

"The chips are gone." They had eaten the last of them, back in the town of Earp. An hour ago? Two hours ago?

"Nobody knows the trouble I've seen," Gerard said, humming.

"Don't do it," Stan warned.

"Nobody knows, 'cept Jesus . . ."

"Gerard . . ."

Silence.

It was like traveling with a child, Stan thought. The bird had all of the stubbornness and unexpectedness of a child. It was exhausting.

They passed train tracks, off to the right.

Gerard made chugging sounds, and a mournful whistle. "I ain't seen the sunshine, since I don't know when-nnn . . ."

Stan decided not to say anything. He gripped the wheel and drove through the night. Behind him, he could see a faint lightening of the sky. That meant he was driving west. And that was where he wanted to go. More or less.

And then in the tense silence, Gerard began again.

"Ladies and gentlemen, mesdames et messieurs, damen und herren, from what was once an inarticulate mass of lifeless tissues, may I now present a cultured, sophisticated, man about town! Hit it!"

"You're pushing," Stan said. "And I'm giving you a warning."

"It's my life—don't you forget!" the bird sang, screaming at the top of its lungs. It seemed as if the whole car vibrated. Stan thought the windows might shatter.

He winced, gripped the wheel harder.

And then the screaming stopped.

"We're so glad to see so many of you lovely people here tonight," Gerard said, sounding like an announcer.

Stan shook his head. "Dear God."

"Let's be happy, happy happy, say the word now.

"Happy happy happy, try it somehow . . ."

"Stop," Stan said.

Gerard went right on:

"Happy, happy, happy, happy, oh baby yes, happy, happy—"

"That's it!" Stan yelled, pulling over to the side of the road. He got out of the car, slammed the driver's door hard.

"You don't scare me, buster," Gerard said.

Stan swore and opened the back door.

Gerard was singing again: "I've got some news for you, and

you'll soon find out it's true, and you'll have to eat your lunch all by yourself—"

"No problem," Stan said, "because you are *out of here*, pal!" He grabbed the bird roughly—Gerard pecked at him viciously, but he didn't care—and put Gerard down on the side of the road, in the dust.

"It looks as though you're letting go, and if it's real I don't want to—"

"It's real," Stan snarled.

Gerard flapped his wings. "You can't do this to me," he said.

"Oh no? Watch me." Stan walked back to the front of the car, opened the door.

"I want my perch," Gerard said. "It's the least you can—"

"Fuck your damn perch!"

"Don't go away mad, it can't be so bad, don't go away . . ."

"Bye, bye, Gerard." Stan slammed the door and shoved his foot down on the pedal, driving off fast, making sure he raised a big cloud of dust. He looked back, but couldn't see the bird. He did, however, see all the bird shit in the backseat. Jeez, it would take days to clean all that up.

But now it was quiet.

Blessedly quiet.

Finally.

The adventures of Gerard were over.

Now that there was silence in the car, his accumulated fatigue hit him. Stan began to doze off. He turned on the radio, rolled down the window, stuck his head out in the cold breeze. Nothing was helping. He realized he was going to fall asleep, and he had to pull off the road.

That bird had kept him awake. He felt a little bad, putting him out in the road that way. It was as good as killing him. A bird like that wouldn't last long in the desert. Some rattler or coyote would make quick work of him. Had probably already done it. No reason to go back.

Stan pulled over to the side of the road, into a grove of pines. He turned the engine off and inhaled the scent of the trees. He fell instantly asleep.

Gerard walked back and forth on the dusty ground for a while in the darkness. He wanted to get off the ground, and several times he tried jumping onto the scrubby sage bushes that surrounded him. But the sage didn't support his weight, and he came crashing down again each time. Finally he half-hopped, half-flew into the air, coming down again on a juniper bush about three feet off the ground. Standing on that makeshift perch, he might have gone to sleep, except the temperature was extremely cold for a tropical bird. And he was kept awake by the yelping of a pack of animals in the desert.

The yelps were coming closer.

Gerard ruffled his feathers, a sign of unease. He looked in the direction of the sound. He saw several dark shapes moving through the desert brush. He caught the glint of green eyes.

He ruffled his feathers again.

And watched the pack come toward him.

The Robinson R44 helicopter descended in a cloud of dust, and Vasco Borden came out, crouched beneath the blades. He got into the waiting black Hummer. "Talk to me," he said to Dolly, who was driving. She'd come down earlier, while Vasco went on that wild goose chase to Pebble Beach.

Dolly said, "She checked into the Best Western at seven-thirty tonight, went to Walston's, where a security guy ID'd the car. She brushed him off with a story about an ex-husband, and he went for it."

"When was that?"

"Little before eight. From there she went back to the motel, gave the kid at the desk a story about someone being in her room. While he was checking, she took his shotgun from under the counter and made off with it."

"Did she?" Borden said. "The little lady has some balls."

"Apparently she had tried to buy a gun in a drugstore, but ran into the ten-day wait."

"And now?"

"We were tracking her cell phone, but she turned it off. Before that happened we got her heading east, toward Ortega Highway."

"Into the desert," Vasco said, nodding. "She'll sleep in her car, and then continue on tomorrow morning."

"We can download sat shots at eight a.m. That's the fastest processing time."

"She'll be gone before eight in the morning," Vasco said. He leaned back in the Hummer. "She'll go at dawn. So let's see." He paused, thinking. "All afternoon she's been driving, and it's basically south. The minute all this began, our lady went south."

"You thinking Mexico?" Dolly said.

Vasco shook his head. "She doesn't want to leave a record, and crossing the border will leave a record."

"Maybe she'll head east, try to cross at Brown Field or Calexico," Dolly said.

"Maybe." Vasco rubbed his beard thoughtfully. Too late, he felt the mascara coming off on his fingers. Damn, he had to remember that. "She's scared. I think she's heading for a place she thinks will give her help. Maybe meet her father down here. Or meet up with somebody she knows. An old boyfriend? School friend? Sorority sister? Former teacher? Former law partner? Something like that."

"We've been checking all the net databases for the last two hours," Dolly said. "And so far we've got nothing."

"How about her old phone records?"

"No calls to San Diego area code."

"How far back?"

"A year. That's all that's available without a special order."

"So whoever this is, she hasn't called 'em in a year." Vasco sighed. "We'll just have to wait for her." He turned to Dolly. "Let's go to that Best Western. I want to find out what kind of gun the little lady got. And we can get a couple of hours' rest, before dawn. I'm sure we'll get her by tomorrow. I got a feeling." He tapped his chest. "And I'm never wrong."

"Hon, you just got mascara on your nice shirt."

"Ah hell." He sighed.

"It'll come out," Dolly said. "I'll get it out for you."

CH077

Gerard watched the dark shapes approach.

They moved with a loping gait, and made a snorting or snuffling sound, and sometimes a mewling sound. Their bodies were low. Their backs were just visible above the sage. They circled his perch, approaching, then sliding away.

But they had clearly smelled him, because they were coming ever closer to him. There were six animals altogether. Gerard ruffled his feathers, partly in an attempt to warm his body.

The animals had long snouts. Their eyes glowed bright green. They had a distinctive musky odor that was unpleasant. They had long fluffy tails. He could see that they were not black but rather brownish-gray.

They moved in closer. "I'm sha sha shakin', I'm shakin' now."

And closer. They were quite close, now.

The largest one paused a few feet away and stared at Gerard. Gerard did not move.

After several seconds, the big animal edged closer.

"You can stop right there, mister!"

The animal stopped instantly, and even took a few paces backward. The other animals in the group backed away, too. They all seemed confused by the voice.

But not for long. The big animal started to move in again.

"Well, hold on!"

This time, there was only a momentary pause. Then the animal kept coming.

"You feel lucky, punk? Do you? Huh?"

The animal was coming very slowly now. Sniffing at Gerard, closer and closer . . . Sniff, sniff . . . The creature smelled awful. The nose was just inches away . . .

Gerard bent and bit hard on the animal's soft nose. The creature yelped and jumped backward, almost knocking Gerard from his perch. He regained his balance.

"Every time you turn around expect to see me," Gerard said. "'Cause one time you'll turn around and I'll be there, and I'll kill you, Matt."

The animal was flat on the ground, rubbing his injured nose with his forelegs. He did that for a while. Then he got up, growling.

"Life is hard, but it's harder if you're stupid."

The whole pack of animals was growling, now. They moved forward in a semicircle. They seemed to be coordinated. Gerard ruffled his feathers, and ruffled them again. He even flapped his wings, trying to make as large and active a shape of himself as possible. These creatures didn't seem to care.

"Look, you fools, you're in danger, can't you see? They're after you, they're after all of us!"

But the spoken voices seemed to have no effect at all. The animals just kept moving forward, slowly. One was loping around behind Gerard. He turned his head to look. Not good, not good.

"Get back to where you once belonged!" Gerard flapped his wings again, nervously, but apparently the anxiety gave him new strength, because there was a bit of lift from the branch he stood on. The growling animals closed in—

And Gerard flapped his wings hard—hard—and felt himself lift into the air. It was weeks since his last feather clip, that was the reason. He could fly! He moved high above the ground, and discovered that he could soar a little. Not much, but a little. The smelly animals were far below, howling at him, but Gerard turned west, following the road that Stan had been driving on. He was heading away from the sunrise toward darkness. With his acute sense of smell, he detected the odor of food, and flew toward that.

Sleeping in the front seat of her car, Alex Burnet opened her eyes and saw that she was surrounded by men. Three of them were peering into her car. They wore cowboy hats and carried big pronged sticks with loops on them. She sat up abruptly. One of them waved for her to be still.

"Jes' a moment, miss."

Alex looked over at her son, Jamie, sleeping peacefully in the seat beside her. He didn't awaken. Nothing woke Jamie.

When she looked back outside, she gasped. One of the cowboys raised his stick. A gigantic rattlesnake, easily five feet long and as thick as a forearm, was wriggling on the end of it, making a sizzling sound with its rattle.

"You can come out now, if you want." He swung the snake away.

She opened the door cautiously.

"It's the heat of your engine," one of them said. "Draws 'em under the car in the mornings."

She saw that there were six men altogether. They each had sticks, and carried large sacks with squirming contents. "What're you doing?"

"We're collecting rattlers."

"Why?" she said.

"For the Rattlesnake Roundup next week. In Yuma."

"Uh-huh . . ."

"Do it every year. It's a contest. Who brings the most snakes."

"I see."

"It's by weight, so you want the big 'uns. Didn't mean to frighten you."

"Thank you."

The group of men was moving off. The man talking to her lagged behind. "Ma'am, you oughtn't to be out here alone," he said. "Though I see you got yourself a weapon." He nodded to the backseat of the car.

"Yes," she said, "but I don't have any ammo."

"Well, that won't do you," the man said. He started toward his car, parked across the road. "Is that a twelve-gauge you got?"

"Yes, it is."

"These'll serve." He gave her a handful of red shells. She stuffed them into her pockets.

"Thanks. What do I owe you?"

He shook his head. "You just take care, ma'am." He turned to rejoin the others. "A black Hummer came up this road about an hour ago. Big guy with a beard, said he was looking for a woman and her little boy. Said he was their uncle and they were missing."

"Uh-huh. What'd you tell him?"

"We hadn't seen you yet. So we said no."

"Which way did he go?" she said.

"Toward Elsinore. But I figure anytime now he'll be heading back."

"Thanks," she said.

He waved. "Don't stop for gas," he said. "And good luck."

TRANSCRIPT: CBS 5 SAN FRANCISCO >>>>>>>>>

Accused Bio-Terrorist Released Today

(CBS 5) Suspected terrorist Mark Sanger was released from Alameda County Jail today on two years' probation for possession of dangerous biological materials. Informed sources say the technical complexity of the government's charges against Sanger led the prosecutors to reluctantly conclude that they might not be able to put the suspect behind bars. In particular, the charge against Sanger that he had genetically modified turtles in Central America has now been thrown into question. We spoke with Julio Manarez in Costa Rica.

(Manarez) It is true that the Atlantic turtles have suffered from genetic modification that produces a purple color in their shells. As yet there is no explanation for how this happened. But the age of the turtles indicates that genetic manipulation occurred five to ten years ago.

(CBS 5) Shortly after his arrest, investigators determined that Sanger had not been in Costa Rica early enough to have carried out the genetic change. He was only there last year. And so Mark Sanger, suspected terrorist, is now free on a five-hundred-dollar fine.

CH079

In **Congressional** Hearing Room 443, while waiting for proceedings to begin, Congressman Marvin Minkowski (D-Wisconsin) turned to Congressman Henry Wexler (D-California) and said, "Shouldn't we have stronger regulations to limit the availability of recombinant DNA technology?"

"You thinking of Sanger?"

"Well, he's the most recent case. Where did he get his stuff, do you know?"

"On the Internet," Wexler said. "You can buy recombinant kits from outfits in New Jersey and North Carolina. Cost a couple of hundred bucks."

"That's asking for trouble, isn't it?"

"Listen," Wexler said, "my wife gardens. Does your wife garden?"

"Now that the kids are gone? She's a fanatic about her roses."

"Local garden club? All of that?"

"Well, sure."

"Plenty of gardeners who used to make hybrids by grafting cuttings onto rootstocks now use DNA kits to carry things a step further," Wexler said. "People are making genetically modified roses all over the world. Supposedly a Japanese company has made a blue rose using GM methods. A blue rose has been a dream of growers for centuries. Point is, the technology's everywhere, Marv. It's in big companies, and it's in backyards. Everywhere."

"What do we do about that?" Minkowski said.

"Nothing," Wexler said. "I'm not about to do anything to make your wife angry. Or mine." He cupped his chin in his hand, in a gesture that always looked intelligent on camera. "But maybe," he said, "maybe it's time for a speech expressing my concern about the dangers of this uncontrolled technology."

"Good idea," Minkowski said. "I think I'll give one, too."

LIPOSUCTION NEWS

Prime Minister's Fat Sells for $18,000
Next: Celebrities to Donate Fat for Charity

BBC NEWS. A bar of soap made from fat liposuctioned from Italian Prime Minister Silvio Berlusconi has been sold for $18,000 to a private collector. The soap is a work of art entitled "Mani Pulite" ("Clean Hands"), made by the artist Gianni Motti, who is based in Switzerland. Motti bought the fat from a clinic in Lugarno where Berlusconi had the liposuction performed. Motti then molded it into a bar of soap, which sold at the Basel art fair to a private Swiss collector who "can now wash his hands with Berlusconi."

Commentators noted that Berlusconi is unpopular in Europe, which may have reduced the price fetched by his fat. The fat of film celebrities would be worth significantly more. "The sky's the limit for Brad Pitt or Pamela Anderson by-products," said one.

Would celebrities ever sell their fat? "Why not?" said a Beverly Hills plastic surgeon. "It could be a charity thing. After all, they're doing the liposuction anyway. At the moment we just throw the fat away. But they might as well use their fat to help worthy causes."

Speedboat Racer Bums Around
The Butt of Many Jokes

WIRED NEWS SERVICE. Wealthy New Zealander Peter Bethune will attempt to set a world record on a speedboat powered by fat from his own backside. His eco-correct

LIPOSUCTION NEWS

78-foot trimaran, *Earthrace,* is powered entirely by bio-diesel fuel made from vegetable oil and other fats. In fact, Bethune's bum will make only a minor contribution to the round-the-world journey. His buttocks yielded a mere liter of fuel. However, Bethune noted that he was badly bruised and said "it was a personal sacrifice" to produce the fuel.

Artist Cooks, Eats His Own Body Fat
Protests "Wastefulness" of Western Society

REUTERS. New York conceptual artist Ricardo Vega underwent liposuction, cooked his fat, and ate it. He said his purpose was to draw attention to the wastefulness of Western society. He also set aside other portions of his fat for sale, noting that this would enable people to taste human flesh and experience cannibalism. Vega did not set a price for his fat, but one art dealer estimated that it would be worth considerably less than Berlusconi's. "Berlusconi is a prime minister," he pointed out. "Vega is an unknown. Besides, this has already been done by the artist Marcos Evaristta, who made meatballs of his body fat."

Marcos Evaristta is a Chilean-born artist living in Denmark. Reports that his body-fat meatballs would be auctioned by Christie's in New York could not be confirmed as Christie's representatives did not return phone calls.

CH080

The ambulance sped south on the freeway. Sitting in the driver's seat, wearing her new Bluetooth headset, Dolly talked to Vasco. Vasco was angry, but there was nothing Dolly could do about it. He'd set off in the wrong direction a second time. He had only himself to blame.

"Look," Dolly said. "We just got telephone records for the last five years. Just got 'em this minute. Alex calls people in this area code named Kendall, Henry and Lynn. He's a biochemist; we don't know what she does. But Lynn and Alex are the same age. We think maybe they grew up together."

"And where are they located?" Vasco said. "The Kendalls."

"La Jolla. It's north of—"

"I know where it is, goddamn it," Vasco said.

"Where are you now?" Dolly said.

"Coming back from Elsinore. I'm at least an hour from La Jolla. Road's so damn twisty. Goddamn it, I *know* she was sleeping on this road somewhere."

"How do you know?"

"I just know. Got my nose working."

"Okay, well, she's probably on her way to La Jolla now. She might even be there already."

"And where are you?"

"Twenty minutes from the Kendall house. You want us to pick them up?"

Vasco said, "How's the doc?"

"Sober."

"Sure?"

"Close enough for government work," Dolly said. "He's drinking coffee from a thermos."

"You check the thermos?"

"Yes. Of course. So—do we pick up, or wait for you?"

"If it's the girl, Alex, leave her alone. But if you see the kid, grab him."

"Will do," Dolly said.

CH081

Bob," **Alex said,** holding her phone to her ear.

She heard a groan at the other end. "What time is it?"

"It's seven in the morning, Bob."

"Aw Christ." A thump as his head hit the pillow. "This better be important, Alex."

"Were you out on a wine-tasting?" Robert A. Koch, distinguished head of the law firm, devoted a great deal of attention to wine. Kept his collection in lockers all over town. Bought at auction from Christie's; made trips to Napa, Australia, France. But as far as Alex was concerned, the whole thing was just an excuse to get drunk on a regular basis.

"I'm waiting, Alex," he said. "It better be good."

"Okay, last twenty-four hours, I got a bounty hunter, huge guy looks like a walking brick, he's after me and my kid, trying to stick biopsy needles in us and take our cells."

"Very funny. I'm waiting."

"I'm serious, Bob. There's a bounty hunter chasing me and my kid."

"This is out of nowhere?"

"No. I think it's related to BioGen."

"I hear BioGen is having troubles," Bob said. "And they're trying to take your cells? They probably can't do that."

"*Probably* is not what I want to hear."

"You know the law is unclear."

"Look," she said, "I have my eight-year-old son here; they're trying to grab him in the back of an ambulance and stick needles into his liver, I don't want to hear *unclear*. I want to hear *We'll stop it*."

"We'll certainly try," he said. "This is your father's case?"

"Yeah."

"Did you call him?"

"He's not answering."

"You call the police?"

"There's a warrant out for my arrest. In Oxnard. There's a hearing in Oxnard today. I need somebody good to go up and appear for me."

"I'll send Dennis."

"I said, somebody *good*."

"Dennis is good."

"Dennis is good if he has a month. This is today, Bob."

"Well, who do you want?"

"I want you," she said.

"Aw Christ. Oxnard? It's so fucking far . . . I haven't had my shots . . ."

"I have a sawed-off shotgun in the backseat, Bob. I don't really care if you think the drive is too long."

"Okay, okay, take it easy," he said. "I have to arrange some things."

"Will you go?"

"Yes, I'll go. You want to give me a hint what this is about?"

"You'll find it in the Burnet file. I assume it has to do with takings, by eminent domain or simple conversion."

"Taking your cells?"

"They claim they own them."

"How can they own *your* cells? They own your father's cells. Oh, I get it. Same cells. But that's bullshit, Alex."

"Tell the judge."

"They can't violate the integrity of your body, or the body of your kid, just—"

"Save it for the judge," she said. "I'll call you later, find out how it went."

She flipped the phone shut.

She looked down at Jamie. He was still sleeping, peaceful as an angel.

If Koch got to Oxnard by late morning, he might get an emergency hearing set for the afternoon. She should probably call him around four p.m. That seemed a very long time away.

She drove toward La Jolla.

CH082

t's the last thing we need, Henry Kendall thought. Visitors! He watched in dismay as Lynn threw her arms around Alex Burnet and then bent over to hug Alex's kid, Jamie. Alex and Jamie had just shown up, with no advance warning. The women were chattering excitedly, arms fluttering, happy to see each other as they walked into the kitchen to get food for Alex's Jamie. Meanwhile, his son Jamie and Dave were playing Drive or Die! on the PlayStation. The sound of crunching metal and squealing tires filled the room.

Henry Kendall was overwhelmed. He walked into the bedroom to think things through. He had just come back from the police station, where he reviewed the playground security camera tape from the day before. The image quality wasn't that good—thank God—because the image of that kid Billy kicking and beating his son was so upsetting he could hardly watch. He had to look away several times. And those other boys, that gang of skaters, they should all be in jail. With any luck, they'd be expelled from school.

But Henry knew it wouldn't end there. It never did. Everybody sued these days, and no doubt the skater parents would sue to have their kids reinstated. They'd sue Henry's family, and they'd sue Jamie and Dave. And out of those lawsuits it was sure to emerge that there was no such thing as Gandalf-Crikey syndrome, or whatever it was that Lynn had made up. It was sure to emerge that Dave was in reality a transgenic chimp.

And then what? A media circus beyond all imagining. Reporters camped on the front lawn for weeks. Chasing them wherever they went. Filming them with spy cameras day and night. Destroying their lives. And around the time the reporters got bored, the religious people and the environmentalists would start in. Henry and his family would be called Godless. They'd be called criminals. They'd be called danger-ous, and un-American, and a threat to the biosphere. In his mind he saw commentators on TV in a babel of languages—English, Spanish, German, Japanese—all talking, with pictures of him, and Dave, in the background.

And that was just the beginning.

Dave would be taken away. Henry could possibly go to jail. (Though he doubted that; scientists had been breaking the rules about genetic testing for two decades, and none had ever gone to jail, even when pa-tients died.) But he would certainly be barred from research. He could be kicked out of the lab for a year or more. How would he support his family? Lynn couldn't do it alone, and her web business would almost certainly dry up. And what would happen to Dave? And his son? To Tracy? And what about their community? La Jolla was pretty liberal (parts of it, anyway), but people might not be understanding about the idea of a humanzee going to school with their kids. It was radical, no doubt about it. People weren't ready for it. Liberals were only so liberal.

They might have to move. They might have to sell their house and go somewhere remote, like Montana. Though maybe people would be even less accepting of them there.

These and other thoughts raced through his mind, to the accompa-niment of cars squealing and crashing into each other, and his wife and her friend laughing in the kitchen. He felt overwhelmed. And in the middle of it, at the center of everything, was his deep sense of guilt.

One thing was clear. He had to keep track of his kids. He had to know where they were. He couldn't risk further incidents like the one that had occurred the day before. Lynn had kept the children at home for an extra hour, intending to let them go to school later, so there wouldn't be any incidents with older kids. That Cleever kid was a menace, and it wasn't likely he was jailed. They'd probably just scare him and give him over to the custody of his father. The father, Henry knew, was a defense analyst for a local think tank and a hard-ass gun nut. One of those intellectuals who liked to shoot things. A manly intellectual. There was no telling what could happen.

He turned to the package he had brought home from the lab. It was marked TrackTech Industries, Chiba City, Japan. Inside were five inch-long polished silver tubes, slightly thinner than soda straws. He pulled them out and looked at them. These marvels of miniaturization had GPS technology built in, as well as monitors for temperature, pulse, respiration, and blood pressure. They were activated by a magnet that you touched at one end. The tip glowed blue once, then nothing.

They were designed to keep track of lab primates, monkeys and baboons. The tubes were inserted with a special surgical instrument that looked like an oversized syringe. They were placed under the skin of the neck, just above the clavicle. Henry couldn't do that to the kids, of course. So the question was, where to put them?

He went back to the living room where the kids were. Drop the sensors in their school bags? No. Down the collars of their shirts? He shook his head. They'd feel them.

Then where?

The surgical instrument worked perfectly. The devices went smoothly into the rubber at the heel of the sneaker. He did it for Dave's sneaker, then for Jamie's, then, on an impulse, went out and got a sneaker from Alex's son, Jamie, as well.

"What for?" Jamie said.

"I need to measure it. Back in a sec."

He inserted another device into the third sneaker.

That left two more. Henry thought about it for a while. Several possibilities came to mind.

CH083

The Hummer pulled up behind the ambulance, and Vasco got out. He walked up to the ambulance.

Dolly slid over onto the passenger seat.

"What's happening," Vasco said, as he got in.

Dolly nodded to the house at the end of the street. "That's the Kendall place. You see Burnet's car in front. She's been in there an hour."

Vasco frowned. "What's goin' on?"

She shook her head. "I could get the directional mike, but we have to be straight on to the windows, and I figured you didn't want me to pull up closer."

"Right, I don't."

Vasco leaned back in his seat. He gave a long sigh. He looked at his watch.

"Well, we can't go in there." Bounty hunters were permitted to enter the premises of the fugitive, even without a search warrant, but they could not enter the premises of third parties, even if they knew the fugitive was there. "Sooner or later," he said, "they gotta come out. And when they do, we'll be here."

Gerard was tired. He had been flying for an hour since his last stop, which had been something of a disaster.

Shortly after dawn, he had landed at a complex of buildings where he smelled food. The buildings were made of wood with faded paint. There were old cars with grass growing up around them. Large animals made snorting sounds behind a fence. He stood on a fencepost and watched a young boy in blue coveralls walking out with a bucket in his hand. Gerard smelled food.

"I'm hungry," he said.

The young boy turned. He looked around briefly, then continued on his way.

"I want food," Gerard said. "I am hungry."

The boy paused again. He looked around again.

"What's the matter, don't you know how to talk?" Gerard said.

"Yes," the kid said. "Where are you?"

"Here."

The kid squinted. He walked over to the fence.

"My name is Gerard."

"No kidding! You can talk!"

"How thrilling for you," Gerard said. He could smell the bucket strongly now. He smelled corn and other grains. He could also smell something else that smelled bad. But his hunger overwhelmed him.

"I want food."

"What food do you want?" the kid said. He reached into the bucket and scooped up a handful of feed. "You want this?"

Gerard bent over, tasted it. He spit it out at once. "Yuck!"

"It's chicken feed. Nothing wrong with it. *They* eat it."

"Do you have any fresh vegetables?"

The kid laughed. "You're funny. You sound like British. What's your name?"

"Gerard. An orange? Do you have an orange?" He hopped back and forth on the fencepost, impatient. "I like an orange."

"How come you talk so good?"

"I could ask the same of you."

"You know what? I'm going to show you to my dad," the kid said. He held out his hand. "You're tame, aren't you?"

"Sink me!" Gerard stepped on his hand.

The kid put Gerard on his shoulder. He started walking back to the wooden building. "I bet we can sell you for a lot of money," he said.

Gerard gave a squawk and flew up to the roof of one building.

"Hey! Come back!"

From inside the house, a voice: "Jared, do your chores!"

Gerard watched as the kid reluctantly turned back to a dirt yard, where he tossed handfuls of the grain from the bucket onto the ground. A group of yellow birds clucked and jumped as the food was thrown to them. They looked incredibly stupid.

It took a moment before Gerard decided that he would eat that food, after all. He flew down and made a loud squawk to drive away the stupid birds, then started eating their grain. It tasted disgusting, but he had to eat something. Meanwhile the kid dived for him, hands outstretched. Gerard flew into the air, pecked the kid hard on the nose—the kid screamed—and then dropped down a short distance away, to eat again. These big yellow birds were all around him.

"Get back! Get back, all of you!"

The yellow birds paid little attention. Gerard made the sound of a siren. The kid dived again, barely missing Gerard. He was obviously a stupid kid.

"Buffeting! Buffeting! Twenty thousand feet, buffeting! I am going to push the stick forward—" Then the sound of a huge, air-shattering explosion. The chickens scattered at that, and he had a moment of peace, eating a little.

Now the kid was back with a net, and was swiping downward with it. That was too much excitement for Gerard, who was feeling sick in the stomach from the horrid food, so he flew quickly into the air, evacuating and hitting the kid perfectly on the head, before he climbed into blue sky and went on his way.

Twenty minutes later, in cooler air, he came to the coast and followed it. It was easier here, because there were updrafts, a blessing to his tired wings. He could not soar, but it helped nonetheless. He experienced a modest sense of peace.

At least, he did until some giant white bird—enormously huge, gigantic—rushed silently up at him, whooshing past, creating spinning turbulence that tumbled him out of control. When Gerard got his bearings again, the bird had glided away from him on huge flat wings. There was a single eye in the center of the head; it glinted in the sun. And the wings never moved; they just remained straight and flat.

Gerard was grateful there was not a flock of these birds, but instead only one. He watched as it circled slowly toward the ground below. And that was when he noticed the beautiful green oasis in the midst of the dry coast. An oasis! It was built at the site of a large cluster of huge boulders. Surrounding the boulders were palm trees and luscious gardens and pretty buildings nestled among the green. Gerard felt certain that there would be food there. It was so inviting, he spiraled down.

It was a kind of dream. Beautiful people in white robes walking silently through a garden of flowers and shrubs, in the cool shade of palm trees, with all sorts of birds flittering about. He did not smell food here, but he was sure there must be some.

And then he smelled—orange! Cut orange!

It took him only a moment to locate another bird, brilliant blue and red, standing on a perch with lots of oranges all around him on a tray below. Oranges, and avocado, and bits of lettuce. Cautiously, Gerard landed next to him.

"I want you to want me," he said.

"Hel-lo," blue-and-red bird said.

"I need you to need me."

"Hel-lo."

"Nice place you got here. My name is Gerard."

"Aaah, what's up, doc?" the bird said.

"Mind if I have an orange?"

"Hel-lo," the bird said. "Aaah, what's up doc?"

"I said, I would like an orange."

"Hel-lo."

Gerard lost patience. He went for the orange. The blue-and-red bird pecked at him viciously; Gerard dodged and flapped away with the orange in his mouth. He sat on a tree branch and looked back. That was when he saw that the other bird was chained to the perch. Gerard ate the orange at his leisure. Then he flew back for more. He came at the perch from behind, then later from the side. He flew in unexpectedly, each time dodging the bird, who could only say, "Hel-lo!"

After half an hour, he was quite satisfied.

Meanwhile, he watched the people in white robes come and go, talking of NyQuil and Jell-O. He said, "Jell-O, the tasty dessert for the whole family, now with more calci-yum!" Two of the people in robes looked up. Someone laughed. Then continued on their way. This place was peaceful; the water gurgled in little brooks beside the path. He would stay here, Gerard felt certain, for a long, long time.

Okay, we got action," Vasco said. Two young kids were coming out of the Kendall house. One was a dark kid in a baseball cap, sort of bowlegged. The other was fair, also in a baseball cap. Wearing khakis and a sport shirt.

"Looks like Jamie," he said, putting the car in gear.

They drove slowly forward.

"I don't know," Dolly said. "Doesn't look quite the same."

"It's the baseball hat. Just ask him," Vasco said.

Dolly rolled down her window. She leaned out. "Jamie, honey?"

The boy turned. "Yes?" he said.

Dolly jumped out of the car.

Henry Kendall was working at the computer, activating the TrackTech, when he heard the high-pitched scream from outside. He knew at once that it was Dave. He bolted up and ran for the door. Behind him was Lynn, running from the kitchen. But he noticed that Alex stayed in the kitchen, with her arms around her son, Jamie. She looked terrified.

Dave was confused by what he saw. Jamie spoke to the woman in the big white car, and then she jumped out and grabbed him. Dave was not inclined to attack females, so he watched as the woman scooped up Jamie, took him to the back of the white car, and opened the back doors. Dave saw a man inside in a white coat, and he saw lots of shiny equipment that frightened him.

Jamie must have been frightened, too, because suddenly he was screaming, and then the woman slammed the back doors shut.

Before the car started moving, Dave screamed and leaped onto the back, grabbing the handles on the door. The white car accelerated forward, going fast. Dave held on, struggling to keep his balance. When he had a good grip, he pulled up, so he could look through the rear windows. He saw the man in the coat and the woman pushing Jamie onto a bed, trying to tie him down. Jamie was screaming.

Dave felt rage flood through his body. He snarled and banged at the doors. The woman looked up in alarm. She seemed shocked to see Dave. She yelled something to the driver.

The driver started to swerve the white car. Dave was flung sideways, barely able to hold on to the recessed door handles. When the car swung him back once more, he reached high, grabbing the lights above the doors. He pulled himself onto the top of the ambulance. The wind blew hard. The surface was smooth. He lay flat, inching forward. The car straightened out, drove more slowly. He heard yelling inside.

He crept forward.

"We lost him!" Dolly yelled, looking out the back window.

"What was it?"

"Looked like an ape!"

"He's not an ape; he's my friend!" Jamie yelled, struggling. "He goes to school with me."

The kid's baseball cap fell off, and Dolly saw that he had dark brown hair. She said, "What's your name?"

"Jamie. Jamie Kendall."

"Oh no," she said.

"Aw Christ," Vasco said, driving. "You got the wrong kid?"

"He said his name was Jamie!"

"It's the wrong kid. Jesus Christ, you're an idiot, Dolly. This is kidnapping."

"Well, it's not my fault—"

"Whose fault do you think it is?"

"You saw the kid too."

"I didn't see—"

"You were looking right out there."

"Christ, shut up. Stop arguing. We gotta take him back."

"What do you mean?"

"We gotta take him back where we found him. It's goddamn kidnapping."

And then Vasco swore, and screamed.

Dave was on the roof of the cab, wedged between the light bar and the slope of the ambulance. He leaned over the driver's side. There was a big side mirror there. He could see an ugly black-bearded man, driving and shouting. He knew the man was going to hurt Jamie. He could see the man baring his teeth in a sign of rage.

Dave leaned down, resting his weight on the side mirror, and swung his arm in through the open window. His strong fingers grabbed the bearded man by the nose, and the man yelled and jerked his head. Dave's fingers slipped, but he lunged back and bit down hard on the man's ear, and held on. The man was screaming at him in rage. Dave could feel that rage, but he had plenty of his own. He pulled hard, and felt the ear come away with a gush of hot blood.

The man screamed, and spun the wheel.

The ambulance tilted, the left wheels came up off the ground, and the vehicle slowly turned over and crashed down on its right side. The sound of screeching metal was incredibly loud. Dave was riding the ambulance down as it fell, but he lost his grip on impact. His feet slammed into the face of the bearded man and one of his shoes went right into his mouth. The vehicle slid to a stop on its side. The man was biting and coughing. The woman inside was screaming. Dave pulled his foot out of his shoe, leaving it in the bearded man's mouth. Blood was gushing everywhere from the man's ear.

He yanked off the other shoe, scampered around to the back of the ambulance, and managed with some effort to get the doors open.

The white-coat man was lying on his side, bleeding from his mouth. Jamie was underneath the man, yelling. Dave dragged the white-coat man out of the car, dropped him onto the street. Then he went and got Jamie, put him on his back, and ran, carrying him back to their house.

Jamie said, "Are you hurt?"

The ear was still in Dave's mouth. He spit it into his hand. "No."

"What's that in your hand?"

Dave opened his fist. "It's an ear."

"Ugh. Eeeew!"

"I bit his ear. He was bad. He hurted you."

"Uck!"

Up ahead, they saw everybody standing out on the front lawn of their house. Henry and Lynn and the new people, too. Dave put Jamie on the ground, and he ran to his parents. Dave waited for his mother, Lynn, to comfort him, but she was entirely focused on Jamie. It made him feel bad. He dropped the ear in his hand on the ground. Everybody was swirling around him, but nobody touched him, nobody put their fingers in his fur.

He felt more and more sad.

Then he saw the boxy black car barreling down the street toward them. It was huge, high off the ground, and it drove right up onto the lawn.

CH086

The Oxnard courtroom was small and so cold Bob Koch thought he would catch pneumonia. He was feeling none too good anyway. His hangover had left a very sour feeling in his stomach. The judge was a youngish guy, about forty, and he looked hungover, too. But maybe not. Koch cleared his throat.

"Your Honor, I am here representing Alexandra Burnet, who is unable to be here in person."

"This court has ordered her to appear," the judge said. "In person."

"I am aware of that, Your Honor, but she and her child are presently being pursued by a bounty hunter who intends to remove tissue from their bodies, and she is therefore in flight to prevent that."

"What bounty hunter?" the judge said. "Why is there a bounty hunter involved in this?"

"We would like to know exactly that, Your Honor," Bob Koch said.

The judge turned. "Mr. Rodriguez?"

"Your Honor," Rodriguez said, standing, "there is no bounty hunter per se."

"Well, what is there?"

"There is a professional fugitive-recovery agent at work."

"With what authorization?"

"He is not authorized per se. In this case he is making a citizen's arrest, Your Honor."

"Arrest of whom?"

"Of Ms. Burnet and her son."

"On what basis?"

"Possession of stolen property, Your Honor."

"To make a citizen's arrest, the possession of stolen property has to be witnessed by the person making the arrest."

"Yes, Your Honor."

"What has been witnessed?"

"The possession of the property in question, Your Honor."

"You are talking about the Burnet cell line," the judge said.

"Yes, Your Honor. As previously documented before this court, that cell line is owned by UCLA and licensed to BioGen, in Westview. The ownership is attested to by several prior court rulings."

"How, then, is it stolen?"

"Your Honor, we have evidence that Mr. Burnet conspired to eliminate the cell lines in possession of BioGen. But whether that is true or not, BioGen has the right to restore the cell lines that it owns."

"It can restore them from Mr. Burnet."

"Yes, Your Honor. Presumably so, since the court has ruled that Mr. Burnet's cells belong to BioGen, they can at any time take more. Whether the property is actually within Mr. Burnet's body or not is immaterial. BioGen owns the cells."

"You are denying Mr. Burnet's right to the integrity of his body?" the judge said, raising an eyebrow.

"With respect, Your Honor, there is no such right. Suppose someone took your wife's diamond ring and swallowed it. The ring is still your property."

"Yes," the judge said, "but I might be required to wait patiently for it to reappear."

"Yes, Your Honor. But suppose for some reason the ring becomes stuck in the intestine. Don't you have the right to retrieve it? Clearly, you do. It can't be kept from you. It's your property wherever it is. Whoever swallows it assumes the risk of retrieval."

Koch thought he'd better move in. "Your Honor," he said, "if I remember my high school biology correctly, anything swallowed is not actually inside the body, any more than something inside a doughnut hole is inside the doughnut. The ring is outside the body."

Rodriguez began to sputter. "Your Honor—"

"Your Honor," Koch said, raising his voice, "I trust we can all agree that we are not talking about diamond rings that have been stolen. We are talking about cells that reside inside the human body. The notion that these cells can be owned by someone else—even if the appellate court has upheld a jury finding—leads to absurd conclusions, as you see here. If BioGen no longer possesses Mr. Burnet's cells, then they have lost them by their own foolish actions. They are not entitled to go back and get more. If you lose your diamond ring, you can't go back to the diamond mine and get a replacement."

Rodriguez said, "The analogy is inexact."

"Your Honor, all analogies are inexact."

"In this instance," Rodriguez said, "I would ask the court to stick narrowly to the issue at hand, and consider the previous findings of the court that are relevant to the issue. The court has held that BioGen owns these cells. They came from Mr. Burnet but they are the property of BioGen. We argue that we have the right to retrieve these cells at any time."

"Your Honor, this argument directly conflicts with the Thirteenth Amendment, against chattel slavery. BioGen may own Mr. Burnet's cells. But they don't own Mr. Burnet. They *can't*."

"We never claimed to own Mr. Burnet, only his cells. And that is all we are asking for now," Rodriguez said.

"But the practical consequence of your claim is that you effectively own Mr. Burnet, since you *do* claim access to his body at any time—"

The judge was looking weary. "Gentlemen, I see the issue," he said, "but what does any of this have to do with Ms. Burnet and her son?"

Bob Koch stepped back. Let Rodriguez bury himself on this one, he thought. The conclusion he was asking the court to draw was inconceivable.

"Your Honor," Rodriguez said, "if the court accepts that Mr. Burnet's cells are my client's property, as I believe it must, then said cells are my client's property wherever they are found. For example, if Mr. Burnet gave blood at a blood bank, the donated blood would contain cells that we own. We could assert ownership of those cells, and demand to extract them from the donated blood, since Mr. Burnet is not legally able to give those cells to anyone else. They are our property.

"Similarly, the same cells that we own—the identical cells—are also found in Mr. Burnet's children and descendants. Therefore we have ownership of those cells as well. And we have the right to take the cells."

"And the bounty hunter?"

"The fugitive-recovery specialist," Rodriguez said, "is making a citizen's arrest on the following basis. If he sees Mr. Burnet's descendants, then, since they are by definition walking around with our property, they are self-evidently in possession of stolen property, and can be arrested."

The judge sighed.

"Your Honor," Rodriguez said, "this conclusion may strike the court as illogical, but the fact is that we are in a new era, and what seems strange to us now will in a few years not seem so strange. Already a large percentage of the human genome is owned. The genetic information for various disease organisms is owned. The notion that such biological elements are in private hands is only odd because it is new to us. But the court must rule in accordance with previous findings. The Burnet cells are our cells."

"But in the case of descendants, the cells are copies," the judge said.

"Yes, Your Honor, but that is not at issue. If I own a formula to make something, and someone Xeroxes that formula on a sheet of paper and gives it to another, it remains my property. I own the formula, no matter how it is copied, or by whom. And I have the right to retrieve the copy."

The judge turned to Bob Koch. "Mr. Koch?"

"**Your Honor,** Mr. Rodriguez has asked you to rule narrowly. So do I. Previous courts held that once Mr. Burnet's cells *were out of his body*, they no longer belonged to him. They did not say that Mr. Burnet was a walking gold mine that could be plundered at will, again and again, by BioGen. And they certainly said nothing to imply that BioGen had a right to physically take these cells no matter who carried them. That claim goes far beyond any implication of the court's prior finding. It is, in fact, a new claim made out of nothing but wishful thinking. And we ask the court to require BioGen to call off this bounty hunter."

The judge said, "I do not understand on what basis BioGen has simply acted on its own, Mr. Rodriguez. This appears hasty and unwarranted. You could certainly wait for Ms. Burnet to appear before this court."

"Unfortunately, Your Honor, that is not possible. The business situation of my client is critical. As I said to you, we believe we are victims of a conspiracy to deprive us of what is ours. Without going into details, it is urgent that the cells be replaced immediately. If the court forces a delay, we may lose an enormous business undertaking in the meanwhile, such that our company goes out of business. We merely attempt a timely response to an urgent problem."

Bob could tell the judge was going for it. All that timeliness crap was working on him; he didn't want to be responsible for putting a California biotech company out of business. The judge swiveled in his chair, glanced at the wall clock, swiveled back.

Bob had to pull it out. And he had to do it now.

"Your Honor," he said, "there is an additional issue that bears on your decision. I would like to bring to your attention the following affidavit from Duke University Medical Center, dated today." He handed a copy to Rodriguez. "I will summarize the contents for Your Honor, and how it affects the issue before you."

Burnet's cell line, he explained, was capable of making large quantities of a chemical called cytotoxic TLA7D, a potent anticarcinogen. It was that chemical that made BioGen's cell line so valuable.

"However, last week the U.S. Patent Office issued a patent for the gene TLA4A. This is a promoter gene that codes for an enzyme that snips out a hydroxy group from the center of a protein called cytotoxic T-lymphocyte associated protein 4B. This protein is the precursor of cytotoxic TLA7D, which forms when the hydroxy group is removed. Unless the hydroxy group is snipped out, the protein has no biological activity. So the gene that controls the manufacture of BioGen's product is owned by Duke University, and they assert ownership in the document now in your hands."

Rodriguez was turning very red. "Your Honor," he said, "this is an attempt to confuse what should be a very simple case. I would urge that you—"

"It *is* simple," Bob agreed. "Unless BioGen makes a licensing agreement with Duke, they cannot use the enzyme made by the Duke gene. The enzyme and its product are owned by someone else."

"But this is—"

"BioGen owns a cell, Your Honor," Bob said. "But not all the genes inside that cell."

The judge looked again at the clock. "I will take this under advisement," he said, "and give you my ruling tomorrow."

"But Your Honor—"

"Thank you, gentlemen. Arguments are concluded."

"But Your Honor, we have a woman and her son being hounded—"

"I believe I understand the issue. I need to understand the law. I will see you tomorrow, counselors."

CH087

The Kendalls were screaming as the Hummer raced forward, but Vasco Borden, snarling through his aching teeth, one hand holding the bandage against his bleeding ear, knew what he was doing. He drove the car up onto the lawn and pulled to a stop, blocking the front door. Then he and Dolly jumped out, grabbed Alex's Jamie off the lawn, pushed the kid's stunned mother to the ground, leapt back into the Hummer, and roared off. While the others just stood there and stared.

"Just like that, baby," Vasco said, shouting. "If you're not inside the house, you're mine."

He roared off down the street.

"We lost our ambulance, so we go to plan B." He looked back over his shoulder. "Dolly, honey, get the next operating room going. Tell 'em we'll be there in twenty minutes. One hour from now, this is all a *done deal*."

Henry Kendall was in shock. There had been a kidnapping right on his front lawn; he hadn't rushed forward to stop it; his own son was sobbing and clutching his mother; and Dave had dropped some guy's *ear* on the lawn; the other kid's mother was getting to her feet, screaming for the cops, but the Hummer was gone, down the street and around the corner, and *gone*.

He felt weak and emasculated, as if he'd somehow done something wrong, and he was embarrassed to be around Lynn's friend, so he went inside and sat down again at the computer. It was just where he had been sitting five minutes before, when Dave screamed and all this started.

He still had the TrackTech web site up, where he'd entered the names and the serial numbers. He had done it for Dave, and for Jamie, but he hadn't done it for the other Jamie. Feeling bad, he did it now.

The web site switched to a blank, featureless map, with an entry spot where you typed in the unit you were looking for. The first unit he entered was Jamie Burnet's. If the sensor was operating, he would have seen it moving down the street. But the blue spot wasn't moving, it was static. The address showed 348 Marbury Madison Drive, which was his own house.

He looked around the living room and saw Jamie's white sneakers over in the corner, with his little travel bag. He'd never even put the sneakers back on.

Next, he typed in the sensor for his own son. Same result. The blue spot was fixed at his own home address. Then it moved a little. And his son Jamie walked through the door. "Dad. What are you doing? The police are outside. They want to talk to everybody. "

"Okay, in a minute."

"His mom is really upset, Dad."

"In a minute."

"She's crying. Mom said to get a tissue."

"I'll be right with you."

Quickly, Henry typed in the third serial number—Dave's number. The screen went blank. He waited a moment. He saw the map as it was redrawn. It now showed roads leading north of town, in the area of Torrey Pines.

The blue dot was moving.

North, Torrey Pines Road, ENE, 57 mph.

As he watched, the dot turned off onto Gaylord Road, heading inland.

Somehow, Dave's sensor was in the Hummer. It either came out of his shoe, or they had taken his shoe. But the sensor was there, and working.

He said, "Jamie, go get Alex. Tell her I need to see her for a minute."

"But Dad—"

"Do it. And don't say anything to the police."

Alex stared at the screen. "I'm going to get that son of a bitch and I'm going to blow his head off. You touch my kid, you're dead." Her voice was flat, cold. Henry felt a chill. She meant it.

"Where's he going?" she said.

"He's left the coast and heading inland, but he may just be avoiding the Del Mar traffic. He may go back to the coast again. We'll know in a few minutes."

"How far away is he?"

"Ten minutes."

"Let's go. You bring that," she said, nodding to the laptop. "I'll get my gun."

Henry looked out the front window. There were three cop cars flashing their lights at the curb, and six cops on the front lawn. "Not that easy."

"Yes, it is. I'm parked around the corner."

"They said they want to see me."

"Make an excuse. I'll be in my car."

He told them Dave needed medical attention, and he had to take him to the hospital. He said that his wife, Lynn, had witnessed everything and could tell them what had taken place. He said he would give a full statement when he returned, but he needed to take Dave to the hospital.

Since Dave's hands were bloody, they accepted it. Lynn gave Henry a funny look. He said, "I'll be back as soon as I can." He walked around the back of the house and cut through the property behind. Dave followed him.

"Where are we going?" Dave said.

"To find that guy. The guy with the black beard."

"He hurted Jamie."

"Yeah, I know."

"I hurted him, too."

"Yeah, I know."

"His ears came off."

"Uh-huh."

"Next time his nose."

"Dave," he said. "We need to show restraint."

"What's re-straint?" Dave said.

It was too complicated to explain. Alex's white Toyota was up ahead. They got in the car. He got in front, Dave got in back.

"What is this?" Dave said, pointing to the seat beside him.

"Don't touch it, Dave," Alex said. "That's a gun."

She put the car in gear and drove off.

She called Bob Koch, on the off chance that he had news.

"I do," he said. "But I wish it were better."

"He let it go?"

"He held over until tomorrow."

"Did you try—"

"Yeah, I tried. He's confused. It's not the usual legal area for Oxnard judges. That's probably why they filed there."

"So, tomorrow?"

"Yeah."

"Thanks," she said, and hung up. There was no point in telling him what she was about to do. She wasn't even sure she would do it. But she thought that she probably would.

Henry was riding shotgun, looking at the computer. Now that he was out here, in a car, the connection sometimes dropped out for a minute or two. He began to worry about losing it altogether. He glanced back at Dave, who was shoeless. "Where are your shoes?"

"They camed off."

"Where?"

"In the white car." He meant the ambulance.

"How?"

"One was in his mouth. The man. Then the car falled."

"And your shoes came off?"

"Yes, they camed off."

Apparently Alex was thinking the same thing, because she said, "Then his shoes are still in the ambulance. Not the Hummer. We're following the wrong car."

"No, the ambulance crashed. It can't be the ambulance."

"Then the signal . . ."

"It must have fallen out of his shoe, and slipped into the guy's clothes. Somehow."

"Then it could slip out again."

"Yeah. It could."

"Or they could find it."

"Yeah."

She didn't say anything after that.

He continued watching the screen. The blue dot went north, then east. Then north. And finally east again, passing Rancho Santa Fe, going back to the desert. Then it curved onto Highland Drive. "Okay," he said. "I know where they're going. Solana Canyon."

"What's that?"

"It's a spa. Very big. Very high-end."

"With doctors?"

"I'm sure. They may even do surgery. Maybe face-lifts, liposuction, something like that."

"Then they have surgical facilities," she said grimly. She stepped on the accelerator.

The one hundred acres known as Solana Canyon represented a triumph of marketing. Only a few decades earlier the region was known by its original name, Hellhole Palms. It was a flat, boulder-strewn region, without a canyon in sight. Thus Solana Canyon had no canyon, and precious little to do with the coastal town of Solana Beach. The name simply tracked better than the other choices, which had been Angel Springs, Zen Mountain View, Cedar Springs, and Silver Hill Ashram.

Compared to the other choices, the name Solana Canyon conveyed a muted, understated quality in keeping with a resort that charged thousands of dollars a day to rejuvenate the bodies, minds, and spirits of its clients. This was accomplished through a combination of yoga, massage, meditation, spiritual counseling, and diet help, all delivered by staff who greeted guests with prayerful hands and a heartfelt "Namaste."

Solana Canyon was also a favorite spot for celebrities to dry out.

Alex drove right past the adobe-style main gate, artfully concealed behind giant palms. They were following the tracking signal, which was going around the back of the resort.

"He's taking the service entrance," Henry said.

"You've been here before?"

"Once. A lecture on genetics."

"And?"

"I wasn't invited back. They didn't like the message. You know the old saying. Professors attribute the intelligence of their students to environment and the intelligence of their children to genes. Same with rich people. If you're rich or good-looking, you want to hear that your genes make you that way. That enables you to feel inherently superior to other people—that you deserve your success. And then you can give other people as much crap as you—hold on, they're stopping. Slow down."

"What now?" she said. They were on a side road, and there was a service entrance up ahead.

"I think they're in the parking lot."

"So? Let's get them right there."

"No." He shook his head. "There's always a couple of security guys at the parking lot. You show a gun, and there'll be trouble." He watched the screen. "Stationary . . . now moving again. Now stationary." He frowned.

She said, "If there's security guards, they'll see Jamie struggling when he gets out."

"Maybe they've drugged him. Or . . . I don't know," he said quickly, seeing the pain on her face. "Wait, moving again. They're going around the back road."

She put the car in gear and drove to the service gate. The gate was open. Nobody was on duty. She drove through, into the parking lot. The back road was at the far corner of the lot.

"What do we do?" she said. "Follow them down the road?"

"I don't think so. If we do, they'll see us coming. Better park." He opened the door. "Let's take a walk through beautiful Solana Canyon resort." He looked at her. "You going to leave that shotgun here?"

"No," she said. She popped open the trunk, found a towel, wrapped the shotgun in it, and said, "I'm ready."

"O-kay," Henry said. "Here we go."

"Goddamn it," Vasco said, stepping on the brakes. He was driving around the back road to park behind the surgicenter. The plan was for Dr. Manuel Cajal to come out of the surgicenter, slip into the Hummer, do the biopsies, and go out again. Nobody sees it, nobody's the wiser.

But now the back road was blocked. Two backhoes, digging some big trench. No way across, and no other road. A hundred yards from the surgicenter.

"Damn, damn, damn," he said.

"Take it easy, Vasco," Dolly said. "It's no big deal. If the road is blocked, we just walk to the center, go in the rear door, and do it there."

"Everyone will see us walking through the resort."

"So what? We're just visitors. Besides, everybody at this place is completely self-absorbed. They have no time to think about us. And if they did, and if they decided to call someone—which they never would—the procedure'd be finished before the call was finished. Manuel can do it faster in there than out here."

"I don't like it." Vasco looked around, stared at the road, then at the spa grounds. But she was right. It was a quick walk through the garden. He turned to the kid. "Listen," he said. "This is how it is. We're going to take a walk. You just be quiet. And everything will be fine."

"What're you going to do?" he said. "To me."

"Nothing. Just take a little blood."

"Are there needles?"

"Just a little one, like at the doctor's."

He turned to Dolly. "Okay, call Manuel. Tell him we're coming. And let's get going."

Jamie had been diligently taught to yell and scream and kick if anyone ever tried to kidnap him, and he had done those things when they first grabbed him, but now he was very frightened, and he was afraid they would hurt him if he made any trouble. So he walked quietly along the path of the garden, with the woman keeping her hand on his shoulder and the big mean guy walking on the other side, wearing a cowboy hat so his ear wouldn't show.

They passed people in bathrobes, women mostly, chatting and laughing, but nobody really looked at them. They walked on through another garden area, and then he heard a voice say, "I say, do you need help with your homework?"

He was so startled he stopped. He looked up.

It was a bird. A sort of gray-colored bird.

"Are you a friend of Evan?" the bird said.

"No," he said.

"You're the same size as he is. What's eleven take away nine?"

Jamie was so surprised, he just stared.

"Let's go, dear," Dolly said. "It's just a bird."

"Just *a bird*!" the bird said. "Who are you calling a *bird*?"

"You really talk a lot," Jamie said.

"And you don't," the bird said. "Who are these people? Why are they holding you?"

"We're not holding him," Dolly said.

"You gentlemen aren't really trying to kill my son, are you?" the bird said.

"Ah Christ," Vasco said.

"Ah Christ," the bird said, exactly duplicating his voice. "What's your name?"

"Let's get going," Vasco said.

"My name is Jamie," Jamie said.

"Hello, Jamie. I'm Gerard," the bird said.

"Hello, Gerard."

"All right," Vasco said. "Let's get a move on here."

"That depends on who's in the saddle," Gerard said.

"Dolly," Vasco said, "we have to keep to our schedule."

"Well, a boy's best friend is his mother," the bird said, in an odd voice.

"Do you know my mother?" Jamie said.

"No, son," Dolly said. "He doesn't. He's just saying things he's already heard before."

"Your story didn't sound quite right," Gerard said. And in a different voice: "Oh, that's too bad, you got a better one?"

But now the grown-ups were pushing Jamie forward. He didn't think he could stay longer, and he didn't want to make a scene. "Bye, Gerard," he said.

"Bye, Jamie."

They walked on for a while. Jamie said, "He was funny."

"Yes he was, dear," Dolly said, keeping her hand firmly on his shoulder.

Coming into the gardens, Alex first passed the swimming pool area. It was the quietest swimming pool she had ever seen—no splashing, no noise. People lay in the sun like corpses. There was a cabinet stacked with towels and bathrobes. Alex took a bathrobe and draped it over her shoulder, covering the towel-wrapped shotgun.

"How do you know these things?" Henry said, watching her. He was nervous. Walking with her while she carried that gun, and knowing she intended to use it. He didn't know if the bearded guy was armed, but chances were that he was.

"Law school," she said, laughing.

Dave walked a couple of steps behind them. Henry turned and said, "Keep up, Dave."

"Okay . . ."

They rounded a corner, passed beneath an adobe archway, came into another secluded garden. The air here was cool, and the path shaded. A little brook ran alongside the path.

They heard a voice say, "Mellow greetings, ukie dukie."

Henry looked up. "What was that?"

"Me."

Henry said, "It's a bird."

"Excuse me," the bird said, "my name is Gerard."

Alex said, "Oh, a talking parrot."

The parrot said, "My name is Jamie. Hello, Jamie, I'm Gerard. Hello, Gerard."

Alex froze, stared. "That's Jamie!"

"Do you know my mother?" the bird said, sounding exactly like Jamie's voice.

"Jamie!" Alex started to shout in the garden. "Jamie! *Jamie!*"

And in the distance, she heard, "Mom!"

Dave took off, running forward. Henry looked at Alex, who stood very still. She dropped the towel and the robe to the ground and methodically loaded the shotgun. She pulled the action bar back and forward, making a *chung chung!* sound. Then she turned to Henry.

"Let's go." She was very cool. The gun was cradled in her arm. "You may want to walk behind me."

"Uh, okay."

She started walking. "Jamie!"

"Mom!"

She walked faster.

They couldn't have been more than twenty feet from the back door to the surgicenter—maybe three, four good paces, no more than that—when the whole thing started.

And Vasco Borden was *pissed*. His trusted assistant just melting right before his eyes. The kid cries "Mom!" and she lets go of him. She just stands there. Like she was stunned.

"Hold on to him, damn it," he said. "What are you doing?"

She didn't answer.

"Mom! Mom!"

Exactly what I was worried about, he thought. He had an eight-year-old kid screaming for his mother, and all these women in bathrobes walking around. If they weren't looking at him and the kid before, they sure as hell were now—pointing and talking. Vasco appeared completely out of place, six-four and bearded, dressed entirely in black, with a black cowboy hat he had to pull down low because his damn ear had been bitten off. He knew he looked like a bad guy in a bad cowboy movie. His woman wasn't helping; she wasn't soothing the kid or leading him forward, and any minute he knew that kid would turn and bolt.

Vasco needed to get control here. He started to reach for his gun, but now more women were coming out of rooms on all sides—hell, a whole damn yoga class was emptying into the garden to look, to see why some kid was hollering for his mother.

And there he was, the man in black.

He was *screwed*.

"Dolly," he snapped, "goddamn it, pull yourself together. We have to take this young man into the surgicenter here—"

Vasco never finished the sentence, because a dark shape came streaking toward him, leapt into the air, swung from a tree branch about eight feet high, and—right about the time he realized it was that black kid again, *that hairy kid*, the one that bit off his ear—the black kid slammed into him, hard as a big rock smashing him full on the chest, and Vasco stumbled backward over some rose bushes and went down on his ass, legs up in the air.

And that was it.

The kid bolted, shrieking for his mom. And Dolly suddenly starts acting like she doesn't know him, and he's cut and scratched, dragging himself out of the rose bushes with no help from her. Can't work up any dignity getting up to your feet with your ass full of thorns. And there's at least a hundred people watching him. And any minute, security guards.

And the black monkey-looking kid is gone. Can't see him any-where.

Vasco realizes that he's got to get out of there. It's finished; it's a fucking disaster. Dolly is still frozen like the fucking Statue of Liberty, so he starts pushing her, yelling at her to get moving, that they have to leave. All the other women in the garden start booing and hissing. Some old broad in a leotard screams, "Testosterone poisoning!" And the others are yelling, "Leave her alone!" "Creep!" "Abuser!" He wants to yell back, "She *works* for me!" but of course, she doesn't anymore. She's dazed and bewildered. And by now the leotard broads are screaming for the police.

So it's only going to get worse.

Dolly is so slow; she might be sleepwalking. Vasco has to get out. He pushes past her, moving through the garden at a half-trot, his only thought now to get away, get out of this place. In the next garden he sees the kid standing with some guy, and in front of the two of them he sees the broad Alex, and she's holding a fucking sawed-off twelve-gauge like she knows how to use it—hand on the stock, hand on the action— and she says, "If I ever see your face again, I'll blow it off, asshole."

Vasco doesn't answer, just keeps moving past her, and the next thing he knows, there's a fucking explosion, and ahead of him the bushes along the path just blast away in a green cloud of fluttering petals and leaves and dirt. So of course he stops. Right there. And he turns, slowly, keeping his hands away from his body.

She says, "Did you fucking hear what I said to you?"

"Yes, ma'am," he says. Always polite to a lady with a gun. Especially if she's upset. Now the crowd is huge; they're three or four deep, chat-tering like birds, craning to get a look at what is happening. But this broad's not going to let it go.

She yells at him: "What'd I say to you?"

"You said if you saw me again, you'd kill me."

"That's right," she says. "And I will. You touch me or my son again, and I will fucking kill you."

"Yes, ma'am," he says. He feels the red rushing into his face. Anger, humiliation, rage.

"You can go now," she says, moving the barrel ever so slightly. She knows what she is doing. A lawyer who goes to the shooting range. The worst kind.

Vasco nods and moves off, quickly as he can. He wants to get away from her, and out of sight of all those women. It's like some nightmare, all these women in robes watching him eat shit. In a moment, he's practically running. Back to the Hummer, away from this place.

That's when he saw the black kid, the one who looked like an ape. In fact, he *was* an ape, Vasco was sure of it, watching the kid move. An ape dressed like a kid. But he was still an ape. The ape was circling around the garden. Just seeing that ape made Vasco's head throb where his ear once was. Without a conscious thought, he pulled out his pistol and started firing. He didn't expect to hit the little fucker at this distance, but he needed to do something. And sure enough, the ape ran, scrambled, went behind a wall, and disappeared.

Vasco followed him. It was the damn ladies' room. But nobody was around. The lights in the bathroom were off. He could see the pool, off to his right, but nobody was there now. So nobody was in the bathroom, except for the ape. He held his gun and moved forward.

Chung chung!

He froze. He knew the sound of a double-action pump. You never went in a room after you heard that sound. He waited.

"Do you feel lucky, punk? Do you?" It was a raspy voice, sounded familiar.

He stood there in the doorway to the women's bathroom, angry and afraid, until he began to feel very foolish and very exposed. "Ah, screw it," he said, and he turned and went back to his car. He didn't care about the fucking ape kid, anyway.

From behind him a voice said, "My, my. Such a lot of guns around town, and so few brains."

He spun, looked back. But all he saw was that bird, flapping its wings as it stood on the door leading to the bathroom. He couldn't tell where the voice had come from.

Vasco hurried to his Hummer. Already he was thinking what he would tell the law firm and the BioGen people. Fact was, it just didn't work out. The woman was armed, she was tipped off, someone had told her in advance. Nothing Vasco could do about that. He was good at his job, but he couldn't work miracles. The problem lay with whoever tipped her off. Before you blame me, take a look at yourself. They had a problem inside their organization.

Anyhow, something like that.

CH088

Adam Winkler lay in the hospital bed, frail and weak. He was bald and pale. His bony hand gripped Josh's. "Listen," he said, "it wasn't your fault. I was trying to kill myself anyway. It would have happened, no matter what. The time you gave me—you did me a big favor. Look at me. I don't want you blaming yourself."

Josh couldn't speak. His eyes were filled with tears.

"Promise me you won't blame yourself."

Josh nodded.

"Liar." Adam gave a weak smile. "How's your lawsuit?"

"Okay," Josh said. "Some people in New York say we gave their mother Alzheimer's. Actually, we gave her water."

"You going to win?"

"Oh sure."

Adam sighed. "Liar." His hand relaxed. "You take care, bro." And he closed his eyes.

Josh panicked, wiped his tears away. But Adam was still breathing. He was sleeping, very peacefully.

CH089

The Oxnard judge coughed in the chilly air as he handed the ruling to the assembled attorneys. Alex Burnet was there, along with Bob Koch and Albert Rodriguez.

"As you can see," he said, "I have ruled that BioGen's ownership of Mr. Burnet's cells does not entitle them to take these cells from any individual, living or dead, including Mr. Burnet himself. Certainly the cells cannot be taken from members of his immediate or extended family. Any contrary ruling would conflict with the Thirteenth Amendment, forbidding slavery.

"Within the context of my ruling, I observe that this situation has arisen out of confusion from prior court rulings as to what constitutes ownership in a biological context. First is the notion that material removed from the body is 'waste' or 'lost material,' which is therefore unimportant to the person from whom it was removed. This view is false. If one considers a stillborn fetus, for example, even though it has left the mother's body, we can well intuit that either the mother or other relatives might feel a strong attachment to the fetus, and wish to control its disposition, whether in burial, cremation, or to provide tissues for research or to help others. The notion that the hospital or the doctor may dispose of the fetus as they wish, merely because it is outside the body and therefore is 'waste' material, is clearly unreasonable and inhuman. A similar logic applies to Mr. Burnet's cells. Even though they are removed from his body, he will rightly feel that they are still his. This is a natural and common human feeling. The feeling will not go away simply because the courts rule according to some other legal concept shoehorned in by analogy. You cannot banish human feelings by legal fiat. Yet this is precisely what the courts have tried to do.

"Some courts have decided tissue cases by considering the tissues to be trash. Some courts have considered the tissues to be research material akin to books in a library. Some courts consider the tissues to be abandoned property that can be disposed of automatically under certain circumstances, as rental lockers can be opened after a certain time and the contents of those lockers sold. Some courts have attempted to balance competing claims and have concluded that the claims of society to research trump the claims of the individual to ownership.

"Each of these analogies runs up against the stubborn fact of human nature. Our bodies are our individual property. In a sense, bodily ownership is the most fundamental kind of ownership we know. It is the core experience of our being. If the courts fail to acknowledge this fundamental notion, their rulings will be invalid, however correct they may seem within the logic of law.

"That is why when an individual donates tissue to a doctor for a research study, it is not the same as donating a book to a library. It never will be. If the doctor or his research institution wishes later to use that tissue for some other purpose, they should be required to obtain permission for this new use. And so on, indefinitely. If magazines can notify you when your subscription runs out, universities can notify you when they wish to use your tissues for a new purpose.

"We are told this is onerous to medical research. The reverse is true. If universities do not recognize that people retain a reasonable, and emotional, interest in their tissue in perpetuity, then people will not donate their tissues for research. They will sell them to corporations instead. And their lawyers will refine documents that forbid the universities to use so much as a blood test for any purpose at all, without negotiated payment. Patients are not naive and neither are their attorneys.

"The cost of medical research will increase astronomically if physicians and universities continue to act in a high-handed manner. The true social good, therefore, is to enact legislation that enables people to maintain disposition rights to their tissue, forever.

"We are told that a patient's interest in his tissues, and his right to privacy, ends at death. That, too, is outmoded thinking that must change. Because the descendants of a dead person share his or her genes, their privacy is invaded if research is done, or if the genetic makeup of the dead person is published. The children of the dead person may lose their health insurance simply because contemporary laws do not reflect contemporary realities.

"But in the end, the Burnet case has gone awry as it has because of a profound and fundamental error by the courts. Issues of ownership will always be clouded when individuals are able to manufacture within their bodies what the court has ruled someone else owns. This is true of cell lines; it is true of genes, and of certain proteins. These things cannot reasonably be owned. It is a standing rule of law that our common heritage cannot be owned by any person. It is a standing rule that facts of nature cannot be owned. Yet for more than two decades, legal rulings have failed to affirm this concept. Patent court rulings have failed to affirm this concept. The resultant confusions will only increase with time, and with the advances of science. Private ownership of the genome or of facts of nature will become increasingly difficult, expensive, obstructive. What has been done by the courts is a mistake, and it must be undone. The sooner the better."

Alex turned to Bob Koch. "I think this judge had help," she said.

"Yeah, could be," Bob said.

CH090

Rick Diehl was trying to keep it together, but everything seemed to be falling apart. The maturity gene was a disaster. And worse, BioGen was getting sued by a lawyer in New York who was smart and unscrupulous. Rick's attorneys told him to settle, but if he did, it would bankrupt the company. Although that would probably happen anyway. BioGen had lost the Burnet line, they had failed to replace it with cells from Burnet's kid, and now it looked like a new patent interfered with their product, rendering it worthless.

At Diehl's request, his wife had come out of hiding and returned to town. The kids were at her parents' house in Martha's Vineyard for the summer. She was going to get custody. His attorney, Barry Sindler, was himself facing a divorce, and didn't seem to have time for Rick these days. There was a big uproar over all the gene testing being done for custody cases. Sindler had been widely denounced for pioneering the practice, deemed unethical.

There was talk in Congress of passing laws to limit genetic testing. But observers doubted Congress would ever act, because the insurance companies wanted testing. Which was only logical, given that insurance companies were in the business of not paying claims.

Brad Gordon had left town while awaiting trial. It was rumored he was traveling around the West, getting himself into trouble.

Rodriguez's law firm had presented BioGen with the first part of their bill, for more than a million dollars. They wanted another two million on retainer, in light of all the pending litigation the company faced.

Rick's assistant buzzed him on the intercom. "Mr. Diehl, the woman from BDG, the security company, is here to see you."

He sat up in his chair. He remembered how electrifying Jacqueline Maurer was. She radiated sexuality and sophistication. He felt alive just being with her. And he hadn't seen her in weeks.

"Send her in." He stood up, hastily stuffed his shirt into his pants, and turned to the door.

A young woman of thirty, wearing a nondescript blue suit and carrying a briefcase, came into the room. She had a pleasant smile, a chubby face, and shoulder-length brown hair. "Mr. Diehl? I'm Andrea Woodman, of BDG. I'm sorry I haven't been able to meet with you earlier but, gosh, we've been so busy with other clients the last few weeks, this was the first I could come. I'm so glad to make your acquaintance." She held out her hand.

He just stared.

CAVEMEN PREFERRED BLONDES

Anthropologist Notes Rapid Evolution of Light Gene
Are Blondes Really Sexier?

A new study by Canadian anthropologist Peter Frost indicates that European women evolved blue eyes and blond hair at the end of the last Ice Age as a way to attract mates. The hair color gene MC1R evolved seven variants around 11,000 years ago, he notes. This occurred extremely rapidly, in genetic terms. Ordinarily such a change would take close to a million years.

But sexual preference can produce rapid genetic change. Competition by women for males, who were in short supply due to early death in harsh times, led to the new hair and eye color. Frost's conclusions are supported by the work of three Japanese universities, which fixed the date of the genetic mutation for blondes.

Frost suspects that blondes have sexual appeal because light hair and eyes are a marker for high estrogen levels in women, and hence greater fertility. But not everyone agrees with this view. Jodie Kidd, 27, the blond model, said, "I don't think being a blonde makes you more ripe for sexual activity . . . Beauty is much deeper than the color of your hair."

Professor Frost's theory appeared in the journal *Evolution and Human Behavior*. His research was corroborated by a WHO study that predicted the demise of blondes by 2202. Subsequent reports contested the results of the WHO study after a UN panel denied its accuracy.

CH091

Frank Burnet walked into the starkly modern offices of venture capitalist Jack Watson shortly after noon. It was as he had seen it on previous visits. The Mies furniture, the modern art—a Warhol painting of Alexander the Great, a Koons balloon sculpture, a Tansey painting of mountain climbers that hung behind Watson's desk. The muted phones, the beige carpets—and all the stunning women, moving quietly, efficiently. One woman stood beside Watson with her hand on his shoulder.

"Ah, Frank," Watson said. He did not stand. "Have you met Jacqueline Maurer?"

"I don't believe so."

She shook his hand. Very cool, very direct. "Mr. Burnet."

"And you know our resident tech genius, Jimmy Maxwell." Watson nodded to a kid in his twenties, sitting at the back of the room. The kid had thick horn-rim glasses and wore a Dodgers jacket. He looked up from his laptop and waved to Burnet.

"How ya doing?"

"Hi, there," Burnet said.

"I asked you to come in," Watson said, shifting in his chair, "because we are very nearly finished with the entire business. Ms. Maurer has just negotiated the license agreement with Duke University. On extremely favorable terms."

The woman smiled. A sphinx-like smile. "I get on with scientists," she said.

"And Rick Diehl," Watson continued, "has resigned as the head of BioGen. Winkler and the rest of the senior staff have gone with him. Most of them face legal troubles, and I am sad the company will not be able to assist them. If you break the law, the company's insurance policy does not cover you. So they're on their own."

"Unfortunate," Jacqueline Maurer said.

"So it goes," Watson said. "But given the present crisis, the BioGen board of directors has asked me to take over, and put the company back on its feet. I have agreed to do so for an appropriate equity adjustment."

Burnet nodded. "Then it all went according to plan."

Watson gave him an odd look. "Uh, yes. In any case, Frank, nothing more prevents you from returning home to your family. I am sure your daughter and grandson will be happy to see you."

"I hope so," Burnet said. "She's probably angry. But it'll work out. It always does."

"That's right," Watson said. Still seated, he extended his hand, wincing a little.

"Everything all right?" Frank said.

"It's nothing. Too much golf yesterday, I pulled something."

"But it's good to take time off from work."

"So true," Watson said, flashing his famous smile. "So very true."

CH092

Brad Gordon followed the crowds that swarmed toward Mighty Kong, the huge roller coaster at Cedar Point in Sandusky, Ohio. He'd been visiting amusement parks for weeks now; this one was the biggest and best in America. He was feeling better; his jaw was almost completely pain-free now.

The only thing that bothered him was he had had one conversation with his lawyer, Johnson. Johnson seemed smart, but Brad was uneasy. Why hadn't his uncle paid for a first-rate attorney? He always had before. Brad had the vague feeling that his life was on some sort of knife-edge.

But he pushed all those thoughts aside as he looked at the track far above him, and the people shrieking as their cars went by. This roller coaster! Mighty Kong! With more than four hundred feet of drop, it gave plenty of cause for people to scream. The line of eager ticket-holders buzzed with anticipation. Brad waited, as was his custom, until two very cute young girls got on line. They were local kids, raised in a milk bottle, healthy and pink-skinned, with little budding breasts and sweet faces. One girl had braces, which was just adorable. He stayed behind them, happily listening to their high-pitched, inane chatter. Then he screamed with the rest of them, as he took the fantastic drop.

The ride left him shivering with adrenaline and pent-up excitement. He felt a bit weak as he climbed out of the car and watched the girls' round little buns as they walked away from the coaster, toward the exit.

Wait! They were going again! Perfect! He followed them, getting on line a second time.

He was feeling dreamy, catching his breath, letting his eyes drift over the soft curls of their hair, the freckles on their shoulders, revealed by their halter tops. He was starting to fantasize about what it would be like with one of them—hell, with both of them—when a man stepped forward and said, "Come with me, please."

Brad blinked, guilty from his reverie. "I'm sorry?"

"Would you come with me, sir?" It was a handsome, confident face, one encouraging him, smiling. Brad was instantly suspicious. Often cops acted friendly and polite. He hadn't done anything with these girls, he was sure of it. He hadn't touched them, hadn't said anything—

"Sir? Please? It's important if you would step over here . . . Just over here . . ."

Brad looked and saw, to one side, some people wearing what appeared to be uniforms, maybe security uniforms, and a couple of men in white coats, like people from a sanitarium. And there was a television crew, or a camera crew of some kind, filming. And he suddenly felt paranoid.

"Sir," the handsome man said, "please, we very much need you—"

"Why do you need me?"

"Sir, please . . ." The man was plucking at Brad's elbow, then grabbed it more forcefully. "Sir, we get so few adult repeaters—"

Adult repeaters. Brad shivered. *They knew.* And now this guy, this handsome, charming smooth-talker was leading him toward the people in the white coats. They were obviously onto him, and he tugged free, but the handsome man held on.

Brad's heart was pounding and he felt panic flood through him. He bent over and pulled his gun from its holster. "No! Let go of me!"

The handsome man looked shocked. Some people screamed. The man held up his hands. "Now take it easy," he said, "it's going to be—"

The gun in Brad's hand fired. He didn't realize it had happened until he saw the man stumble and start to fall. He clutched at Brad, hanging on him, and Brad shot again. The man fell back. Everybody was screaming all over the place. Somebody shouted, "He shot Dr. Bellarmino! He shot Bellarmino!"

But by then he was very confused; the crowd was running away, those cute little buns were running; everything was ruined; and when more men in uniform yelled to him to drop his gun, he fired at them, too. And the world went black.

At the fall meeting of the Organization of University Technology Transfer officers (OUTT), a group dedicated to licensing the work of university scientists, philanthropist Jack B. Watson gave the stirring keynote address. He struck his familiar themes: the spectacular growth of biotechnology, the importance of gene patents, keeping Bayh-Dole in place, and the necessity of preserving the status quo for business prosperity and university wealth. "The health and wealth of our universities depends on strong biotech partners. This is the key to knowledge, and the key to the future!"

He told them what they wanted to hear, and left the stage to the usual thunderous applause. Only a few noticed that he walked with a slight limp and that his right arm did not swing as freely as the left.

Backstage, he took the arm of a beautiful woman. "Where the hell is Dr. Robbins?"

"He's waiting for you in his clinic," she said.

Watson swore, then leaned on the woman as he walked outside to the waiting limousine. The night was cold, with a faint mist. "Fucking doctors," he said. "I'm not doing any more damn tests."

"Dr. Robbins didn't mention anything about tests."

The driver opened the door. Watson climbed in awkwardly, his leg dragging. The woman helped him in. He slumped in the back, wincing. The woman got in on the other side. "Is the pain bad?"

"It's worse at night."

"Do you want a pill?"

"I already took one." He inhaled deeply. "Does Robbins know what the hell this is?"

"I think so."

"Did he tell you?"

"No."

"You're lying."

"He didn't tell me, Jack."

"Christ."

The limousine sped through the night. Watson stared out the window, breathing hard.

The hospital clinic was deserted at this hour. Fred Robbins, thirty-five and handsome as a movie star, was waiting for Watson with two younger physicians, in a large examining room. Robbins had set up light boxes with X-ray, electrophoresis and MRI results.

Watson dropped heavily into a chair. He waved to the younger men. "You can go."

"But Jack—"

"Tell me alone," Watson said to Robbins. "Nineteen fucking doctors have examined me in the last two months. I've done so many MRIs and CAT scans I glow in the dark. You tell me." He waved to the woman. "You wait outside, too."

They all left. Watson was alone with Robbins.

"They say you're the smartest diagnostician in America, Fred. So tell me."

"Well," Robbins said, "it's as much a biochemical process as anything. That's why I wanted—"

"Three months ago," Watson said, "I had a pain in my leg. A week later the leg was dragging. My shoe was worn on the edge. Pretty soon I had trouble walking up stairs. Now I have weakness in my right arm. Can't squeeze toothpaste with my hand. It's getting hard to breathe. In three months! So tell me."

"It's called Vogelman's paresis," Robbins said. "It's not common, but not rare. A few thousand cases every year, maybe fifty thousand world-wide. First described in the 1890s, by a French—"

"Can you treat it?"

"At this point," Robbins said, "there are no satisfactory treatments."

"Are there *any* treatments?"

"Palliative and supportive measures, massage and B vitamins—"

"But no treatments."

"Not really, Jack, no."

"What causes it?"

"That we know. Five years ago, Enders's team at Scripps isolated a gene, BRD7A, that codes for a protein that repairs myelin around nerve cells. They've demonstrated that a point mutation in the gene produces Vogelman's paresis in animals."

"Well, hell," Watson said, "you're telling me I've got a genetic deficiency disease like any other."

"Yes, but—"

"How long ago did they find the gene? Five years? Then it's a natural for gene replacement, start the coded protein being made inside the body . . ."

"Replacement therapy is risky, of course."

"Do I give a damn? Look at me, Fred. How much time do I have?"

"The time course is variable, but . . ."

"Spit it out."

"Maybe four months."

"Jesus." Watson sucked in his breath. He ran his hand over his forehead, took another breath. "Okay, so that's my situation. Let's do the therapy. Five years later, they must have a protocol."

"They don't," Robbins said.

"Somebody must."

"They don't. Scripps patented the gene and licensed it to Beinart Baghoff, the Swiss pharma giant. It was part of a package deal with Scripps, about twenty different collaborations. BRD7A wasn't regarded as particularly important."

"What're you saying?"

"Beinart put a high license fee on the gene."

"Why? It's an orphan disease, it makes no sense to—"

Robbins shrugged. "They're a big company. Who knows why they do things. Their licensing division sets fees for eight hundred genes that they control. There's forty people in that division. It's a bureaucracy. Anyway, they set the license high—"

"Christ."

"And no laboratory, anywhere in the world, has worked on the disease in the last five years."

"Christ."

"Too expensive, Jack."

"Then I'll buy the damn gene."

"Can't. I already checked. It's not for sale."

"Everything's for sale."

"Any sale by Beinart has to be approved by Scripps, and the Scripps office of tech transfer won't consider—"

"Never mind, I'll license it myself."

"You can do that. Yes."

"And I'll set up the gene transfer myself. We'll get a team in this hospital to do it."

"I really wish we could, Jack. But gene transfer's extremely risky, and no lab will take the chance these days. Nobody's gone to jail yet over a failed gene transfer, but there have been a lot of patient deaths, and—"

"Fred. Look at me."

"You can get it done in Shanghai."

"No, no. Here."

Fred Robbins bit his lip. "Jack, you have to face reality. There's less than a one percent success rate. I mean, if we had done five years of work, we would have the results of animal tests, vector tests, immunosuppressive protocols, all kinds of steps to increase your chance of success. But just shooting from the hip—"

"That's all I have time for. Shooting from the hip."

Fred Robbins was shaking his head.

"A hundred million dollars," Watson said. "For whatever lab does it. Take over a private clinic out in Arcadia. Just me, nobody knows. Do the procedure there. It works or it doesn't."

Fred Robbins shook his head sadly. "I'm sorry, Jack. I really am."

The overhead lights came on in the autopsy room, bank
after bank. It made a dramatic opening shot, Gorevitch
thought. The figure in the lab coat was distinguished-
looking in a severe way: silver hair, wire-rim glasses. He was the internationally renowned primate anatomist Jorg Erickson.

Using a handheld camera, Gorevitch said, "Dr. Erickson, what are
we doing today?"

"We are examining a world-famous specimen, the putative talking
orangutan of Indonesia. This animal is said to have spoken in at least
two languages. Well, we shall see."

Dr. Erickson turned to the steel table, where the carcass was draped
in a white cloth. He pulled the cloth away with a flourish. "This is a
sub-adult or juvenile *Pongo abelii*, a Sumatran orangutan, distinguished
by its smaller size from the Borneo orangutan. This specimen is male,
approximately three years of age, in apparent good health, with no
external scars or injuries . . . All right, now we begin." He picked up a
scalpel.

"With a midsagittal incision, I expose the anterior musculature of
the throat and pharynx. Note the superior and inferior belly of the
omohyoid, and here, the sternohyoid . . . Hmmm." Erickson was bent
over the animal's neck. Gorevitch found it difficult to maneuver for a
shot.

"What do you see, Professor?"

"I am looking now at the stylohyoid and the cricothyroid muscles, here, and here . . . And this is quite interesting. Ordinarily in *Pongo* we find the anterior musculature poorly developed, and lacking the fine motor control of the human speech apparatus. But this creature appears to be a transitional case, bearing some features of the classic pongid pharynx, and some features more characteristic of the human neck. Notice the sternocleidomastoid . . ."

Gorevitch thought, *Sternocleidomastoid.* Jesus. They would have to dub in a voice-over. "Professor, perhaps you could say it in English?"

"No, the terms are Latin, I don't know the translation—"

"I mean, can you explain in layman's terms? For our viewers?"

"Ah, of course. All these superficial muscles, most of which attach to the hyoid—that is to say, the Adam's apple—these muscles are more human than ape-like."

"What could account for that?"

"Some mutation, obviously."

"And the rest of the animal? Is it more human, as well?"

"I have not seen the rest of the animal," Erickson said severely. "But we will get there, in due time. I shall be especially interested to inspect any rotation of the axis of the foramen magnum, and of course the depth and arrangement of sulci of the motor cortex, to the extent that gray matter has been preserved."

"Do you expect to find human-like changes in the brain?"

"Frankly, no. I do not," Erickson said. He turned his attention to the top of the skull, running his gloved hands over the sparse hair of the orang's scalp, feeling the bones beneath. "You see, in this animal, parietal bones slope inward, toward the top of the cranium. That is a classic pongid or chimp finding. Whereas humans have bulging parietal bones. The top of their heads are wider than the bottom."

Erickson stepped back from the table. Gorevitch said, "So you are saying this animal is a mixture of human and ape?"

"No," Erickson said. "This is an ape. It is an aberrant ape, to be sure. But it is merely an ape."

JOHN B. WATSON INVESTMENT GROUP

For Immediate Release

John B. "Jack" Watson, world-famous philanthropist and founder of the Watson Investment Group, died today in Shanghai, China. Mr. Watson was internationally lauded for his charitable work and his efforts on behalf of the poor and downtrodden of the world. Mr. Watson had been ill for only a short time, but he suffered from an extremely aggressive form of cancer. He checked into a private Shanghai clinic and died three days later. He is mourned by friends and colleagues around the world.

STORY, DETAILS TK

Henry Kendall was surprised that Gerard could help Dave with his math homework. But that wouldn't last long. Eventually, Dave would probably need special schooling. Dave had inherited the chimp's short attention span. He found it increasingly difficult to keep up with the other kids in class, particularly in reading, which was agony for him. And his physical prowess put him in another league on the playground. The other children wouldn't let him play. So he had become an excellent surfer.

And by now, the truth was out. There had been a particularly distressing article in *People* magazine, "The Modern Family," which said, "The most up-to-date family is no longer a same-sex family, or a blended family, or an interracial family. That's all so last century, says Tracy Kendall. And she should know, because the Kendall family of La Jolla, California, is transgenic and interspecies—creating more excitement in the household than a barrel of monkeys!"

Henry had been called to testify before Congress, which he found a peculiar experience. The congressmen spoke to the cameras for two hours. Then they got up and left, pleading urgent business elsewhere. Then the witnesses spoke for six minutes each, but there were no congressmen there to hear their remarks. Later, the congressmen all announced they would soon deliver major speeches on the subject of transgenic creation.

Henry was named Scientist of the Year by the Society for Libertarian Biology. Jeremy Rifkin called him a "war criminal." He had been excoriated by the National Council of Churches. The pope excommunicated him, only later to discover that he wasn't Catholic; they had the wrong Henry Kendall. The NIH criticized his work, but the replacement for Robert Bellarmino as head of genetics was William Gladstone, and he was much more open-minded and less self-aggrandizing than Bellarmino had been. Henry now traveled continuously, lecturing about transgenic techniques at university seminars around the country.

He was the subject of intense controversy. The Reverend Billy John Harker of Tennessee called him "Satan incarnate." Bill Mayer, noted left-wing reactionary, published a long and much-discussed article in the *New York Review of Books* entitled "Banished from Eden: Why We Must Prevent Transgenic Travesties." The article failed to mention that transgenic animals had been in existence for two decades already. Dogs, cats, bacteria, mice, sheep, and cattle had all been created. When a senior NIH scientist was asked about the article, he coughed and said, "What's the *New York Review*?"

Lynn Kendall ran the TransGenic Times web site, which detailed the daily life of Dave, Gerard, and her fully human children, Jamie and Tracy.

After a year in La Jolla, Gerard began to make dial-tone sounds. He had done it before, but the tones were mysterious to the Kendalls. Evidently they were the tones of a foreign telephone exchange, but they failed to identify which country. "Where did you come from, Gerard?" they would ask.

"I can't sleep a wink anymore, ever since you first walked out the door." He had become enamored of American country music. "All you ever do is bring me down."

"What country, Gerard?"

To that, they never received an answer. He spoke some French, and he often talked with a British accent. They assumed he was European.

Then one day one of Henry's graduate students from France was having dinner at their house, and he heard Gerard's tones. "My God," he said, "I know what he is doing." He listened for a moment. "There is no city code," he said. "But otherwise . . . let's try." He pulled out his own cell phone, and began to key in numbers. "Do it again, Gerard."

Gerard repeated the tones.

"And again."

"Life is a book, you've got to read it," Gerard sang. "Life is a story and you've got to tell it . . ."

"I know this song," the graduate student said.

"What is it?" Henry said.

"It's Eurovision. Gerard, the tones."

Eventually, Gerard did the dial tones. The graduate student placed the call. His first guess was to try Paris. A woman answered the phone. He said in French, "Excuse me, but do you know of a grey parrot who is named Gerard?"

The woman began to cry. "Let me speak to him," she said. "Is he all right?"

"He is fine."

They held the phone by Gerard's perch, and he listened to the woman's voice. His head bobbed excitedly. Then he said, "Is this where you live? Oh, Mother's going to love it here!"

Gail Bond arrived to visit a few days later. She stayed a week, and then returned alone. Gerard, it seemed, wanted to stay. For days afterward, he sang:

> *My baby used to stay out all night long,*
> *She made me cry, she done me wrong,*
> *She hurt my eyes open, that's no lie,*
> *Tables turn and now her turn to cry,*
> *Because I used to love her, but it's all over now . . .*

All in all, things were working out much better than anyone expected. The family was busy, but everyone got along. There were only two worrisome trends. Henry noticed that Dave had developed a few gray hairs around his muzzle. So it was possible that Dave, like most other transgenics, might die earlier than usual.

And one autumn day, while Dave was walking with Henry at the county fair, holding Henry's hand, a farmer in overalls came up and said, "I'd like to get me one of them to work on my farm."

That gave Henry a chill.

Author's Note

A t the end of my research for this book, I arrived at the
following conclusions:

1. *Stop patenting genes*. Gene patents might have looked reasonable
   twenty years ago, but the field has changed in ways nobody could
   have predicted. Today we have plenty of evidence that gene patents
   are unnecessary, unwise, and harmful.

   There is great confusion about gene patents. Many observers
   conflate a call to end gene patents with anticapitalist and anti-private
   property sentiments. It is nothing of the sort. It is perfectly reasonable for industry to seek a mechanism that will ensure a profit on
   productive investment. Such a mechanism implies a restriction
   on competition involving a created product. However, such protection does *not* imply that genes themselves should be patented. On
   the contrary, gene patents contradict long-established traditions of
   intellectual property protection.

   First, genes are facts of nature. Like gravity, sunlight, and leaves
   on trees, genes exist in the natural world. Facts of nature can't be
   owned. You can own a test for a gene, or a drug that affects a gene,
   but not the gene itself. You can own a treatment for a disease, but
   not the disease itself. Gene patents break that fundamental rule. Of
   course one can argue about what's a fact of nature, and there are
   people paid to do that. But here's a simple test. If something exists

for millions of years before the arrival of Homo sapiens on earth, it's a fact of nature. To argue that a gene is in any way a human invention is absurd. To grant a gene patent is like granting a patent on iron or carbon.

Because it's a patent on a fact of nature, a gene patent becomes an undeserved monopoly. Ordinarily, patent protection enables me to protect my invention but encourages others to make their own versions. My iPod doesn't prevent you from making a digital audio player. My patented mousetrap is wood, but your titanium mousetrap is allowed.

This is not what happens with gene patents. The patent consists of pure information already existing in nature. Because there has been no invention, no one can innovate any other use of the patent without violating the patent itself, so further innovation is closed. It's like allowing somebody to patent noses. You couldn't make eyeglasses, Kleenex, nasal sprays, masks, makeup, or perfume because they all rely on some aspect of noses. You could put suntan lotion on your body, but not on your nose, because any modification of your nose would violate the patent on noses. Chefs could be sued for making fragrant dishes unless they paid the nose royalty. And so on. Of course, we would all agree that a patent on noses is absurd. If everyone has one, how can anyone own it? Gene patents are absurd for the same reason.

It takes little imagination to see that monopolistic patenting inhibits creation and productivity. If the creator of Auguste Dupin could own all fictional detectives, we would never have had Sherlock Holmes, Sam Spade, Philip Marlowe, Miss Marple, Inspector Maigret, Peter Wimsey, Hercule Poirot, Mike Hammer, or J. J. Gittes, to name just a few. This rich heritage of invention would be denied us by a patenting error. Yet that is exactly the error in patenting genes.

Gene patents are bad public policy. We have ample evidence that they hurt patient care and suppress research. When Myriad patented two breast cancer genes, they charged nearly three thousand dollars for the test, even though the cost to create a gene test is nothing like the cost to develop a drug. Not surprisingly, the European patent office revoked that patent on a technicality. The Canadian government announced that it would conduct gene tests without paying for the patent. Some years ago, the owner of the gene for Canavan disease refused to make the test widely available, even though families who had suffered with the disease had contributed time, money, and tissues to get the gene identified. Now those same families could not afford the test.

That is an outrage, but it is far from the most dangerous consequence of gene patents. In its heyday, research on SARS (Severe Acute Respiratory Syndrome) was inhibited because scientists were unsure who owned the genome—three simultaneous patent claims had been filed. As a result, research on SARS wasn't as vigorous as it might have been. That should scare every sensible person. Here was a contagious disease with a 10 percent death rate that had spread to two dozen countries around the world. Yet scientific research to combat the disease was inhibited—because of patent fears.

At the moment, hepatitis C, HIV, hemophilus influenza, and various diabetes genes are all owned by some entity. They shouldn't be. Nobody should own a disease.

If gene patents are ended, we can expect screams of outrage and threats that business will abandon research, that companies will go bankrupt, that health care will suffer and the public will die. But it is more likely that an end to gene patents will be phenomenally liberating to everyone, and will result in a burst of new products for the public.

2. *Establish clear guidelines for the use of human tissues.* Human tissue collections are increasingly important to medical research, and increasingly valuable. Appropriate federal regulations to manage tissue banks already exist, but courts have ignored federal rules. Historically, the courts have decided questions about human tissues based on existing property law. In general, they have ruled that once

your tissue leaves your body, you no longer maintain any rights to it. They analogize tissues to, say, the donation of a book to a library. But people have a strong feeling of ownership about their bodies, and that feeling will never be abrogated by a mere legal technicality. Therefore we need new, clear, emphatic legislation.

Why do we need legislation? Consider a recent court ruling on the case of Dr. William Catalona. This eminent prostate cancer physician assembled a collection of tissue samples from his patients so he could work on the disease. When Dr. Catalona moved to another university, he tried to take the tissues with him. Washington University refused, saying that it owned the tissues; the judge upheld the university, citing such trivial facts as some of the releases' being printed on Washington University stationery. Patients are now understandably outraged. They believed they were giving their tissues to a beloved doctor, not a shadowy university lurking in the background; they thought they were giving tissues specifically for prostate cancer research, not for any use, which the university now claims the right to do.

The notion that once you part with your tissue you no longer have any rights is absurd. Consider this: Under present law, if somebody takes my picture, I have rights forever in the use of that photo. Twenty years later, if somebody publishes it or puts it in an advertisement, I still have rights. But if somebody takes my tissue—part of my physical body—I have no rights. This means I have more rights over my image than I have over the actual tissues of my body.

The required legislation should ensure that patients have control over their tissues. I donate my tissues for a purpose, and that purpose only. If, later, someone wants to use them for another purpose, they need my permission again. If they can't get permission, they can't use my tissues.

Such a rule fulfills an important emotional need. But it also acknowledges that there may be significant legal and religious reasons why I do not want my tissue used for another purpose.

We should not fear that such regulations will inhibit research.

After all, the National Institutes of Health seems to be able to conduct research while following these guidelines. Nor should we accept the argument that these rules impose an onerous burden. If a magazine can notify you that your subscription has run out, a university can notify you if they want to use your tissues for a new purpose.

3. Pass laws to ensure that data about gene testing is made public. New legislation is needed if the FDA is to publish adverse results from gene therapy trials. At the moment, it cannot do so. In the past, some researchers have tried to prevent the reporting of patient deaths, claiming that such deaths were a trade secret.

The public is increasingly aware of defects in the systems we use to report medical data. Research data has not been made available for other scientists to inspect; full disclosure has not been required; genuinely independent verification of findings is rare. The result is a public exposed to untold unknown hazards. Bias in published studies has become a bad joke. Psychiatrist John Davis looked at the trials funded by pharmaceutical companies in competition for the most effective of five different antipsychotic drugs. He found that 90 percent of the time, the drug manufactured by the company sponsoring (paying for) the study was judged superior to the others. Whoever paid for the study had the best drug.

This should not be news. Review studies conducted by those who have a financial or other interest in the outcome are not reliable because they are inherently biased. That fact should be addressed by an information system that does not permit biased testing, and takes steps to ensure that it does not occur. Yet gross bias remains far too common in medicine, and in certain other areas of high-stakes science as well.

Government should take action. In the long run there is no constituency for bad information. In the short run, all sorts of groups want to bend the facts their way. And they do not hesitate to call their senators, Democratic or Republican. This will continue until the public demands a change.

4. *Avoid bans on research*. Various groups of different political persuasions want to ban some aspect of genetic research. I agree that certain research ought not to be pursued, at least not now. But as a practical matter, I oppose bans on research and technology.

Bans can't be enforced. I don't know why we have not learned this lesson. From Prohibition to the war on drugs, we repeatedly indulge the fantasy that behavior can be banned. Invariably we fail. And in a global economy, bans take on other meanings: even if you stop research in one country, it still goes on in Shanghai. So what have you accomplished?

Of course, hope springs eternal, and fantasies never die: various groups imagine they can negotiate a global ban on certain research. But to the best of my knowledge, there has never been a successful global ban on anything. Genetic research is unlikely to be the first.

5. *Rescind the Bayh-Dole Act*. In 1980, Congress decided that the discoveries made within universities were not being made widely available, to benefit the public. To move things along, it passed a law permitting university researchers to sell their discoveries for their own profit, even when that research had been funded by taxpayer money.

As a result of this legislation, most science professors now have corporate ties—either to companies they have started or to other biotech companies. Thirty years ago, there was a distinct difference in approach between university research and that of private industry. Today the distinction is blurred, or absent. Thirty years ago, disinterested scientists were available to discuss any subject affecting the public. Now, scientists have personal interests that influence their judgment.

Academic institutions have changed in unexpected ways: The original Bayh-Dole legislation recognized that universities were not commercial entities, and encouraged them to make their research available to organizations that were. But today, universities attempt to maximize profits by conducting more and more commercial work themselves, thus making their products more valuable to them when they are finally licensed. For example, if universities think they have a new drug, they will do the FDA testing themselves, and so on. Thus Bayh-Dole has, paradoxically, increased the commercial focus of the university. Many observers judge the effect of this legislation to be corrupting and destructive to universities as institutions of learning.

Bayh-Dole was always of uncertain benefit to the American taxpayers, who became, through their government, uniquely generous investors. Taxpayers finance research, but when it bears fruit, the researchers sell it for their own institutional and personal gain, after which the drug is sold back to the taxpayers. Consumers thus pay top dollar for a drug they helped finance.

Ordinarily, when a venture capitalist invests in research, he or she expects a significant return on investment. The American taxpayer gets no return at all. The Bayh-Dole legislation anticipated that the public would receive a flood of marvelous life-saving therapies such that the investment strategy would be justified. But that hasn't happened.

Instead, the drawbacks far outweigh the benefits. Secrecy now pervades research, and hampers medical progress. Universities that once provided a scholarly haven from the world are now commercialized—the haven is gone. Scientists who once felt a humanitarian calling have become businessmen concerned with profit and loss. The life of the mind is a notion as quaint as the whalebone corset.

All these trends were perfectly clear to observers fifteen years ago; no one paid much attention back then. Now the problems are becoming clear to everyone. A good first step toward restoring the balance between academia and corporations will be to repeal Bayh-Dole legislation.

Bibliography

Excellent books on genetics are available to the general reader, including many written by researchers. This bibliography emphasizes texts I used to research this book. I relied particularly on the work of law professor Lori Andrews, authors Matt Ridley and Ronald Bailey, and scientists John Avise, Stuart Newman, and Louis-Marie Houdebine.

Andrews, Lori, and Dorothy Nelkin. *Body Bazaar: The Market for Human Tissue in the Biotechnology Age.* New York: Crown Publishers, 2001. For many years, Andrews has been the most wide-ranging and authoritative legal scholar on genetic issues. Dorothy Nelkin is a professor at New York University. Their book is comprehensive.

Andrews, Lori B. *The Clone Age: Adventures in the New World of Reproductive Technology.* New York: Henry Holt and Company, 1999. If you want to know about the real cases that are fictionalized here, read her book.

Andrews, Lori B., Maxwell J. Mehlman, and Mark A. Rothstein. *Genetics: Ethics, Law and Policy.* American Casebook Series. St. Paul, Minn.: West Group, 2002. A legal text on genetic issues.

Avise, John C. *The Hope, Hype, and Reality of Genetic Engineering.* New York: Oxford University Press, 2003. Despite the awkward title, this is one of the best books on genetic engineering for the general reader. It covers the entire field from crops to pharmaceuticals to human gene therapy; it is admirably clear, and the author explains exactly what procedures are being carried out at the genetic level. Most books do not. If you are asking yourself, "What exactly are they *doing*?" this is a good place to begin.

Bailey, Ronald. *Liberation Biology: The Scientific and Moral Case for the Biotech Revolution.* Amherst, N.Y.: Prometheus, 2005. A scientifically informed critique of bioconservatives—those individuals from both the political left and right who wish to constrain the field. Bailey's counterarguments cite scientific realities; he is respectful of opponents and ultimately entirely persuasive, in my view. I regard his book as the clearest and most complete response to religious objections to biotechnology.

Buller, David J. *Adapting Minds: Evolutionary Psychology and the Persistent Quest for Human Nature.* Cambridge, Mass.: MIT Press, 2005. A critique of evolutionary psychology.

Chesterton, G. K. *What's Wrong with the World.* San Francisco: Ignatius Press, 1910. Bon vivant, wit, and tireless author, Chesterton lost the debate about the future direction of society to his contemporaries H. G. Wells, Bertrand Russell, and George Bernard Shaw. Chesterton saw the implications of their vision of twentieth-century society, and he predicted exactly what would come of it. Chesterton is not a congenial stylist to the modern reader; his witticisms are formal, his references to contemporaries, lost in time. But his essential points are chillingly clear.

Chesterton, G. K. *Eugenics and Other Evils: An Argument Against the Scientifically Organized Society.* Edited by Michael W. Perry. Seattle: Inkling Books, 2000. Originally published in 1922, this astonishingly prescient text has much to say about our understanding of genetics then (and now), and about the mass seduction of pseudoscience. Chesterton's was one of the few voices to oppose eugenics in the early twentieth century. He saw right through it as fraudulent on every level, and he predicted where it would lead, with great accuracy. His critics were legion; they reviled him as reactionary, ridiculous, ignorant, hysterical, incoherent, and blindly prejudiced, noting with dismay that "his influence in leading people in the wrong direction is considerable." Yet Chesterton was right, and the consensus of scientists, political leaders, and the intelligentsia was wrong. Chesterton lived to see the horrors of Nazi Germany. This book is worth reading because, in retrospect, it is clear that Chesterton's arguments were perfectly sensible and deserving of an answer, and yet he was simply shouted down. And because the most repellent ideas of eugenics are being promoted again

in the twenty-first century, under various guises. The editor of this
edition has included many quotations from eugenicists of the 1920s,
which read astonishingly like the words of contemporary prophets of
doom. Some things never change—including, unfortunately, the gull-
ibility of press and public. We human beings don't like to look back at
our past mistakes. But we should.

Forgacs, Gabor, and Stuart A. Newman. *Biological Physics of the Developing
Embryo.* Cambridge, England: Cambridge University Press, 2005.
A college-level text on a crucial subject.

Fukuyama, Francis. *Our Posthuman Future: Consequences of the Biotechnology
Revolution.* New York: Farrar, Straus and Giroux, 2002. Critics on
both the left and right perceive impending dehumanization from
biotechnology. Fukuyama argues that we can control biotechnology,
and should. While I agree that one ought not to assume that technology is uncontrollable, in this case I doubt control is possible.

Hamer, Dean, and Peter Copeland. *The Science of Desire: The Search for the
Gay Gene and the Biology of Behavior.* New York: Simon and Schuster,
1994. A book as curious and oblique as the discovery that prompted it.
Rambling, good-natured, informative.

Horgan, John. *The End of Science.* Reading, Mass.: Addison Wesley, 1996.
A remarkable book, willfully misread by most of its attackers.

———. *The Undiscovered Mind: How the Human Brain Defies Replication,
Medication, and Explanation.* New York: The Free Press, 1999. Horgan
is one of the brightest and most iconoclastic observers of science today.
His prose is bracing and his viewpoint subtle.

Houdebine, Louis-Marie. *Animal Transgenesis and Cloning.* Hoboken, N.J.:
John Wiley and Sons, 2003. A clear discussion of transgenesis that is
accessible to the interested, not-very-technical reader. Inserting genes
into embryos is immensely complex.

Knight, H. Jackson. *Patent Strategy for Researchers and Research Managers.*
2d edition. Chichester, England: John Wiley and Sons, 1996.

Krimsky, Sheldon, and Peter Shorett, eds. *Rights and Liberties in the Biotech
Age: Why We Need a Genetic Bill of Rights.* Lanham, Md.: Rowman and
Littlefield, 2005. This collection of very brief essays identifies a range
of concerns among those who feel that biotechnology must be limited.
Some essays address science; others raise philosophical or legal issues.

Krimsky, Sheldon. *Science in the Primate Interest: Has the Lure of Profits Corrupted Biomedical Research?* Lanham, Md.: Rowman and Littlefield, 2003. Krimsky was one of the earliest, and has been one of the most persistent, critics of the commercialization of biology. A thoughtful, important book that indicates the complexities within the trend to academic commerce.

Larson, Edward J. *Summer for the Gods: The Scopes Trial and America's Continuing Debate over Science and Religion.* Cambridge, Mass.: Harvard University Press, 1997. Few events in American history are as misunderstood as the Scopes trial. Today it is emblematic of a war between science and religion. In fact, it was nothing of the sort; the truth is far more amusing, complex, and provocative. A gem of a book.

Midgley, Mary. *Evolution as a Religion.* London: Methuen and Co., 1985. Our attitude toward genetics is closely tied to our understanding of evolution. A long-simmering philosophical debate concerns the way we think about evolution and what lessons we draw from it. I find this debate more interesting than the debate that gets all the media attention, which has to do with the mechanisms of evolution. Midgley, a British philosopher who has addressed scientific subjects all her life, does not hesitate to take on sacred cows and those leading lights whose thoughts she regards as uninformed or shallow.

Moore, David S. *The Dependent Gene: The Fallacy of "Nature vs. Nurture."* New York: Henry Holt and Company, 2001. A psychologist aggressively attacks notions that genes and environment interact in any simple or even measurable way. His assessment of such terms as *hereditability* make this book worth reading. One may conclude that the author protests too much; nevertheless, he exemplifies the deep passions that characterize the nature/nurture debate.

Morange, Michel. *The Misunderstood Gene.* Cambridge, Mass.: Harvard University Press, 2001.

Mueller, Janice M. *An Introduction to Patent Law.* New York: Aspen Publishers, 2003.

National Research Council of the National Academies. *Reaping the Benefits of Genomic and Proteomic Research: Intellectual Property Rights, Innovation, and Public Health.* Washington, D.C.: National Academies Press, 2006. Gene patents endanger future research.

Petryna, Adriana, Andrew Lakoff, and Arthur Kleinman, eds. *Global Pharmaceuticals: Ethics, Markets, Practices*. Durham, N.C.: Duke University Press, 2005.

Pincus, Jonathan H., and Gary J. Tucker. *Behavioral Neurology*, 4th edition. New York: Oxford University Press, 1974.

Ridley, Matt. *Genome: The Autobiography of a Species in 23 Chapters*. New York: HarperCollins, 1999. Ridley is that rarest of science writers, one who is able to be entertaining and also not simplify the material. An easy and readable style, good humor, rich anecdotes, and a generally lively mind.

————. *The Agile Gene: How Nature Turns on Nurture*. New York: HarperCollins, 2003. How do genes interact with the environment? What constitutes an environmental or a genetic effect? With brilliant examples, Ridley takes the reader through the intricacies.

Sargent, Michael G. *Biomedicine and the Human Condition: Challenges, Risks, and Rewards*. New York: Cambridge University Press, 2005.

Shanks, Pete. *Human Genetic Engineering: A Guide for Activists, Skeptics, and the Very Perplexed*. New York: Nation Books, 2005. Balanced, straightforward, easy to read.

Stock, Gregory. *Redesigning Humans: Our Inevitable Genetic Future*. New York: Houghton Mifflin, 2002. A UCLA biophysicist embraces this new technology while attempting to clarify the reasons why others oppose or fear it.

Tancredi, Laurence. *Hardwired Behavior: What Neuroscience Reveals About Morality*. New York: Cambridge University Press, 2005. The author is experienced in both medicine and law, and presents a brisk, engaging overview. He distinguishes clearly between present realities and future possibilities.

U.S. Department of Commerce. *Patents and How to Get One: A Practical Handbook*. New York: Dover Publications, 2000.

Wailoo, Keith, and Stephen Pemberton. *The Troubled Dream of Genetic Medicine*. Baltimore: Johns Hopkins University Press, 2006.

Watson, James D. *The Double Helix*. New York: Touchstone, 2001. A classic. A memoir as brilliant as the discovery itself.

Weiner, Jonathan. *Time, Love, Memory: A Great Biologist and His Quest for the Origins of Behavior*. New York: Knopf, 1999. Too many books fail to give any sense of how science is actually done. This delightful book focuses on Seymour Benzer and his work.

West-Eberhard, Mary Jane. *Developmental Plasticity and Evolution*. New York: Oxford University Press, 2003. The relationship of plasticity to evolution is central to our understanding of how evolution actually occurs. It is a difficult subject here made clear in an excellent text.

ARTICLES, PRESS

Attanasio, John B. "The Constitutionality of Regulating Human Genetic Engineering: Where Procreative Liberty and Equal Opportunity Collide," *The University of Chicago Law Review* 53 (1986): 1274–1342. I ordinarily dislike far-out speculation, but this essay, now twenty years old, remains remarkable for its detailed and complex presentation.

Charlton, Bruce G. "The rise of the boy-genius: Psychological neoteny, science and modern life," *Medical Hypotheses* 67, no. 4 (2006): 679–81.

Dobson, Roger, and Abul Tahar. "Cavegirls Were the First Blondes to Have Fun," *The Sunday Times* (U.K.), February 26, 2006.

Marshall, Eliot. "Fraud Strikes Top Genome Lab," *Science* 274 (1996): 908–910.

Newman, Stuart A. "Averting the Clone Age: Prospects and Perils of Human Developmental Manipulation," *Journal of Contemporary Health Law and Policy* 19, no. 1 (2003): 431–63. A scientist presents the anti-cloning case.

Patterson, N., Daniel J. Richter, Sante Gnerre, Eric S. Lander, and David Reich. "Genetic evidence for complex speciation of humans and chimpanzees," *Nature* (advance online publication), DOI: 10.1038/nature 04789.

Rajghatta, Chidanand. "Blondes Extinction Report Is Pigment of Imagination," *Times of India*, October 3, 2002.

"Scientist Admits Faking Stem Cell Data," *New York Times*, July 5, 2006.

Stern, Andrew. "Artist Seeks to Free His Glowing Creation—Rabbit," Reuters, September 23, 2000, http://www.ekac.org/reuters.html

Wade, Nicholas. "University Panel Faults Cloning Co-Author," *New York Times*, February 11, 2006.

————. "Journal to Examine How It Reviewed Articles," *New York Times*, January 11, 2006.

Neng Yu, M.D., Margot S. Kruskall, M.D., Juan J. Yunis, M.D., Joan H.M. Knoll, Ph.D., Lynne Uhl, M.D., Sharon Alosco, M.T., Marina Ohashi, Olga Clavijo, Zaheed Husain, Ph.D., Emilio J. Yunis, M.D., Jorge J. Yunis, M.D., and Edmond J. Yunis, M.D. (2002). "Disputed maternity leading to identification of tetragametic chimerism," *New England Journal of Medicine* 346, no. 20: 1545–52.

INTERNET SOURCES

"Berlusconi's Fat Becomes Soap." http://www.ananova.com/news/story/ sm_1424471.html

"'Berlusconi's Fat' Moulded to Art." BBC News, June 20, 2005. http:// news.bbc.co.uk/2/hi/entertainment/4110402.stm

"Blonde Extinction." http://www.snopes.com/science/stats/blondes.asp

"Blondes to Die Out in 200 Years." BBC News, September 27, 2002.

"Extinction of Blondes Vastly Overreported, Media Fail to Check Root of 'Study.'" Washington Post, October 2, 2002.

"Genetic Savings & Clone." http://www.savingsandclone.com/

"Marco Evaristti, Polpette al grasso di Marco, 2006 (to fry in his own fat)." http://www.evaristti.com/news/meatball.htm

"It Really Hauls Ass." Wired, May 2006. http://www.wired.com/wired/ archive/14.05/start.html

Marshall, Eliot. "Families Sue Hospital, Scientist for Control of Canavan Gene." http://www.sciencemag.org/cgi/content/summary/290/5494/1062

"The Cactus Project." http://www.thecactusproject.com/images.asp

"Tissue Engineering: The Beat Goes On: Nature." www.nature.com/ nature/journal/ v421/n6926/full/421884a.htm

WHO. "Clarification of erroneous news reports indicating WHO genetic research on hair color." October 1, 2002. http://www.who.int/ mediacentre/news/statements/statement05/en/